FEB / 2020

D0890702

FAR AWAY
BIRD

A NOVEL

DOUGLAS A. BURTON

Silent Music Press, LLC
7600 Burnet Rd, Suite 290
Austin, TX 78759
SilentMusicPress.com

Cover art and illustration by George Frei, Treehousemachine.com
Cityscape provided by Byzantium1200.com
Book cover and interior design by Monkey C Media
Publishing consulting by Jeniffer Thompson
Edited by David Aretha
Author photo by Korey Howell Photography

First Edition
Printed in the United States of America

978-1-7330221-0-1 (trade paperback)
978-1-7330221-1-8 (eBook)
Library of Congress Control Number: 2019908827

ACKNOWLEDGMENTS

This book would have been impossible if it wasn't for the support, counsel, and feedback from my wife, Crystal Burton, my mother, Sharon Burton, and my best friend, George Frei. And to the brilliant, wonderful women who helped bring Theodora and all her complexities to life ... thank you Caroline Sears-Bridges, Carrie Newberry, Luci Williams, Kathie Giorgio, Eleanor Adams, Jeniffer Thompson, and Sara Kocek.

PART 1

HIPPODROME

ONE

512 A.D.
CONSTANTINOPLE, BYZANTINE EMPIRE

Theodora had heard the word "rebellion" before, but now she listened to the deafening roar of a real one, not far off, and it exhilarated her. The very sound evoked in her mind the image of a bear, as big as a mountain, snapping its head, opening its maw, and spewing thunder upon the whole city. Only this roar went on and on, never waning, and she felt an urgent need to see it. From her perch at the edge of the rooftop, Theodora craned to get a glimpse of the upheaval, but a wall of apartment dwellings obstructed any view. So, she glanced instead at the spaces in between the buildings, at the mouths of alleyways, where the ominous rumble spilled into her neighborhood.

"Careful, Theodora," said her older sister, Comito, her black hair lashing in the chilly breezes. "Do you want to fall and kill yourself?"

"I can't see anything, but it sounds so close," she said without looking back at Comito. Although her sister had a boy's name, Theodora knew she hated the activities of boys, things like prowling on rooftops to spy upon the city. "Besides, you heard Pata. He wants to go out there and fight," Theodora said as she leaned further over the roof's edge to peer down at the front portico. Her neighborhood street was mostly empty, a sight at odds with the distant mob noise.

"Pata wouldn't be fool enough to join a riot," said Comito. "What good is a bear trainer in a street fight anyway?"

"That's the whole idea of a rebellion. Pata says that when the factions fight the emperor, everyone gets called into the battle." But before she could explain further, Theodora spotted their father—or rather, the top of their father's balding head as he appeared suddenly below. He stepped out and looked both ways down the street. "There's Pata," she said and pointed.

"Where?" Comito dared to lean forward for a look, but quickly pulled back. "Maybe he just wants to see the uproar for himself."

"I don't think so." Theodora's father sometimes spoke of rebellion with his friends in the Green faction, but always in whispers and always after much drinking. Her father once told her that the Green faction was one of the city's civilian militias, one that rebuilt city walls or put out deadly fires when the city was under attack. But the faction could also be amassed to oust an emperor if need be. He assured Theodora that such a dangerous scheme would never happen. And yet, here it was . . . unfolding out there somewhere.

Theodora watched a group of about thirty men march up the street and toward her father. They carried swords and wore the olive-colored sashes of the Green faction. Her pata had his own green sash tied around his bulging belly. In his hand, Theodora spotted a coiled whip, one of many he used to keep the circus bears at bay. The approaching partisans howled and chanted with fists in the air. How confident the men all looked, she thought, working men who seemed to think themselves indestructible. Theodora stared at them for a long while. She admired the world of men, all the strength and vitality and, admittedly at times, even the violence. The world down below was their world after all, but how she wished she could join them.

And when Theodora saw the faces of individual men, the hard creases around their eyes, the thick, black beards of their jaws, and the girth of their arms below their tunics, she instinctively grabbed her hood and pulled it over her head. Even at age fourteen, Theodora understood that her face attracted peculiar attention from men, both wanted and unwanted. She had dark olive skin in an unvaried hue, with obsidian black hair, long and plush, both gifts of her mother's Greek Cypriot descent. Her eyes, though, were hazel like her father's, with a natural black line that encircled them and made them prickly with lashes. The eyes of men always seemed to find her and linger on her, and though her mother didn't know it, Theodora often smiled back. Because she found men interesting, because she wanted them to find her interesting. Men were daring in the way she was daring. Men went out into a world that she desperately wished to be a part of. Such desire filled her belly as a constant and nagging exuberance, an urge to be part of these goings-on, to be regarded as important. Her pata always remarked that Theodora had an overly female nature, but her mother came to the opposite conclusion, likening Theodora to boys due to a fearlessness and knack for troublemaking.

And now, such trouble came sweeping right into her neighborhood, right where she could almost touch it. Theodora's heart raced when she watched her father hail the approaching men and step into the streets.

"He's joining the partisans," said Theodora excitedly.

The men greeted him with cheers and swats on the back as if to say *even the bear trainer is out amongst us.* Strange energy bloomed inside Theodora's chest—an anxiety, an elation, a sudden fear for her father.

"Oh, Pata, don't go," Comito said in a childish whine.

Theodora stood and brushed the dirt from her hands. "I'm going down there to stop him."

"We can't go down there now in these silly disguises. Mother needs our help with Anastasia and—"

"Anastasia's asleep with a fever," said Theodora, referring to their younger sister, who'd been sick since that morning. "You don't have to go. I'll be back before anyone even knows I'm missing."

Theodora and Comito both knew women weren't allowed on the public streets of Constantinople unaccompanied. The sight of a young woman in the streets was reserved only for beggarly children and the thieving daughters of vagabonds.

"You think you can just sneak around like some alley rat?" said Comito, who looked frightened. "You'll be seen and maybe even killed."

"I've done it before—you just never knew."

"When?"

And then, the ominous roar of the city erupted, like the Hippodrome crowd when one of the chariots won a race. Louder than that. More frightening than that. Theodora and Comito snapped their attention to the south, and for an anxious moment, neither spoke.

Theodora knew her sister would never do anything daring unless forced to. So, she spun and ran toward the adjacent roof edge. When she came to the end, she leaped into the air, spanned the thin chasm between apartment buildings, and landed surefootedly upon slanting clay tiles. "Let's go!" said Theodora. "Pata's already turning onto the Street of the Candlemakers. We'll lose him if we don't hurry."

Comito ran toward Theodora, but more out of panic. She also leaped across the chasm, but awkwardly and without grace.

Theodora's idea to save her father now had a moral imperative, one even her sister couldn't refuse. She scrambled across the sloping roof, scattering pigeons and clattering the pottery-like tiles with every step. She kept her eyes fixed upon her pata, tracking his path, as surely as a hawk follows a field mouse. How suddenly alive she felt. The mysterious and colorful world enveloped her on all sides. Below her, the streets beckoned with the prospect of a deadly fall, while above, the autumn skies dizzied her with an immovable blue, teetering her sense of balance. Just as she turned to check on Comito, one of the clay tiles cracked beneath her foot and slid away. Theodora slipped and landed hard on the rooftop. She then felt an airy terror in her belly as she slid toward the edge of the roof, her body rattling over the ridged surface, her fingertips grazing tile after tile. She finally grabbed one firm tile, and her body jolted to a stop. Her dread, though, turned to

awe as a panoramic, unobstructed view of the city rebellion lay now before
her.

Constantinople had gone mad.

Thousands, no, tens of thousands of men crowded the city center,
pitching and roiling like an angry ocean. Interspersed above the masses, she
spotted swords jabbing skyward, matching the cadence of an unintelligible
chant. Some men hoisted effigies of the emperor above the meshing throngs,
doll-like bodies that blazed in whipping flames. Rocks sprang into view,
hurled aimlessly from one side of the street to the other. Theodora also saw
random fires burning unattended in the streets here and there, with crowds
forming wild circles around each one. And everywhere there was smoke,
wafting through the expanse in sickly black and ghostly white.

Above and behind the riotous horde, Theodora raised her eyes to gaze
upon the Great Hippodrome of Constantinople, the monumental char-
iot-racing stadium that loomed over everything. The Hippodrome glowed
with the orange hue of dusk, a marble leviathan that lay in a pool of its own
spectators. Theodora pressed a hand against her chest as if to suppress the
anxiety that burned there.

"Let's turn back."

Theodora flinched and turned to see Comito, who crouched behind her
with unblinking eyes.

Her sister continued. "Look at them all."

Theodora needed a moment for the mesmerizing sight of violence to
release her. Her sister was right. The streets seemed warlike and full of chaos,
but she noticed that their father and his friends had stopped where the
Street of the Candlemakers faced out to the city center. They now stood like
statues as they gazed upon the rebellion.

"He's having second thoughts," said Theodora with certitude. "If he sees
us, he'll have no choice but to walk us back home. It's worth the risk," She
then scanned the roof line until her eyes came to rest on the bushy top of a
cypress tree. "Come on."

Theodora jumped into the tree, which swayed terribly against her
weight. Limb by limb, she climbed down through the mossy fragrance of

cypress, but she kept thinking about her pata. He wasn't a fighter. The sight she beheld only a moment ago was far beyond her father, a domain of young and dangerous men, soldiers, criminals, and tavern brawlers.

Theodora finally slipped from the tree limbs and landed on the ground like a cat, splashing up puddle water. She stood in the debris-ridden corner of an alley that faced out to the lawless Middle Way. *We're coming, Pata!* She crouched and studied the foot traffic, trying to judge her best route through the crowd, and fully aware of the danger she was about to pass through. When a frightened Comito drew up behind her, Theodora had to shout. "He's across the street. Stay close!"

Comito didn't seem to hear Theodora. She held a fearful face and glanced distractedly at all the chaos around them. Theodora tugged at her sister and then darted out of the alley, making her way openly through the crowd. Torsos and chest plates and hips with sword hilts moved past her vision. Several times, she collided with bodies that appeared suddenly in the maze of crisscrossing people and open spaces. She glanced over her shoulder and saw Comito struggling to follow, hunching up, and reaching out as if to seize the other side of the street with her hands.

The waning sun cast strong orange light and shadows against the citizens on the street. Theodora glanced up as she raced, staring at the faces of countless men, getting such good looks at their features this time, getting right up close like never before. One man steadied a massive basket atop his head as he observed the rioting. Another man led an elderly blind man away from the area, while beardless young men pushed by, hoping to join the fighting. The people were all so fascinating to Theodora. Her chest burned with excitement as she passed among them for these precious few moments, as if she were a ghost, unseen, yet in full view. Passing through cook smoke, eyes burning, colliding into pack animals, hearing excited voices from all directions, breathing in the heavy aroma of wax from the candlemaking shops, feeling the chill of wet air on her hooded face, her senses were overwhelmed.

As she drew up to the violent crowd, she pulled her hood low to cover her feminine face. Nary an eye could see her. Then she spotted two men brawling in the street, right up close. They moved so fast as they grappled, with rose-red blood upon their faces and knuckles. Veering away from the scuffle, Theodora spun into an empty arched doorway and pressed against one side. She peered around the edge of the doorway as Comito finally crashed in behind her. They were so close. Pata had been standing across the street right in the area she now stood, but a mass of bodies obstructed her view. All the faces were unfamiliar. "I think I lost sight of Pata," said Theodora, feeling a sudden bout of panic.

"Oh, Theodora, what are we doing out here?"

But then, Theodora noticed the two brawling men stop fighting and slowly rise to their feet. Strange that they would forget their fighting, Theodora thought. Their attention shifted northward, toward a common sight. The riotous crowd around them suddenly cleared away, as if retreating. Theodora turned to follow their gaze and spotted something that made her breath stop. A fully armed column of Roman soldiers approached up the Street of the Candlemakers, as if out of nowhere. Perhaps two hundred soldiers now advanced ominously, with shields lifted to cover the bottom half of their faces, spears aimed skyward with glistening tips. She heard the shout of the commanding officer, who seemed to be preparing the soldiers for a clash against the rioters.

Theodora suddenly realized that she and her sister were caught between the rebellious mob and a company of Roman troops. A rock whizzed by and banged against a Roman shield, then another.

"You've trapped us!" said Comito, squeezing her eyes shut. "I hate you for this."

Theodora pulled her sister into the doorway and fell over her protectively. She suppressed her own panic just as rows of Roman soldiers marched by them, sweeping autumn air into the doorway, the rhythmic sound of their footfalls and the clank of their armor overtaking all other sound.

Each soldier wore heavy-looking shirts of chain mail that hung from their shoulders down to their belt line with white sleeves and tunics beneath. Steel helmets shaped like half of an egg crowned their heads and shadowed their faces, while strips of red leather bounced off their thighs. Worse yet to Theodora, the soldiers appeared ready for violence. The front ranks lowered their spears, which settled between each red oval shield. An officer shouted so closely and so loudly that Theodora and Comito both covered their ears.

"Form up! Get the auxiliaries into position!"

Theodora finally spotted her father turn and flee into the thousands of rioters. *Not that way*, she thought as the column of troops moved by her and took up a pitched position in the street. She reached over and took up Comito's cold, shaking hand. "I just saw Pata."

"Spears!" shouted the commander.

And Theodora watched the troops in the front line suddenly hoist their spears up to their ears, rear back, and hurl the weapons through the air.

She gasped and leaped from the doorway to trace the arching path of the spears through the sky. "No," she muttered to herself.

She heard howls of agony as the spears plunged into the faceless mob. The rioters broke ranks in all directions, while the Roman troops formed a shield wall and marched forward again. Theodora didn't even flinch when a brick struck the street near her feet and skipped away. Smoke gusted into her eyes, and she couldn't see her father anywhere. She spotted a few rioters lying on the ground and bleeding, spear shafts sticking out from their bodies. None were her father though.

"Pata!" Theodora screamed as frantic people ran passed her. She called out for him again and again, but a strange sense of futility grew inside her. Just then, someone wrapped her with both arms, heaved her into the air, and spun away from the street. Before Theodora could react, deafening hoofbeats clamored by her, followed by a cold gust of wet leaves and air. When she opened her eyes again, she saw the buttocks of a dozen white stallions as Roman cavalry guards galloped by.

"Do you want to be trampled, child?" said a man's harsh voice.

Theodora realized that she was in the arms of another soldier and so she kicked and twisted until he set her down. But her hood had come off, and the soldier stared right into her eyes. He had no violence in his countenance, but his big brown eyes burned with intelligence and authority. His face was clean-shaven, like a rich man's, Theodora thought—intense, but not battle-ready like the other soldiers she'd just witnessed. He wore the white and purple armor of a Palatine guardsman, an imperial guard of the Daphne Palace. And he was completely handsome, which made Theodora stare, despite her anger.

"You girls need to run," he said as if issuing a command. "There's nothing but bloodshed out here tonight."

"We're trying to get home, Commander," said Comito, who took the lead, grabbing Theodora by the arm and pushing by the Palatine guardsman. "Please. We're so sorry." Theodora let herself be guided away but kept her gaze on the dashing Roman. She couldn't take her eyes off him. She found herself hating his natural authority over her and hating even more that striking face beneath the shadow of his helmet. At the last instant, not knowing how else to defy him, Theodora stuck out her tongue. The gesture was childish, she knew, but it reassured her against following some order.

Finally, Theodora turned away and raced after Comito. "We're sorry, Pata," she said aloud but didn't dare look back.

TWO

The skies were black and full of stars by the time Theodora made it back to her neighborhood. She and Comito had slipped through the faction lines and finally made it back to the so-called "First Hill," their small neighborhood on the north end of the city. But she'd come so close to dangerous men and their violence that the exhilaration still burned in her chest.

"Do you think Pata's all right?" said Comito between breaths.

"You heard the people talking back there. The emperor's going to speak to all the men at the Hippodrome. That old beggar with the cat said the emperor would take back the law that caused the revolt."

"But what about Pata?"

Theodora raised her voice. "I told you I didn't see him. I saw wounded men in the streets," she said, recalling the sight of so many blood puddles on the cobblestone. "But he wasn't there. So, he must be in the Hippodrome with all the other men. That's what I'm telling Mother anyway."

Theodora looked again. At the end of the street, facing southward, she saw the dark upper rim to the Hippodrome of Constantinople in the distance. The Hippodrome looked as black as ink, with an orange glow above the racetrack, like a mist. Tens of thousands of men were chanting something ominous in there. During the daytime, this massive structure shone pale white, with columns that split the beams of the sun and banners that flapped among the birds. Normally, Theodora heard that crowd chanting, "Nika! Nika! Nika!" a drunken, maddened Greek word that meant "victory," but on this strange night the crowd noise roiled without horse sport. "All this madness over the emperor," said Theodora. "Why do we even have one?"

"Because the empire has to have an emperor. We've always had one. Come on, let's cut through the alley."

Sometimes Theodora despised her sister's ignorance to the larger world. Comito somehow fretted intensely over simple matters of the domicile or crooned sympathetically for street beggars, and lately, she took to babbling about the prospects of a husband. Yet in the city of Constantinople, Theodora understood that it was the will of the people that mattered, it was the factions that mattered, and it was the Christian god who mattered most.

Theodora turned into a dark alley with high plaster walls, chipped and showing exposed bricks beneath. Timber beams framed many dark doorways, any one of which could hide a knifeman of the Blues or Greens. Both she and Comito walked quickly. The night sky above her looked like a river of stars beset on each side with the black monolithic shapes of the insula, the blocks of city apartments.

When they came out on the other end, and when they saw their own apartment dwelling, Theodora finally removed her hood. Her family lived in a dwelling above a workshop that spun colorful fabric for use in the theaters. At that hour, though, the spinning wheels lay still and looms empty in the darkness. Most of the dwelling windows above the workshops were aglow from candlelight.

When the two sisters finally reached the dark entrance to their family's apartment, the door swung open, a soft light pouring out, and their mother, Maximina, stood there with blazing eyes.

"You girls get in here," she said with flushed cheeks. "You ran off while drawing water from the wells, didn't you? And here you come back late and with not even a bucket."

Her mother's words were thick with a Cypriot accent, a sound in her language that was absent from Theodora and her sisters. The apartment was a dark place in the candlelight, a cramped place, with a crumbling hearth and spit over embers. The floors were hidden beneath many rugs that were darkened from years of long use.

"We're completely unhurt, Mother," said Theodora.

"Don't be so calm when you speak to me," she said. "The streets are full of violence and here you make me worry like some fool. Where's Acacius?"

"Pata's in the Hippodrome."

Maximina went to the lone window on the wall and craned to stare through the wooden grille.

Theodora heard men say that Maximina was a comely woman for her age, despite the exertions of bearing three daughters. Theodora's mother had once been a dancer at the theater and still dressed to emphasize her body. She wore a lacy jerkin with strings untied, each half of the white linen flayed carelessly to either side. The opening trailed down to her navel and highlighted a buxom chest. Several layers of necklaces—gold, silver, seashell, and elephant teeth—filled the space at her collar. She looked most like Comito, but older, heartier, a woman whose strong face bore creases from much life, both joy and toil alike. Maximina had dark eyes, almost black, with dark moles around the mouth that complemented rather than diminished her looks. Her lavish hair was black like Theodora's, but with noticeable grays, hanging unkempt from beneath a red and gold head wrap, and jingling with copper charms.

Maximina continued. "What happened out there?"

Comito stepped in and hugged Maximina. "Oh, Mother, all the men have gone mad, worse than anything I've ever seen. They filled the streets and were fighting everywhere and then soldiers came out—"

Maximina stiffened. "Soldiers?"

"You were right to tell Pata to stay home," said Comito. "I think he's in terrible danger."

Theodora disliked her sister's fawning manner toward their mother, so she walked over to her younger sister Anastasia, who was resting in sickness in the corner. Anastasia was still awake and smiled when she saw Theodora. She was a timid girl who lacked the pretty features of her mother and older sisters alike. Right away, Theodora felt the fire-hot skin of her sister's forehead from the fever. She adjusted thin blankets, which were damp with sweat, and when Theodora saw a flea appear on her sister's exposed skin, she caught and killed it.

"Theodora, is this what you saw of your father as well?" said Maximina.

"Yes, but I'm not mad at Pata like you both."

"You dare defend your father in this?" said Maximina.

"Well, yes. All the men are out there and Pata's part of it. I think it's good that he's standing up to the emperor. You should have seen how happy the faction men were when Pata joined them."

"Those friends might get him killed," said Maximina. "Acacius doesn't need to be out in this foolish revolt, not with his bad foot. Now I want you girls to listen to this city." Maximina pointed at the ceiling, but her finger signaled the distant commotion at the Hippodrome. For a moment, no one spoke and the pulsing chants of the Blues and Greens boomed like sporadic thunder, before fragmenting into ever louder ovations. "That is the sound of the people against the emperor. If the Blues and Greens go too far in this, if they tread too heavily, then your precious father might be arrested by those soldiers you saw, or worse. What do you think of that, Theodora? If Acacius goes to prison, we'll be begging in the streets. Will you go visit Pata in the prisons? Show him what a good beggar you've become? You can bring him what bread you did not eat and watch him eat it like an animal with shackles on his wrists. Is that what you mean when you speak of this *thing* that goes on?"

"Stop, you're scaring poor Anastasia," said Theodora.

"Oh yes. Make a show of your worry for your little sister while dismissing your mother. Go on then."

"I will."

"Mother's right to be scared for Pata," said Comito. "She didn't tell you, but this morning when we threw alum powder into the flames, Mother saw the shape of a black scorpion in the smoke. Now look, the fortune has come true. The city has been stung by some kind of poison."

"How can I argue such a thing?" said Theodora. "For I have no smoke with different shapes in them to prove otherwise."

"Do you mock me?" said Maximina.

Theodora didn't answer. She knew her mother still held bizarre superstitions from her home island, beliefs of future portends of the world, predictions based on strange alchemy and dark, pagan arts. Although her mother told certain friends that the family was Christian, Theodora knew they'd never been baptized. Her mother believed that baptism was a dangerous charm upon the forehead that left people prone to drowning. Maximina couldn't swim and so feared water. Even Theodora's name and the names of her sisters were meant to foretell the future of the empire. She named Comito after the comet, a celestial object of the night skies, revered by the old pagans. Theodora was the only daughter with a clear, Christian name, meant to please the Hebrew father now worshiped by the Romans. And finally, Theodora's youngest sister was named Anastasia, the feminine version of Emperor Anastasius. Theodora knew that to Maximina, Anastasia was only sick because the emperor was sick, or at least his reign was sick with rebellion. So then, Theodora's mother honored the three great powers of the fading empire and, in so doing, ensured the proper tributes to whichever power finally emerged supreme. But Theodora often wondered which power that would be—the old gods, the new god, or the emperor?

Theodora wanted to climb up to the rooftops to watch the revolt. But she knew her mother would stay up into the late evening. When she glanced up, she saw that Maximina still awaited some kind of response.

"What do you wish me to say?" said Theodora. "It's just powder burning in a fire."

"No, not tonight," said Maximina, pulling away from Comito and stepping in close to Theodora. "Tonight, you respect the old ways for your father's sake. Even the Christians are kneeling in prayer right now."

Theodora stroked the cheek of Anastasia, whose eyes became heavy. "I understand, Mother."

That seemed to be the end of the confrontation for a while. After a quiet moment, Comito moved to the hearth in the center of the room and stirred the embers. Maximina stepped to the window, which was covered by a patterned wooden grille. She leaned against the dark wall and listened to the sound of the distant Hippodrome.

As Anastasia breathed heavily under the weight of sleep, Theodora watched her mother and felt small pangs of guilt. Even though Theodora thought little of fortune-telling, there was something in her mother's passions that she still respected. Comito and Anastasia might have been more polite to Maximina, more blindly obedient, but it was Theodora who understood her mother best because they were the most alike.

Her mother came to Constantinople from Cyprus as a migrant, crossing the rugged coastline of Anatolia, and carrying an infant Comito in her arms. Maximina knew the pleasures and dangers of life outdoors, alongside the crumbling imperial highways. She often told Theodora of a time when she saved Comito from a wolf attack in the night, beating off the animal with a rock, even after being dragged several paces from within the jaws of the animal. Comito said she remembered their mother's battle with the wolf, but Theodora doubted the claim, herself having no memories at such a young age.

Only after that journey ended did Theodora arrive at her mother's breast, a pure urban girl who never saw those distant shores nor slept beneath that open air. She knew not the fragrance of the wild soils or timbered ships, though she often tried to imagine them. No, Theodora was conceived behind the walls of civilization, a child of music, of alleyways, of bricks and rats, of bronze statues and cobblestone, but perhaps most importantly, she was a true child of their pata, Acacius. Comito's father was a different man, an unknown man, whose name was never uttered by Maximina.

This gave Theodora a special bond with her pata, despite his less impressive story. Acacius had traveled the Via Egnatia alongside the wine caravans and refugees from Italy, joining those weary Romans who abandoned the western empire after the fall of Rome. Theodora's pata knew how to train bears the way that many Christians knew how to train dogs. Acacius made his living on the Middle Way, directing his bear to walk atop wooden barrels or stand upright in the garb of a Persian soldier.

But it was Maximina who insisted Acacius save his earnings to purchase a true post, the bearkeeper post for the Green faction. Now, Theodora loved that her pata set his skills upon the spectators of the Amphitheater. This gave Theodora's family a modicum of status in Constantinople—no longer wandering migrants, but *citizens.*

Theodora saw her mother as a woman of will and vitality, one who scavenged across a wild earth like an animal, only to somehow triumph, to pull out of street poverty and build a family, who should have had boys instead of three girls. Yet Theodora never sensed disappointment from her mother at having daughters. Maximina expected Theodora and her sisters to survive in the world, to learn their letters while other girls frolicked, and to think, as men did, about the goings-on beyond the domicile.

So, when Theodora watched her mother at the window, she knew that Maximina was something of a commander at the moment, watching and waiting for news of a distant battle, one that, if lost, could threaten all that she built up from nothing.

And that was why, when the revolt ended, when the men finally filtered out of the Hippodrome that night, and when Acacius did not come home, Theodora wept first for her mother, before succumbing to grief for her missing father.

THREE

Theodora, her sisters, and Maximina found Acacius in the morning. He lay on the wet cobblestone streets along with a hundred others, arranged in a row in front of the Hagia Sophia Basilica, face up, peaceful, as if sleeping. He had a wooden plate atop his chest that held the gnarled remains of a candle. Whatever colors paint a man's face and hands in life, they were gone, replaced by a stony shade of gray.

Christian priests worked through the night to dress the wounds of the dead, laying them out in repose and uttering benedictions. Theodora knelt with her sisters and mother beside Acacius. She pressed her head into her father's autumn-cold chest and cried. How could she have been so wrong about him? How could she have been so sure he'd come home? She listened to the solemn hymns from the monks who lined up in the forum. They graced the chill morning with graven music; a choir of masculine voices made sweet, rising and falling in eerie but distinctive Christian melodies, their breath misting at each Latin word.

Theodora saw that Anastasia shivered in the cold, despite her layers of cheap scarves and shawls. She embraced her sister, to comfort as well as to warm her. Her sister's body felt hot beneath the clothing and she pulsed irregularly with sobbing. The thought came to Theodora that her frail sister could soon lose a bed to sleep in. What then? Would she be forced to heal outdoors in the constant cold of winter?

And then Theodora agonized at the thought of her pata lying on the street throughout the night, last night, out where the light rains pelted him, out there in the weather, no different than debris in an alley. The sight of grieving women and children over a motionless man repeated all around Theodora. Were any of them thinking about their families when they joined in the revolt? she wondered. Then she stared again at her pata and recalled how only last night she watched him lumbering out to the rebellion. He looked so happy. And Theodora had been so proud of him. Now she would forever know that she was watching her father walk out to his death.

In the distance, Theodora heard street cheering. She lifted her head and stared off in the direction of the celebratory noise. She realized that the rebel citizens who were in the Hippodrome last night now reunited all along the Middle Way to revel in their apparent victory. They could cheer because they survived, thought Theodora. They weren't in the Augustaion, grieving for the dead. She no longer liked that sound, the sound of a great host bellowing in madness. To her, it was the sound of a creature with many tentacles, one that made the city shudder as it clashed blindly against the emperor as well as itself . . . a murderer of men, a taker of fathers.

When the sun finally slipped into the western skies, blurring the horizon with stripes of vermillion, orange, and lemon-yellow, the deacons came out from the church. Some carried golden thuribles that smoked with frankincense, while others flung water droplets upon the corpses. Then they loaded the dead, one by one, onto funeral carts.

"Take a good look, girls," said Maximina as the priests lifted Acacius from the ground. "Your pata leaves us now for good." As the corpse of

Acacius rolled to rest atop another in the back of a cart, Maximina broke forward and struck the cart repeatedly. "You left us with nothing, you fool! Nothing!" Theodora watched as deacons calmly, solemnly took her mother by the arms and moved her away from the cart. Maximina fell to her knees and sobbed. Comito, Anastasia, and Theodora all crowded around their stricken mother, a new and disturbing sight.

Theodora looked around and noticed other members of the Green faction who gathered nearby. They lit handheld candles for the coming funeral procession, but looked over at Maximina regretfully, before looking away again. *Just another widow . . . so sad,* they all seemed to be saying. They sympathized in a way that came to nothing, with a care that slipped off with their brief attention. Theodora glowered at them all. In a way, the overwhelming grief pressing in on her family seemed to just blend in, becoming common and somehow insignificant.

Then she spotted a face she recognized. Magister Origen. He was a high-ranking noble, a Judge of the Ward, who went by the title "Magister." After a moment, she realized that he noticed her watching him. He stared back, his eyes flitting back and forth between her, her sisters, and Maximina. He didn't look away like the others but held a stoic expression. He excused himself from his colleagues and approached.

The man had oiled dark-honey hair that clung to his scalp and intense eyes that seemed to bore through whatever he looked at. He moved gracefully, slowly, as if gliding through a sea of lesser men, a man of favors and acquaintances. Theodora's pata had told the girls that Magister Origen would one day become a senator and powerful friend of the family. One day.

He drew up and embraced Maximina, offering condolences. Theodora watched the two speak inaudibly to one another, her mother nodding, the magistrate holding her at the shoulders. Then he looked down at Theodora and her sisters. "I'm so sorry, girls. Acacius was a good man and beloved by all."

That was all he said. Afterwards, Theodora and hundreds of solemn families followed the funeral procession to a mass grave north of the city, just inside the Red Gate, called the Place of Many Men. Acacius, the bearkeeper of the Greens, was given a burial that Theodora thought unfitting. He was dumped into a pit in the earth, there to lay atop a heap of other dead men.

The dancing masters from both factions made quite a show of their grief. But they didn't pay the same price, did they? Their rebellion was over; the funerals were over; so they returned to their lives.

But Theodora returned to a home without a father.

FOUR

Theodora struggled for days to find some solace. The death of her father came suddenly and with devastating possibilities. For once, her mother had no answers, no plan that would keep the family off the streets, and no source of income. When Theodora suggested that perhaps her mother could return to the theater and dance again, Maximina viciously scolded her. She lifted her shirt to reveal a patch of wrinkled skin at the belly, skin she carefully hid with cloth belts. "The stage is no place for a mother of three, you foolish child! Men would only pay me to *leave* the stage," she said, before weeping again.

The family had a trifle of gold left over from Acacius, but those coins would soon dwindle.

Three days after the funeral, when the neighborhoods settled into stillness and silence, when widows grieved behind empty windows, when the streets filled with frolicking children once again, Theodora saw that her mother no longer wept, but sat for long hours, still as a statue, while a square of sunlight from the open window moved across her. She didn't eat much. When she did move, it was to tend to Anastasia, who lay asleep on the mattress, a blanket atop her shape, breathing the scantest of breaths. The domicile felt barren and cold.

Theodora and Comito stayed outside. There, they sat among the pigeons in the street when Magister Origen suddenly appeared on horseback from out of the foot traffic. He had a bodyguard beside him.

Theodora pointed. "Look. It's that man again."

"What's he doing here?" said Comito.

Theodora stood up, watching the magistrate dismount, but he didn't see her. He then climbed a flight of stairs and knocked on the door to Theodora's dwelling. Maximina let him inside.

"Maybe he's here to help us," said Theodora. "Pata said that Magister Origen's rich."

"I hope he's here to help," said Comito. "I really don't want to beg in the streets."

"Come on. Let's go to the back window. We can hear what they're saying."

"Good idea."

With that, Theodora led Comito down the street, slipped between two apartment buildings, and paused in a dark corridor so narrow, she barely fit. Stray foot traffic passed by, and none noticed the two sisters in the crevice. Then, Theodora scaled the plaster and brickwork, navigating the crooks and crops in the masonry until she reached the window to their dwelling. It was an opening with a wooden lattice shutter, slightly ajar. There she secured her feet on a wood beam ledge that ran horizontally along the wall. If she fell from that height, she'd be seriously injured. Leaning her head in slowly, allowing only one eye to peer inside, Theodora saw her mother sitting at the table with Magister Origen. Behind them, Anastasia stirred and then stilled from the blankets.

"Theodora," called Comito, half-whispering, half-shouting. "I can't climb this. How did you get up there?"

"You just have to figure it out," said Theodora. She then held a finger to her lips and pointed at the window.

Comito put her hands on her hips and sighed. "Tell me what they are saying, will you?"

Theodora nodded at her older sister and then turned her full attention to the meeting inside her home. She got a good look at Magister Origen. He had a fascinating, striking face, with a slight weathering of his skin from age, which was most obvious at the corners of his eyes. The furrows complemented him and gave him a stately, highly experienced air. He squeezed Maximina's hand on the tabletop and there seemed to be a heartfelt sadness between them both.

"When I heard that Acacius had been slain, my heart sank," said Magister Origen. "Truly. Acacius was a favorite of the Greens. He trained his bears quicker than any prior keeper I've ever known. And whenever the emperor attended festivities in the Hippodrome and bears were part of the show, it was always your husband's bears they used." He nodded as if thinking privately to himself. "He loved his family. I can't tell you how often he doted on his three girls. The hazel-eyed girl, what's her name?"

Theodora gasped. He was talking about her.

"That would be Theodora, my second born."

"Yes," he said and lowered his voice. "I dare say Acacius favored his Theodora."

Maximina wiped her eyes. "That's because she's like him, headstrong with too much will."

"No, she's just young, and the young have the luxury of being headstrong."

Theodora listened intensely. She liked that her mother compared her to Pata, and she liked even more that the magistrate defended her.

"But men of rank don't have that luxury," continued Magister Origen. "Acacius never shared the passions of other faction members over religious matters, so I was surprised to see him among the dead. What he did, he did for the Greens, for his friends."

Maximina's gaze slipped to the floor.

He continued. "How many men left their families behind and in need?

Had I not seen you grieving, I doubt I could've understood the nature of this tragedy so clearly, so personally. I thought to myself, *By God, this beautiful family could lose their foothold in life*. And I just haven't been able to shake the thought."

"But there are hundreds of families like ours right now, grieving as we do," said Maximina. "Why come to me?"

"Because your situation is dire. You have no sons you can look to. So that's why I wished to visit you in your home to offer assistance."

Theodora leaned over and whispered down to her sister. "He's going to help us."

"He is? How?" said Comito.

Theodora held out a finger and then returned her attention to the conversation beyond the windowsill.

"That is an option, of course, for widows and their children," Magister Origen was saying. "There is the Orphanage of Zoticus, but that may be a harsh life for the girls. The blessed Sampson, a personal friend of mine, takes in many people, but even he is overwhelmed these days with more sick and dying than homeless. And now, after the revolt . . . ," he said and flung up a hand. "I've come up with a more preferable course, one that I hope you won't find improper."

Maximina twitched. "Improper?"

"I ask your permission to speak plainly about these sensitive matters."

Maximina dabbed her eyes with a cloth. "Of course, Magister Origen."

The magistrate nodded and placed his hands flat on the table. "With the tragic passing of your husband, the fact remains that the bearkeeper post is now vacant. The Greens need to fill the post soon. There's already been much politicking and sums being offered. We have a list of candidates for the post, names the dancing master has already approved. One of these candidates is a man named Samuel. He's a good Christian and hard-working. Now, the detail that matters here is that Samuel, unlike the other candidates, is not yet betrothed."

"What are you saying?" said Maximina.

"I'm suggesting you marry this Samuel and keep the bearkeeper post in your family. I'll plead your case. Marry Samuel. Keep the post. Keep your family off the streets."

Maximina covered her mouth and squeezed her eyes shut. Theodora couldn't tell if the emotion was fresh grief or rekindled hope. But the thought. She tore her gaze away from the scene within and froze. Would her mother bring a different man into their dwelling? Theodora didn't like the thought. Pata was her father and no other. She ignored Comito's demands for information and peered back through the window.

"I feared you would be offended at my suggestion of marrying another man. I half-expected to be rebuked," said Magister Origen with a friendly smile. Then he grew serious again. "I hope you understand the full weight of this path. A marriage would have to be arranged quickly in order to get the post while it's still vacant. So, you would not be afforded the proper period of mourning, grounds I'm sure for harsh gossip."

"Gossip I can stand," said Maximina. "I saw a future for my girls that was so bleak, Magister Origen, bleak as the night is black. And here now, all I must do is to marry another?"

"You're the widow of a very popular bearkeeper, and the mother of three daughters, no less. I'd give my support for Samuel, and my recommendation holds much weight with Dancing Master Asterius."

"How would I pay for the post?"

"Samuel pays for the post."

Maximina looked confused. "What do I owe you then? Surely, you want something in return, Magister."

He's just being nice, thought Theodora. *Why did Mother always make people uncomfortable with her doubts and suspicions? Why couldn't she just accept the magistrate's help?*

Magister Origen continued. "You would owe me nothing and be in no debt. I do, however, have a request, not a condition, one I hope you'll oblige me on."

"There had to be something," Maximina said.

"Let me bring your two oldest girls in front of Dancing Master Asterius. I know you saw him at the funeral and—"

Maximina interrupted. "I know the dancing master well, Magister."

"Well, your late husband mentioned on several occasions that his daughters were quite talented, especially that Theodora of his," said Magister Origen. "You may not believe it, but women earn surprising sums of money these days. A premier actress could even support her entire family."

Theodora spun away from the window, pressed her shoulders flat against the hard wall, and held her breath. Her chest constricted as if a belt tightened around her.

An actress!

She'd thought about such a thing so many times, but Maximina always scolded her. *That's what I did,* her mother would say. *That's not how you girls will do it. You girls need a good mind, not a stage.*

"What is it?" asked Comito from below, but Theodora didn't answer.

Me.

On stage for all to see. Someone beautiful and important.

Theodora eagerly readjusted her position and bits of plaster sprinkled poor Comito.

"Have you heard of Helladia?" said Magister Origen. "She's only nineteen years old, but performs at the great Amphitheater, right up the street. Anyway, Helladia earns more with her pantomiming than her father earns as a shoemaker." Origen rapped his knuckles on the table. "At the theater."

Maximina didn't brighten at the comments. "I'm sure she does, Magister. She probably works hard for many patrons to earn so much. I'm no stranger to a theater. Actresses serve the public in a variety of ways, but you and I both know that not all services are on stage."

Theodora furrowed her brow. Again, her mother grumbled when she should be humble with appreciation.

Magister Origen continued. "I'm talking about sending them to a dance school, a koitṓna, for prestigious training."

"But my girls would be around that shameless theater life. I was part of an acting troupe myself once. I know what goes on backstage. That's why I want husbands for my daughters."

"How has that worked out for you?" said Magister Origen curtly. But when anger flashed over Maximina's face, he winced and shook his head. "I'm sorry. I just meant that there are risks even along the safe path you sought. No need to skirt around it. We both know how many ways a girl may earn. But you danced in the pavilions outside the city in your day, where things are a bit more free-spirited. I'm talking about the Amphitheater, a long-standing institution here in Constantinople. Women are beginning to garner serious respect as performers. They're no longer just stage decorations for off-stage activities. In some neighborhoods, the audience prefers women to men, especially with pantomiming. These are very different times we live in. I believe your girls have a chance to earn in a respectable way."

Maximina shook her head and sighed. "I'll remarry to keep the bear-keeper post, but I don't want that theater life for my girls. It mingles too closely with the brothels—"

"I want to do it," shouted Theodora, revealing herself and crawling in through the window.

Maximina sprang to her feet. "Theodora!"

"I want to go to the theater, Mother. I'll earn money for all of us. Please don't say no."

Maximina grabbed Theodora by the arm. "What are you doing at that window? Don't you know that a fall would kill you? Where's Comito?"

"Outside."

Maximina marched toward the window, pulling Theodora behind her, and then stuck her head out. "Comito, you get up here! Why did you let your sister climb up here?" Then she looked over at the magistrate. "I'm so sorry."

Magister Origen arose. "No apologies needed," he said and turned to face Theodora. "You listen to your mother. Becoming an actress is no easy thing."

"But I want to do it," said Theodora as she twisted free of her mother's painful grip. She took a step toward the magistrate and sweetened her voice. "And I think you're being most kind with your offer."

"Theodora! Sit down!" said Maximina, surprisingly harsh.

Theodora obeyed but kept her eyes on the magistrate. She smiled at him and he returned the smile.

He then shifted his gaze to Maximina. "Let me take them to the dancing master. I'm giving you a chance to keep the bearkeeper post and this one request is all I ask. Remember, Dancing Master Asterius could turn your girls down outright. He's a very particular man with an exacting eye for talent. But if he agrees that your daughters can be trained, then you should pounce on the opportunity. Your girls could earn as handsomely as if they were sons. But, you're their mother and I'll defer to your wisdom on the matter."

In the background, Anastasia moaned as she awoke.

The magistrate heard the moan and then looked back at Maximina with renewed concern. "Give me your answer soon, Widow of Acacius," said Magister Origen.

Theodora saw that her mother stared at her with a look of concern and contemplation.

FIVE

wo weeks later, Theodora watched the betrothal of her mother to this Samuel, a fat and balding man who looked like the bears he trained. Unlike Pata, Samuel was no passive believer in Christianity. He made the family say prayers before each meal, traced the sign of the cross over the food they ate, and invoked the Trinity whenever Maximina spoke obscenities.

Each day, Theodora went through the routine of waking, coming out of a fog, only to remember that her pata was dead and that another man lived in her home. When the household slept and the mice rustled throughout the domicile, Theodora opened the wood shutters and slipped out the window into the chilly night air. Once outside, she climbed to the roof, laid flat against the cold clay tiles, and stared up at the stars. Her breath pulsed like mist and wisped away, yet the stars remained. Christians believed the dead traveled up to a place far above the earth. Perhaps her pata was up among those stars somehow. But since Theodora couldn't see or touch heaven, such a place interested her less. She listened instead to a lonely hymn from a monk in the distance, somewhere out in a dark neighborhood, where a man's bell-like voice rose and fell so beautifully. The monk sang verses of a canticle until eventually his voice fell silent, but only for a moment, when another monk, who relieved the first, took up a new canticle. In that way, a single voice penetrated the city throughout the night.

To Theodora, there was something special about the night, about being awake while civilization lay hidden in the dark. She crawled to the edge of the roof, set her chin in her hands, and observed whatever goings-on she pleased, and for as long as she pleased. Her eyes traced the nightly ships that passed along the horizon, visible by the lanterns on each mast, like fireflies, casting luminance upon a sea of black ink. Every now and then, she heard an echo of laughter or a shout from a dark corner of the city. Sometimes, Roman patrollers lumbered down her street on foot. They wrapped red capes around their shoulders, covering their mouth to keep warm, with metal armor jingling at each step. They never thought to look up, she noticed. But the most frightening moments came when a fire broke out somewhere in the city. Nothing was more terrifying to a city of wood than fire. Sometimes the fire would appear as a smoke plume that covered the star field, while other times, Theodora watched violent flames leap up from a rooftop, only to spread to another, burning, lashing, while silhouettes hurled water buckets.

But Theodora sensed that something about her childhood life was slipping. Change had come. The aristocrat, Magister Origen, set new and exciting possibilities into motion. Theodora and Comito were to leave soon and attend a dance school, there to join other girls of talent. She'd join a colorful segment of society, one of Greek marble seats and smiling masks, elegant costumes, music, and applause. Now, Theodora dared to imagine Magister Origen one day observing her dance performance. And when the audience cheered heartily, Theodora would single the magistrate out in the crowd and offer a theatric bow.

Eventually, though, the applause fell silent in her imagination. After a yawn, she returned to the cramped dwelling, where her sisters breathed in deep sleep, and where fleas lay waiting in her blanket.

So, two weeks after her mother's marriage to Samuel and one month after the death of her father, Theodora left her childhood home behind.

She and Comito hugged their mother and a sobbing Anastasia in the streets before climbing into the back of a covered wagon. The last thing Theodora remembered was the sight of Maximina and Anastasia standing in the street, weeping as the wagon turned a corner. She felt anxiety at the uncertain future. And while Comito sobbed, Theodora stared at the wintery city passing by outside the wagon.

The dance school was on the northeast side of the city near the Amphitheater, a rickety old building called a koitóna. There was no going home now, not unless the head of the koitóna permitted the excursion and provided a male escort.

A strange man came out of the koitóna to greet them, though he said not a word. He was a slight man, but his face frightened Theodora. He stared at her through one brown eye, while the other was as white as a boiled egg. Below the ghostly eye, where the cheekbone protruded, Theodora saw a shadowy hole, like a knot in a tree, where an arrow must have struck him long ago. She winced as the man led her from the wagon to the koitóna.

When she and Comito entered the koitóna, warmth greeted them. The interior of the place looked better than the exterior. Theodora smelled burning incense mixed with a stale wooden odor. There were at least three floors, with each level encircling the bottom floor like a balcony and looking down into a common room. Colorful rugs hung over almost all the wall space, while more overlapped the floor. Ornate, metal lanterns dangled from the rafters and cast dots of luminance, like stars, throughout an otherwise dim interior.

"Come here, girls," said a woman's voice.

Theodora turned to see an old woman in a red robe, seated on a large, pillowed bench. Blue smoke drifted up from brass incense bowls at the base of the bench, curling around her like ghostly serpents. And Theodora gasped when she noticed an antelope fawn curled up and sleeping beside the older woman.

Four other girls stood nearby. One of them, a girl of about eleven, shook a cluster of ostrich feathers to stir the air. The other girls were Comito's age. Their silhouettes stood behind the incense smoke with watchful but unwelcoming gazes.

"You must be the new girls from Magister Origen," the old woman said.

"Yes. I'm Theodora and this is my older sister, Comito."

"Well, I'm Madame Glyceria. I'm the mistress of the girls here. I'm your instructor and new mother. Now, let me get a good look at you," she said.

And here the woman sat forward, pushing her face through the smoldering mist. Theodora thought Glyceria looked hideous but glamorous. Her eyes bore the mysterious shape of the Asian folk, like two sunken diamonds that bristled with lashes. As elderly as Glyceria's face looked, her hair, which hung straight like curtains against her cheeks, was dyed like fabric, as black and shiny as a young woman's hair. Perhaps the woman had been a beauty once, but now her face was old, spotted, wrinkled, and worn.

"You're a pretty one," the woman said and grabbed Theodora by the chin, angling her head left and then right. "Very pretty. The magistrate's girls don't always make the stage, but they're always pretty. You have much of the daystar, girl."

"That's what my mother says, Madame," said Theodora.

"Let's see what the ashes say." The woman licked her thumb and dipped it in incense ash. Then she traced a line along Theodora's eyebrow line, cheeks, and chin. With a strange posture of her hand, she seemed to measure the distance between Theodora's nose and ears. "How old are you?"

"Fourteen."

"Address me as *Madame Glyceria*," she said without breaking her study of Theodora's face. "What season were you born in?"

"In the winter, Madame Glyceria."

"Well, there's something interesting," the woman said. "The heat in your neck, the large size of your eyes? It could mean your heart is of the wolf."

Theodora wrinkled her nose. Her mother always used the Greek word for "wolf," *lýkaina*, to describe flirtatious women.

Then Madame Glyceria shifted her attention to Comito. "You're less pretty than your sister but still handsome enough. Yes, plain, but handsome.

Let me see your face." As Madame Glyceria repeated her study of Comito's features, she seemed to lose interest. "You're good with chores, aren't you? Have you girls been baptized?"

"My mother didn't want it," said Comito.

"Good. Your mother is wise to refuse such water magic. The theater is not favored by the goatherder's god, for Christians don't want you in their world or near their men. In here, you'll give love and homage to Tyche. She's the ancient guardian of this city and a protector of feminine beauty." Glyceria drew in a luxurious breath and appeared suddenly wistful. "And beauty is the only thing worth worshipping in this life, ever-rich if you have it, and ever-haunting if it proves elusive. Look around you. I turn the beauty of girls into motion and thought, into a living art form. And eventually, I'll make real women out of you, one way or another. You, pretty one, touch my robe."

Glyceria grabbed Theodora's hand and slapped it against the cherry-colored fabric of the sleeve. The material felt surprisingly cool on Theodora's skin, shimmering like a pool of red oil in the dim light, as smooth as polished marble, but soft as a cat's fur.

"It's silk, little wolf, the most expensive fabric in the world. Follow my teachings exactly and one day you'll wear such finery."

Theodora rubbed the fabric in her fingers as the sleeping antelope fawn resettled in its position.

Madame Glyceria pushed Theodora's hand away. "Now I am burdened with turning you into women that men will pay to see perform. Do either of you think you can hold the attention of men?"

"I can, Madame Glyceria," Theodora blurted.

The old woman lifted her chin, apparently intrigued by the confident answer. Then she looked over Theodora in full and smirked. "A little wolf indeed. Because men have the money and we have the beauty," she said and sat back again. "Now, Magister Origen may have brought you to me, but I must spend to maintain you both. That means you both took on a debt when you came here, a debt to me. You'll repay me when you become fully trained women, but new girls cover my expenses through labor. You'll both upkeep the koitóna with the maidservants and learn the ways of the place. Work well, and I'll promote you to the dance lessons." Then Madame Glyceria leaned forward again. "I need constant reassurance that I spend wisely on you. Otherwise, all you'll do is chore work. And never think of leaving here without my permission. Because I'll ruin you."

Theodora glanced at the front door. That man stood there, guarding the koitóna's only exit. He stared back at Theodora without expression. She couldn't tell if his good eye saw her fear of him, or whether his ghostly eye saw through her, into her thoughts, perceiving Theodora's willingness to challenge his superiority of that door, if it came to that.

"Do you understand me, girls?" said the Madame.

Theodora snapped back to attention. She answered in unison with her sister. "Yes, Madame Glyceria."

SIX

Theodora and Comito slept in separate rooms after that day. Each sleeping chamber had four cots, but in Theodora's room, the remaining three cots lay empty. The room was on the third floor, reached only by two flights of wooden stairs that warbled like sparrows with each step. Glyceria said those stairs alerted the door guard to any girl who tried to leave the koitộna, and thus far, no girl ever succeeded in escaping.

But escape was for girls who had no future here, thought Theodora. She had a future. So, she focused on learning her duties. She was responsible, however, for more than she imagined. As a new member of the koitộna, she had no status among the other girls, and even though some of the girls were younger than Theodora, they all had primacy in rank. And while the other girls spent long hours training for the theater, Theodora and Comito spent their days working to upkeep the old koitộna.

Theodora didn't understand the overarching reasons for her arduous duties, but she certainly felt the effects. She had so much work that, by day's end, she felt bodily exhaustion unfamiliar to her. She awoke each morning before the sun rose. In the dark morning, which was always so cold, Theodora and Comito both descended the noisy, warbling stairs under the corpse-like gaze of the door guard. Beside the Madame's bedchamber, Theodora noticed other sleeping quarters that looked like rooms at an inn, and these needed tending first, even though none in the koitóna ever used them. Then, the sisters went to the outside well in front of the koitóna to fill buckets of water. Usually, women of the neighborhood gathered there in the chill morning, pulling up water to a chorus of birds, while the girls waited their turn. Of course, the door guard always followed them, standing nearby, never looking at anyone else. Theodora couldn't help but stare back. The man seemed to watch her the most, through seemingly lidless eyes, both challenging and alert. If Theodora ran, she knew he'd chase her down relentlessly. But again, she reminded herself, she had no intention of escaping.

As the sky filled with beautiful colors of dawn, the sisters separated. Theodora hung the red awning that covered the entrance to the koitóna, while Comito opened all the windows. By the time daylight befell the city, when people bustled upon the street, Theodora was to prepare the back parlor, known as the salóni. There, she jealously watched the older girls busy themselves with cosmetics and clothing, assisted by a young eunuch boy named Pontíki.

It was during this part of the day that envy pestered Theodora. For as the young girls put paint on their faces, their appearances tilted decisively toward womanhood, and even simple faces radiated with beauty. Theodora felt more like a street beggar as she ground the colored powders and refilled oil vials, so clearly separate from the other girls. Once the dancers left for training, Theodora collected their clothing, washed them in a wooden tub, and hung them on ropes that stretched over the alley. Theodora often stole peeks during lyre practice. She watched the girls pluck strange harp-like instruments that made ghostly notes, like rain, elegant and otherworldly. Sometimes Theodora rested her head against a doorpost and privately listened to the melodies, wondering when she'd get her turn.

After lyre practice, Glyceria sent Theodora outside to clear away any horse dung that collected in front of the building. On race days, Theodora did her chores under the deafening roars of the nearby Hippodrome, eruptions of madness and passion that mixed with the muted thudding of countless horse hooves.

By the late afternoon, Theodora and Comito were reunited to help the maids cut vegetables, portion spices, and heat water for cooking. Once the food was prepared, the sisters swept the floors.

At the Vesper's Hour, Theodora lit and hung the lanterns throughout the koitóna, and Comito collected the dry linens outside. By day's end, Theodora was filthy, foul-smelling, sweaty, and no closer to anything that resembled a stage.

At night, while the other girls slept, Theodora lay awake and thought of her mother and dead father. All the powerful feelings from her pata's death stalked her at night. Only at the dance school, there was also loneliness. Theodora languished in a wearisome place where no one laughed at her jokes, nor smiled when she entered a room. And those thoughts were often interrupted by a mysterious warbling of the main staircase. Someone descended or climbed those stairs and Theodora wondered whether it was Madame Glyceria patrolling, like soldiers upon the street, or whether that noise came from an unseen spirit that roamed the dark koitóna at night.

On the final Holy Day of Epiphany, Theodora knew enough about the koitóna that she formed a strange idea. She took it upon herself to move a cupboard halfway between the kitchen and dining hall. This cut the distance the maids had to walk to gather dishware before a meal and saved time when they put the dishware away. The maids were so happy with the idea that Theodora changed her approach to chores altogether. Instead of trying to just get through the day, a soulless pursuit, she decided to work harder, not for the koitóna, not for Madame Glyceria, but for herself.

Two days later, Theodora cleared debris from an upstairs room that no one used, where part of the roof had collapsed years earlier. She found coils of hemp rope that she traded for henna oil with a passing merchant, which was an important cargo for the koitóna. And she added the damaged wood slats to the day's firewood, saving Glyceria the day's firewood stipend. Her whole attitude toward manual labor changed. Theodora felt less like a pack animal and more like a person who was useful and needed. Whenever she was alone, Theodora hummed the melody of the lyres. Whenever she was in the presence of the other girls, she smiled, even when those smiles were unreturned.

But Comito didn't like the changes. "Why do you try so hard in this place?" she asked. "While Mother toils alone with Anastasia?"

Theodora shrugged. "I want to feel like I *did* something at the end of the day."

"I wish we could see Mother or speak with her," said Comito. "Don't you miss home?"

Theodora always answered "yes," but in her heart, she knew she missed her home less and less. Her thoughts and attention were on the koitǫna.

And it was noticed.

At breakfast one morning, Glyceria announced that Theodora was to be promoted and join the other girls for the pantomime exercises. It was the moment that Theodora had awaited since arriving.

She knew that pantomiming was a type of performance dance with specific gestures and elegant contortions of the body. But learning these physical expressions didn't come so easily. The morning exercises took place in the courtyard, where Pontiki tapped rhythmically on hide drums while the girls practiced. Madame Glyceria issued voice commands and Theodora had to strike certain poses. One posture flowed into the next, arching, twisting, and sweeping along invisible lines. Then she'd have to stop and assume an unnatural stance, holding the pose until her muscles ached and legs quivered. Balance alone became the most difficult task. Any twitch or falter in balance and Theodora heard "clumsy girl" or "graceless" or "it's like watching a pack mule." Out of step and inexperienced, she fumbled through the day, whispering questions to nearby girls, who shushed her. Everyone else seemed to belong at the koitǫna, except her; she felt like an imposter, a poor and awkward girl in the company of trained dancers.

But Theodora proved better at the foot exercises, which taught a girl to be nimble when leaping into the air and soft-footed upon landing. Years of bounding over rooftops and climbing trees at least prepared her for one aspect of dance.

"Theodora, face your audience," said Madame Glyceria, cuing Theodora to stand before the other girls and demonstrate a series of pantomimes. The old woman circled her, observing each transition. "Just look at that, girls. Despite her slack postures," she said as the girls all snickered. "Silence! Theodora has what most of you don't, a *speciosa vi*. Look at the vitality in her eyes and arrogance of her posture. She almost dares you to engage her." The room was now silent. "*How* a girl takes the stage can be as important as what she does upon it. Thank you, Theodora. You may sit."

Speciosa vi was a Latin phrase that meant "beautiful force." Madame Glyceria singled out Theodora for this elusive quality day after day. At times, Theodora even considered that the Madame valued stage presence above all else.

Comito, though, wallowed in the drudge of chore work. Theodora rarely spoke with her older sister, and when she did the two were of different minds. She had brimming optimism, while Comito wished only to go home. Theodora eventually devised a plan to help her sister, but the plan fell asunder when Madame Glyceria brought the most exciting news.

"In a few days, I'm taking a few girls to the Hippodrome, yourself included. One day, you may be hired to perform at that racetrack, so all girls must see it firsthand. I've watched many young dancers collapse the first time they trot out there. They find themselves encircled by the fearsome gaze of tens of thousands. The feeling will strike you here," said Madame Glyceria, tapping Theodora center chest. "It'll hit you like an arrow and send you reeling to the ground. I've seen it. Any girl who wishes to perform must know the perils of such a large audience. So, are you ready to see this spectacle?"

Theodora often wondered what was inside the marble enigma at the center of the city, the place where men could go and she could not. She cleared her throat. "Yes, Madame Glyceria."

SEVEN

T heodora sprung up in bed and threw aside her blanket. Today, she was to see the Great Hippodrome firsthand. That morning, Madame Glyceria took Theodora to the salóni, where the other dancers readied themselves for a foray into the open public. The room was arranged with roughly ten desks, where a girl sat before a cloudy mirror. Cosmetic tools, vials, and bowls of colored powders cluttered each desk. As Theodora entered the salóni, she noticed the glances in the mirrors as she passed, both unwelcoming and curious.

"Theodora's coming with us this morning," said Madame Glyceria. "You girls all remember your first time out, so welcome her. Pontíki, gather some raiment from the wardrobe."

The eunuch boy of about twelve years turned toward Madame Glyceria and nodded. He had a powdered face, rouged cheeks, and oiled hair. "Yes, Mother," he said, giving Theodora a cursory glance.

Pontíki opened the large wardrobe and, moments later, had square folds of clothing piled up to his chin. Theodora undressed until she wore only her undergarments, an act that would be forbidden in front of a boy, but clearly, this boy was exempt from such rules. He shook out an under-frock and the smell of lavender wafted by Theodora. The material wrapped tightly around her neck and collar, loosened at the torso, and hung down to her ankles. Strange that mere fabric should feel so heavy. Then, Pontíki draped her in a brown woolen robe that went over the under-frock, but parted at the front, tied together at the navel. She felt awkward, even foolish, in the presence of the other girls, dressing as they dressed. As Theodora stood there, being clad in fragrant garb by the soft-mannered boy, she noticed that the other girls kept a wary eye on her. She wondered why they were looking at her like that.

Pontíki cut Theodora's unruly hair and then wrapped her locks in a veil. Afterward, he lined Theodora's eyes with black kohl and added rose coloring to her lips. The transformation in her appearance from these colors was extraordinary. Finally, she saw why the other girls took so much interest in her preparations. When Theodora looked again at her reflection in the mirror, she saw a strange girl looking back at her, a girl with well-trimmed and oiled black hair, a polished face, one that burst with vibrant beauty. She realized that she was looking at a different person. No longer did Theodora see the girl in tattered clothes who climbed trees; she saw now a girl who belonged on a stage.

Pontíki had Theodora stand, and he arranged a white shawl over her shoulders and arms. Finally, he rubbed oils against her neck, her upper chest, and the insides of her wrists, but Theodora noticed how the fragrance filled her nostrils with spicy air, the overwhelming scent of flowers. Quickly, though, the potent fragrance faded into a sweet smell that clung to her clothing.

She recognized jealousy in the eyes of the other girls. Perhaps they feared it was Theodora who bore the most beauty in the koitóna, unmasked and presented for all to see. And in the society of girls, Theodora understood that beauty meant status.

When Theodora walked out of the musty salóni, she spotted Comito enter the koitóna, struggling to bring in the buckets of cooking water. Her sister looked miserable as she pulled off her hood and paused to warm her hands. When Comito saw Theodora, her eyes took in the sight with a cold indifference. Then, Comito smiled apologetically and nodded as though the world made sense.

"You look wonderful, sister," she said as she walked near to Theodora. "If Mother could see you."

Theodora beamed. "Don't worry, you're next."

"I don't think so," said Comito, aware that the other dancers listened in. "Madame Glyceria needs me more for chores."

"Every girl begins with maid duties. Please don't lose heart."

Comito shook off her sister's encouragement. "Theodora, this is your day. You're going to the Hippodrome of all places, where Pata used to work."

"Comito?" said Madame Glyceria, descending the chirping staircase. "Do you always distract my pupils while neglecting your duties at the same time?"

"No, Madame Glyceria," Comito said with a bow. She then turned and crept away toward the kitchen. Theodora didn't like the new disparity between herself and her sister.

"Come," said Madame Glyceria. "The Hippodrome is still a distance from here. We can arrive by the tenth or eleventh race if we depart now."

Madame Glyceria led six painted girls and Theodora outside, where a gray-speckled horse and wooden carriage awaited. The carriage looked like a large wooden box with a curved roof and two large wooden wheels. Theodora entered last and sat on a wooden bench. She shivered. Two unglazed windows filled the cabin with bright morning sunlight, floating dust particles, and chilly autumn air. The girls bunched in so close that despite the discomfort, Theodora welcomed the body warmth.

Once the carriage lurched forward and rooftops slid by beyond the window, Theodora had to hide her fluttering excitement. Even her mother never got painted and escorted in a carriage her whole life.

Theodora listened to the cacophony from the outside streets, but when she heard a deafening cheer erupt just outside the carriage, she knew they had arrived. Pontíki slid open the rear curtain and assisted Madame Glyceria and the girls out of the cabin. Theodora stood upon the Middle Way, a street that ran down the slope of the hill and emptied into a great intersection at the city center. Here, the Hippodrome, the Great Church of Holy Wisdom, and the Daphne Palace all came together and faced a common public square. Citizens milled about all around her, while pairs of Roman soldiers trotted by on horseback, wading through the bustling throngs. When Theodora turned to gaze upon the Hippodrome, she had to lean way back to stare up at the towering white walls, pillars, and shadowed arches.

Before Theodora even finished taking in the full sight, Madame Glyceria whisked her and the other dancers into a side entrance meant for the entertainers. Performers of the Green faction carried about their duties in the torchlight, their countless conversations echoing loudly off the stonework. Theodora also recognized a strong animal odor in the air, the same smell that once lingered upon the clothing of her pata.

When she glanced back, she spotted Magister Origen suddenly emerge from the foot traffic and greet Madame Glyceria. The magistrate stood with a small entourage of other men all clad in the white togas of imperial station-holders. None but the city officials ever wore togas anymore, so these men stood out in the crowd and simply radiated prominence.

Strange, she thought—she stood in the world of men. They all gathered here in their leisure to jest or mingle about their professions, dressed in public attire, with all the pageantry and sport for them alone. Women shared in none of these things.

When Magister Origen looked her way, Theodora finally experienced the exhilaration of knowing she looked beautiful in the presence of a man she admired. A warm and airy feeling blossomed throughout her body.

"How's this one's training going?" he asked Madame Glyceria.

The old woman glanced at Theodora. "Stunning, is she not? Her dance steps are lacking. But by the favor of Tyche, I'll make a dancer out of her."

"Look at you," Magister Origen said, his dark brown eyes flitting over Theodora's face and attire. "As I expected."

At last, she got her chance to smile and bow with all the glamour of her recent daydreams.

"Superb," said Magister Origen. Then his attention slipped onto a different girl as though he forgot about Theodora.

As he spoke to the girl named Sara, Theodora's smile faded. She looked on as Sara beamed under the magistrate's attention. A foul feeling surged in Theodora's belly, as though she'd lost a contest of a kind. Perhaps it wasn't beauty alone that gave a girl her power, but attention...attention from men.

"Now take notice, little wolf," said Madame Glyceria, turning Theodora to face a different direction. "The man beside Magister Origen is Dancing Master Asterius. In this city, he's the one who manages all entertainment for the Green faction."

"I know," said Theodora, trying not to listen to Magister Origen and Sara. "My father answered to him as well, before he died."

"Yes, well, Asterius holds all the power in our little world," answered Madame Glyceria. "And Magister Origen is one of his closest friends. So, that's why we keep Magister Origen happy, no matter what. Understand?"

Theodora nodded and looked again at Origen, who stood out, even among this crowd. It was as if his esteem had somehow rubbed off on Theodora and granted her a special status. She felt a strange warmth at knowing such a striking and influential man took an interest in her. She wanted more of his favor, if possible. Asterius, by contrast, had the face of a boy, with taut skin at the cheekbones and a deep cleft in his chin. He looked unnaturally thin at the neck and shoulders, with sunken brown eyes that mocked whatever and whomever he looked at, like a spoiled child who mixed amusement with cruelty. Yet his luxurious attire projected esteem and high rank.

Magister Origen finally stopped talking to Sara and pointed up ahead. "Why don't we take a brief look at the track? Porphyrius is warming up out there. He's racing for the wretched Blues today, the old crow." The magistrate then turned into an entourage of togas, while the dancers of the koitóna followed behind.

As the dark corridor brightened with sunlight, Theodora craned to see what lay ahead.

And then she saw it.

EIGHT

Theodora's breath stilled as she caught her first glimpse of the great and mysterious spectacle. At the end of the tunnel, framed in a black arch, she saw a wheat-brown racetrack bathed in sunlight. She approached at the same level of the track with the spectator benches above her. Theodora heard and even felt the terrifying rumble of horse hooves, and a moment later, a practicing chariot flashed across the portal with such speed and noise that her skin prickled.

When she emerged from the tunnel, Theodora was awestruck. The animal roar of civilization enveloped her every sense, making her dizzy in the head and sick in the belly. The whole of the Hippodrome sat nakedly before her. Such an extraordinary environment, she thought, an arena built with precise shapes, hard angles, and vivid colors, so monumental in size that it teemed with tens of thousands.

Theodora heard the shrill whinnies of horses pierce the din. Across the track from her, not far off, she watched muscular charioteers lean against their chariots, coolly observing their competitors at practice. Others adjusted and tightened the leather straps on the horse teams, a quadriga of four horses tethered together. A man with an announcer's cone stood near the charioteers, booming out words that made the spectators above Theodora's head suddenly cheer out. And all the while, dust from the track, heavy with the sweet stink of horse, filled her mouth and nose.

The whole sight left Theodora breathless.

She finally blinked. Pushing ahead of the other girls, Theodora leaned further out the tunnel and peered in both directions. From her far left to her far right, the swarming benches encircled the track in an oblong U-shape, dotted with black sockets from tunnels along the promenade. Centered in the racetrack, a white marble median separated the two straightaways, atop which sat obelisks, statues of crocodiles and elephants, gold pylons, and a bronze column of braided snakes that split into three serpentine heads.

On the far north end, Theodora saw the starting gates with ten horse stalls. From there, the track stretched into a long dirt straightaway that ran southward toward the first and only turn, the sphendone, a semicircle that curved into a second straightaway, and back to the starting gates. There, the chariots would have to lean away from the gates, hug the median, and turn again onto the first straightaway.

Theodora could imagine the scene at last: men, horses, and chariots circling in violent laps, around and around they would go, whips lashing, clouds of dust trailing in their wake, and bringing all the fury of war before a frenzied, cheering public. And she felt it too, inside her, a quickening of her pulse, followed by a strange urge to bare her teeth and scream. This was it, she realized, this was the source of the lunacy that had killed her pata.

But what does it all mean? The whole view seemed overwhelming, dazzling, yet bizarrely incoherent.

She didn't see a single Christian cross on the walls, nor priest in the crowd. The piety of Christendom showed nowhere in the Hippodrome, as if the racetrack stood apart from religion, a brazen reminder of Constantinople's brutal Roman roots. No, the Hippodrome was a temple of its own, she thought, a place where men came to worship chaos, where they denounced all restraint and cast off any moral code that suppressed their violence, their vitality, and their barbarity.

Theodora felt a hand on her back and glanced up to see Magister Origen staring down at her. He bent forward so that his mouth was beside her ear. "What do you think, Theodora?" he shouted over the din.

Unexpectedly, she blurted, "I think it's the most wonderful sight in the world." She'd always assumed that she'd condemn the Hippodrome, not fall under its spell.

"Do you think you could perform before such a crowd as this?" said Magister Origen.

Theodora looked again. A group of bearded dwarves wearing horse costumes around the waist now chased each other, prompting a surge of laughter. This time, she tried to imagine all those spectators staring down at her instead. "I think so," she said. "I think I could do it."

"What about that man?" Here, the magistrate leaned closer, aiming his finger across the track at a large viewing box centered in the stands. "That's the Kathisma, where the emperor himself sits among us. Could you dance before a mighty gaze such as his?"

Theodora squinted. She saw the shaded silhouette of a man. He lifted a chalice to his lips but turned and conversed with others who stood behind him. "Yes," said Theodora. She bounced with a girlish exuberance. "I want to do all of these things. Do you really think that'll happen, Magister Origen?"

"I do," he said. "Once you're trained, I suspect you could handle just about anything. Would you like to see where the charioteers are quartered?"

"Oh, could we?" Theodora said.

The magistrate stood upright and then asked the same question to all the girls. Madame Glyceria brightened at the idea and quickly herded the girls back through the tunnel. The deafening noise of the crowd fell quieter, and Theodora heard a trumpet blare in the distance. They were clearing the track for a race, and she'd miss it.

Magister Origen led Madame Glyceria and the girls through a torch-lit network of corridors. The Hippodrome was so large that Theodora could barely believe she was inside something built by men. As she walked, she listened to Magister Origen explain that the Daphne Palace was connected to the Hippodrome, where the emperor could pass from the palace to the viewing box at will and watch the same horserace as the common citizens of Constantinople. Magister Origen spoke proudly of this last part, Theodora noticed.

"Sometimes, the Blues and the Greens will accuse the emperor of wrongdoing right here in the Hippodrome," he said. "And when necessary, we'll challenge the emperor with rebellion."

Rebellion.

That word burned at the fore of Theodora's thoughts. The Hippodrome had been at the center of the lawlessness that had killed her father. Now she saw that the arena could be a cauldron of boiling water that could froth over, releasing all those wild citizens against the emperor. Theodora quickened her pace so that she was beside the magistrate. "Why did the people revolt last time?" she asked.

Magister Origen looked down at her, intrigued.

"Theodora, quit pestering the magistrate," said Madame Glyceria.

"No, no," he said. "It's a just question. She lost her father in the last rebellion and wants to know why."

Theodora smiled at him for defending her.

"You see, Emperor Anastasius tampered with the sacred words of the Trinity," said the magistrate.

"Which words?"

"The emperor declared that Jesus Christ came *from* God, rather than being *of* God." He held up a finger. "*From*, not *of*."

Whereas Theodora expected the cloud of confusion to lift, she now felt utterly lost. "But how could a word start a rebellion?"

Magister Origen placed a hand on Theodora's back. "Think about it. If Jesus Christ came *from* God, he'd be a second divine being. We'd have two divinities, each with a nature of their own, a father and a distinct and separate son. However, if Jesus Christ is *of* God, then he and God are one and the same, a simultaneous father and son."

Theodora spoke as if cursing. "So what?"

"Christianity cannot have two gods. That's polytheism, and it shatters the First Commandment issued at Mount Sinai. We Christians can have only one god. That's why Orthodox men in both factions rose up against the emperor."

"But then why is the emperor still ruling?"

"Because the emperor withdrew his heretical decree and begged for forgiveness, right here in the Hippodrome. That's why the factions allowed him to stay in power."

Theodora recalled the sight of the emperor only a few moments ago, so calm, sipping wine, about to watch a chariot race. "So my father died over one word? And the emperor just went home?"

The magistrate must've seen Theodora's pain and bewilderment. "No," he said. "Acacius didn't die for the word. Acacius died for the Greens, beside his friends in the faction."

Theodora didn't know what to think about the revolt now. The thought of murder over a single word was beyond belief. She knew that there was another commandment that said men couldn't kill either. Breaking one commandment to defend another seemed senseless to her.

Magister Origen shifted his attention back to the other girls. "This is where the charioteers sleep after long hours of practice," he said.

They stood in a long passageway with very little foot traffic. By the muted sound of cheering above, another race was underway. Theodora saw some of the girls scatter down the hallway, rising on tiptoes, and peering into each room through the windows of the doors.

"Why don't you go on ahead, Madame Glyceria," said Magister Origen. "Perhaps it's best if I answer some of Theodora's questions without the other girls listening."

Madame Glyceria looked down at Theodora. The look on the old woman's face was peculiar, she thought, perhaps even a look of jealousy.

"Yes, of course, Magister. We'll be near the tunnel," she said, and then gave a scolding look to Theodora. "Now you listen to the magistrate, girl. Do you hear me?"

Theodora nodded. "Yes, Madame Glyceria."

A moment later, Theodora watched the other girls dally down the passage and into the distance, some even giving her challenging looks. Inside her chest, though, arose a feeling of excitement. She liked being singled out.

"Would you like to see the quarters of the great Porphyrius?" he asked.

Theodora raised her eyebrows in amazement. "Would I?" she said. "Yes, yes, and yes!"

NINE

Magister Origen opened a thick wooden door, making the iron hinges creak, and Theodora entered. The room faced away from the track with a small unglazed window on the back wall, one that glowed with light blue sky. Throughout the room, Theodora saw objects a charioteer might use. Leather whips hung in coils from the wall, an enamel water bowl sat in the corner, and a leather jerkin and helmet adorned a wooden dummy. She realized that while the spectator stands were above them, this wing of the Hippodrome, where the charioteers resided, was similar to her own koitóna.

Theodora wandered in front of a strange ax. The item was set into wood pegs and suspended on the wall. As far as she knew, charioteers were not gladiators and didn't use weapons. "What is this for?" she said.

"That's a mattock. They use that to cut a man free if he becomes trapped in his reins or beneath his chariot."

Theodora sensed Magister Origen watching her, most likely noticing her beauty just as she herself noticed in the mirror that morning. The way the magistrate spoke to her earlier felt more like a man speaking to a woman, not a girl. He saw her the way she always wanted to be seen, and now the world was following suit. She liked the feeling.

"Madame Glyceria tells me that you're doing exceptionally well," he said. "That you've been assigned pantomime training ahead of your older sister."

"Yes, Magister. But the training is so very difficult," she said, trying to adopt a mature tone in her voice. "So much to learn."

He sat down on the bedstead of Porphyrius, whose blankets shone with bright patterns and fine woolen layers. "Yes, well, you've entered a much larger world," said Magister Origen. "And you're rising to the new challenges and becoming a woman."

Theodora turned to face the magistrate and smiled, knowing her beauty was having a pleasant effect on him. His fascination with her seemed to be sweetening the bond that had already developed. "Thank you, Magister. We all owe you so much," she said, smiling, absently scratching at the flea bites on her forearm.

"Surely those are going away," he said and reached out his hand. "Let me see."

Theodora went over to him and held out her arm.

Magister Origen took Theodora's wrist in his one hand, a strong grip, and pulled back her sleeve with his other hand. Then he slid his fingers gently along the top of her forearm, feeling the small bumps that sprinkled her skin, making her flesh prickle. "Your father would be proud of you, you know?"

Theodora stood in front of the magistrate, their eyes taking each other in. But she felt anxiety growing inside her at this proximity. When she smiled, she noticed that Origen's look changed. His face became stoic, but his eyes burned with intensity as if something insulting had just been uttered. She sensed the look to be a man's look, a hard look, focusing on her prettiness. She tried to hold his eye contact, but the room fell silent. Theodora felt an iciness at the back of her head, one that spread over her whole scalp, blending an awareness of danger perhaps, but with a kind of mesmerizing calm. Her gaze unsteadied and moved about rapidly now—at him, away from him, at him again, at the floor.

Magister Origen tucked his finger under her chin and lifted her head to face him. "Look at me," he said, warmly. "You're very beautiful, you know, for a girl your age."

Theodora never heard such silkiness in a man's voice before.

Still gripping her wrist, the magistrate pulled Theodora closer to him, his intense eyes observing her every expression. The wool and linen of his white toga crumbled as he pulled her into the space between his knees, the fabric encircling her like water in a pool, and creating a stealthy sound in the quiet room. She noticed that the chalk he used to whiten his toga rubbed off on her brown outer-frock, proof that she came into questionable contact with a man.

"Magister," said Theodora, alarmed. "You're getting chalk on my dress."

"How old are you?" he said.

She looked him in the eyes again, trying to appear undaunted, pretending as he did that everything still unfolded within normal boundaries. "Fourteen," she said.

Magister Origen took a breath in through his nose and seemed to appraise her again with those dark, authoritative eyes. "Fourteen," he repeated as he exhaled.

The silence that followed made her swallow involuntarily.

"I've rescued many girls from a life of destitution," said the magistrate, still clutching Theodora's arm. "And I've seen them flower into beautiful women. Now that I see you with paint on your face, I cannot stop looking at you. Even with these little blemishes on your arm, you're entirely striking," he said.

Then his hand drifted up from her exposed forearm and slid into her hair, just above the ear, and his stony fingers opened and closed so gently. Theodora jerked and stiffened. She knew he shouldn't be touching her like this, that such contact wouldn't be acceptable in the presence of others, and yet the magistrate carried on unabashed, as though his behavior was perfectly normal. But this was a man she liked, a Judge of the Ward, and he was treating her like a woman, spending this time with her instead of others. So, Theodora stood perfectly still and tried to mimic Magister Origen's calm, despite the awkwardness.

"When a man tells a woman she's beautiful, usually the woman responds with gratitude," he said.

"Thank you," Theodora said, quickly, almost defensively. Were this any other man, she'd have pushed him away and called him a fool. But she couldn't do that to Magister Origen. This was the man she had to keep happy for the sake of the koitóna. Rare confusion crashed in on Theodora and she realized that she felt more fear now than flattery. Her heartbeat quickened and her body seemed to weaken.

Deep down, Theodora knew that to break this strange pleasantry would spark unseen forces from the magistrate. His eyes warned her of those forces. Any show of disapproval on her part would surely turn his eerie kindness into what it really was, a terrible reality, one where a fourteen-year-old girl would have to contest the full power of a grown man, and in that reality, Theodora sensed futility and terror. She was being cornered in an unfamiliar way.

Theodora glanced at the closed door. "I think we should go," she finally said, but her voice sounded weak and unconfident, a paralysis of the throat.

"Glyceria knows you're safe with me," said Magister Origen. "You do feel safe, don't you?"

"Yes," Theodora blurted. Somehow the opposite words kept coming out.

"Good girl," he said. "My brave little woman. It's perfectly normal to feel a little uneasy when you're alone with a man. But I'm more than that. I'm your benefactor, Theodora."

Perhaps the magistrate was just overbearing in his concern for her. *But then there were those eyes.* His stately figure seemed strong and tightly coiled, ready to spring out like a snake. Thoughts of striking the magistrate faded from her conscious mind, for it seemed that any blow would merely glance off of him, as in a dream, as harmless as a feather fall. "We're all very grateful, Magister," she said. "Me especially." Then Theodora risked a decisive move away from him.

But Magister Origen jerked her closer, revealing that hidden strength she feared and had no answer for. She flinched and stared at him.

"How dare you," he said. "I was talking to you."

She instinctively leaned away from him. But Magister Origen yanked her back again, drawing her in closer than before, his face looming up into her vision. Theodora placed her hands on his hard chest and pushed. "What are you doing?" she said.

"Growing impatient with you," he said. "You mutter half-hearted gratitudes and then openly disrespect me?"

"I didn't mean to—"

"Do you think that you can just milk me for your own self-advancement, like some kind of cow?" he said, his voice raised. "You can't just retreat from this, Theodora."

"Retreat from what?" she said.

"Oh, you know what." Magister Origen's hand reached to the back of her under-frock, fumbled through the garment, and then, to Theodora's utter horror, settle firmly on her backside. He squeezed her there and his look became one of authority. "Girls don't follow men into an empty room unless they want to favor him," he said. "And you have a lovely favor to give me."

She looked at him, stunned. "No, Magister. I don't have anything," she said and pushed harder this time. He barely moved. The enthusiasm she felt all morning at her blooming womanhood suddenly receded, leaving her again as a pure child. "Please . . ."

"Come now, you're a smart one, Theodora. I see a woman's ambition behind those pretty little eyes of yours. Ambitious girls must learn to favor the men who help them."

Theodora's mind went blank. She knew he referred to vulgar things, but never imagined such words set upon herself. "You misunderstand, Magister Origen."

"Not at all," he said as his hand against her rump grew even livelier. He nodded as though he understood something about Theodora that she didn't know about herself. "You don't need to pretend to misunderstand. You're letting your fears get in the way of your curiosities, and you're close to spoiling a perfect opportunity for you. Stop it."

"Let go of me!" Theodora said, this time making a serious attempt to break free. "You're not yourself, and you're hurting me. Let me go." Theodora squirmed but heard herself make a whimper, an awful sound, one that triggered another escalation. Magister Origen tightened around her like ropes going taut. Theodora felt bodily heat from beneath his toga, a suffocating proximity, while his breath stank of wine. She winced as her feeble struggle failed to break his embrace and she suddenly wanted to cry, to fall into an all-consuming anguish as if she were a child half her age.

"Little whore. You'd be begging in the streets if it weren't for me," he said, his voice cold with anger.

Suddenly, the Hippodrome crowd burst into a sustained roar right above her. At that moment, the magistrate pressed his face against hers, moving and contorting his mouth against her lips, half-angry, half-impassioned. Wetness blossomed all around her mouth and chin. She pivoted her head to one side and then the other.

"Stop struggling," he said. "This is what you wanted."

"I don't . . . want this," Theodora said, trying to turn away.

"Oh yes, you do," he said, releasing her wrist and wrenching her hair to keep her head firmly in place. "And don't stand here and lie about it, just because you're having second thoughts. Confess it! Tell me you wanted this."

Theodora could no longer hide her fear. She breathed rapidly now, and her scalp hurt where he pulled at her hair. "Magister, don't," she said as tears came.

"Crying will only ruin the paint on your face, you stupid girl. Now say it," he said.

"No."

She felt Magister Origen shake her angrily, let go of her backside, and move his hand around to her front. Then he pressed his fingers firmly against her maidenhead. She folded forward, but he had her now. He held her there with overwhelming strength, and here, now, Theodora's worst fears came on in a rush.

"Admit you wanted this," he said again, rubbing his hidden fingers against her.

The soft skin between her legs felt like searing fire as his fingers tried to bore into her. She squeezed her thighs closed, but it only held Magister Origen's hand in place. "Please stop," she said, wincing and looking away.

"Somewhere in your little mind, you knew what this was. Just admit that part of you wanted this and I'll stop. Now say it!"

Theodora finally broke, cringing through her tears. "I wanted this," she said amidst the outside cheers.

"I didn't hear that. Say it again."

"I wanted this," she said.

"Of course you did."

Theodora had uttered the false phrase only to make him stop asking, but now that she said it aloud, a powerful misery overtook her. She somehow made the phrase true, somehow validated the magistrate's corrupted beliefs about her, creating a false truth that he willed into existence, an illusion as powerful as reality, but born at her expense. She felt his fingers slipping inside her, just a bit, and to her utter horror, she felt her body respond to the touch, inside, despite her utter revulsion and pain. *How could that be?* And she watched the magistrate return an approving nod. He seemed encouraged by something Theodora's body was doing on its own that she couldn't control. Ashamed, she squeezed her eyes shut and turned away. Her eyes filled with water until a few heavy tears fell like raindrops.

"You see?" he said. "You did want this, so stop crying."

I wanted this.

She tried not to think the words, but they kept on repeating. The more she tried to silence her thoughts, the more the phrase echoed in her mind.

I wanted this.

Down where his hand worked to further betray her, Theodora felt a pinch. The pain was slight but shot through her like an arrow. She cringed and then looked down and away, her throat and cheeks sore from the crying, unable to wish the nightmare away.

"Stop tensing," he said, leaning his mouth alongside her ear and lowering his voice. "Soon you'll look forward to this. You'll dream about it when you're alone, I promise. Now come on. Either favor me like a woman, or I'll treat you like a whore. Your choice."

With all strength gone, all will to resist broken, Theodora felt the magistrate turn her around, her body moving freely now, like a doll stuffed only with hay. A great hand pressed against the middle of her shoulder blades, bending her until her chest flattened against the fabrics atop the bedstead. Magister Origen lifted both of her frocks and cool air wafted over Theodora's lower body.

As the man fumbled over her with more deliberate actions, tugging and pressing and adjusting her, Theodora's eyes befell the mattock, the ax the charioteers used to free themselves when trapped, just as she was now trapped. The weapon sat on the wall as an object of salvation, the only object in the world at that moment, but one she couldn't reach. Her eyes fixed on that mattock. Then she cringed and pressed her wet face into the bed. She knew she wouldn't do anything else.

Now was the time to surrender in full. To panic, to fight weakly, or flail about in crude hysterics would only make it worse. She calmed. In her mind, she was preserving some kind of dignity by not struggling, just as she saw men do before a public hanging. Now she understood. There had to be a point of acceptance. And once she accepted, Theodora's feelings started to wash away, the fear and shock all began an inevitable erosion, just as structures of sand do against the lapping seas. Only a bitter, sick shame remained inside her.

She heard him spit into his hands. She winced when she felt him against her. And then came the painful intrusion. A sound slipped up from Theodora's throat that she wished she didn't hear herself make, a miserable grunt, not from a girl, but inhuman.

She could sound like that.

Theodora clenched her teeth as the magistrate continued wordlessly, assuredly, as if he was not crushing her, nor destroying so thoroughly a bright vision she had of herself since the beginning, an optimistic belief that she was a special girl, a good girl, someone admirable. Those beliefs collapsed in a rush. She was fornicating with a grown man like a dog, right there in the room, irrefutable. She squeezed her eyes shut as warm blood trailed down the inside of her thigh, like a long tear.

Theodora couldn't be in that room a moment longer, not in her waking mind anyway. And so she looked out the lone circular window set high on the wall. Sky shone there. The sounds of trumpets and spectators could be heard. Somewhere in her head, Theodora left that room, drifting up and out that window, up where clouds cruised through blue heavens, up where no one could touch her. She imagined herself reforming as a glittering bird and ascending toward the sunlight. Feathers for fingers, wings for arms, she soared alone. And her bird was a beautiful bird. It flew freely overhead, unburdened, there to circle until her body might again be her own.

When the lunatic roar of sixty thousand voices erupted from the Hippodrome stands, the awful sounds in the room were finally drowned out. And so, Theodora flew, looking down upon them all, watching from high, high above.

TEN

The rest of that day meant little to Theodora. The vividness of the Hippodrome, the tremors of frenzied spectators, they all passed through her body like a ghost, numbing her enthusiasms and dulling any sense of wonder. She felt as though by some illusion, a great tabletop adorned with banquet food had been revealed to be nothing more than rotten heaps left in the dark for flies. The magistrate took her back, and Theodora made no effort to hide her broken appearance. Madame Glyceria saw her; the girls all saw the smeared kohl at her eyes, the chalk on her frock, and the misshapen strands of her hair. None said a word. And then Madame Glyceria *looked away*. Magister Origen patted Theodora's backside before slipping off to the spectator benches. She watched him leave and for a moment, didn't want him to go, because he had shielded her from the other dancers. But he left, no longer even a tormenting conspirator. Theodora just stood there, burning with pain, her eyes affixed on nothing. She didn't even twitch when chariots rumbled by, when a wild gust swept over her, blowing her hair over her face. She couldn't get past the truth of the moment. Madame Glyceria and the girls all seemed to perceive what had taken place, but somehow, they all understood that this ugly thing was to be ignored, unaddressed, and denied. In each passing moment, Theodora felt more isolated and insignificant.

When the girls returned to the koitóna, Theodora went straight to her bedchambers. When she saw herself again in the mirror that day, painted in the beautiful colors of elegant womanhood, she clenched her teeth in anger. All she saw now was a stupid girl who'd allowed herself to be tricked and degraded.

Theodora suddenly covered her face with both hands as a surge of desperation overcame her. Heat poured into her cheeks. She wanted to disappear, to go away, to un-exist. Even after a long while passed, she found that she lost the will to remove her hands. They stayed pressed against her face, there to hide her in the darkness forever, if possible, never to be seen again. Her optimistic opinion of herself, which was so ingrained, now clashed completely with what she'd just done. After a great length of time, Theodora thought to remove her hands, but couldn't bear to see her face in the mirror again. So, she angrily rubbed off the colors from her cheeks and eyes and lips, her palms smearing her skin, rubbing, erasing, until her whole face burned with pain.

The next night, while the others slept, Theodora climbed up into the old bell tower of the koitóna. She stared through the slats at the starry sky and white crescent moon and wept openly.

Theodora was either a stupid girl not to recognize the trap, or she was a whore, the kind of girl who schemes with the trap-setter.

I wanted this.

The words of a conspiring girl, spoken aloud with a grown man's hands vulgarly upon her body. She had stood there patiently, obediently, while Magister Origen cleaned up the blood upon her groin and thighs. She even thanked him when he finished. And she nodded when he told her she was a woman now, even though she felt more soiled and childlike than ever before. He did save her family, so she gave him what he wanted, what he deserved, because she had to. She knew that she offended him with her refusal but didn't like what he was doing. Around every corner, Theodora saw only her own fault.

So she let slip the dangerous contemplation: *What if I went through it willingly?* Would she feel as bad as she did now? Surely the girls who smiled at men didn't feel devastated afterward. Those girls had power in such a situation. Yet, when she imagined herself acting calm as he touched her, or worse, slipping into a conspiring smile, distress sent Theodora into a dizzying, panicky state.

And who could she tell?

No one. *I must stay silent*, thought Theodora. Silence left the whole thing in the darkness, where it could stay hidden and unspoken, as though it had never happened.

Over the next few days, Theodora avoided Comito's gaze. She could see her sister was concerned, but Theodora stayed distant. Once at night, Theodora heard Comito calling her name in a whisper. But she pretended to sleep and cried instead at her inability to answer. When Theodora watched Comito pass from the entrance to the kitchen the next morning, she wanted to grab her sister by the arm, drag her into the back hall, and tell her . . . but tell her what exactly? That she had allowed a man to force himself upon her? That her physical body did what the magistrate wanted it to do for the act to transpire? Wouldn't that only prove she *did* want what happened? The great edifice of Theodora's superiority would come crumbling down. Comito would see Theodora as weaker than they both believed, not a girl to admire, but a girl capable of either an egregious error or previously unknown and perverted desires. She couldn't speak to her sister about such things, even if she wanted to.

Without confidence, Theodora felt as though she never woke for the day. She faltered in her pantomime lessons, forgetting steps and holding slack postures. The *speciosa vi* that had made Theodora stand out from the other girls seemed to have winked out, like a candle flame, replaced by disinterest. Often, Theodora's thoughts wandered away from the koitóna and back to that room in the Hippodrome, only to feel the smack of Madame Glyceria's baton.

After a week of poor showings at practice, Madame Glyceria promoted Comito into the dance lessons. Theodora knew the Madame meant to incite a rivalry between the sisters, but she didn't care. She allowed herself to show poorly in front of her sister. And surprisingly, Comito proved to be a great learner who followed directions exactly. Theodora figured Comito took pleasure in her first brush with excellence, finally getting a chance to imagine herself as the greater of the two sisters. And where the other girls despised Theodora for an inborn quality, her *speciosa vi*, they admired Comito because her sister plodded as they plodded, over something tangible, something more attainable ... disciplined instruction. As Comito grew in favor at the koitóna, and as Theodora declined, any lingering thoughts of telling Comito about the magistrate fell off.

And Theodora's nightmare wasn't over.

Pontíki woke her in the night. He leaned over Theodora and whispered in her ear to wash up and go downstairs, that Madame Glyceria wanted to see her. When Theodora complied, she went down those chirping stairs and found both Magister Origen and the Madame seated at a table, their faces aglow from a lantern. Theodora's breath quickened, while heat singed her face and neck. *Was she dreaming?*

"You have new duties here," said Madame Glyceria, nodding and aiming her head toward one of several rooms behind Magister Origen. Those rooms that Theodora had once cleaned every morning finally revealed their purpose. A private room where a girl could lay with a man was called a fornice. "I warned you when you first arrived here not to miscarry your lessons."

Theodora's breath drained from her body. She stared hopelessly at the candlelit fornice behind the magistrate. Her whole body seemed to constrict. Now she knew the nightly ghost that tread the warbling stairs was no ghost at all, but her fellow pupils being summoned to the fornices. And now Theodora was one of them.

"The first of many," Madame Glyceria told her with all the elegance of a compliment. "I didn't think we would need to do this with you so early, but since your lessons are becoming a farce, this will be our arrangement," Madame Glyceria said. "Girls who can't earn on stage must earn off stage."

Theodora tore her stunned gaze away from the fornice and finally looked at Magister Origen, her head drooping in timidity. She gazed into those black eyes and saw the hunger dancing there, a subtle glint she'd seen before, occasionally, even in front of her mother here and there, but now that look was sustained, intense, certain. He could come for her and have her now at will. When Theodora took a fearful step backward, she heard a man clear his throat. She turned to see the door guard, his eye, like a wet pearl, staring at her.

Madame Glyceria arose and approached Theodora. She spoke quietly. "You'll do whatever the magistrate asks because he's your patron now. If I hear otherwise, I'll offer you up to other men, who pay less than him. You'll be a busy girl. So, it's time to grow up," she said and gave Theodora a half-friendly, half-scornful shove toward the magistrate.

As Theodora approached that dark room, she felt Magister Origen's arm go around her, his hand pressing against her lower back, and a chill settled over her body. He owned her.

As with the first experience, her body felt torn and vile. She remained silent and lay still, as if dead, forced to listen to the rapid breathing of the magistrate. He was heavy upon her, his chest undulant near her eyes, his mouth grazing her scalp. And again, her body betrayed her by accommodating the disgusting penetration, something beyond her control to suppress, as involuntary as breathing or blinking. She hated the act so surely, but why then was her body doing this? Maybe she was a corrupt girl, after all, she thought. Maybe Magister Origen was right about her.

I wanted this.

But Theodora didn't want this. *So why?* She welled up again with tears of shame as her confusion became unbearable. So, she lifted into the air above Magister Origen, gliding past the door guard, and through the front door. Then turning and aiming upward, Theodora flew into the night, transforming into a glittering bird. Her wings were like sails upon the cool air. There, she circled among the stars and looked upon the sleeping city below, just like she used to from her rooftops. Her bird was a beautiful bird. Something majestic. Free and serene. And far away.

Theodora fell asleep afterward in a daze, and for the first time, sleep interested Theodora more than waking life. Feeling nothing at all came to be her only solace, a barren luxury, private and untouched. And so she faded from herself, adrift from within.

Madame Glyceria explained that Magister Origen came from an old Greek family, a deep-rooted aristocracy in Old Byzantium before the Romans came, before the city became an imperial capital. With ties to the dancing master of the Greens, Origen was a precious client.

Seeing the whole city not only accept but accommodate such open evil, that men like Origen could freely enter a place where girls slept and be welcomed as a guest, burned a hole in Theodora's thoughts. The world allowed it; her body allowed it; while she alone helplessly opposed it. There was no one she could tell, no one who would listen, and nothing that would be done to stop the nightmare. Whenever she watched Madame Glyceria drag the magistrate's coins across the table until they dropped into her velvet purse, Theodora clenched her teeth behind an expressionless face. The Madame sold something she didn't own. Theodora now saw her life following a very different path, one where she'd perform for men she hated, and quietly, in the shadows where no one looked or cared.

After the magistrate's fourth nightly visit, Theodora took matters into her own hands.

ELEVEN

To escape the koitǫna, Theodora knew she'd have to contend with the chirping staircase that alerted Madame Glyceria to creeping footfalls. So far, each time Theodora had been summoned for a nightly visit, she'd always descended that noisy stairwell in full view. If she could smuggle a weapon down into the fornice, she could use it against the magistrate and make a run for it. Once outside, the darkness of the night would cloak her flight from the koitǫna, concealing her all the way back home to her mother. Surely, her mother would know what to do next, she thought.

After her pantomiming exercises for the morning, but before the baths, Theodora slipped inside the kitchen. While the elder maids huddled in the corner for their midday meal, Theodora stole one of the carving knives. She hid the knife in the folds of her frock and smuggled it back to her bedchambers. There, she hid the knife beneath one of the wood slats in the floor.

For the rest of the day, her mind was bent on that knife. She performed so poorly during posture training that Madame Glyceria made her sit on the floor near Comito, there to study her sister's proper form and precise dance steps. But the humiliation no longer bothered Theodora, because her thoughts were elsewhere, fixed on the task ahead.

In the silence of night, when the stairs chirped for another girl's descent, Theodora imagined holding the carving knife in her hand, having the courage to thrust it into the flesh of the magistrate. She calculated each step of the plan. Magister Origen would be sitting in the fornice, alone in the dim lantern light. Then he'd arise and shed his toga. At that moment, when his hands and arms were occupied within the fabric, for just a few beats, Theodora would pull out the knife, rush forward, and plunge the blade into the man's chest. She'd have to be fast, she knew. Fast and strong. Then she'd have to get past the door guard, the man with a ghost for an eye. He looked older, fifties perhaps, an ex-soldier, but she sensed he'd be quick and aggressive. At night, though, he wouldn't expect her attempt to escape. As long as she was quick, Theodora believed she could get past him.

On the following evening, Pontíki came for Theodora, but she was already awake, terrified at the seriousness of her plan.

She tucked the knife into her night frock without Pontíki seeing the act. Theodora descended the warbling stairs in a daze, eyes unblinking, and feeling her heart pound in her throat. Once again, her body seemed to betray her will to fight back. Her legs felt weak, and her face felt hot beneath the skin. Even her breathing changed, coming out unevenly, more like gasps and sighs. And the door guard watched her as he always did, creepily, suspiciously.

When Madame Glyceria saw Theodora, she seemed to study her pupil's face. "What's wrong with you, girl?"

"I'm not well, Madame Glyceria," said Theodora.

"You're healthy enough for a visit. Now let's go. He's been waiting for you in the fornice," said Madame Glyceria, her tone scornful.

Theodora walked into the dark room and saw Magister Origen. He was seated on the bed, already naked, and attuning the oil lantern. The room grew brighter with a nightly hue of orange. Theodora panicked. With his toga already off, the moment of her attack was no longer possible. She saw that Origen's arms were free to ward off any attack. As terror befell her senses, the impulse to flee the fornice grew urgent.

Magister Origen looked up and studied Theodora for a moment, perhaps suspiciously, but then smiled. His grin showed stubbled dimples and white teeth, his eyes hard upon her. "There you are, sweet one," he said. "I was growing impatient."

"I don't like your visits," she finally confessed. "You think I do, but I don't."

"Theodora, I'm not your enemy. I'm your patron," he said with that air of gentle authority. "I take care of you and make sure you have what you need. And now and then, you and I will lay together. It's the way of it."

He stood, and his naked chest darkened as the lantern light fell behind him. He became a silhouette of a man with eyes like two points of smoldering light. At the edge of her vision, Theodora saw that the magistrate's manhood took its full form, and a wave of revulsion swept through her.

She swallowed involuntarily. The magistrate hadn't asked her to undress. Paralysis struck, just like before, and her arms hung like dead weight as the magistrate came within a few steps of Theodora. She meant to reach for the knife, still tucked behind the rope at her beltline, but couldn't. Stabbing a man wasn't so easy a thing to do after all.

He slid one hand along Theodora's hip, his fingers passing so near to the knife. Then he leaned down to kiss her. His lips ate cautiously at her mouth, but his eyes stayed open, as did hers. A strangeness rose up between them as if the magistrate saw Theodora's intentions in her gaze. The seductive glitter in his eyes melted into one of suspicion. As Magister Origen pulled back, Theodora finally broke.

She frantically reached under her belt and grabbed the knife handle.

He looked down.

As he did, Theodora pulled out the weapon—suddenly as light as eiderdown—reared back, and *plunged* it deep into the man's bare chest.

Only the blade never actually struck Magister Origen. He held her wrist firmly in his grip. Theodora realized that he'd caught her hand in time to stave off the attack.

"You," he said, the word hissing out of his mouth like a slow wind. "Little whore. You thought to stab me?"

Theodora pulled back as hard as she could to break free of his grip. Instead, the powerful magistrate swung her around and flung her onto the bed, crashing against the back wall. Panic-stricken, Theodora scrambled to her knees and thrust the knife out, warning him to stay back, but saw that Magister Origen hadn't moved.

She had bumped one of the lanterns that hung from the ceiling when he threw her and so points of light rocked back and forth across the room, across the magistrate. He stood motionless, like one of the marble statues of the city, his eyes still and malevolent, his mouth tight from clenched teeth.

Madame Glyceria peeked through the cloth partition and gasped. "Theodora! Put that knife down!"

But Magister Origen raised his arm to bar the old woman. "No. She wants to threaten me. It's her decision—let her make it. Let her see what happens when I sever the cord that holds her life in place."

Madame Glyceria continued. "Theodora, give me—"

"Silence!" shouted the magistrate, causing both Theodora and the Madame to jolt. Magister Origen took another step toward Theodora. "Do it, little whore. It's what you wanted, isn't it? To stab me? To make me your enemy?"

Theodora saw the knife blade quivering uncontrollably in her hand. She could never control her damn body when she needed to.

The magistrate approached her, his steps calm, but his gaze frightening. He then thrust his chin out. "Go on. I'll give you one try. And then I'll teach you what it means to be truly worthless in this world."

As the room fell silent, Theodora suddenly understood the price she was about to pay: her life at the koitóna, her hopes of becoming an actress, her dreams, all forfeit in exchange for a single moment of botched revenge. She'd pulled a knife on an imperial administrator. There was no turning back now.

Knowing that she had only a few moments left before the magistrate subdued her, she raised the blade, feeling a surge of wild energy.

"There you go, little one," he said, but didn't flinch nor falter. "Now, come on. Don't back out now. Don't make me intervene again."

With her heart thudding against her chest, Theodora lunged and slashed the blade across the magistrate's face. His head turned sideways. She saw a small spray of blood and heard a scream from Madame Glyceria. Then, Theodora took flight, leaping past the magistrate, who grabbed for her, racing past Madame Glyceria and into the next room. The girls were already awake, probably from the magistrate's shouting, and now they all peered down at her from the upstairs railings. Theodora spotted Comito, whose startled eyes seemed to be asking, *What have you done, Theodora?*

The door guard appeared from nowhere, reaching out, but Theodora instinctively ducked. She flung herself below his hand, darting out the door and into the chill night air.

The guard spun after her.

As the blackened shapes of Constantinople wheeled around her, Theodora became disoriented. She was barely outside when she felt a powerful grip on her arm, and then a yank. "Let me go!" she screamed. Terrified, Theodora looked up at the door guard, hanging from his grip. And that pale white eye stared back at her, wide with accusation.

He looked over his shoulder, then back at Theodora, and unexpectedly released her. "Go!" he said in a whisper. "Get out of here."

Theodora backed away, not knowing what to think. Then she picked a direction and ran. She ran as fast as she could.

TWELVE

Theodora fell, exhausted, into the debris of a dark alley. The outside sky was so black, the area around her so dark that she lost all her bearings. An awful sensation overcame her in flight; a panicked feeling that no step was fast enough, that pursuers closed ever in, that she was exposed, visible, and moments from capture. She looked back at the end of the alleyway, expecting to see Magister Origen and Roman soldiers appear beneath the light of torches, spotting her and racing toward her. Theodora shivered uncontrollably as she crept through a labyrinth of dark streets. She took care to avoid the gaze of late-night bystanders but couldn't get a sense of direction in the dark. *Where was her home?*

Strange, she thought. The city at night always looked so peaceful when viewed from the safety of a rooftop; yet once submerged into the thick darkness at ground level, Constantinople took on a far more menacing front. At the end of street corners, she saw men huddled around dim pockets of light, like fluttering moths, probably knifemen of the Blues or Greens. Above the rooftops, the Hippodrome appeared as a stripe of obstructed stars. The starting gates end of the track faced her, which meant that her apartment, and her mother, were to the north.

After hours of hiding, of waiting, and of skulking through shadows, step by step, Theodora made her way home. Not until sunrise did she see her apartment building.

When the door opened, and when Theodora finally saw Maximina, she fell into her mother's arms and took in the familiar scent. The feelings of relief made her dizzy.

"Theodora! What are you doing here? Are you injured?"

Theodora shook her head.

"Did something bad happen to you?"

Theodora resisted responding because nothing bad ever happened to Theodora.

"Answer me. Did something bad happen to you?"

Theodora nodded and felt Maximina stiffen and then embrace her tightly. She pressed her face against her mother's chest, and tears suddenly came.

Maximina's voice grew icy. "Was it Magister Origen?"

This time, Theodora nodded right away.

Maximina then rested her head on Theodora. Somewhere outside of the embrace, Theodora was aware that Samuel and Anastasia watched her in silence. They all saw the invincible Theodora laid low.

After a while, Maximina draped Theodora in a wool blanket and placed a soup cauldron on the fire. Anastasia too, hugged Theodora even though she didn't understand what had happened.

Maximina asked a few questions about the magistrate, but Theodora sensed her mother somehow figured out the entire ordeal. Perhaps her mother saw the events in her powders and smoke, or perhaps just understood the world in ways that Theodora didn't. In whispered voices, she told her mother about the knife, the attack, and the flight from the dance school. Maximina listened but never once scolded Theodora.

After Samuel left that morning, Maximina explained the situation to

Theodora. "Attacking a magistrate with a knife is a serious crime," she said. "And we haven't the money to persuade the judges for mercy."

Her mother didn't say it, but Theodora knew no one would believe a fourteen-year-old girl over an aristocrat of Old Byzantium. Even if anyone did believe her claims, none would dare say it aloud. Again, the whole world was willing to look away, always looking away . . .

Maximina continued. "But a man like Magister Origen might not publicly admit that a girl injured him."

Someone knocked at the door.

Terror struck Theodora, who arose and backed away from the sound. Magister Origen could be there. Soldiers could be there.

"Go hide," said her mother.

As Theodora made for the window, prepared to scale to the roof, she heard the voice of Comito instead.

She'd been expelled from the koitóna.

Theodora returned to see that her mother now embraced Comito. She saw that her sister's mood, though, was not sorrow, but scorn.

"Madame Glyceria told me that Theodora was stealing coins from the coin chest and quarreling with patrons," said Comito in tears. "She yelled at me in front of the other girls, saying she couldn't trust the daughters of transients. She called us fornicators and thieves."

"She lies," said Theodora.

Comito then turned on her sister. "I know this is your fault. You started laying with Magister Origen like a whore. I know what the bad dance students do with men at night. And you thought you were better than the rest of us. Did you quarrel with him? Is that why you ran off?"

"Comito!" said Maximina, more stunned than angry. "How dare you speak like that of your sister."

Theodora stepped in and pushed Comito. "A few weeks ago, you couldn't wait to leave the koitóna—now you're crying because you left?"

"Stop it. Both of you!" said Maximina, separating her daughters.

"You lifted your frock for the magistrate at the Hippodrome," Comito said. "Right there in public. The other girls told me everything. They said you had his toga chalk all over you. Admit it! Admit that you got jealous because I was doing better than you in the lessons."

Theodora had never seen Comito so infuriated. Her sister usually yielded to Theodora, but here, suddenly, in the aftermath of Theodora's nightmare, Comito came on strong.

"You were gossiping about me?" Theodora shouted back. "My own sister? You should defend me from such lies when I'm not there to defend myself," she said and shoved Comito.

"Why would I defend a whore who spreads her legs for men in public?" And Comito, unexpectedly, shoved Theodora back.

"Girls!" shrieked Maximina.

Theodora lunged at Comito, grabbing her by the hair and yanking with all her strength. Both girls tumbled to the ground, pulling at clothes, straining, clawing, and screaming. Even though she was the smaller of the two, Theodora got atop Comito, grabbing her sister's hair in both hands, twisting until Comito howled in pain. "I'll kill you!" said Theodora.

Maximina ripped Theodora off of Comito. "Stop it, or I'll beat the both of you!" she screamed. "What evil has befallen this home?"

For a while, the two sisters only glared at each other and tried to catch their breath. Anastasia stood behind Maximina, fingers over her mouth, her eyes wide with wetness and fear.

So, thought Theodora, the other girls knew what had happened at the Hippodrome and blamed Theodora. And Comito was there, eager to listen, eager to believe, willing to condemn. Now that Theodora heard the falsity spoken aloud, she felt numb, her downfall complete.

"You're getting worked up over lies, Comito," said Maximina in an accusing voice. "You know nothing about what's going on, and yet your mouth is the loudest."

"You weren't there, Mother," said Comito. "I saw her with the magistrate last night myself."

The conversation was interrupted when Samuel burst through the front door. He carried his bear-training whips and other tools in his arms. He should have been at the Hippodrome, training the bears. "I've been removed from my post," he said.

Maximina looked terrified. "What?"

"The dancing master wants Marcien to have the bearkeeper post instead. Marcien of all people. He'll get mauled in a week."

Theodora forgot that Magister Origen arranged the transfer of the bearkeeper post from her pata to Samuel. She forgot a lot of things lately. And the girls, who expected to earn silver on the stage in the coming years, suddenly had no prospects. The family was outcast.

Maximina stumbled backward, settling into a chair with her mouth agape. Theodora's eyes widened, waiting for her mother to say something, anything that would stave off the rush of misfortune. But no words came. The family had an enemy that couldn't be beaten, and Theodora knew she'd caused it all. Had she just laid with the magistrate willingly, instead of being so stubborn, everything would've remained unbroken.

"I have no post," said Samuel. "All that silver I paid to get the post, it's just gone." He lowered his heavy body onto a chair. "I haven't had a single incident during any of the shows. I don't see how this could've happened."

"Ask Theodora," said Comito.

Samuel looked at Theodora. "Does this have something to do with last night?"

Theodora looked to Maximina, unsure how to answer. To say anything would be to risk words that brushed by the unspeakable memory. How could Theodora say such things aloud to a stepfather she barely knew? What words could she even use, especially when Comito need only speak "whore" and the very truth that should exonerate Theodora would ruthlessly incriminate her instead?

Maximina spoke up. "Theodora didn't do this, Samuel. Magister Origen did this."

"Magister Origen?" said Samuel. "He's helped us at every turn."

"He's controlling us with his help," said Maximina. "And it costs him nothing."

"But why?" Samuel looked into his lap. "Someone better explain this to me. I cannot forgive what transgressions I know nothing of."

Comito answered. "Because Theodora lifted her frock—"

"Be quiet, you spiteful child!" Maximina shouted and slapped Comito across the cheek, spinning her daughter's face sideways.

Theodora jumped. Maximina never slapped any of the girls before and so now her mother loomed large in the room. But Theodora also felt relief. Her mother killed the false phrase in midair, turning the lethal gossip into brutal silence. Comito stood, stunned, redness appearing on her cheek as Anastasia began crying.

"Comito, I forbid you to speak on this matter," said Maximina. She then shifted her gaze to Theodora. "And you, you don't understand how it is for women. When others speak ill of us, people believe it. The harder you try to clear yourself, the worse it becomes. Gossip can make any girl look suddenly suspicious. Quiet girls become schemers, and carefree girls are all promiscuous when gossipers begin to whisper. You see? It's the *possibility* that drives them mad. Worse, you'll find that gossip will be all the more convincing when it's completely untrue."

Maximina stepped in and touched Theodora gently on the cheek and lowered her voice. "So, you see, a girl like you, who's bold, intelligent, and most of all capable, is a girl of many possibilities. And a girl who can do so many things can be said to do anything, Theodora . . . no matter how incredible, and others will believe it." She looked again at Comito. "That's why such wicked words ring true when said of Theodora. You let yourself be deceived by these girls who know nothing of your sister. But they're just wicked words, Comito, and you'll never speak them in my presence again."

Comito lowered her head. "Yes, Mother."

Theodora listened. Her mother seemed so suddenly frightening, wise, and gentle all at once.

"So why did I lose my post?" said Samuel.

Maximina turned and faced her husband. "Because Magister Origen is punishing my daughter. But the fault is not hers."

Samuel's face darkened, and for a pulse, he hesitated to speak, as if afraid to say what he thought. Then he held up one finger. "Our entire betrothal was based on that post."

Theodora spoke. "You'd never have gotten that post if it weren't for my mother."

"Young woman," said Samuel. "Never getting a post and losing a post are two very different things. Now, please, show me some respect."

"Why can't you go to the Greens?" said Maximina. "Can't the faction help?"

Samuel winced in disbelief. "Magister Origen's family is a great benefactor of the Green faction. Not a soul alive would cross him for our sake," he said and suddenly stood up with fists clenched.

Theodora thought her stepfather might batter down any object in his path. He went to the window, lowered his head, and slowly dropped his fists onto the sill. Then, just as quickly, he drew in a breath, and a calm befell him. "I forgive you," he said. "Damn the whole thing, I forgive you. The post and silver are important, but so are other things," he said and turned around. He stared at Theodora and then at Maximina. "Whatever happened, we must have faith that God will provide."

Theodora wondered if she was observing the peculiar thinking of a Christian.

"Your god isn't going to solve this, Samuel," said Maximina. "We have to solve this."

"Our best hope rests in the will of God," Samuel said, more certain with every word. "We'll go to Hagia Sophia and beg for His mercy."

"Samuel, no," said Maximina.

"Woman, I could blame your daughters for this misfortune, but I haven't," he said without raising his voice. "I've forgiven you all, and so now you'll heed my judgment. We have no power. God does."

Maximina stared at Samuel with hard eyes. Then she looked down, squeezed shut her eyes, and nodded.

And that's when Theodora knew that her fierce mother had lost all hope.

THIRTEEN

Later that evening, Theodora found herself inside the Great Church of Holy Wisdom, the Hagia Sophia. The giant building stood across from the Hippodrome, smaller, humbler, and simpler. From the outside, the church looked like a monumental stable for giant horses, with box-like walls, a stone-gabled roof, and a row of feeble lambs carved into the edifice. She never felt impressed by the shabby Christian churches. The buildings were large, but plain, nothing like the converted pagan temples that scattered the city. For some reason, the old gods still had better temples.

Maximina had allowed the girls into the church before, but only to learn letters in secret from a priest she paid, something no other mother did for their daughters. Theodora and her sisters never came there to worship. Now she took in the sight of the temple as a person who sought favor from the god that dwelt within. The interior bore a meditative calm, with light that glittered and winked at her from countless colored tiles. Mosaics of solemn angels with circles behind their head covered every wall. There were so many of these angels that Theodora had the sensation of being ever-watched.

Overhead, Theodora saw what looked like giant carriage wheels, laid flat as a tabletop, wreathed in candles, and held in place by chains that hung from the ceiling. Benches faced the front sanctuary, just like an amphitheater, as though a show were being performed. But there was no performance to watch, only a giant crucifix set in the shadow of a half-dome. And the audience did not cheer or clap. They sat silently, some with heads bowed, some staring forward peculiarly as if they saw something. Whereas the pagans worshipped outdoors in full view with public festivities, the Christians preferred their ceremonies indoors. Maximina always told her daughters that worshipping in privacy was the way of treacherous devotees who conspired against the public.

Now Maximina conspired with them. So, Theodora wondered whether that made them all Christians now.

Samuel led the girls toward the front, where the crucifix hovered high above, facing the congregation. Samuel knelt first, clasping his hands together and closing his eyes. When Theodora watched her mother get down on her knees in the Christian fashion, she felt a sudden wave of dread and despair. She sensed and even felt her mother's desperation, but seeing such willing surrender now frightened Theodora. Comito and Anastasia quickly knelt beside Maximina, and although none looked back to observe her, Theodora finally knelt as well. This is what the Christians did.

They knelt.

The whole gesture seemed awkward, though, and Theodora snuck glances at her mother. Maximina only squeezed her eyes shut and mouthed inaudible words, hoping once more to ward off a descent into scarcity, sickness, need, hunger, cold, facelessness . . .

Theodora clasped her hands together and looked up, unsure of what to do.

When she looked up, she saw the statue of Jesus Christ unchanged. His eyes were closed, his head slumped forward, his ribs scarred and bleeding. So strange an image for a god, she thought, nothing more than a lifeless man with a gentle face. Over the years, Theodora had heard the stories Christians told of their god—strange stories. Their god spoke of mercy and forgiveness. He didn't fight back when the Romans came to kill him. She even heard that the son begged the father not to punish, but to forgive the Romans, even as they crucified this god like a common criminal.

Forgive.

Is that what Jesus Christ expected her to do in this temple? She closed her eyes, and the face of Magister Origen was there, holding power over her, even in her imagination. Then she opened her eyes.

She knew.

She couldn't forgive the magistrate for what he did. Never. Not him.

Theodora glared at the sleeping face of Jesus.

How dare you ask me to forgive Magister Origen? You only suffered once and became a worshipped god. How easy for you.

Forgiveness was an arrogant decree, she decided. Jesus Christ died upon the cross, his humiliation honored, his disgrace revered, his physical body *restored to new* on the third day, unlike her own body, as if such human injuries were but smudges upon the skin, and so easily washed out. And he, the son, was carried up to heaven in an exalted state, while she, Theodora, was left to linger on below, broken and marred, there to suffer the will of an evil man, her tormentor free and unpunished. She couldn't simply retreat to heaven for eternal shelter. Jesus suffered in full view while his followers wept. And there in the church, they still wept for him . . . his single degradation . . . five hundred years in the past. Yet Theodora sat right among these people, alive, her humiliation fresh, known by some and unacknowledged by all. She had been quietly disavowed for her suffering. And none wept for her.

Theodora cried because she saw the darkness inside her now, a new capacity for cruelty, a desire to hurt back, a feeling of hatred. She knew what she would do if given the chance, and it was not forgiveness.

There was the son, but she also heard about the father. And he was a jealous god, one of harsh judgment, a creator and a destroyer alike. She'd heard how the father had made skies rain until cities perished. The father turned rivers to blood, wrought plagues upon nations, and purged entire armies with the sea when he declared injustice. That's what she needed, to know that a god would act with authority, that a god acknowledged a time for wrath, for heaven was a kingdom, after all, and this god did not share power.

Theodora glanced up into the blackness of the ceilings and cried.

Why won't you help me? Don't you care about girls? I'm called evil by evil people, and yet you give them total power over me? They get to destroy me and my family so easily? If you're real, why would you ever allow that? Theodora's anguish choked her, and she lowered her head, tears falling freely to the floor. She truly wanted answers to these questions that she would never ask aloud. *Because why is it my fault? Why am I the guilty one? Why wouldn't you give someone like me all the power there is to strike down an evil man? I just don't understand. If you're going to help someone, help me.*

And how did the Christians end their prayers? With a word.

Amen.

FOURTEEN

Night came.

Theodora prayed for revenge, but she should have prayed for simple firewood. The hearth sat empty, the ashes cold. She and her family gathered in the dark domicile and ate only bread and drank only water. After supper, Samuel lit a single candle, and they all watched the wax make tears until the candle was no more. Wax became a precious commodity by then. Wax for darkness, wool for cold, water for thirst, and bread for hunger. Those were the four final luxuries until the silver ran out, which Samuel said would be in a few days. All of this misery came only one week after Theodora fled the koitǫna.

So rapid the slide to destitution.

Anastasia lay curled in Theodora's arms. Her younger sister was the first to be stricken by hunger. Theodora gave her portion of bread to Anastasia, but it was not enough. Now she too, felt the onset of hunger; a deep ache in her belly and throat, a merciless preoccupation of the mind, a desire to eat, a desire to chew, and a weakening of her body. She considered the coming days. Samuel and her mother would lead them from the dwelling and take them to the place beside the aqueduct, where the hungry and dispossessed gathered. She imagined a cold, vacant plot where the weeds pushed through the cobblestones, where the foot traffic no longer took notice, there to share the earth with mice and beetles. And the hunger, she thought, the hunger would be there every day, lurking inside, thinning her body until bones pushed through her skin. Would she soon look like so many of the stray dogs that scavenged through the Sacred City, the city guarded by God?

"I'm so hungry," said Anastasia in a sad, brittle voice.

"Me too," Theodora said.

Comito, who sat with her chin on her knees, glanced up. "How much longer until they make us leave?"

Theodora looked over at her mother. Maximina and Samuel held each other, backs against the wall, eyes closed, but it was Samuel who spoke. "Two days. By now, the landlord's been told of my dismissal. It seems that everyone knows we've angered someone from the nobility. But God will provide, children. We must be strong in our faith and not doubt His will. He is a merciful God who shelters the weak and feeds the hungry. He will bring salvation to us."

Then why are there so many hungry and poor in the city? God hasn't saved them.

Theodora also saw her mother's eyes. She saw that Maximina didn't share Samuel's faith. "Go to sleep, girls," she said. "Sleep will free you from hunger tonight."

Hunger.

Just the thought of the word pricked Theodora's imagination with bleak and unanswerable agony. Eventually, though, Theodora fell to sleep, and when she did, she dreamed.

She found herself on an unfamiliar street, running, escaping the koitóna once again. She glanced backward to see the magistrate bearing down on her. No matter how desperately she ran, the magistrate drew closer, as if his hand need only to reach out and grab her.

Theodora came upon the Hippodrome, dark with night, empty. She ran inside the vacant archway and through black tunnels while the magistrate's voice and footfalls echoed all around her. Suddenly, Theodora burst through the tunnel and out onto the darkened horse track. The great stadium, though, was nothing more than charcoal gray shapes in the night. The sounds of pursuit also fell silent behind her. For a moment, Theodora was alone. Only a crescent moon shone overhead.

Then she saw a single silhouette approaching her upon the racetrack, closing fast. As the silhouette drew up, Theodora saw a barrel of a belly and then her pata's face slip into the moonbeams. He crouched down, and she ran to him. She embraced her father. When Theodora pulled back, she saw that Acacius appeared untroubled, almost playful. For a moment, Theodora basked in the memory of being her pata's favorite daughter, a secret they each knew, but none spoke aloud.

"You left us with nothing, Pata," she said to him. "You went off and died, and now we're ruined."

He stared back at Theodora with a father's guilt. "I'm sorry, my little gift from God." That was what he always called her, the Latin version of her name. "I know I failed you."

"Oh, Pata, we're to beg in the streets."

"Theodora," he said, brushing his daughter's hair. "Don't worry yourself so. It hasn't happened yet."

"But it *will* happen, and I'm the cause of it all," she said.

"No, no. I'm the cause of it all, Theodora."

"But I'm so hungry," she said, glancing down. When she looked up, her father was gone. "Pata, no!" she screamed and spun in place. The sound of her voice echoed further and further away, out beyond the roof-line of the Hippodrome.

And then she saw a torch catch fire on the far side of the stands. Then another. One by one, torches ignited, and a wave of fiery luminance spread across the Hippodrome stands, revealing countless shadowy citizens. They just stood there. From the Kathisma, where the emperor would sit, Theodora watched in horror as Magister Origen stepped out. He stared at Theodora with eyes that glowed white. A pure and primal panic gripped her in an awful but familiar paralysis. He had her trapped again.

"No!" she shouted and sat up, awake. She was breathing hard and sweating.

Maximina reached over and brushed her hand through Theodora's hair. "Shh," she said. "You had a bad dream."

"I saw Pata. He was in the Hippodrome."

"Yes. He'll visit you in your dreams as my father still visits me sometimes. My mother too. We're all orphans one day."

Maximina and Theodora spoke in whispers while Samuel snored through an open mouth. The rest of the apartment was dark and quiet.

"I also saw *him*," said Theodora and looked up at her mother. "He was in the emperor's box." The fear came back to her as she recalled the sight.

Maximina hushed her.

For a long while, Theodora and her mother sat awake in the night. She figured they both fell into distraction at the bleak prospects of the coming days. After recalling her dream, an odd thought stuck in Theodora's imagination, one that lingered, pestered, and became an idea of scale. "Mother," Theodora said. "Who decides who gets Samuel's bearkeeper post?"

"That would be Dancing Master Asterius. Why?"

"So, Magister Origen convinced Dancing Master Asterius to take the post away from Samuel?"

"Yes."

"There might be a way to get the dancing master to change his mind," said Theodora.

Maximina paused in her stroking of Theodora's hair. "How?"

"Pata died because the people rose up and pressured the emperor to change his mind. The revolt ended in the Hippodrome when the emperor gave in. In my dream, Magister Origen was in the emperor's box. So, maybe Pata's trying to tell me that we could use the factions to pressure Dancing Master Asterius to change his mind too."

Maximina slipped into a compassionate smile. "A revolt against the dancing master, you say?"

"We could go to the Hippodrome. In between the races, we could beg the Greens to give the post back to Samuel. We could try and turn the crowd against Dancing Master Asterius."

Maximina didn't answer, but only stroked Theodora's cheek. "Why don't you get some sleep. We can talk about this tomorrow."

The silence gave way to Theodora's endless thoughts. But stealthy sleep crept in and finally stilled her weary mind.

She awoke to a shouting voice. Samuel.

"Beg God, not men, you childish woman!" he said. "Even if I did humiliate myself before the whole city, and even if I did get my post back, who could ever respect me again after such a disgusting, such a dishonorable sight?"

Theodora sat up, noticing the strange scent of flowers in the dwelling. She watched as Samuel moved toward the door while her mother followed him.

Samuel continued. "Have you no dignity? No man would stoop so low that he'd beg for his post like some spectacle."

"Well, I'm not a man!" Maximina shouted back. "I'm a mother of three daughters, and I've kept them off the street my whole life. I'll take the girls by myself if I have to."

"Before the entire Hippodrome?" Samuel laughed and opened the door. "If begging suits you, then beg of God. That's where I go."

The door slammed, and Theodora jumped. Comito and Anastasia sat awake beside her. "What's happening?"

Comito answered. "Samuel's going to the church, but Mother's going to the Hippodrome."

Theodora's stomach twisted. "She is?"

Maximina turned and approached the girls. "Get washed up," she said. "I want you girls to look your best today."

Theodora and her sisters didn't question Maximina. They washed in the cold water of the wooden washtub since they had no more firewood. When Theodora finished, she saw that her mother now donned a white dress. The sight stunned her. Her mother never wore such an innocent color. She set out three other white dresses for the girls, attire the Christian girls wore on holy days, weddings, and feasts.

"Where did you get those?" asked Theodora.

"I borrowed them. Put them on, girls."

The sisters complied. Maximina came to Theodora and adjusted the strange gown at the shoulders, collar, and waist.

"What is all this, Mother?" said Theodora.

"I was up late last night," she said and took up a bowl of black powder. She then outlined Theodora's eyes in kohl. "I thought about your idea and believe it was an omen."

The smell of kohl powder reminded Theodora of the salóni and the koitóna. She felt an uneasy flutter in her belly. "I don't like wearing paint on my face."

"Be quiet. You're going to wear your paint." Maximina rubbed rouge on Theodora's cheeks. "Then I will take you and your sisters to the Hippodrome."

"You're really going to do it?"

"The streets are full of women who have been pushed aside, but not me, not *us*. No one's going to fight for us, so we must fight for ourselves." Maximina dabbed Theodora's cheekbones with a cloth. "In the end, all battles are social battles, Theodora. We just need to win that crowd today."

But the morning brought sobriety to Theodora. "How are we going to turn so many against Dancing Master Asterius?"

Maximina tapped her finger against Theodora's temple. "With wit and courage," she said and grabbed a garland of flowers. She slipped the garland over Theodora's black silky hair, like a crown. "You were the only one who came up with an idea last night. And no matter how ridiculous or far-fetched, I would be damned for the rest of my life if I did not try to carry it out. I'm your mother. In this life, who, if not your mother?"

Theodora felt warmth course through her body. She'd been feeling so worthless, so low, so ashamed. Maximina could've easily blamed Theodora for the ruin that had befallen the family. And here? Here, her mother was instead going into battle against the men who threatened the emperor, who filled the stands in the tens of thousands...

Maximina then tended Comito and Anastasia, who wore the same white gowns and garlands. She gave each of her daughters a basket filled with sweet-smelling, white flower petals, freshly picked. She must've strung the garlands together that morning, thought Theodora, because the flowers looked so bright and smelled so fragrant. There were pink apricot blossoms, lavender snow flowers, green fig leaves, and beautiful crocus flowers with imperial purple petals and lemon-yellow centers.

"The Christians prefer saintly women, so that's what they'll get," said Maximina. "We'll get there by foot and draw many strange looks, but do not look back at them, girls. Keep your heads high. If anyone offers you alms, refuse. We're *not* street beggars."

Theodora exchanged a glance with Comito and Anastasia. Perhaps her sisters wanted to see something in Theodora's face, some show of confidence, a haughty sparkle that assured them that she believed in her plan. Instead, Theodora cast her eyes toward the south, at the bone-white brim of the Hippodrome, where the zealots of sport and rebellion awaited her.

FIFTEEN

When Theodora, her sisters, and her mother arrived at the Hippodrome, and when from behind a wall of marble the crowd burst into a deafening roar, Theodora sensed the full weight of the battle to come.

There, they met with a man named Nilus, a stall-keeper for chariot horses and friend of the late Acacius. He led them into the Hippodrome through the southwestern gate and into the torch-lit tunnels. The moment Theodora saw the glow at the end of the tunnel again, a crushing anxiety filled her chest. Nilus guided Maximina to the mouth of the tunnel, where the dirt of the track mixed with the hard stone of the floor, where the mighty crowds cheered and roared above them. A group of male acrobats stood near the entrance, hands on hips, chatting as they stared out at the track. They gave no more than cursory glances at the decorated girls and their mother.

A race was in progress.

Theodora saw how Comito, Anastasia, and her mother gaped at the sights and sounds. Not only would they be going into battle, but for them, the unfamiliar battlefield humbled them with awe.

Then Theodora heard the soft rumble of galloping horses growing closer, quaking the ground until the rumble became earsplitting. In a sudden gust, several horses and chariots thundered past the tunnel, one after the other, with whips snapping, wooden axles straining, horses grunting, and charioteers shouting their onward cries. With so many chariots racing at full speed at the same time, the noise was deafening. Their passing was so loud that Theodora covered her ears. And just as quickly, the fury moved away from them, sweeping clouds of dust into the tunnel.

Theodora brushed off her dress, but then trumpets blared at the far end of the Hippodrome. Maximina jerked in alarm. Above them, the Green spectators burst into a riotous "Nika" chant, since a Green chariot apparently won. Eventually, though, the spectators fell into a disorderly murmur, their attentions fracturing into private conversations. As Maximina tried to shake out the fright from the chariots, Theodora knew with certainty that her mother was overmatched.

Nilus darted across the horse track. He spoke with the announcer, pointed at the tunnel, and gave the announcer a coin. The announcer for the Greens then wandered to center track and raised the voice cone to his lips. "Victorious Greens! We have a sad matter to bring before you," he boomed in a dramatic voice, placing his hand over his heart. "A widow! Her three daughters! Destitution! Women who have sacrificed their very dignity to come before you and beg like dogs..."

From the mouth of the tunnel, Theodora witnessed raw terror on her mother's face. Her sisters must have also felt the panic, because they both turned and faced their mother, shifting on unsteady feet and frantically awaiting instruction.

Maximina bent down. "Listen to me, my daughters. Stay close. When I give you a signal, throw your flower petals at the stands as if saluting an emperor," she said.

The announcer waved Maximina forward. She drew in a deep breath, placed her hand flat against her collar, and stepped out onto the track. Theodora and her sisters followed.

Sunlight crashed upon them as the crowd murmured at sight of them.

When the girls reached the center of the track, where Theodora saw trampled horse dung and treads in the dirt from chariot wheels, Maximina turned her daughters around to face the crowd. Theodora fell into a stunned stupor, as did her mother. Tens of thousands of people stared down at them from the Hippodrome benches, as if the sky had become a great host of wild men and staring eyes.

Theodora saw Anastasia swoon slightly with flush cheeks. "Close your eyes," she said and steadied her sister.

The announcer handed Maximina the voice cone, and Theodora saw it shaking in her mother's hand. But Maximina held it to her lips. "Where is Dancing Master Asterius?" she called out in an unexpectedly loud and commanding voice. "Show yourself, Dancing Master."

Theodora and her family stood in the semicircle turn of the track, a place called the sphendone. There, the entire south section of the hippodrome quieted at Maximina's voice.

Theodora spotted Asterius in the front row, surrounded by wealthy Greens. He paid no attention to Maximina, but merely sipped his wine and carried on a private conversation with none other than Magister Origen. The sight of him made Theodora take a step back. His face looked bright in the sun. He squinted and nodded as he spoke, unaware of Theodora's presence on the track. But she felt exposed, visible. Whereas she suddenly wanted to run and hide, her mother's voice drew in more attention.

"You came to my late husband's funeral, oh Dancing Master!" roared Maximina, her voice powerful and clear. "The Greens remember my late husband, the great Acacius, who was bearkeeper for ten years and two!"

At that, the crowd responded with polite applause. Theodora exchanged a glance with Comito. Applause was good.

"And after gracing our family with your generosity, you've suddenly turned us away, Dancing Master!" Maximina said. "You sold my new husband's post without warning and turned us into the streets!"

Magister Origen finally looked out on the track. He glanced, turned, and glanced again, his surprise settling into a disturbing stare at Theodora. She held her breath as she met his dark eyes. The magistrate sat in the first row, high up as if from a low balcony, and not far away. He was close enough for Theodora to see the knife cut along his cheek. Asterius too, now eyed the women, but leaned toward Magister Origen, as if receiving an explanation as to Maximina's presence.

Finally, Theodora noticed some spectators signaling the dancing master, urging him to respond. He twisted around to look at them and shrugged, irritation showing plainly on his face.

"Dancing Master," said Maximina. "Is our hunger unworthy of your briefest attention? Are three starving girls so insignificant that you cannot pause from your own feasting?"

Asterius gestured to Magister Origen, pausing their conversation, and nodding as though he now understood the situation. Then he dabbed the wine from his lips and looked out onto the track. For a long while he pretended to stare as if he couldn't see the girls, long enough for some in the crowd to laugh.

Maximina pulled her daughters in closer, forming a protective embrace. Theodora saw how the white gowns spilled down like milk upon the dark brown of the track, her mother rising above. "We're over here," Maximina said. "Perhaps we have grown too thin from hunger that you barely see us. Look down here, Dancing Master, down at the track. Even someone as drunk as you should be able to see us."

The crowd bellowed in laughter and even clapped, seeming to appreciate the defiance of Maximina. More spectators took notice of the exchange because now the benches hushed to hear more.

Maximina pressed him. "I see Magister Origen is in your ear, oh Dancing Master! Now there's a man who cares for the pretty young daughters of our fine faction. His concern is so deep that it's almost, how shall I say," she said with a dramatic pause, "suspicious?"

At this, the crowd laughed and taunted Origen and Asterius.

"For a man who loves little girls so much, surely he advises mercy for *three!* We beg the mercy of the Greens!" said Maximina to applause. At that, she signaled Theodora and her sisters.

But when Theodora saw her mother's eyes, she gasped. The black center of Maximina's eyes overtook the brown, making her look like a wild animal. She realized that her mother was in the grip of battle-fright, clinging desperately to her wits. Yet she and her sisters did as they were bid. They stepped forward and flung the white flower petals into the air, the white blossoms catching in the breeze and scattering about on the track.

"We beg the emperor of the Greens for mercy," said Maximina and the crowd clapped again at her plea.

A few voices in the stands now shouted at the dancing master. "Mercy," they said. "Show them mercy!"

Anastasia opened her eyes now to see, while Theodora and Comito exchanged a smirk.

Mother was winning.

The dancing master finally stood and raised his hand, like a man about to address the Senate. The Greens who jeered him fell silent. He then leaned in and studied the women with an exaggerated gaze. After a moment, he feigned a revelation. With both hands, he gestured as though he held and juggled two breasts at his chest. He turned to the crowd, mocking the very notion of womanhood and drawing attention back to the odd presence of women inside the Hippodrome. The crowd, which were all men, mostly drunk, roared with laughter. The dancing master then performed a vulgar pantomime, thrusting his hips with exaggerated rhythm, and gathering ever louder laughter. He concluded by pointing to the Blue section of the stands as if directing prostitutes to their rightful clients. This made the Green spectators erupt in hilarity, and at that moment, Theodora sensed a shift in approval away from her mother. The men laughed, mouths agape, some with food in their teeth. Magister Origen clapped calmly at the jest, amused by the dancing master's clever pantomime.

"Dancing Master," called out Maximina, but the crowd's laughter drowned her out this time. "Dancing Master!" she said again. Some of the men now dismissed the girls with arrogant waves of their hands and defaming calls of "Whores!"

"Dancing Master," said Maximina again, but this time her voice quavered and her eyes glazed over in terror. And Theodora saw the great wave of her mother's bravery crest, break, and ebb back.

Just like that, the crowd turned against them, sentencing her family to life on the streets at last. The dancing master never even uttered a word. What power, thought Theodora as she watched Asterius take his seat.

Magister Origen arose and clapped at the dancing master, in the manner of giving his friend an ovation. Others joined him. He looked back at Theodora, his eyes mocking her.

She couldn't stand that look. Theodora bent down and grabbed an apple-sized chunk of dried horse manure. Then she flung it into the stands at Magister Origen. He leaned aside and watched the dung strike a spectator behind him. The crowd oohed at the defiance.

"Shall the Green faction feed these beggars?" said Magister Origen. He grabbed a bread loaf from a nearby spectator, tore off a piece, and tossed the bread at Theodora. More laughter. Before Theodora could react, most of the Greens, too many of them, showered the track with bread bits. She turned and saw her sisters holding their arms up defensively. But her mother stood motionless, eyes downcast as bread bits pelted her and collected all around her.

"No!" Theodora shrieked at the sight. "Stop it!"

All battles are social battles. That's what Maximina had told her. Now, she understood what that meant—she, her sisters, and her mother were on the lowest rung. Maximina came close, but the battle was lost.

The announcer, taking his cues from the waning interest in the crowd, waved the women off the racetrack.

But a single parade-ground voice split the air. "You heartless Greens! Is this how you treat the mothers of your children?"

Theodora spun around. There, on the opposite side of the Hippodrome, she saw a single man standing tall on the Blue side of the benches. He cupped his hands as he called out to the Greens. "No wonder the Green faction is a litter of bastards and criminals! Are you blind to this woman's courage?"

The Blue section now laughed and applauded their own champion.

Magister Origen waved him off. "Be silent, you Blue, you son of a whore!"

At the sound of the challenge, many other Greens stood up and shouted obscenities at the Blues.

The lone Blue continued his taunt. "You show your cruelty, you Greens! You turn your women out into the streets and mock them! Only motherless men would show such hatred to this woman and her daughters!"

Theodora stared at the man in the stands. He stood at the edge of the concrete lip, one hand outstretched.

"The Blue faction are Jews and Manicheans!" said Magister Origen. "How laughable that you speak against cruelty!"

"Then let the Blues teach you a lesson in mercy, you sheep-lovers!" said the Blue. "I say, girls, come here! We would honor a mother with your courage!"

"The Blues always did give their highest honors to whores," said Magister Origen to thunderous laughter.

The other man continued. "We Blues have a vacant bearkeeper post that we'll give your husband! You need only renounce the Green faction!"

Maximina lifted her head as if she barely understood what was happening.

"Come on, Mother," said Theodora, who saw with perfect clarity the opportunity at hand. She tossed aside her flower basket and raced across the dirt track. She glanced over her shoulder to see Maximina, Comito, and Anastasia breaking forward after her.

The Greens jeered and shouted obscenities at the fleeing girls. As Theodora drew near the other side of the track, she saw the face of the man in the stands. The Blue bore an unexpectedly familiar face. He was the handsome Roman officer who had captured her and Comito the night of the rebellion. He wasn't in uniform, but Theodora never forgot his face, clean-shaven, intelligent, commanding. Theodora lowered her head to keep the garland from blowing off, but her heart felt buoyant as her eyes fixed on that one face. How magnificent this man looked in that moment, standing in a sea of people, waving her forward as if he alone cared for her welfare.

When she reached the wall, the man in the stands reached down and the crowds waved her up. As the Blue section urged her on, Theodora felt Maximina grab her by the waist and hoist her into the air.

Not knowing what else to do, Theodora pulled the garland from her head and tossed it at the man in the stands. He caught the garland and the spectators around him roared with laughter and applause. Theodora drew back and blushed at the riotous attention she was getting.

"May God shine upon the merciful Blues!" said Maximina.

The Blues cheered and mocked the Greens, while the Greens hurled vicious insults in return. A fight broke out in the stands where the Blues and Greens meshed, causing Roman soldiers to rush into the fray. But the crowd's fleeting attention was drawn away by the blare of a horn.

The next race was about to begin.

As Theodora, her sisters, and her mother were ushered off the track, this time on the Blue side, she looked back. Magister Origen still stood at the edge of the promenade, his hands upon the barrier and staring across the track. After a second blare of the horn, he gave a disinterested wave, turned back to the benches, and vanished into the teeming masses. He seemed so far away now, drifting ever further.

Perhaps now she could forget the magistrate. Perhaps the anguish and shame of what he did to her could disappear as if nothing ever happened. Perhaps she could be reborn entirely, emerging renewed and unspoiled, up from the wellspring of that marvelous new color . . . Blue.

PART 2

UNDERWORLD

SIXTEEN

Theodora hurried through the dark passageway as the sounds of the Amphitheater grew louder. She heard the lone stage voice of her sister, Comito, followed by light audience laughter. She was late and more than a little drunk. As she entered the portico behind the stage, she slipped and fell. Theodora's sudden appearance in the portico drew giggles from her thespian friends, while a black-haired boy of about fifteen scrambled to help her up.

"Thank you, Bacchus," she said. "Please don't tell me I missed the scene."

"No, but you're about to miss it."

Theodora got to her feet and stumbled into the dark portico. The nighttime air was warm and pleasant, but she had a light sweat on her forehead. Through the stone pillars behind the stage, she saw Comito standing in costume with a few other actors before a late-night audience. Beyond her sister, hazy spectators filled the semicircle of benches.

Then she noticed the stage master glaring in her direction. He was a white-haired Roman who wore a fine blue tunic over his small frame. Theodora saw that he meant to rebuke her, so she quickly removed her robe, leaving her naked except for a girdle that covered her genitalia. At nineteen years old, she knew the sight of her unclothed body always caused a man's eyes to glaze over, even here in a theater where nudity was not uncommon. She grinned at the stage master and turned to face him in full. When he said nothing, Theodora reached out and grabbed her costume from Bacchus, who was himself bashfully stealing glances at her body.

Theodora shook her hair out and slipped on a slave boy's tunic, a thin muslin costume scantily arranged with the lower half of the garment barely reaching her thighs. The Blue faction was performing *Assemblywomen*, the same Greek comedy they'd been performing all spring, a play about women running the government of old Athens.

Comito won the lead role of Praxagora, an Athenian woman who established an all-female government and attempted to dole out egalitarian rights to the citizens.

"Men of Athens!" declared Comito in her crisp stage voice. "You are hereby granted the rights of sexual equality as requested. Any man has a right to bed any woman of the city at least once."

The male audience cheered the decision.

"However," Comito cut them off. "Only after the elderly and unsightly women are serviced first."

The audience laughed and cawed at the cruel caveat. Comito turned to stage left and summoned her slave boy.

That was Theodora's cue.

She shimmied off the girdle around her waist, her only undergarment, and tossed the item to the side. Then, dressed as the slave boy, she cantered out of the shadows and onto the firelit stage. Immediately, the crowd came to life at the sight of this "slave boy." Theodora knew the audience could see through the thin muslin of her slave tunic, where her breasts jostled beneath the loose-fitting attire, and where the silhouette of her lower body showed the missing undergarment. A law banned actresses from appearing onstage without a girdle, so Theodora looked out at the audience and theatrically covered her mouth in mock surprise. She spun once as she walked so her tunic lifted in the air, flashing her bare figure briefly to the crowd. The audience, Blues and Greens alike who were pleasantly humored, now burst out with cheers, whistles, and howls of admiration. She heard men shouting out her newest moniker, the *Notorious* Theodora, hailing her scandal.

When Theodora reached Comito, she dropped into an ill-mannered bow. Comito's eyes were ablaze with anger.

The slave boy role was but a trifle in *Assemblywomen*, an extra part with no speaking lines. But now that Theodora had showed herself to the crowd and enticed all those masculine eyes, she'd receive invitations for sexual services. This had long become her routine. Since all actresses were expected to sell their services after the play, the Notorious Theodora would be their first choice. Comito may have won the stage, but Theodora always won the crowd.

She turned sideways to the audience and bowed formally as she placed the scroll in her sister's hand, bending so that the edge of her tunic crept ever upward, revealing a full side view of her nude backside once it slipped out from the tunic. The audience cheered her on, begging her to show more.

In an attempt to maintain character, Comito gestured to dismiss her annoying "slave boy," but this met with a chorus of disapproval from the audience. Theodora, giddy from wine, ignored her sister, pointing out that the crowd wished for her to stay. Barely clinging to her character, Comito pushed Theodora back toward the stage entrance, but Theodora reached down and pinched Comito's bottom, sending her sister springing backward in surprise. Thunderous laughter encircled the two. Theodora went to repeat the jest, and Comito retreated. The other actors and actresses on stage stepped away as the play devolved, Theodora sensed, into a disorderly farce. Comito finally broke character and signaled the stage master.

Theodora waved off Comito, as though her sister was no fun, causing another round of laughter. One man arose and pulled apart the flaps of his shirt to reveal a dark, bristly chest and then cried out a confession of love for the Notorious Theodora. She pressed her hand to her lips and waved at the admirer. She then gestured for payment, and the man held up a few glinting silver coins.

"Hardly enough!" she said to a riot of laughter.

With a waggle of her fingers, Theodora finally scampered off stage, while her adoring patrons clamored in disapproval.

Once Theodora was again backstage, the stage master struck her in the back of her head, a painless blow. "Impudent girl," he said in a singsong Latin accent. "I'll get fined for that. You go out there, you show your legs, and you get off stage."

"I tried," said Theodora. "But they insisted I stay—"

The stage master struck her on the top of the head again. This time, the blow stung. "You show your legs and get off stage."

"Oh, don't be so angry, Stage Master," she said. "Your audience was nearly asleep. I just woke them up."

Bacchus grinned at Theodora's quip.

The stage master stepped in at Theodora and shoved the girdle into her hands. "Now put it back on."

"I know you were watching the show too," she said, slowly lifting her tunic again. Though the stage master clearly tried to resist, his eyes slipped down to look at her, and she laughed mockingly. "Just admit that you love me, Stage Master."

"I love the extra silver you bring in," he said, turning back to the stage to gauge the mood of the audience. "Every time I parade you out there, I attract a big audience, but also risk vulgarity, which is the very opposite of art."

"Yet you keep me in your play," said Theodora.

"Don't do it again," said the stage master, turning now to address the male actors nearby. "I miss the days when only men were actors. Now they want women, and once you let women into any profession, the trade naturally degrades. Such are the times. But where one sees decay . . . only a fool will blame the maggots."

"I'll know when you are serious, Stage Master," said Theodora, grabbing a wine jug and filling a wood cup, "the day you actually remove me from a performance. Until then." She toasted him.

The stage master ignored Theodora to observe the current scene. As far as Theodora was concerned, all the quarreling between herself and the stage master was a kind of unspoken theater, a pantomime of real life. With the money and patrons she brought in, the Blues would never dismiss her, no matter how much Comito or anyone else complained. The others may have toiled for stage time, but not Theodora. She found her own way. Her *speciosa vi* and now her matured body were the only things she needed. She stood among the actresses of the stage, yet she was apart from them, unlike them.

Theodora noticed Bacchus smiling admiringly at her, so she puckered her lips at him in a mock kiss. Then she leaned against one of the pillars, wine cup held at the chin, and looked out at the audience. The benches rose upward and backward until the faces in the distant upper seats dimmed in the darkness of night. She searched over the faces in the crowd, an act that was sometimes unconscious to her. She always hoped to spot the unforgettable face of that man in the stands, the man who had defied a host of Greens at the Hippodrome with naught but words, stealing away their cruelty and defeating Magister Origen. But she never saw either man since that one day. Theodora always hoped, even assumed, that one day the mysterious man who saved her family would be seated up among the spectators at the Amphitheater, gazing down at the stage, and upon seeing her would pay for an evening alone with her. She was a woman now and could reward the man with more than a silly garland. Ever since the gloss of girlhood smeared off so abruptly, Theodora wasn't prone to daydreams. But somehow, this one fantasy persisted.

Theodora's thoughts were interrupted when timpani drums signaled the end of the scene. She watched as Comito turned away from the audience and stormed off the stage, pulling the wig from her head.

"How dare you spoil the scene," said Comito. "Showing up drunk and trying to steal all the attention with your nothing of a role."

Theodora feigned surprise.

"Calm yourself," said the stage master. "I've already dealt with Theodora."

"Stage Master, you don't understand," Comito said in a pleading voice. "My character is at the head of the Athens government. How can anyone take me seriously if my lowly slave, some bawdy harlot, lingers on the stage and mocks me? It undermines the whole play."

Theodora filled a fresh cup of wine. "Oh please. You're playing a woman at the head of government. What could be more comical than that?" Then she lowered her voice a bit. "With a little help from me, we finally got them laughing."

Some of the actors laughed at Theodora's haughty remark, though discretely. Comito silenced them all with a threatening look.

"Come now, Comito," said the stage master, who approached her and took the wig from her hand. "You are the lead actress. You must handle your higher post with better grace."

"I don't want her in that scene anymore," Comito said. "Use Antonina or Chrysomallo. They do those kinds of roles. Only they understand that the audience isn't there for them."

Theodora laughed sarcastically. "I guarantee you, that audience wants to see a lot more of me and a lot less of you."

Comito waved a hand at her sister. "Go! Empty another cup of wine. Go find some slaves to lay with backstage. You lurk around the theater, pretending you have talent, and all the while you force Mother to tend your daughter."

"Snake," she said and stepped in at Comito, who stepped back. Her sister promised never to mention the baby in front of the troupe.

The stage master clapped his hands twice. "Professional women, everyone. Aren't they wonderful? Comito, get focused on the upcoming scene. Theodora, get out of here. Your little scene is done. When we get requests for you, Bacchus will call for you."

"She has more offers than I could take," said Bacchus. "One is from the Palace."

Theodora toasted the stage master and Comito and then emptied her cup of wine. "I won't take any patrons until I've had some fresh air."

"A palace client, Theodora," the stage master warned. "Freshen up, but do not make him wait."

"For me, men would wait all night." She then took up the amphora, a double-handled ceramic wine jug, and walked away. No one stopped her.

Theodora left the portico behind the stage and slipped outside into the breezy night air. She realized that she still held her girdle, so she threw the undergarment angrily into the thickets. The area outside the Amphitheater was wooded and pulsed with the sound of crickets and distant street music. Unlike the Hippodrome, which boldly occupied the city center, the Amphitheater was surrounded by a forested urban park and smelled of cypress and moss. Fireflies and thespians moved about the trees and pavilions, while lanterns hung from low tree branches.

And how dare Comito mention that damn child?

The other actresses chided the Notorious Theodora for allowing such a thing as a baby to come between her vulgar theater and the stage. The pregnancy was a complete embarrassment. For months, Theodora stayed with her mother, while Samuel worked at the Hippodrome and a gaunt Anastasia hovered around Theodora, always touching her belly and suggesting various names for the coming baby. And during that time, Comito reigned over the Amphitheater alone. Theodora could only lay there like an ailing horse, removed from all publicity.

When Theodora heard the applause as the play resumed, she scoffed. Comito took her performances so seriously, even though the real purpose of the theater was to draw men together to pay for women like herself. Maybe that was what she needed tonight, a man, and not one who paid her.

Theodora took another gulp from the amphora and decided not to wait around the theater for patrons, palace client or not. The last palace client was a mere tax collector. Instead, she walked toward the sound of the street music.

Theodora followed the stone walkway around the perimeter of the Amphitheater and down a wooded pathway that passed beneath the aqueduct. Stage craftsmen, jugglers, and acrobats came and went. Many eyes followed her as she wandered through the night-blackened arcade. She smiled at each of the theater men, seeing whether any were bold enough to give her attention that promised more than just flirtation. None were. So she continued, stumbling from too much wine.

Finally, the stony pathway opened up into a bright shimmer as Theodora entered the festive Forum of Leo. The night revelers, mostly peasants and transients, already abandoned themselves to the music, dancing and laughing and creating a spirited din together. This was a different kind of vitality, thought Theodora, a pulse of life far more exciting than the pretentious theater.

And there arose a wonderful music, a lively clamor that Theodora warmed to. A group of street musicians gathered beneath the giant marble pillar of Emperor Leo, which was centered in the forum. She studied the faces of each musician as they barked and yipped at one another, each man invigorated by the brash music he made. The lead man held a V-shaped pipe to his lips from which blared a shrill, reedy tune, rising, winding, falling, fluttering. His shoulders bounced at his ears while his cheeks puffed rapidly at each breath from the mouthpiece. To his side, a dark, shirtless man smacked the canvas of a wood drum between his thighs. He held his eyes wide and stared off at nothing, his head lurching forward in a cadence of his own. Another man slapped a tambourine hard against his palm, and a fourth swayed his hips while plucking a lute.

Theodora felt freedom in the music.

So many gathered and shared the elation with barely a word passing between them. Nowhere did there exist a structure to be learned, nor was there a master. There was no rank among them in the laughter and merriment, she thought. The forum displayed a beautiful chaos that happened without any guidance at all, a *speciosa vi* of the masses. And so, Theodora let herself be drawn into the active and colorful forum, a space for those who cast aside restraint and embraced a joyous spirit.

Theodora set down her wine jug, trotted into the crowd, and began dancing. She still wore the slave tunic from the play and so attracted instant and excited male attention. A set of strong hands squeezed her just above the hips, lifting her, swinging her in an airy circle before setting her back down and letting go. She moved from one person to the next, twirling, laughing, and staring into the black eyes of men.

Before she even knew it, Theodora slipped into a crowd of young street men who were loosely dressed, like transients. She coiled her arms around one man's neck, her hair hanging freely, her tunic loose and untidy. She kissed one of the men and then turned and kissed another. Theodora felt their hands upon her body, squeezing her breasts, sliding heavily across her stomach, and cupping her between the legs, where she wore no girdle. And her body responded. She was drunk, and the suffocating movements, the vigorous breathing, the body heat, and the feel of muscled skin enlivened her. So, she allowed the sexual spell to overtake her. The wine and music made the night feel like a dream.

Theodora finally met the eyes of a seated man, who looked at her with the ill intent she sought. He looked like a former slave by his stoic face and muscular build. Theodora straddled his lap, tossed her hair to one side, grabbed his chin, and kissed him. She rested her arms on the man's shoulders, flexing her hips and rubbing her bare loins slowly against his. He parted her scant slave tunic at the chest and eagerly took one of her breasts into his mouth, and then the other. Theodora arched her back so that her bosom pressed harder against the man's face. She closed her eyes and exhaled.

Then Theodora reached out and traced her fingers down the bare chest of another man, who watched her nearby. He drew in, and so she kissed him too. She heard the excited chatter of nearby onlookers but didn't care. She couldn't stop herself now anyway. This was what she wanted—no, needed. She liked that others saw her like this; for any bystander would only witness a woman who feared nothing, who was not ashamed, who partook where other women recoiled. As the numbness of drink blurred her thoughts, and as the stifling exertion of her body fell into an urgent animal rhythm, Theodora entered a private, distant place inside her mind. There, she heard only the music and the accompanying sound of her hurried breathing.

And the silly Amphitheater seemed far, far away.

SEVENTEEN

Theodora returned later that night. She lived in a brothel on a seedy but festive street known as Harlot's Row. She rented a small sleeping chamber from the brothel-keeper, a former charioteer named Tiberius. Although Theodora wasn't a common prostitute, she was still expected to earn money by laying with men, as did all actresses. So, her brothel was lively with thespians and late-night revelers who greeted her as she passed. She declined their offers to join them. She was quite drunk and needed to clean herself.

Theodora stumbled into her room and lit a small candle. Then she took out a rag from a bowl of rosewater and wiped the sweat of the night from under her arms, her neck, her stomach, and between her legs.

Someone rapped at her door and Theodora snapped to attention. "Who is it?"

"It's me," whispered a soft and elegant voice. "Macedonia."

Theodora opened the door. Macedonia was a beautiful Greek woman, famous for her bronze-like skin and long, silken black hair. She appeared stately, seasoned with age, not yet old, but no longer young. She stood erect and glided into the room, taking a quick assessment of Theodora's sleeping chamber. Although she stood a bit shorter, Macedonia's controlled mannerisms made Theodora feel a bit boorish by comparison.

"Forgive my late calling," said Macedonia. "But I saw you come in alone."

"I don't mind being alone once in a while."

Macedonia smiled warmly. "Are you all right, despina?"

Despina was the feminine word for "despot" or "mistress" and was spoken around the theater as a friendly term among women. "How sweet is your concern? You remind me of my Persian client, who insists I need to be rescued from Constantinople's dark underworld."

Macedonia laughed. "Do you at least tell him how heroic he is for trying to save you?"

"I tell him that he's an idiot. Wine?" Theodora said, filling two wooden cups. She liked and admired Macedonia. The woman was a performer in the chorus line and, like Theodora, she entertained men privately afterward. Yet Macedonia somehow retained a rare dignity within the station. Most importantly, though, she paid Theodora for information about certain bed clients. "So, I've guessed your purpose here and, well, I do have a rumor or two for you."

"Oh?"

"I laid with an officer today who mentioned the rebel Vitalian," said Theodora. "He said Vitalian seeks to raise another army."

Macedonia raised a single eyebrow and took the cup of wine. "Whatever else you learn about Vitalian will be met with silver. But Theodora, something's come up that I want to talk with you about." Macedonia set her wine atop the dressing station without taking a sip. "It could mean quite a lot more pay for you."

Theodora saw the seriousness in Macedonia's dark brown eyes. "What?"

"You'll hear about this tomorrow from the stage master, so I wanted to tell you first. You made a mistake tonight, during the play."

"Oh, that's just a farce. I show my figure and pull in better-paying clients."

"Yes, well, a *very* wealthy, *very* highly ranked man summoned you tonight. Only you were nowhere to be found."

Theodora nudged Macedonia. "Tell me, you tease. Who was he?"

Macedonia sat on the bed and tapped the space beside her. Theodora sat. After a moment of silence, Macedonia reached into her robe and pulled out a pinch of gold coins. The candlelight gave the gold a liquid-like shimmer. She then dropped the coins into Theodora's open palm, which drooped from the weight.

"Theodora, I work for a powerful client within the Blue faction. This client is special to me, and he's a man to whom I'm fiercely loyal, so I'm trusting you by even having this discussion. Can I count on your trust?"

"Yes," said Theodora as she closed her hand around the coins.

"This client keeps watch on certain happenings in the city and pays his collaborators well. As much as he's ever paid me, he's never asked me to lay with him nor made any advances." Macedonia looked away. "Nor accepted when I offered. Either way, it's my client's task to gather information about certain powerful people in the Green faction."

"So, he's spying on them?"

Macedonia didn't answer. "This evening, a man we've been watching for some time now came to the theater. After seeing you, he sent for you, but no one knew where you were."

"Damn," said Theodora, recalling the mention of a palace client. The other girls called it "bedding Zeus" whenever one of them captured the desires of the extremely wealthy. A single evening's pay could match a month's work at the theater.

Macedonia continued. "The man who called upon you is of great interest to my client. If you were to lay with this man, my client would pay for any information you could obtain."

"Well, just who is this great man of the vile Green faction?"

"The second highest Green there is," said Macedonia with a tilt of her head. "Hypatius, the eldest nephew of Emperor Anastasius and heir apparent to the empire."

Theodora's grin faded as her breath caught in her throat. "You want me to spy on the emperor's nephew?"

"Yes."

Theodora thumbed over the emperor's profile etched upon the gold coins. The Greens held most of the political power because the emperor was a Green, leaving the Blues to suffer every indignity and inequity in the courts. She then arose and whirled to face Macedonia. "Isn't that dangerous?"

Macedonia also stood. "Extremely. That's why the payments are substantial. Of course, you could say no and I'll never raise this question again. But, Theodora, if you do help us, you'd become one of our most important informants. It's the rarest of opportunities. Whisper has it that Hypatius was quite smitten by you and that's no small thing. He's been one of the most difficult men to get near to."

Theodora took a generous sip of wine and rubbed her forehead, where she felt a terrible aching. "Would your client use my information against the Greens?"

"Yes."

"That would give me great pleasure."

Macedonia placed a hand on Theodora's shoulder. "Does that mean you'll help us, despina?"

"If I do this, what then?"

Macedonia looked down and seemed to clear her head for a moment. When she looked back up at Theodora, her face shone with sternness. "Then we'd have some serious work to do, Theodora. Very serious work."

"Like what?"

"As it stands, Hypatius is the heir apparent to the throne. Laying with this man is nothing like laying with regular patrons." She paused long enough to catch Theodora's attention. "And it's different still from pleasuring two men at the Forum of Leo."

Theodora shook her head as if to wake from nodding off. "What?"

"When I heard that Hypatius requested you, I ran out to find you."

Theodora paused for a long while, remembering her rather public sexual encounter, but now, she felt the pangs of indignation. "You dare to judge another woman? You of all people. I do the same things you do every night."

"Clearly, you do more. Normally I wouldn't care about who you lay with or how. But that was before," Macedonia said. "You have a higher calling now. For all your beauty and intelligence, you have habits that foster much wildness, Theodora, in yourself and others. When my client asked me whether you were suited to this task, I said yes, but that you'd need training."

"Training?" said Theodora and laughed. "There isn't a living man who can refuse me if I want him. I should be training you."

"That's finely my point, despina. You're confusing a man's lust with a man's loyalty. Any beautiful woman with the will can get a man to lift his tunic. But capturing a man of power for months or even years at a time, gaining his confidence despite his suspicions, getting him to share secrets even when he knows better, or getting him to betray another man? These skills are beyond you."

"So, you ask for my help, offer to pay me generously, and I agree to it," said Theodora, "and now you stand here and tell me I haven't the talent for the job?"

"I'm offering to train you in the tradecraft of espionage, but only if you accept my authority."

Theodora felt heat in her face. Just like at the Amphitheater, others always tried to tell her that she needed improvement, always tried to establish some hierarchy—with Theodora, naturally, at the bottom. And Theodora always defied them, finding her way without any wearisome training. She stepped back from Macedonia. "Not even the stage master tells me what to do. I live at my own pleasure. Obviously, I can attract Hypatius without any training. All you're trying to do is get in between the transaction. If you want me to do this petty spy work, then I do it my way."

"No, Theodora. The man I work for isn't an easy man like the stage master. He and his constituents are powerful and serious men. And yes, your beauty caught the eyes of Hypatius, but you couldn't carry out the arrangement because you left your post. You're not your own master, nor living at your own pleasure, as you say. You're a slave to whatever pleasure is at hand."

"So?"

"It makes you unreliable."

Silence followed, and Theodora considered throwing her wine at the woman.

Macedonia continued. "Now I think you could be a highly skilled informant for us, but you need guidance."

"A chorus line girl wants to be my master," said Theodora. "You embarrass yourself with such a suggestion. If you have the skills, then go seduce Hypatius yourself."

"Always on the attack, aren't you?"

"I'll refuse you."

"Then you'd be a fool, Theodora, and I would've misjudged you."

"You're jealous of me. You know full well that once your special client lays his eyes on me, he'll forget all about you. I'm younger. I'm more beautiful. And obviously, I attract the men you can't."

Surprisingly, Macedonia didn't appear flustered by the insult. Theodora was used to dominating other women in this way, cutting them low with scathing words and smothering them in conceit. Yet Macedonia didn't react at all.

"You think you can take the payments of my client, yet deny the quality he means to purchase? Well, that's something he won't allow, nor will the powerful Blues he serves. There's no room for debate on the matter." Macedonia held out her hand.

Theodora dropped the coins into Macedonia's palm. "Pathetic. You use your station like a man, trying to enrich yourself. If your precious client wants my services, then he can visit me himself."

Macedonia closed her hand around the gold. "I'd hoped this wouldn't happen. But as you are, you're entirely unsuited to this task. If I were a jealous woman as you propose, then I would've just gotten the better of you. Being so easily provoked lets others push you into bad decisions. You see?

Even now, you can't act in your own best interest. All you get is to stand there like a fool, too proud for your own good."

"I do as I will."

"So you say."

"Get out!" Theodora flung open the door to her chamber.

"You are smarter than this, Theodora," said Macedonia. Then she bowed and departed. Theodora watched Macedonia's elegant form vanish down the hallway. Even in retreat, the woman stayed dignified and unshaken. Apparently, such a woman was worthy of higher tasks, and Theodora was not. She wanted to hurl one final insult at Macedonia but slammed the door instead.

Once again, Theodora felt the dull thud in her chest that followed rejection. A fellow prostitute passing judgment on her was too much to bear. And here now, Theodora burned with anger at knowing that she was being watched and judged on a private matter. Macedonia couldn't understand—no one did—but Theodora needed her so-called habits. She had to do it for her own reasons, and sometime tomorrow, Theodora knew, she'd do it again.

EIGHTEEN

Theodora blew out the candle and collapsed onto the small bed. She tried to fall asleep, but no sleep came. Her thoughts persisted in the drunken blackness that pitched like a boat in the harbor. Macedonia's departure still bothered her. In a contest of sexual dominance, Theodora always won. Yet when she exerted this advantage upon Macedonia, it was Theodora who was left feeling low. How did the older woman, some lowly chorus line dancer, strike such a decisive blow? How did she remain so undaunted? Just what did Macedonia have that Theodora did not?

After a while, Theodora relit the candle by the bed and her sleeping quarters came to life with a soft luminance. She walked over to the tall mirror in one corner, a mirror that usually showed her full and vivid beauty before she set out each evening. Now the reflection showed a tired woman, her eyes drawn and glassy from wine.

Theodora let slip the slave boy tunic that covered her body. The fabric whispered as it fell, pooling at her feet, while the cool night air made her skin prickle. She flattened her palms against her hips and, in a well-rehearsed routine, she went about admiring her body in the mirror.

Statues of women in the city were less impressive.

Theodora's eyes moved up her long legs, which were slender below the knee, but thickened at the thighs, unmuscular and silky in the light. Her gaze drifted up, where she appreciated the beautiful symmetry of her breasts, where the skin was glossy, the shapes accentuated by the coin-sized nipples that crowned each one. She traced the outer edge of her figure, where her skin met the darkness, where her ribs tapered inward, curving in crescent-like before protruding outward again at the hip. And her lower belly tapered downward to form an elegant arrowhead shape, the bare skin so soft, so alluring. The sight only confirmed to Theodora that each line and shadow of her body, every mysterious curve and contour had the effect of pulling the eyes, unbidden, toward that small point of focus, the very center of her sex.

She reminded herself that this was the source of a woman's power in the world, and nothing else. This was the sight that men sought of her, after all, the sight that burned in their imaginations whenever they stared at her. And once seen, men drew in close, whether desperate, greedy, or timid; they desired to touch her, to feel her body as if blind. Men touched her body all the time now and somewhere along the way, Theodora came to accept their desire for her.

Yet her body wasn't perfect. Theodora moved her hand up to cover the tiny area of loose skin at her belly. It was her body's most unforgiving drawback. The mark reminded Theodora of the nine months she carried an unwanted child, when her body was not beautiful, but swollen and burdensome. Her belly twitched with new life, yet she sought its death, the child inside merely an unconscious existence from an unknown father. She tried so many remedies to stop the child from growing inside, from ever being born, but her body overruled her, as it always did, forcing an outcome she didn't want. If a man was guilty for acting against her consent, what then did that say about her own body?

The pregnancy also reminded Theodora of the rift that arose between her and Maximina. For Theodora had been a victim of Magister Origen, a powerful man, and her mother fought him in full view of the city over Theodora's honor. So, pregnancy by another man, so soon after the contest in the Hippodrome, broke her mother's heart.

When Theodora's daughter was born, she wondered whether she'd feel what other women felt, some kind of natural connection to the baby. But, of course, she felt nothing.

Theodora rubbed her belly more angrily.

Because no one noticed that Theodora suffered long after Magister Origen. They all missed it. No one saw that invisible things festered. When her girlhood shattered and gave way to womanhood in a rush, Theodora soon struggled with the invisible forces that lurked inside her, like hunger, like thirst, mysterious and confusing forces that seemed to move her closer to the very men she feared most. Magister Origen, for all his evil, at least knew Theodora's darkest and most shameful secret. He shared that with her. Good men wanted to see her as pure or motherly or innocent, which left Theodora feeling estranged from them, as though these men ignored or denied something crucial to her. She needed to be understood by those men who knew the dark things below the surface.

And there was no way to explain this to anybody because *no one* talked about these matters. Theodora understood, perhaps all women did, that going forward would be a path she'd tread alone, without comfort or advice, without a friend or ally. So, she sought men out on her own.

As Theodora continued to look at her nude body in the mirror, she thought back to the first time she exposed herself to a man on purpose. He was an older man, a guildsman passing through the neighborhood at dusk. When Theodora saw him taking lengthy notice of her, she pulled down her shirt and showed him her breast. She didn't know why she did it, but Theodora felt enlivened as she stood there, watching the man look on her. When he approached, she suppressed a surging anxiety and allowed the guildsman to touch her. She offered no resistance when he led her into the alley and carried out his desires.

Her mother eventually noticed the changes in Theodora, but by then it was too late. The fixation had taken hold.

Theodora scoffed aloud. Then she poured a cup of wine until it spilled over the rim and splattered the ground. When the amphora was empty, she took the wine cup and emptied it in a long gulp, the liquid running over her chin and continuing down to the naked skin of her chest and belly. She caught her breath and dropped the cup.

Theodora simply couldn't lay with men the way other women did. Other women spoke as though they found intimacy and closeness, pleasure or tedium. But that's not what Theodora felt.

No.

Few women understood the brute exhilaration of giving in to the most corrupt demands. For compulsion erased coercion, and extreme encounters were neither intimate nor close, nor pleasurable nor tedious. Theodora didn't have to disappear anymore, like some scared little girl. She could stay present, alive, waiting for her body's responses to slip beyond her control. That's what Theodora so desperately needed to feel—that slippage, that proof she wasn't actually in control, not of her body, not of her life, to experience that vicious, visceral truth again and again.

And as a woman, she now also needed to feel the relief that came afterward. Indeed, the more obscene the act, the greater her relief . . . liberating, sweeping, and final. Because order was restored. Because she was not ashamed anymore. Shame itself became pleasure since Theodora couldn't live in a world where shame destroyed her. *Shame had to be made good*, and violation, a sacred ritual.

And because nothing would change.

Men would continue to see her carnal beauty and come for her, blind to the injury upon her soul, an expendable woman's soul, while she'd continue to find her only pleasure in repeating the injury.

Theodora grabbed the mirror and flung it to the floor. The piece only thudded harmlessly onto its side, but the motion swept the candle flame out. She just stood there in the darkness for a long while.

Alas, there were two Theodoras, the one who laid face down, her clothing half-removed, while a thief entered her body, a weak girl who knew the sound and feel of her most worthless, lowest self; and then there was the other Theodora, the one in the mirror only a moment before, who basked in her nudity and acted with daring, who wasn't afraid of dark rooms with wicked men, a woman of extraordinary sexual power.

Perhaps that's what Macedonia did tonight that bothered her so. She had stirred the buried shame again, and that was *not* hers to stir. Macedonia drew again the line between two types of women—a woman of worth and a worthless woman. And tonight only reminded Theodora, unequivocally, which kind of woman she meant never to feel like again.

NINETEEN

The next morning, Theodora was relieved not to feel the weight of her private torments. Now and then such anguish swept in to stifle her spirits, but the melancholy often faded with the new sun. Now, sobriety replaced the drunken anger.

As you are, you're entirely unsuited to this task . . .

That's what Macedonia had said. Last night, the woman offered Theodora a chance to become a well-paid informer, a secretive second profession, one that Theodora definitely wanted. The sale of certain information was a good supplement for a girl's pay, sometimes equaling the full fee of a man's pleasure. Apparently, a man's secrets and a man's pleasure had similar values in Constantinople. But rumors circulated that some women didn't just pass on petty gossip for a handful of bronze; some earned gold as professional spies. Macedonia admitted as much to Theodora last night, trusting her with the delicate secret about her private dealings.

The men may have had the Hippodrome and city streets, where the

Blues and Greens warred against each other with naked fists and knives, but the women had the bathhouses and brothels, where that same war was fought in the perfumed darkness, in between the panting and the giggles. Theodora had heard that these spies worked as actresses and prostitutes, indistinguishable from other women, but served in powerful circles, and some possibly serving the emperor himself. In a very real way, the post offered change, or at least something noble in an otherwise ignoble profession.

Yes, she wanted to outshine Comito, and yes, she wanted the gold, but in her heart, Theodora simply wanted to be trusted with something important. She wanted a task that made demands upon her mind, rather than her body alone.

First, though, Theodora needed to wrest back the offer, which meant she needed to find Macedonia before the woman found a different girl for the post.

Theodora arrived at the bathhouse much earlier than usual and found the place more crowded than she was used to seeing. The interior of the bathhouse smothered her in humidity, filling her lungs with thick air, and causing instant perspiration on her forehead. Right away, she heard women's voices floating and echoing in the dome above her head and hoped that one of them would be Macedonia's.

Except for helpful eunuchs, there were no men in this section of the bathhouse. Here, the professional class of women, from the Amphitheater to the Hippodrome, from the brothels and arcades, from the forums and marketplaces, all came to soak in hot waters and relax in the casual society of women. And everywhere there was steam.

Theodora wrapped white linen around her waist and entered a cloud of hot mist. She trod through the maze of sweaty, nude women and their arrogant glances. Mosaics of mystic moons and stars adorned the walls, while high above, set within a great dome, a giant yellow sun with watchful eyes peered down at Theodora through the steam. But no Macedonia.

Along the perimeter, Theodora peeked inside private rooms where women knelt at wall spouts, filling wooden bowls with water. Then they poured the steaming liquid upon their bare arms, chest, or scalp, savoring the ancient pleasure of flesh and hot water.

When Theodora entered the dressing chambers, she spotted Macedonia occupying one of the benches. Right as Theodora drew up close, a very different voice interrupted the pursuit.

"What are you doing here so early?"

Theodora turned to see Comito being dressed by the bathhouse girls. She stood nearby, surrounded by other actresses and dancers of the theater.

"Don't you usually sleep with the stagehands until midday?" said Comito.

Her sister was the last person Theodora wanted to see. "I'm here to speak with a friend," she said.

Comito turned and studied Macedonia. "Usually the old women come at sunrise," she said and looked back at Theodora. "And the infantry whores don't show until midday. By this reckoning, neither of you should be here at this hour."

The other actresses giggled.

Theodora smiled at the jest. "If only you could make an *audience* laugh."

Comito turned to the woman nearest her. "Should I tell her now or let her find out later?"

A dark Syrian woman with long black hair smirked and eyed Theodora. "I say tell her now."

"Very well," said Comito. "The stage master is removing you from the play. Chrysomallo will take over that stupid slave boy farce."

"You think the stage master has a strong opinion over a small bit."

"Exactly. Small. Your talents are easily replaced."

Theodora noticed Macedonia dressing quickly, but listening, her expression impossible to read. She feared that the petty exchange and news of a demotion only confirmed Macedonia's harsh judgment.

"You won't get the stage master to change his mind this time," said Comito. "But you're free to try."

"I hear she's free half the time anyway," said the Syrian.

"Why would such prominent actresses care so much about a side role?"

"We care about all roles," said Comito. "Because we care about the stage."

Theodora meant to press her sister further but saw Macedonia turn to depart. A subtle flash of Macedonia's eyes and a shake of the head, so soft, so barely perceptible, told Theodora not to follow.

She turned back to Comito "Be assured. I'll be back on that stage tonight. I'll make it extra memorable for you." Theodora made a rude gesture and left the dressing chamber, ignoring the obscenities volleyed at her back from her sister.

But Macedonia was gone.

By that hour, nothing more could be done. The time came for work. She still had to earn so she could pay Tiberius his nightly fee. Since Theodora couldn't rely on a theater cameo to draw men, she went to the arcades around the Forum of Leo, where she'd find men the old-fashion way. There, she donned a red sash to identify herself as a prostitute and mingled with the Amphitheater crowd. This was a temporary measure, she told herself, just until the stage master restored her role.

And so, Theodora beckoned the foot traffic that came and went around the theater. The daylight hours were typically the lowest paying, as the city streets were dominated by the working Christian men of Constantinople, many of whom scoffed at women of the red sash, seeing the girls as a nuisance. Theodora managed four clients that afternoon. The first was a Roman officer summoned from a mountain post in Krusovos. After him, she had a shy stable master, then a former aquarius who knew the aqueducts and cisterns of the city, and finally, an imperial bricklayer who had recently moved from Antioch and still sought work, but somehow had money enough for Theodora. These men all paid her fairly well, just enough for Theodora to pay Tiberius a believable portion of income. More importantly, though, she realized just how much information these men carried with them and how willing they were to discuss their duties with a woman they didn't know.

As the waning sun cast a golden sheen upon Constantinople, Theodora made her way backstage to the Amphitheater. Already, actors and actresses milled about, half-dressed in costumes, conversing and adjusting wigs. She approached Chrysomallo, who also filled marginal roles, standing near the costume station. The girl was a long-legged actress with thick ringlets of golden hair and Gothic blue eyes. She already wore Theodora's slave boy tunic.

When Chrysomallo saw Theodora, she stiffened and looked around for help. When she saw no one, she took a nervous sip of wine instead. "Theodora," she said. "They told me you weren't in the play tonight."

Theodora sidled up alongside Chrysomallo and folded her arms. "I'm not supposed to be."

"Then what are you doing here?"

"Showing up anyway."

Chrysomallo nodded. "I didn't ask for this, Theodora, I promise. You know how your sister is."

"Comito hates anyone who isn't Comito," said Theodora, reaching to pour a cup of wine. Before she took her first sip, Bacchus raced up to the girls.

"I have a summons for you already," he said, confused.

"But Theodora never even went on stage yet," said Chrysomallo.

The boy looked uncomfortable but leaned into Theodora's ear. "It's a woman."

Macedonia. She was using the privacy of the fornices to arrange a meeting.

But a booming theatrical voice interrupted. "Theodora!"

Theodora, Chrysomallo, and Bacchus all glanced up to see the stage master descending the steps that ran down through the Amphitheater benches. He shuffled along at a hurried pace as if to intercept Theodora before trouble began. "You're out of the play."

"Says who? You or Comito?" said Theodora.

"You've caused too much of a stir within the troupe," he said. "The time has come for you to focus on your other talents."

Theodora's smile faded. "I bring so many patrons to this stage."

"I know," he said. "But you insulted one of our most important patrons last night. I looked like a fool for not knowing your whereabouts." He came to a stop in front of Theodora and smiled sympathetically. "Come now, we both knew this day would arrive. You're just not an actress, Theodora."

The cold verdict uttered in front of the whole troupe sent heat into Theodora's face. If she could no longer call herself an actress, then she'd slide down further, to that of a common prostitute. Everyone listening understood the distinction. Theodora looked at Comito on the far side of the stage, who now appeared to pity her. She looked at Chrysomallo, who looked away. Then she stepped forward and flung her cup of wine at the stage master. The crimson liquid splashed onto his fine white toga, followed by a chorus of gasps. The man stepped backward and raised his arms.

Before the stage master even responded, Theodora turned, grabbed the amphora of wine, and hoisted the vessel at him. She heard the delicate burst of shattering pottery. "All of this over one little role," she said. "I hope it's worth it, because look at yourself now, you old fool."

The stage master came at Theodora but slipped. He landed on the ceramic shards from the broken wine jug and cried out. When Theodora instinctively tried to help him up, a male actor pushed her aside.

She knew she had gone too far. Theodora didn't wait for the matter to get resolved. She turned, grabbed Bacchus by the arm, and hurried off the backstage, lifting her gown as she scampered down the stairs.

"You said a woman was waiting for me. Where is she?"

Bacchus rushed to keep up with Theodora. "She's waiting in the Nymph House, seventh room."

Good, thought Theodora. She gave a silver coin to Bacchus. "For your silence," she said.

Bacchus snatched the coin.

Theodora left Bacchus and turned into the foot traffic of the arcade. She slowed to a brisk walk and tried to blend in. Other prostitutes occupied the area, dipping their gowns to show a bare breast at the pedestrians, or flirting conversationally with men. Theodora's friend, Antonina, trotted over, smirking as if she sensed mischief was afoot. The girl had braided brown-honey hair and the greenest eyes, almost luminous. "What are you up to, Theodora?" she said. "I can always tell when you're in trouble."

"If anyone comes looking for me, make sure the other girls keep quiet," said Theodora.

"What happened?"

"I threw wine on the stage master."

"You didn't," said Antonina, covering her mouth, eager for the gossip.

"The bastard gave my role to Chrysomallo. All because of my stupid sister and her stupid friends."

"I love you, Theodora. We dream of doing these things to the stage master, but you actually do them. None of us will peep."

"Thank you," said Theodora, glancing over her shoulder. No one followed her, so she entered the brothel. She made her way down a narrow hall with curtained doors lining both sides. When she came to the seventh room, Theodora brushed the wrinkles from her gown, took a deep breath, and ducked into the fornice.

Macedonia stood in the center of the room. "Good evening, Theodora."

But she wasn't alone. Someone else whirled to face Theodora, the fragrance of male perfume wafting afresh, the lovely scent of wealth.

"I'd like you to meet my special client," said Macedonia.

A man stepped forward. When his face came into the light, Theodora froze. She stood face to face with the man from the Hippodrome stands that day so long ago, the heroic Blue who had saved Theodora's mother from public humiliation, who had saved her family from ruin, a man she never got to thank, who had vanished as if he never existed. His face had been marooned in her girlhood memory, the face of a secret guardian who came back only in dreams, more mythical than real.

But there he was.

Theodora's heart quickened as heat coursed through her body.

"A pleasure, Theodora," he said in that unforgettable voice. "I'm Justinian."

TWENTY

Theodora stood in the fornice, staring up at Justinian. Well, at least now she knew his name, a piece of the puzzle that seemed unsolvable, and most excitingly, he knew her name, said it aloud. She saw that Justinian dressed as a Roman noble, clean-shaven, crowned in oiled brown hair, with a long crimson cape spanning his broad shoulders. He towered above Theodora, looking down at her with imperial authority. She searched his beautiful brown eyes for some hint of familiarity, some sign that he recognized her as the girl from the Hippodrome. She wanted to hear that he remembered her, that he'd looked for her and finally found her after five years of searching. But he only looked at her with a formidable air.

"We haven't much time," he said in that perfect Latin Theodora remembered. "Macedonia tells me that you want to elevate your involvement with the Blues."

Theodora glanced at Macedonia, who stared back without expression.

"She told me you showed interest, but questioned her authority," he said.

"I don't like being talked down to," said Theodora.

Why do I sound like a child?

Justinian turned to face Macedonia and then swung back to face Theodora. "Was that the only reason?"

"Well, yes, but I'm past all that now. I've had time to think."

"Theodora," he said. "I need to know that you can handle straight talk from a woman like Macedonia."

"I can."

"Because she'll give you directions and you'll be expected to follow them. It's the only way we'll be able to work together."

Work together? That sounded so wonderful to Theodora, who stood with a younger girl's tenseness, both vulnerable and exuberant. "I understand," she said. "I think Macedonia just caught me off-guard is all."

"Are you easily caught off-guard?" he said.

"Not usually, but she visited me late in the night, and I drank a lot of wine, and—" Theodora trailed off, not wishing to speak anymore. Everything she said sounded so foolish in front of Justinian.

"If you wish to work with the Blues in this capacity, then you cannot afford to be unprepared," he said. "Not anymore. Even good reasons to be off-guard are bad reasons. Do you follow?"

"Yes."

Justinian continued to speak, but Theodora's eyes widened as she stared at him, her belly churning with disbelief. She noticed the commanding way he controlled his body when he spoke, his lips contorting to each word in precision, his voice doing all the work. She saw how he aimed his head downward with both eyes fixed squarely upon her, as surely as if he held her in place with his hands. She liked being the focus of his attention. Most men held Theodora's gaze with a stark awareness of her beauty, either timid, malevolent, or admiring. But this man, Justinian, peered right into her, bypassing the beautiful outer self that Theodora constructed. She felt more naked in those few moments than at any time without clothes on her body. For the first time in a long time, Theodora couldn't be certain whether her beauty granted her any power over this man. "So you're the Blue with money for secrets," said Theodora with a smile, trying to break his control of the conversation.

"I pay for information," he said, unaffected. "But I don't operate alone. I'm part of a much larger association within the city and throughout the empire. I'm among certain Blues within the Blues."

Theodora nodded.

"Macedonia vouched for you," he said. "She's the only reason I'm here and the only reason I'm bothering to reconsider this arrangement."

Anxiety settled in. Theodora's girlish enchantment was being replaced with a womanly awareness that she was in a critical negotiation. Justinian wasn't just another man of rank in the city, but a serious man with forceful intelligence. "Well, I'm grateful to you both." She was going to say more, but Justinian interrupted.

"I care nothing for gratitude, I assure you. I want what you and I don't have. Trust. Trust takes time, and by the grace of God, should we one day establish trust, you'll be in danger for the rest of your life. Do you understand what I just said?"

Theodora blinked. This was the man who had taken on a legion of Greens with his voice and words, and now as they stood in the dimly lit fornice, he set his voice and words against Theodora. Whatever flutters of girlishness that lingered in her stomach now faded. She managed a nod. "I understand."

"Because some girls collapse under the pressures of the post," he said. "A relentless fear of getting caught can break a person. I don't want to put you through that hell. I need a certain kind of woman."

She saw that he looked at her as if searching for something in her eyes, some quality. "I think I can be that kind of woman, Magister Justinian," said Theodora. "What exactly are you asking of me?"

"To deliberately betray powerful men who trust you. These men will have high imperial stations, and they'll tell you things in confidence that you'll turn around and tell me. If these men discover who you are or what you're doing, you could be killed. I want you to let that settle in because

I can't afford any confusion. This is a deadly profession that won't allow second thoughts once you've committed."

The room grew silent. Theodora broke eye contact from Justinian and looked at Macedonia.

"He wants you to know what you're getting into, despina," said Macedonia.

Theodora finally found the courage to look Justinian in the eyes again. "I wouldn't be afraid of these situations, and I'm certainly not afraid of any man."

Justinian took one step closer. "No? Some men aren't men at all, young woman. Some men are demons. I know them personally, and you better damn well be afraid of them."

Theodora felt a tingle in her scalp.

Justinian triggered a terrible feeling that swelled in Theodora's body, the chill sense of being cornered by a man. She felt that blank state of existence where she could endure anything, do anything, disappear. She recovered and narrowed her eyes. "I'm not afraid of those men either."

Justinian seemed to notice the shift in Theodora's demeanor because his head ticked to the side. He looked right into her eyes and held her gaze for an uncomfortable length of time. Theodora knew not to be the first to break the silence or to look away from him.

Finally, Justinian turned to Macedonia. "Train her," he said.

Justinian studied Theodora for another moment, eyeing her with a peculiar expression. She suddenly wondered whether he recognized her. Did he see traces of her girlhood face through the veil of five years?

Then, as though he came to some silent conclusion, he broke forward, striding past Theodora in a draft of perfumed air, ducking out of the fornice, his crimson cape billowing behind him.

Theodora stared at the exit with pangs of disappointment. She wanted to keep speaking with Justinian, to continue looking into his eyes for long durations. But Macedonia called her name twice now. Collecting herself, she turned to face her new mentor.

"So now you've met my special client," Macedonia said. "He's an industrious man who rarely lingers. You'll get used to that."

"Who is he?"

"A Blue of rising status."

That answer told her nothing. Theodora slipped into a broad smile, revealing her relief and slight fluster. "He seems so intense. So serious. Does he ever smile or laugh?"

Macedonia returned a look of warning. "Theodora, I have to go over a few things with you briefly."

Theodora cleared the smile on her face. "Go ahead."

"Never try and seduce him."

Theodora was stunned.

Macedonia continued. "He's not interested."

"Is he interested in men?"

"Not at all. You'll see. You'll know by the way he looks at you sometimes, but you must never act on it. He's a man with unusual self-control, but he is still a man. I learned the hard way, Theodora, so heed my advice to the utmost. The Blues can arrange to have you removed not only from the post but Constantinople if they will it. You're to serve the post, Theodora, never just one man."

"I see," she said but felt some of her excitement draining out.

"I hope you do," said Macedonia. "An imperial agent such as he can't become involved with his informants. Otherwise, he risks becoming a liability to the Blues. Powerful people will accuse you of working for the Greens. Never muddy those waters. Tell me that you understand."

Theodora tried to downplay the warning. "I understand."

Macedonia did not look convinced.

She knows. She sees me. "When you say that you learned the hard way, am I to understand that you broke this rule?" said Theodora.

"In a moment of weakness, I confused our trust and intimacy for something more than professional. The Blues were so upset with me that they arranged to have me sent to Antioch."

Theodora considered that Macedonia had loved Justinian and worse—

perhaps still did. Women may fool men in matters of the heart, but they can't fool each other. Macedonia saw Theodora and Theodora saw Macedonia on the matter. Somehow, Macedonia learned to suppress her desires and kept her feelings locked away, like a prisoner, like the beasts that Theodora's pata once marched into their cages at the day's end.

"How did you convince the Blues to keep you in Constantinople?"

"I promised to never again act in such a way," said Macedonia. "And for five years, I've honored that promise."

"That must be difficult," said Theodora. "To bury something like that." But Theodora knew exactly how to bury any part of herself where pain dwelled.

"We find a way, despina," said Macedonia. "We have to. Our great contributions aren't public knowledge. We're quiet allies who are easily expendable, a hard truth you must never forget."

Theodora nodded. So, in this matter, they would not be rivals. She wanted to ask whether Justinian was married or had a woman, or whether he hid all his personal affairs, but knew better than to press. She smiled sympathetically instead. "So, what next?"

"We need to prepare you for what's ahead, despina," she said. "But this won't be so easy. You'll still need to make your daily wages and maintain all that you do now."

Theodora looked down. "That may be a problem."

"Why?"

"You heard my sister. I've been dismissed from the troupe."

"That should work to our advantage because you and I will need to meet and conduct our training."

"How do we do that?"

Macedonia lifted her hands, palms up. "We have a profession where privacy is assured. Discretion, secrecy, privacy are tools we already have at our disposal. I'll show you how to use them all. You'll see. Women can have great power in Constantinople if they know how to use it."

Theodora liked hearing that women could have power.

"Every day at midday, you'll go to the Wolf's Head Brothel across from the Amphitheater. Go upstairs to the Chamber of Cupid just as if summoned by a regular client," said Macedonia. "The Blues will pay you ten follis for each of our meetings. I'll train you on how to get information and how to start handling yourself as an informer. We need to change many of your habits."

Theodora hated hearing anyone suggest that she was lacking. "You speak of me as though I'm some barbarian whore from the West."

"You've no discipline," said Macedonia. "If you wish to influence men, you must first learn how to control yourself."

"How do I do that?"

Macedonia's gaze sparkled with surety in her answer. "You must learn how to think and act like a queen."

Theodora slipped into a smile that she couldn't suppress.

TWENTY-ONE

The Chamber of Cupid was on the second floor of a brothel that overlooked the Amphitheater and Harlot's Row. The room itself, though, was spacious, if not barren at that hour. The red plush sofas were empty, and the smell of burnt sandalwood still lingered in the air. Theodora saw a low table that looked more like an oversized silver platter centered in the room. At night, the platter would be topped with colorful fruits, sweetmeats, and jugs of wine.

"We need a little light in this place," said Macedonia.

Theodora watched her cross the room and swing open the wood shutters, letting in the sunlight and the sounds of the city below. The air was cool, but pleasant that morning. Beyond the open window, Theodora saw the distant upper rim of the Hippodrome over the wooden rooftops, which reminded her of the view from her rooftop when she was a girl.

Theodora sat on a rug, her head at eye level with the empty silver platter. Macedonia, though, sat on the cushioned bench along the wall, so that Theodora had to look up at her.

"I have one question that's been bothering me," said Theodora.

"Yes? What?"

"How did you know that I changed my mind about the post?"

Macedonia leaned sideways and inclined on a mound of colored pillows, her head held elegantly erect. "You never changed your mind. You were drunk, Theodora. I drew you into a fight on purpose, one you couldn't win. Does that bother you?"

"Yes," said Theodora curtly.

"Good. Some women cling to a belief that they are special, or that they are above other women. Such a belief can turn into arrogance or, God willing, it can be honed into great ability," said Macedonia, who pulled out the four gold solidi from the other night. She scattered them across the silver table top, the coins clinking and wobbling to a stop. "Those are for you."

Theodora reached for the coins, but Macedonia raised a finger. "First we talk."

Theodora nodded and met Macedonia's stern gaze.

"Do you work with anyone else?"

"No," said Theodora.

"You've never been approached by the Greens or any other member of the Blues for information?"

"Not like this."

"If you're ever approached by anyone else going forward, you're to tell me immediately," said Macedonia. "Is that understood?"

"Yes."

"Good. Now stand up."

Theodora did so.

Macedonia arose from the bench and circled her. The woman seemed to study Theodora's posture, face, and clothing.

"You are beautiful," she said. "But that is a gift that often brings as much harm as it does favor." Macedonia tugged at Theodora's gown in a few areas before scooping a handful of hair and letting the strands slip through her fingers. "I overheard that squabble with your sister at the bathhouse. I've watched you both for a long time now. She certainly enjoys her higher station. Comito is less impressive but better trained."

"She's always been less impressive," said Theodora with a satisfied grin.

"But better trained," said Macedonia and slapped Theodora. The blow was soft and painless, but enough to shock. "This is nothing to be proud of. Comito is at least someone who can follow instructions without letting her pride get in the way."

Theodora's eyes narrowed on Macedonia as she exhaled through her nose. "Then go recruit her."

Macedonia nodded. "And there it is. The defiance you believe is serving you but has betrayed you all your life. Stop it. I've seen your dance steps if you want to call them that. You're a sloppy woman if truth be told. You compensate with the brute force of your wits and beauty. A child's game, Theodora, one that won't work with men of the aristocracy. If I'm to bother training you, I need to know why you failed in your previous training."

Theodora flinched in confusion. "I didn't fail."

"Oh, yes you did. You have an extraordinary stage presence and nothing more. Why?"

"Because I came from a rotten koitǫ́na."

"You came from the same koitǫ́na as your sister and she's the lead. If you're so special, how do you explain doing bit parts before being dismissed from the Amphitheater?"

Burning anger filled Theodora. She met Macedonia's eyes but knew the woman was trying to provoke her. So, against all her instincts, Theodora kept quiet.

But Macedonia pressed her. "Or do you believe that talent is inbred, like beauty, a gift from God that makes one woman superior to another? Well, it isn't. Talent is the result of devastating hours and painstaking practice."

"I understand that. If you'd let me finish," said Theodora. "Some lessons are overly simple."

"Wrong again. Only a fool gives up because the task is too simple, Theodora. You see, people like you can justify quitting anything. So how do

I know you won't quit whenever my training gets to you? Or is it that, deep down, you're frightened I'll find out that beneath all that beauty and wit, you're just another stupid girl with a pretty face?"

"Enough," said Theodora.

"Is that what you are?"

"No!" Theodora finally shouted. "I just lost confidence, all right? I lost my confidence when I was a girl and never got it back. And I hate it."

Macedonia pulled back.

"I hate it," Theodora said again in a whisper.

Theodora felt Macedonia gently grab her chin and lift her head. She finally looked into the older woman's strong brown eyes and recognized the potency of the look; it was her mother's look, a fighting woman's look.

"I know strength when I see it," said Macedonia. "And I know what it looks like when the strong ones hide. But you must first learn how to let go and become a pupil again."

Once more, here was a demand for submission and Theodora still resisted giving anyone such devastating power over her. She shook her head and glanced away.

"Look at me, Theodora," said Macedonia. "We can get lost out there, just as you have gotten lost. I've dealt with many women, and too many of us hide our pain and weaknesses, especially from other women. And so, each of us becomes an island, sealed off and silent." Macedonia collected herself and sighed. "There is a type of mask, one I see on the face of too many women, especially in our profession. I call it a mask of shame."

Theodora looked up, intrigued, but waited to see what Macedonia meant.

Macedonia nodded. "You wear yours well, despina, better than anyone I've ever met. It took me a while to see it, but I realized that you indeed wear this heavy mask. So brazen. So bold. Who would ever believe that shame could wound the Notorious Theodora? But I realize now how perfectly it all fits. You're hiding too. But you hide right out in the open, right in plain sight."

Theodora thought about herself on stage all those times, flashing her bare body before so many eyes. *But what am I hiding?*

"You say you lost your confidence? Well, we're going to take it back, despina. You and I. Theodora, the prostitute, is just an invention, a powerful one in your case, but an invention all the same. She's not the real Theodora. Or have you forgotten that?"

"No," she said, but wasn't sure. Macedonia seemed to know about the two Theodoras. There had been two for some time now, the Theodora who dominated and the Theodora who foundered. And here, Macedonia called out to the weaker of the two, the unwanted girl who followed silently at a distance, like a beggarly child. How could *that girl* be entrusted with anything of importance?

"I don't want to deal with the Notorious Theodora," said Macedonia. "She's all the pageantry and noise that could ever surround a bitch in heat. Unbridled. Arrogant. Reckless."

Theodora finally nodded. "She's all those things. But she isn't weak."

"Not today, she's not," said Macedonia and turned away. She paused at the window, leaned against the sill, and fixed her gaze upon the Hippodrome. The distant cheers from a chariot race filled the room. "But I fear she'll be just like all the rest . . . beautiful, spectacular, and then one day forgotten."

"What else is there?"

"The real you," said Macedonia. "Men mentor each other with brutal honesty. We'll do the same," she said. "So, let this be your first lesson, despina. Be present for me. Weakness, your weakness, is the only starting point I know of. If we face it honestly, you'll gain incredible strength."

Theodora liked hearing that. If Theodora the prostitute was just a role, then maybe there was indeed a place in the world for Theodora the woman after all.

TWENTY-TWO

Every midday, Theodora met Macedonia in the Chamber of Cupid under the pretense of entertaining a high-paying client. Every time Theodora opened the doors to the chamber, she hoped to see Justinian standing there in his crimson cape, hands clutched behind his back and turning to set his commanding gaze upon her. Each time, though, she was disappointed, and each time, Macedonia stood alone, awaiting her. Soon, though, even the sight of Macedonia became as welcome a sight as any because the training gave Theodora a sense of empowerment.

Macedonia was obsessed with control over the body, preferring stillness to motion in most situations. No longer was Theodora allowed to let her raw female vitality govern her body language. The way a woman took her seat, arose from the table, poured a cup of wine, drank from her cup, and ate her food all mattered. This was more difficult than she'd imagined. In Theodora's mind, her overly expressive nature and boldness were the very things that made men adore her. She worried that her humor and her playful nature would be erased under such stifling control.

"Most of those charms are simply ways you draw attention to yourself," said Macedonia. "In our line of work, your boldness inspires men also to act boldly. But once he does act, he's in command. You then try to regain power by agreeing to everything *he wants*. That's your pattern. That's why you value fearlessness so much. But your manners give men a signal to follow. So, the more under control you are in the presence of a man, the more under control he becomes. You are establishing power in a subtle way. Your constant state of self-control makes a man more and more dependent on signals from you to guide his actions. This will leave him open to suggestion over time, and eventually into accepting your direction. Ours is a soft authority, but it is authority."

Theodora nodded. "I wish they taught us these things in the brothel."

"This lesson is not for those girls, who pleasure men for a short period. You won't be working out of the brothel with me, despina," said Macedonia. "You'll be working in the presence of powerful men in wealthy estates. Men of the aristocracy are different. In public, like at the Amphitheater, a woman may stand out with a lot of noise, but in the presence of the nobility, she must learn their social rules or else they'll tire quickly of her antics. As a woman who's paid for her company and pleasure, power over the body is your first advantage."

But power over the body had always been the problem.

Macedonia taught Theodora how to stand with a good posture, remaining still for long hours, and only moving when necessary. She also learned how to wear her robes properly, and how to fold them at the day's end, all the details that men and women of the aristocracy would notice if done incorrectly. Macedonia showed her how to arrange her hair so that the soft curve of her neck, just below the ears, lay exposed, lightly powdered, and lightly perfumed. Apparently, this part of a woman's body also had a strong effect on men that Theodora never considered.

Other lessons, though, were more common and dealt with everyday activities. Macedonia taught Theodora how to drink her wine slowly so she didn't become drunk. For an informer, tipsy was best, drunk ... forbidden. Even the common men she laid with during the day became men to study.

She learned to sit in stillness and look a man in the eyes until he became uncomfortable. And if she said nothing, it was he who wished to know why.

Theodora learned a powerful truth. Sobriety and self-control gave her an unexpected sharpness of the mind, an expanding power of perception, a wit of another kind.

TWENTY-THREE

After weeks of training, Theodora entered the Chamber of Cupid to find Macedonia sitting with a eunuch boy. He sat with his forearm slung over a lanky knee and a drowsy look in his eyes. Set out before him was a pair of wood drums.

"Theodora," said Macedonia. "Now that you have learned some control over your body, we must circle back to dance."

Theodora's confidence waned. "I've never been a good dancer."

"That was before. And this is about more than just dancing," said Macedonia as she closed the shutters and drew the curtains. "This is about seduction. It's an exercise meant to harness a woman's two conflicting desires, a desire to dominate and be dominated. It's your dark feminine, Theodora, your *feminam in tenebris*, and it's unique to each woman. You'll bring to bear all your body's sexual powers and align them with a special focus, which I'll teach you today. You'll learn to impose your own will on others, instead of the other way around. The purpose of seduction, after all, is authority." Macedonia let down her hair. "A seduced man will tell you anything you wish to know, even when he knows better, even if he suspects you of being an informer. A proper seduction will block the influence of all others, no matter how persuasive. I've seen men fiercely defend the woman who betrayed them, even after discovering that she cheated him out of a fortune or left him in disgrace. Fantasy can be more powerful than reality." Macedonia removed a rose-colored shawl from her body, revealing her naked belly. "Stand next to me."

Theodora did so.

Macedonia then raised her hands above her head and nodded to the eunuch. The boy thumped rhythmically on the hand drums. At once, Macedonia moved with the music, her hips rocking back and forth, her belly undulating, her hands in motion, her eyes and head as still as a statue. "This dance exhibits all the disciplines of the body you've learned. Move your hips."

Theodora tried to mimic the movements but felt foolish as her dancing always seemed a little clumsy.

"Don't think," said Macedonia. "Let your body circle and pitch like the sea, but under your direction. Let go of any discomfort."

Theodora tried to focus on the cadence of the hand drums, just like when she was a girl at the koitóna. But the music and her body, as always, mismatched the drums. She stopped.

"Again," said Macedonia. "Don't stop unless I command it."

Frustrated, Theodora raised her hands and tried again. She felt the pangs of embarrassment but continued.

"Men look on your body with fascination," said Macedonia. "But their eyes flit from one part of your body to the next, desperate and brief. That means your body alone isn't the true source of power over a man."

This was the exact opposite conclusion that Theodora had reached.

"There is only one place a man will look on you with unblinking obsession," said Macedonia. "It's not your body, but your eyes. Your very essence as a woman is found there, and it can be made to dominate him. You must channel it. He's aware of your body, especially when you are dancing, but you capture him with your eyes."

Theodora's body fell in sync with the drums.

Macedonia pivoted around to face Theodora, her torso's alluring motion never breaking, her eyes unblinking. "Look at me. Focus. To make this work, you must know your dark feminine with utter clarity and find the will to use it. True seduction requires almost no deceptions at all. We're not tricking men. We speak sincerely. We use honesty, not truth. In this work, no one is entitled to the full truth, if there is such a thing. So, do you remember what we spoke of yesterday? About masks?"

Theodora felt suddenly guarded. "I remember."

"If I'm correct, then your dark feminine will be most impressive. Now, this may seem contradictory, but I want you to put on the mask we spoke of. Can you do that? Here now in this room?"

Theodora continued to dance while Macedonia watched her. She had no desire to summon up memories of something so personal and hated. Besides, those memories only resurfaced when she was by herself. But then, as if a black ghost entered the room, Magister Origen's eyes flashed in her mind, the feel of a strong hand on her wrist, her cheek against the bedstead, a lone mattock upon the wall...

Theodora's skin prickled. She felt a cramping in the back corners of her jaw and a tightening of the throat. That familiar tumult came rolling through her, crashing against an invisible wall before ebbing back, and dissipating.

"That's it, despina. No emotion," said Macedonia. "Now dominate him. Command him with just your eyes. Your authority over him exists here and now."

The hand drums seemed to quicken. Theodora thought Macedonia looked younger than usual, more beautiful, more vivid.

"The unskilled woman tries to take command of a man through protest, decrying what she dislikes. Not us," said Macedonia, drifting closer. "We take command of a man at his most virile, at the peak of his strength and power, with all his violence at the ready. His will to dominate will shatter against you. His need to worship shall be made to worship you. In this space," and Macedonia stepped closer, "there is only you."

Theodora felt the heat of the woman's body as if her skin were made of candle flames, her breasts grazing Theodora's. The drums, the heat, the perfume, and the vivid white of Macedonia's eyes all excited Theodora. And Macedonia drew in closer still.

Does she mean to kiss me?

Theodora had kissed women before, but always as an exhibition to rouse men. She never did it in private. Theodora leaned in slowly, her lips parting slightly. Then she touched her lips to Macedonia's, their fire-hot breath mixing as they danced. When she moved to intensify the erotic sensation, Macedonia drifted backward, as if a soft tide pulled her out to sea. Theodora stopped dancing, and a moment later, the gawking eunuch stopped patting the drums.

"A seduction took place," Macedonia said, coming to a rest. "But not by you."

Theodora sighed, more out of exasperation, to flush away the momentary excitement. "I don't understand. What just happened?"

"I taught you two things at once. I showed you how to incite someone to action where you remain in control. As a woman, your inexpressive face may be interpreted many ways. Are you warning him? Or are you inviting him? You force the action while he is unsure, just like I did to you," she said. "And that's what you want—uncertainty out of him, and a display of total control from you. Do you see now that control over your body lends itself to authority?"

Theodora stared ahead, retracing the moments that led up to the almost kiss. She saw again the enchanting face of Macedonia.

"Which brings us to the second part of the lesson. What did you feel when I asked you to wear the mask?"

"Something," Theodora said, confused. "Or nothing. It was an empty feeling."

"Yes, as the darkness enters in, emotion will recede. All seduction is about authority, and authority is cold and absolute. Your will . . . imposed upon others."

"I don't understand the lesson," snapped Theodora. "That mask, as you call it, makes me feel less in control, less confident, less of everything."

"That's why I focused you on dancing. I wanted to see your face as it would appear in the darkness, alone," said Macedonia. She relaxed her veneer, looked down, and stepped away. "For reasons of my own, I came up with the idea of masks as a little girl. There was a mask of anger, a mask of sadness, and so on. I practiced every possible mask in front of a mirror until I mastered each one. But I happened to notice, quite by chance, that there were two masks that, whenever I wore them, appeared to be identical. So alike were these two masks that I concluded that they were indistinguishable. One is the mask of shame, despina," she said and paused. "But the other is the mask of power."

Theodora raised her eyes until they again met Macedonia's. "Power?"

"Yes, Theodora. I believe your dark feminine is power. Both masks are perfectly stoic, unfeeling to an extreme. Both look on weakness with a merciless contempt. And both masks hide a mind plagued by heavy thought."

Theodora looked away. "But how could that be?"

"Whatever the reason, shame and power share something," said Macedonia, who adjusted Theodora's dress in several places. "There is a critical difference between these two masks, though."

"What is it?"

"The mask of shame directs a devastating judgment inward, at the self. But the mask of power projects it outward, at others. This subtle distinction doesn't show on the face, but it's very different in here," said Macedonia as she tapped the center of Theodora's chest. "Perhaps one day, you'll remove the one mask and take up the other. But you're not ready just yet, despina. So, until you've mastered yourself, I want you to wear the mask you know."

Theodora's thoughts still dwelled on the blankness of the feeling behind the mask. Was power truly as emotionless as shame? After a long silence passed, she sighed. "If I'm able to succeed with Hypatius, if I gain his trust, what then?"

"Direct him," Macedonia said with a smile that broke the tension. "When demands are made of a queen, her subjects must learn she has demands of her own."

TWENTY-FOUR

Theodora and Macedonia stood side by side, sweeping through a series of dance stretches. "You must engage men directly," Macedonia said. "This is not so easy for some women because it involves confrontation. But you must learn how to oppose a man and to let your opposition strengthen your position with him."

"What does that mean?"

"There are three basic roles to any relationship," said Macedonia. "A master, a servant, and a peer. These roles are very defined among men, but with you, he will always assume himself the master. The world has taught him this and now you must teach him otherwise. Put a man in conflict, and he'll work his way out, one of their great strengths, but you'll use it to your advantage. When you learn what drives each man, you must challenge him on his ground. You're to become the impetus," she said and pulled out of the dance stretch. She turned to Theodora and lifted her chin. "If he is arrogant, doubt him. If he is ignorant, correct him. If he worships you, command him. If he is timid, embolden him. If he is judgmental, discredit him. If he is broken, console him. If he is withdrawn, ignore him. If he is a dreamer, inspire him. If he is irritated, pester him. If he is demanding, deny him. If he is threatening, turn and face him," she said. "Too many women challenge men *as the servant*, using anger without power, and a powerless woman will eventually falter. Men are prepared for confrontation, and so too must you be. And when he responds to your opposition, you will remain composed, unflinching, and assertive."

Theodora sighed and asked the inevitable question. "But what if he becomes violent?"

"Then he seeks authority over you, Theodora. If he strikes you, stand tall and dare him to do it again."

That wasn't the answer Theodora was looking for.

"Remember, we're speaking about a man with whom you've established some level of trust and rapport. He'll be a friend, a relative, or lover. If that man should turn against you, if he should strike you, you *must* confront him immediately." Macedonia repeated herself, but slowly. "Stand tall and dare him to do it again. The power of violence is not the violence itself, but whether you accept his sole authority afterward. And you will *not* accept it. With each blow you defy him. His authority is collapsing, even while he believes he's enforcing it."

"And if he kills you?"

Macedonia stepped in close again and grabbed Theodora's robe. "Then let this be your burial shroud. Wear it proudly. If you desire power, Theodora, then you better know the price. You go all the way. The wellspring of all power in this world comes from a willingness to face death for your own autonomy in this life. That is the covenant. No person or nation has ever risen without facing this brutal and powerful truth."

Theodora stared back at Macedonia, stunned, feeling the weight of her mentor's lesson more heavily than normal.

Macedonia continued. "And why should women fear death? We stare death in the face to bring life into this world, and we do so willingly. So, tell me, which is the better burial shroud? The one you wear now, or the one you'll wear as an old woman who feared death and died anyway? Because I say that a woman who dies on her feet never really dies." Macedonia blinked and glanced above Theodora as if she saw something there. "She is swept up from the earth in a magnificent gale, and she'll leave this world sovereign." Macedonia reset her eyes on Theodora. "An unconquered woman."

Unconquered.

The smaller of the two Theodoras heard the word. She circled her thoughts around it. But like a wolf drawn in by a bright and mesmerizing fire, she feared to go any closer.

TWENTY-FIVE

The next day, Theodora arrived for her lesson, but Macedonia wasn't there. Her mentor was never late.

Theodora opened the shutters and gazed down upon the streets. Men waved when they saw her at the window, and Theodora waved back, smiling and flirting. Most of the foot traffic headed north toward the Hippodrome. The day's races were underway because a light cloud of dust drifted up from the horse track and blended into the blue skies. At that hour, they must've been on the eighth or ninth race.

Theodora heard the door open behind her and turned to see Macedonia.

"You're going to get your chance," said Macedonia. "Whether you're ready or not." She shut the doors, strode to the water bowl, and splashed her face.

"What chance is that?"

"Hypatius. We know where he's going to be and it's time we dangled you in front of him again."

Theodora clasped her hands together, feeling anxious. "When?"

"Tonight," said Macedonia. "There's going to be a sex party at the home of Olybrius Anicii. Do you know who he is?"

"No."

Macedonia patted her face with a cloth. "Olybrius Anicii is a member of one of the wealthiest families in the empire. Decades ago his father was even a western emperor, and his family has ties to Emperor Anastasius. He has relatives in the Church, Army, and Senate. Olybrius is also a man of intense sexual appetite." Macedonia looked into a mirror and quickly brushed her hair. "I've arranged for you to be the *actus initium*, the act that starts the sex party. I want Hypatius to get a good look at you."

"Am I to dance?" said Theodora.

"No, Olybrius prefers a live sex show."

"How do you know Hypatius will be there?"

"Justinian's informers tell us that he'll be there along with his brother, Pompeius. Both are Greens, so it's intriguing that the brothers are attending a party hosted by such a prominent Blue."

Theodora took a deep breath and smiled uneasily at Macedonia.

"What's wrong?"

"I'm just tense is all. I've laid with men in every possible way and place," said Theodora. "But this feels different."

"Because it's not about sex this time," said Macedonia. "Don't worry, despina. I've trained you for this, and I believe you're ready."

Theodora prepared herself for the evening. Macedonia helped her purchase a beautiful silk robe that was blue with gold squares speckling the fabric. The robe had loose sleeves and was tied at the waist by a white silken belt. Theodora learned that, besides the obvious areas of a woman's body, men of the nobility had a particular fascination with the forearms, so she rubbed a rosewater cream on her skin until it looked smooth and shiny. Unlike the daytime, when she worked around the Amphitheater, Theodora wore her hair up, exposing the neckline in the fashion of aristocratic women.

Theodora and Macedonia traveled to the House of Olybrius later that night in an elaborate horse-drawn carriage. Since a winter cold still gripped the city, Macedonia quickly lit the hanging lantern and pulled out the animal hides for blankets.

After some time, the carriage passed through large iron gates of a massive estate and came to a stop. Theodora and Macedonia shuffled into the villa through a side door and walked through candlelit hallways. Her eyes wandered over all the signs of opulence. Ornate wood furniture occupied spaces throughout the villa as if it were not meant for use, adorned with upright gold plates, bronze figurines, and vases. She saw marble statues in arched nooks, and double doors flanked by elephant tusks, winding upward like warped pillars. Down one hallway, the oar of an old Carthaginian warship ran the length of the wall at eye level. Theodora strode through a place far above her station. At least for one night, she intersected the world of the aristocracy. For one night, she belonged there.

Theodora finally entered a small room with walls covered in vivid frescoes that depicted all manners of copulation. Inside the room, she saw unfamiliar actresses mingling, half-naked and changing into various costumes.

"Ah, Macedonia," said a voice. "Is this the one for the *actus initium*?"

Theodora turned to see a slender, clean-shaven man with light brown skin and black hair that circled his head in a straight line. She thought his face looked vulpine, clean, and overly manicured.

Macedonia bowed. "This is her."

The man ran his hand along the side of Theodora's ribs, pausing on her hip and looking over her body as if inspecting furniture. "Remove your clothes for me."

"You're an eager one," said Theodora.

"I need to see that you're free of scars or deformities."

Theodora held the man's gaze. With deft fingers, she unfastened all the buttons and knots that held her new and finest garment in place. Apparently, she didn't much need it, she thought, as the gown fluttered to the floor.

"What a stunning woman," he said, no longer smug, but incredulous. "Where do you work?"

"Wherever I want."

Macedonia interjected. "She's known as the *Notorious* Theodora."

The man raised his eyebrows and smiled. "How promising. Young woman, do you know 'The Virgin and the Faun'?"

"Of course," she said.

"Well, that's our little act tonight. It's simple. The other girls know what they're doing already. We have minstrels for a few lyrics, and you're our virgin. I doubt you need direction for the final act. Just do what you do," he said, examining her body again. "Stand near the front so we all get a good look at you."

Theodora smirked at the man but continued to stare at him. She realized he served as a stage master of sorts. And judging by his leisure attire, he was likely a participant in the party as well.

"Here, put this on," he said and handed Theodora a folded garment. "And Macedonia, shall we retire to the great hall?"

Macedonia smiled demurely. "I'll be with you shortly."

The man bowed and departed.

"Remember," said Macedonia, lowering her voice to a whisper. "The show will make you desired by all tonight, but you're to stay focused on Hypatius."

Theodora leaned in. "Which one is he?"

Macedonia slid the curtain aside with two fingers and searched the vast chamber beyond. She pointed. "There."

Theodora saw dozens of men and women standing and mingling. Most of them wore scant clothing, but a few were nude already. The man that Macedonia pointed out was tall with thinning silver hair above his ears and a glossy scalp; the baldness, though, appeared regal and even appealing to Theodora. He wore a white evening gown with notes of imperial purple and had a small crowd around him. As she looked at the man's eyes from afar, the reality of her task finally struck her. He was a stranger, hopelessly above her station, and she had to capture his attention.

"I'll be watching the show as well," said Macedonia. "You'll be fine, despina." At that, she ducked through the curtain and joined the festivities.

A shadow fell over Theodora as a man leaned over her to get his own look into the main hall. She saw a faun mask with two black horns tucked under his arm and knew he was the male lead. He was an enormous eastern Goth with white skin common to their race. He wore a faun costume, complete with a jerkin that was shaggy with brown hair, open at the chest, revealing a thick torso and well-muscled midsection. "And who might you be?" she asked.

"I'm Badwila," he said, but his Latin was skewed with a heavy barbarian drawl. "I've not seen you here before."

"So?" she said, loving his accent. "I'm here tonight."

Badwila shrugged his big shoulders. "First time?"

"I haven't been asked that for some time now, Master Faun," she said with a promiscuous smile. "Anything I need to know?"

"See that window over there?" He pointed with his head. "At the wall behind those slaves. It's for people to watch the party in secret."

A secret audience, she thought, for a secret kind of theater. Theodora let the curtain slip from her fingers. "Well, I hope you're ready to go, Master Faun. I know I am."

Badwila smiled at Theodora as he slipped on his faun mask. "I'm always ready to go. My gift and curse."

"Mine too," she said, more to herself.

Theodora donned the white headdress of a Vestal Virgin, a bygone order of Roman priestesses, who remained celibate for thirty years, else be buried alive. For a costume, the fabrics were heavy and suggested authentic religious garb.

The show began with a darkening of the outer room as candles were extinguished, replaced with a fire basin, which was supposed to be the eternal flame of Vesta. A chorus of female minstrels then sighed out with a surprisingly beautiful melody. And then Theodora heard a single pan flute play an ethereal melody, fitting for a pagan temple.

Theodora and nine other dancers filed out through the curtains, their heads bowed in devotion. Theodora felt all those eyes upon her, like wolves' eyes in the dark, yellow and glinting, watching her and the girls with animal-like anticipation.

In the middle of the performing area, Theodora saw a large Roman altar wreathed in shimmering candles. As the white-robed Vestal Virgins lined up in two rows, Theodora took her place in the front row, on stage right. She met the eyes of the audience that stood so close by. She spotted Hypatius near the front, just as the temple pan flute fell hush.

Silence.

Then the voice of a female singer sang a verse in Latin:

Virgins beware
Virgins beware
A faun has entered in

Theodora knew the play. At the back of the performing area, Badwila, clad now in the full costume of the faun, appeared from the shadows, taking stealthy steps forward. He twitched his head from side to side as he crept into the row of virgins. He tried to look the girls in the eye, but each priestess seemed to wilt, turning their heads aside, casting their eyes downward, too pure to acknowledge a trespassing demon.

Theodora suddenly felt the presence of the faun at her left shoulder. But she broke the pattern of the other priestesses and didn't turn away from the faun. Instead, she blinked slowly and raised her head into the light, her eyes straying to gaze up at the faun. And for a breath, the music went quiet, but only for a breath.

Then a drum boomed out with the military cadence of Roman war drums.

Theodora saw the drummer behind the minstrels, a mere silhouette of a large man dropping two mallets against two drum tops, marching her toward the darkness, inescapable. Wood blocks then accompanied the drums, a hurried insect-like clacking that echoed in repetition. Her skin prickled as the music dominated the room.

Danger beside you!
Danger beside you!
He sees you are intrigued

Theodora lifted her chin defiantly at the faun, staring at him with insolent eyes. He circled her, and she felt a great tension rising in the room. And the elephantine pounding of the drums reverberated in her chest, already evoking the forceful impacts of sexual union. As if sensing danger, the other priestesses cleared away from Theodora, their white robes billowing as they scurried to the side of the performing area.

But Theodora held her ground, alone, staring boldly back at the faun. Now she heard the impish twangs of lute strings plucking and picking amongst the relentless percussion. This was followed by the eerie wail of a reed pipe and the flutter of a pan flute. Theodora thought the instruments conjured an evil music—beautiful, dark, and oppressive.

Why do you not flee?
Why do you not flee?
If you stray, you can't return

Badwila's blue eyes almost glowed through the sockets of the faun mask, but Theodora also saw violence there. Like herself, he too was becoming his character, summoning up the darkness inside him, becoming the faun, and so the turn passed to her to become the impure girl, the public sacrifice of innocence. This role she knew. But she was a woman now, and where there had once been a paralyzing fear, there was only a burning fever of the body.

Theodora closed her eyes and slackened, swaying fluidly now with the thumping, thumping, thumping of the drums. Her mind became a blank, black sky with a rising plume of crimson smoke. She felt the faun press against her from behind, his horned head curling over her shoulder, his neck hot beside her own. She reached backwards and wrapped her fingers around one of the horns, feeling a pleasurable eagerness inside her flesh now. Then his hand was upon her, a brown, bearded hand that slid up her belly, over her breasts, up along her exposed neck, before toppling her white headdress. Theodora felt her long black hair spill down, a sight that would excite the men in the audience. She gasped as if shocked by her willingness to feel the sensation of the faun's hand upon her, unopposed. On both sides of the stage, the other priestesses covered their mouths in alarm, yet watched in fascination.

The faun leaned down and kissed Theodora on the mouth. She tasted the wine he'd been drinking. But she kissed him back, without modesty, her tongue outstretched and meshing with his, the charcoal paint around his mouth smearing onto her own skin. The hand of the faun was inside her robe now, working its way up. She pulled away from the kiss and looked down, where the fabric rippled as if spiders crept upward from beneath. Theodora's Vestal robe slipped slowly from her shoulder, exposing a breast, the air cool upon her nipple, the fire hot upon her skin. The faun squeezed and rubbed her breast, and she let him. Through the slits of her half-opened eyes, she saw the nearby audience standing in their shadowed postures, like statues, as they looked on. She excited them, but now it was they who excited her. She felt her breath quicken.

Finally, the faun wrenched the robe from Theodora. She stood fully naked, covering herself, elbows at the belly, fists at the chin, knees together. After this initial shock, she lowered her arms and stood upright, ready to be seen. Pleased, the faun took Theodora into his arms and carried her to the sacred Altar of Vesta. She settled onto her back while the dark faun crawled up and over her, gazing down at her with bestial eyes. Then he knelt upright. He removed his black tunic and revealed his enormous phallus and the full state of his arousal. This triggered an astonished murmur throughout the room, but Theodora stayed focused on Badwila's eyes.

And the music came to a hush.

Theodora felt Badwila force her knees apart and press himself into her, slowly, then all at once, her skin going taut with pain and pleasure alike. When she gasped, the music suddenly resumed, but with all the instruments at once. The war drums commenced while the hand drums pattered like rain. The faun writhed in the familiar throes of sexual passion, and soon after, Theodora watched the other Vestal Virgins approach the altar, now curious of these carnal pleasures. Soon the priestesses caressed Theodora's naked arms, chest, and legs as if to soothe her virginal transformation. The faun bid each priestess to remove their robe, which one by one they did.

A temple falls!
A temple falls!

The gods, alas, are gone
A temple rises!
A temple rises!
The Temple of the Faun

As the music quickened, as the faun became more forceful, Theodora saw that even the musicians and minstrels stared at her, their mouths agape and eyes wide. The whole world, it seemed, men and women alike, wanted to see this. Revulsion at the corruption melts away, and their minds tilt toward fascination.

Then she turned her head to face the secret window in the corner. There she saw the silhouettes of many heads framed within; countless eyes stared back at her, dotted like orange stars. Those were not the eyes of men. Darkness was a woman's camouflage, a way of being close to danger, but not in danger, fascinated by violence, but safe from destruction, a watchfulness, without being watched, to witness one woman's overindulgence of her body, yet never risking the slipping away of their own willpower. To be worshipped as a pure sexual object was the most forbidden desire. The window was the final boundary between their private curiosity and the brazen sexual reality Theodora exhibited for their entertainment. Both worlds came closest together at that dark, little window. Theodora stared back at them, enraptured, taunting, unafraid. She wanted them to see the woman upon the altar. But did they behold a woman ascending in her liberation or sinking further into her enslavement? To Theodora, it was always both . . . because there were two Theodoras . . . the one upon the altar and the one behind the window.

Finally, Theodora felt the faun nearing his climax and returned her attention to him. The music fell off until only the hand drums rattled like a downpour of rain. The faun suddenly withdrew from her body, cried out, and emptied upon her bare belly, his torso inflating and deflating rapidly.

As Theodora panted heavily with Badwila, chatter and applause spread through the room. They were always there for her at the end, she thought, adoring of the beast and mesmerized by the willing girl.

And with that, the party commenced.

TWENTY-SIX

Behind a curtain at the back of the stage, Theodora cleaned herself thoroughly and changed into an outfit of sheer red muslin. She heard a man, who must have been Olybrius, quiet the room. "To become gods, first you must kill the gods," he said, followed by light applause. "Mock them! Make their temples your own, for the sole purpose of a god is to threaten the outside world with fears of tomorrow. In this place, we hold only the present to be sacred. So, set aside your restraints. Eat and drink as you will. Indulge! Indulge in the body of your neighbors, and they will indulge in yours."

Theodora then heard sweeping hedonistic music, the big drums rapping softly, like earthen tremors, accompanied by pleasant tambourines and plucked harps, all mixing with the murmur of conversation. The host provided her with real gold necklaces, rings, and earrings. She'd have to return them, but for now, Theodora admired her reflection in the mirror, turning her head from side to side and watching the star-like glints where gems touched her skin.

When Theodora emerged from behind the curtain, a eunuch boy led her into the mysterious lair of the aristocracy. The interior chamber was larger than she thought, with green garland spiraling Roman pillars, and the roasted torso of a full-size bull in the corner, suspended over an enormous hearth. Bowls of fire gave the room a bright and shifting light, clearly meant to show as much of the shocking sight as possible.

And Theodora *was* shocked.

She saw perhaps fifty people, mostly nude, and gathered together in the center of the great hall. They created a labyrinthine mass of bare skin, intermingled with a chaotic pattern of dark-haired scalps, exposed nipples, and sparkling jewelry. But Theodora's eyes fell most upon the black seams of so many bare buttocks, which gave the sight its peculiar aura—partly beautiful, yet undeniably obscene.

Although the environment fostered luxury and social normalcy, it occurred to Theodora that nothing about the party looked natural. Even in the lowly theater and brothels, nudity was still a private affair, fulfilling animal impulses in hidden rooms. But this was widespread, brightly lit, and communal. The revelers lounged and spoke freely, as if clothed, with intertwined legs, heads resting in naked laps, and hands stoking lengths of bare skin. Theodora thought the excessive nudity somehow drew a sharper contrast between the taller, larger men and the slender, feline women; all variety of male and female, aimlessly interwoven.

As the eunuch led Theodora toward the gathering, she searched for the distinctive face of Hypatius among the crowd but didn't see him. Theodora watched a nearby woman suddenly kneel and bend low to kiss another woman, who was already laid flat in slow copulation. As the first woman settled into the kiss, a man in a gold mask drew up behind her, sweeping his hand across the curve of her upturned and bare backside, and then gently enter her. The woman never even looked at the man, but merely reached back, dragged her fingers down his forearm, before clutching him at the wrist and falling into a bodily cadence. Behind them, Theodora watched a man pull out of a dark-skinned woman, then give a friendly nod to another man as they exchanged places. The woman greeted the newcomer with friendly surprise but quickly succumbed to thoughtless panting. These unusual interactions repeated all around Theodora. Some of the men and women took notice of her approach, waved her over, and moved aside to make room.

The surrender of restraint still mesmerized Theodora. She felt a falling sensation in her lower belly and genitalia, a rising exhilaration of the body. She could turn herself over in totality...

"Not that one," said a voice over the light music and din. "That one's all mine."

The spell broke, and Theodora turned to see Hypatius. He stood beside an elevated marble platform, one of many that surrounded the room. The platform was covered in pillows, partitioned by red curtains and occupied by a few other people. She smiled as the eunuch led her over to him.

Hypatius was taller than she thought, his face freshly shaven, the top of his scalp like polished stone. He wore a thin white robe with a pattern of purple lines running along the seam. He looked sophisticated to Theodora, a man in his sixties, yet unimpressive—handsome, but unimposing. Perhaps good clothes and grooming alone gave the man his aristocratic air because he didn't intimidate her the way Justinian did.

"This is the one I want," Hypatius said in upscale Latin.

"And what if I wanted to join the main gathering?" said Theodora as the eunuch bowed and departed.

"The Notorious Theodora indeed," he said. "You live up to your name."

Hypatius, who smelled faintly of lotus flower, grabbed her hand and guided Theodora onto the platform covered with rugs, animal pelts, and colored pillows. The other revelers cleared space for Theodora as she laid sideways onto the soft fabrics, while Hypatius knelt.

"Just what have you heard about me?" she said.

"You have an appetite for sex that exceeds a man's. That there's nothing you fear in matters of the body, as I witnessed here tonight."

Theodora saw that an older eunuch stood nearby, holding a tray of silver wine chalices. She grabbed two. "I'm just like any woman, only honest about what I like. When I lay with a man, I expect pleasure from him."

A few nearby guests giggled at her bold remark to the emperor's nephew.

Hypatius also laughed, but with the bluster of disbelief. "You expect pleasure? You're the giver of pleasure, not the receiver. And ultimately," he said, sounding more like a parent correcting his child, "you're the one who's paid."

Theodora handed Hypatius his wine chalice and arched in close to him. She looked him right in the eyes. "I'm the one they pay because I'm the one they want." She smiled. "That changes nothing for me. I still expect a man to satisfy me."

"What a clever bit of thinking," said Hypatius. "But the lowly soldier doesn't devise the battle plan."

If he is arrogant, doubt him.

She kept her gaze on him without blinking, a difficult trick, but one that she mastered in her training. "Well, as amused as you may be, Magister Hypatius," she said, recoiling and sipping her wine, "the battle plan, as you call it, is certainly your own. But even the lowly soldier demands a victorious general."

Hypatius darkened. "A soldier dare not question his general."

Theodora placed her hand on the man's leg. "Well, I *am* questioning him."

He darkened. "You'd like that, wouldn't you? Accept a hefty payment and then make demands of your patron."

The payment gave him all the power, she realized.

Hypatius moved to sip his wine and Theodora placed her hand over his chalice, pressing her lips beside his ear. "And what if you didn't pay me? What if it was just you and me, alone, and I was in need? What then?"

He looked at Theodora, obviously confused and uncomfortable, an unusual look for a noble, for the nephew of the emperor, no less. His gray eyes flitted about, searching for some answer. Theodora was surprised to see that the wealth, the rank, the luxurious pedestal of pure Roman pomp all melted away from him.

"You're not seriously suggesting that I withhold your evening's fee?" he said.

He doesn't know how to respond.

Theodora lowered her voice to a whisper and crawled alongside him, facing him, demanding action from him, the way that Macedonia did to her. This was the moment to wrest power, she thought. "For a true man, for a victorious general, I'll forgo my fee. Or does that frighten you?"

"I'm not afraid of a woman."

But he was afraid.

Then Hypatius fell upon her as if struck unconscious. She absorbed his weight and leaned backward until they lay in the feathery folds of silk and eiderdown. Hypatius wasn't heavy, but Theodora enjoyed the feel of his cool robe through her sheer gown and loved the sound of meshing fabrics. He kissed her passionately for a moment and then stopped.

"We need more wine," he said.

Many men preferred drunkenness whenever they lay with a woman. The practice was a dangerous gamble, she thought, for a sober man could be a dull man, but a drunk man could be worthless when it came to pleasure. As Hypatius gulped down a cup of wine, Theodora removed her muslin gown and laid back. He then hurriedly pulled off his silk robe, crawled over Theodora, and kissed her more aggressively.

"Relax," she said, dropping her wrists upon the back of his neck. "There's a long night ahead of us."

He pressed a hand against one of Theodora's breasts, cupping and rubbing it. His touch was gentle and admiring rather than greedy, but she could feel a slight tremble in his fingertips. He kissed her softly on the nipple and then upon the mouth—a boyish kiss, she thought, but sweet and tender. She couldn't help but notice that Hypatius was a fawning man for his older age, and not the commanding noble she prepared herself to face tonight. She heard stories of how some men in the ruling class could be cruel at such parties, preferring pain to pleasure, or gathering many women only to issue humiliating commands. So Hypatius was nice, thought Theodora, even if lackluster.

"I saw you before tonight, you know?" he said. "In a play, and I knew I had to have you."

Theodora locked her fingers behind his neck and pulled her face up to his, smiling. "Then worship me, Hypatius."

Curiously, Hypatius grew uneasy. He looked around to see if anyone else nearby paid any attention to him. He delayed. At that moment, Theodora understood what was happening. This man, so frail-looking in his naked state, was struggling to become aroused. She experienced this from time to time at the brothel, where a man would sometimes fail to swell up, only to become demoralized or angry. But here? From a man of such power?

He slowly lifted his eyes to meet hers, and Theodora saw an unmistakable shame in them. But she couldn't afford his failure. Not tonight. He'd avoid her forever if she let him retreat. This turn of events wasn't what she'd expected for the evening, but the task had changed.

If he is timid, embolden him.

Theodora placed her palms on both sides of Hypatius' face, stilling him. She closed her eyes and let out a soft moan and then another. In such a place, people would be distracted by their own private company, she figured. No one would care about Hypatius unless he drew attention to himself. When she opened her eyes, she saw the confusion on his face. Theodora moaned again, as though thoroughly pleasured, nodding and giving him a reassuring smile. He reluctantly took her cues. He laid flat upon her, dropping his head beside hers, moving as though he were inside her, but periodically checking the attention of those nearby. Convinced his troubles remained secret, he continued with the contrived act. Theodora moaned his name slowly, hoping he may yet become aroused but to no avail. He avoided her eyes for the duration. After a short while, he pretended to conclude and came off Theodora, throwing his robe over his shoulders and pouring another glass of wine.

Theodora sighed with satisfaction. "That was wonderful, Magister Hypatius," she said so that others heard.

Hypatius glanced at her with contempt. "Please, the praise is yours alone."

She saw he was upset but managed to keep him talking. There were six other nobles on the private vista and so conversations sprouted up. Talk always focused on other people, like gossip at the bathhouse, occasionally slipping back into sexual couplings. While the others coalesced bodily, Theodora and Hypatius reclined and succumbed to drinking, caressing, and kissing. None interrupted, she noticed, probably due to his station. But in the later hours, the glassy-eyed revelers spoke of rebellion from outside the city and then politics. Theodora pretended to be ignorant of politics, so made light of such things with jests. Even Hypatius laughed at her witty remarks at times, his hand gently stroking her thigh. Soon, though, most of the unclothed people in the center of the hall fell asleep in their exhausted and drunken state, while some slipped off into other wings of the villa.

"Where are they going?" said Theodora.

"Olybrius has many bedrooms for those who want privacy afterward," he said. "Only the very bold stay here to awaken together. I'm told some of these people will continue through the day tomorrow. I don't know how they do it." Hypatius stood to depart.

Theodora arose and took Hypatius by the hand. "Take me."

He looked confused. "I think I'm done for the evening, Theodora. I don't normally attend this kind of party anyway, so I'm not used to a full night. Regardless of what was said earlier, I'll be sure you're paid for the evening."

Theodora stepped in close to him. "Take me."

He lowered his voice to a whisper. "Theodora, I'm *non bonum*." He shrugged. "I can't."

"Take me," Theodora said with finality.

Hypatius sighed. Then he took her hand and led her out of the banquet room. On the way out, Theodora passed right in front of Macedonia, who was unclothed and reclining idly with two naked men. She traced Theodora's departure with her eyes, never moving her head. For the first time, Theodora saw the woman differently, not as a sexual servant to her wealthy masters, but an intelligent spy lounging among the men who ran the empire, breasts bare, ears open. Macedonia winked without a smile.

Theodora knew not to respond. Then she followed Hypatius out of the hall and into a private place where she'd have him all to herself.

TWENTY-SEVEN

H ypatius led Theodora past a bowing male chamberlain and into a doorway off the main hallway. She couldn't suppress her awe at the interior of the bedchamber. In her experience, sleeping quarters weren't unlike the fornices she worked in—small, practical, and disconnected from the world. But this chamber was cavernous. The ceilings hovered high above, like a fisherman's net of timber beams. A fireplace occupied the back wall; only this one had an ornate marble mantel adorned with numerous shimmering candles. In the middle of the room was the largest bed that Theodora had ever seen. The bed and canopy looked like an enormous green cube with each face of the cube parted down the middle, its curtains forming a triangular opening that showed a silken bed within. Beside the bed, Theodora spotted silver jugs and chalices.

"Wine?" she said and filled two cups.

"Yes, please. Though I doubt there's enough wine in the empire to drown out the memory of this evening."

She handed him a chalice of wine that trickled over the rim. "Stop it. It's hard to love another person when others are watching."

"Is that what you call it? Loving another person?" He laughed and guzzled the wine, allowing trails of the red liquid to run alongside his mouth and drip from his chin. When he finished, he wiped his face. "And is that what it was on stage tonight with that man in the faun costume? Love?"

"Yes," said Theodora, undaunted. She took a quick sip of wine, slipped out of her gown, and crawled onto the bed. The feathery fabric enveloped her naked skin like a cool and soothing caress. She laid onto her back with arms stretched out above her head, raising one knee and smiling at Hypatius. "I've loved an aspect of every man at one time or another. I find the attractive part of him, and that's the part I love."

Hypatius avoided climbing onto the bed, preferring to stand beside it. "I think I know which part of a man you love."

"That's not always a man's best feature. I might love a man's arms, his eyes, or his air of confidence."

"Dare I ask," he said. "What part of me would you find attractive?"

Theodora noticed that Hypatius stared across the bedchamber at nothing, fearing to look her in the eyes, fearing her answer.

"Your vulnerability," she said. "Despite your high rank."

He considered her words for a moment, then laughed and took another gulp of wine.

"That's no small thing to me," said Theodora in a more serious tone. "There's something honest about it. You're not the only man who's had difficulties. Only most men run off, embarrassed. You stayed with me."

Hypatius sipped his wine and turned to face her. Though his look was timid, he seemed desperate to know whether Theodora was being honest with him or merely offering up a rehearsed phrase meant to pacify him. "Perhaps I don't have the sense other men have," said Hypatius.

"Running away is the least attractive of all." Theodora moved so that she lay sideways, her head in one hand, her naked hip arching in the shadows. She patted the bed.

Hypatius looked in her direction. "I want to get into that bed with you. But I know nothing will happen."

"Come lay with me anyway," she said.

He sighed in frustration and finally climbed onto the bed, pulling himself alongside Theodora and resting his head in his hand.

"See?" said Theodora. "Even if we're just talking, closer is better."

"I know what you're trying to do," he said. "I don't think it'll work. I wish I knew what's wrong with me. I've taken many women in my life. In my youth, I can honestly say that I was the best lover for some women. And now, alas, I can say that I've been the worst."

Theodora stroked his shoulder with only her fingertips. "Sex isn't the only way a man and woman can love each other. Intimacy can also be exciting."

She needed to get him talking. According to Macedonia, almost anything said in bed could be valuable information. Usually, men loosened up after sex, so here now, she'd have to loosen up Hypatius without it.

Theodora watched him look over her body. He reached out and pressed his palm against one of her breasts, feeling her body there before sliding his hand along a length of her bare skin, over her hip, down her leg, and then back again. And again, Theodora found his touch to be surprisingly soft and sensual.

"I dreamed of taking you tonight. When I saw you at the Amphitheater some while back, I filled with such a desire for you. I figured that a woman as beautiful as you would surely make me able to . . ." He trailed off, and his hand slid from Theodora's body, flopping on the bed like a lifeless object. "And now I have you in this bed, and I'm a ghost."

"Stop. Tonight doesn't have to be a grand event," Theodora said, rolling onto her stomach and kicking up her feet.

Hypatius sat up and suddenly flung his chalice at the fireplace. The cup clinked and ricocheted off the mantel as he cursed.

Theodora remained cool. She sat up and slid next to him, putting her arm around him and letting her long black hair spill down the front of his chest. "When was the last time you had a woman?"

Hypatius grabbed his scalp with one hand and rubbed in frustration. "Almost two years. Ever since I came back from the front."

To Theodora, this was further proof that Macedonia's training was correct. She said that the essence of a woman was more powerful than her physical body. Perhaps the same was true for men; perhaps there was something internal for them too, something within that could overpower their physical body. "What happened?" she said.

Theodora felt his body rise and sink with a defeated breath. "I doubt you'd understand. You're a prostitute."

She let the insult go uncontested and kissed his neck. "I know."

"I lost a military battle. Do you see? I led a great army against the rebel Vitalian and not only did I lose the battle . . . I was captured and taken hostage." Hypatius turned and seemed to gauge Theodora's reaction. "Me. I was taken hostage and held for ransom. Better had I been slain. I didn't realize it then, but my name and standing were destroyed forever. Reputation has no meaning to a prostitute like you, but to a man, his name is everything."

"But Vitalian was defeated when he attacked the city," she said.

"Yes, but not by me. General Marinus gets that accolade. I'm talking about a battle that took place before Vitalian ever made it to the city gates. You're probably too young to remember it," Hypatius said as he slid away from Theodora. He wandered toward the fireplace and stood with his back to her. "I was supposed to be an emperor."

The room grew silent, and Theodora didn't know what to say, so she held her tongue.

"I was groomed for succession. I'm the eldest nephew to an emperor who bears no sons," he said. "The House of Anicii backs my claim to the throne through my wife, which ensures the backing of other houses. I held the position of Consul. I have *everything* to make my ascension an absolute certainty. And yet somehow, I squandered it. Somehow, I let it all slip right out of my hand." Theodora watched him clench his fist while staring vacantly into the flames.

"Did the emperor come out and say that he no longer wants you as his heir?" said Theodora.

Hypatius turned to Theodora. "Worse. He never said anything about it ever again. Nothing. Before I was taken hostage, magistrates and nobles circled me as though I was an emperor already. I dealt with powerful families who sought my favor, lavishing me with gifts and promising support. Members of the church were eager to know of my stance on religious doctrine, and the empire's best generals spoke of military campaigns against the Persians or barbarians." He suddenly raised his voice. "I was goddamn important!"

His words echoed in the ceiling, causing the chamberlain to peek his head in from the doorway. Theodora quickly waved him off.

"And then Vitalian released me. I came back from the front," said Hypatius. "After Anastasius paid my ransom, of course. Slowly, day by day, the meetings fell off, the discussions, the gifts, and dinners. Now no one comes to me anymore. When I attend parties, the nobles look at me with mocking eyes. Conversations wilt like unwatered flowers. It's the exact opposite of everything that came before, and all because of Vitalian, the swine. So you see, the emperor need say nothing."

"What about your wife?" said Theodora. "And her family? You said they're important people."

"No, she's been good to me," he said. "She stood by me, and her family would still back me, I'm sure, but it's not enough. I'd need guaranteed support from the army . . ." He punched his palm. ". . . which I no longer have. Besides, the House of Anicii backs all imperial candidates. That's how they maintain favor, no matter who sits on the throne. I'm just a ghost in the Daphne Palace now. Is this what you wanted to hear? Because I'm sure you have seasoned advice on these matters."

Theodora looked down. His problem was much bigger than she'd anticipated. "No."

"I didn't think so. Ever since I came back," Hypatius said and nodded to himself, "I haven't been able to enjoy a woman. And if a woman as beautiful as you can't cure me, then I can't be cured."

"Maybe it's not the woman," she said.

Hypatius faced away from Theodora; his eyes fixed on the flickering fire. She saw that his thoughts drifted elsewhere, perhaps out to some soggy battlefield far away.

"I know it feels hopeless," she said. "But over time, you'll find your way back. Believe it or not, I understand a little bit about the pain."

Hypatius stiffened as if offended. "What do you honestly know about my pain? A prostitute. What's the worst that could happen to a lowborn woman like you?" He turned away from her. "Someone slaps you around a bit? Some bastard fucks you in a humiliating way? Forces your mouth down onto him for pleasure? I mean, humiliation is your profession."

Theodora climbed off the bed and faced Hypatius. "I'm trying to help you, and you belittle me," she said. "Women don't choose this life, you fool. We come into it."

"Fool?" he hissed, anger kindling in his eyes. "You dare address *me* as though speaking to a common man?" Hypatius slapped her, a weak hit for a man, but it stung nonetheless.

Theodora recalled Macedonia's training.

When he responds to your opposition, you will remain composed, unflinching, and assertive . . . stand tall and dare him to do it again . . .

Theodora slowly straightened her posture until she stood at full height. Her face muscles relaxed until she stared back at Hypatius with a stoic gaze void of all feeling, void of all fear. She didn't shrink, nor blink, nor breathe.

"I don't want to hit you," he said, his hand suspended, ready to strike again.

"Then don't. But make up your mind whether you like me or hate me."

He lowered his hand, and to Theodora's surprise, Hypatius broke. His shoulders dropped, and he covered his face. She saw him squeeze his eyes shut in shame, crestfallen. "I don't hate you," he said. "I know you're only trying to help. It's just proof that I've fallen so far if my final *consiliarius* is a prostitute."

Theodora knew that it was his own self that Hypatius hated, his own weakness that haunted him. She understood in full.

If he is broken, console him.

Although her cheek still stung, Theodora guided Hypatius over to the bed, and they both sat down. "Look," she said. "You're right. I know nothing of emperors or battles, but I do know what it feels like to lose yourself."

Hypatius twitched his head. He was listening.

Theodora continued. "It's a terrible, suffocating feeling . . . like death, but you're still alive. Just a living deformity of yourself. It seems like every little thought is a sip of the same damn poison. And the notion that you once thought highly of yourself becomes the most hated thought of all." Theodora paused, feeling the heaviness, the heat and constriction settle over her. "Your mind is bent on recovering the time that came before, when you were unruined, when everything went your way. Only you can't go back. Deep down, you tell yourself you'll outlast the nightmare, and in time, you'll return to your former self. But then years bleed out. Eventually, the terrible realization comes to you at last . . . it was your former self who was the dream all along; and the deformity is the real you, the only you, a lowly creature exposed for *all* to see. Those who spoke ill of you are suddenly wise, while those who thought highly of you look away. And in your heart, you know . . ." Theodora sighed and looked down. "You died. You died without even a fight. You died in disgrace."

Hypatius stared ahead in silence, his eyes glassy. "It is a death, isn't it?" he said. "An invisible murder right out in the open."

Silence passed in the bedchamber and the log in the hearth came apart, crumbling to orange embers.

"When the person you were is dead, what then?" he asked.

Theodora ducked down to meet his gaze. "Then you *must* come back anew," she said.

Hypatius seemed to ponder her answer. "Can I ask what happened to you? Actually, don't tell me. I won't make you speak of such things aloud."

"It was when I was a little girl," said Theodora anyway. "By someone of wealth and rank. By someone who could go through life without ever having to answer for what he did."

"People like that get away with it. They wreak havoc on the world and the world lets them." Hypatius finally looked fully on Theodora. "Do you ever . . . dream of revenge?"

Theodora pulled back, a chill upon her skin. "Oh, yes."

Hypatius nodded and fought back another wave of sorrow, pressing the back of his wrist over his mouth. "It's terrifying. Such dreams only unmask a part of you that you didn't know was there, showing you what dark things you're capable of doing. Murder even. If I had my way, if I could ever get to Vitalian, I'd kill him. If one cannot be great . . ." But Hypatius didn't finish the line of thought. He sighed and stood up. He poured two new cups of wine and handed one to Theodora. "To revenge."

She toasted back and took a sip, staring at Hypatius over the rim of the cup.

"The Notorious Theodora of the stage," he said with a smile. "A worthy advisor for the vexed. I've never spoken to a woman of such things, not even my wife."

"Well? Are you ashamed?"

Hypatius considered the question. "No. I keep these thoughts to myself, but they eat at me from the inside."

"You should speak with your wife. She can help you too."

"No. Mary is still a woman of the high aristocracy," Hypatius said. "I can't have her sharing my worries and fears with others in the House Anicii. Any sign of weakness is the kiss of death when you are among the nobility. They're ruthless. They'll circle a foundering man, chew him up, and spit out the carcass for the vultures to have their turn." He then set his eyes upon Theodora. "That is why I must ask you never to speak of these matters to anyone. Can I trust you?"

Theodora smiled warmly and put her hand on his shoulder. "Of course you can trust me."

TWENTY-EIGHT

Theodora sat across from Justinian and Macedonia in the Chamber of Cupid. He appeared more at ease than the last time she saw him, when he marched out of the fornice in a hurry. Now, he sat back in his chair with a relaxed look, neither stern nor intense, but focused.

"Can you see Hypatius as emperor?" asked Justinian.

"No," said Theodora, stroking the skin along her collarbone.

Justinian.

Theodora recalled the sight of Justinian in a sea of spectators, his voice booming, the crowd reacting to his every word. She refocused on the calmness of the current moment, where that same Hippodrome crowd cheered in the distance and that same man sat in stillness across from her. Now Justinian ruminated on her answer, one hand upon the table, absently tracing a finger back and forth in repetition, his attention on her alone.

"Give me your impressions," said Justinian. "Is he an ambitious man?"

"Maybe at one time. But his mind is bent on his lost status among the army. He thinks of nothing else. We never even slept together."

"You spent the night in his bed but didn't sleep with him?" said Macedonia.

"No. He wasn't able to, you know," Theodora said, making a gesture with her finger. "An issue he blamed on Vitalian. He said he was captured by Vitalian during a battle a couple of years ago."

"That's right," said Justinian. "Emperor Anastasius was forced to pay an embarrassing ransom to get his bungling nephew back."

Theodora nodded. "That's exactly what he told me. He said that ever since that ransom was paid, he lost all his support."

"Interesting. I wonder if Hypatius has enough backing inside the Palace."

"He doesn't think so."

"Good," said Justinian. "Let him brood. What else did he say?"

"He constantly compared himself to the general, Vitalian."

"To the rebel," said Justinian, correcting Theodora. "Vitalian *was* a Roman general until he turned his army against Emperor Anastasius. Then he became a rebel."

Theodora nodded. "Well, he blames the *rebel* Vitalian for costing him the throne."

"War hostages don't exactly earn the respect of the army," said Justinian. "That's the main reason the emperor won't name Hypatius as his successor right now."

"What happens if Emperor Anastasius never names a successor?" said Theodora.

Justinian glanced at Macedonia and then back to Theodora. "If Emperor Anastasius dies without naming a successor, then the people of the city will invoke Greek democracy," he said. "Constantinople isn't Rome. Most of the people here aren't Romans. Go down to the ship docks and listen for yourself. The men bark at one another in Greek, not Latin. The Roman Empire wasn't founded here, but here it survives. The local population has its own traditions to fall back on. If Emperor Anastasius dies without naming an heir, the next emperor will be *elected* in the Hippodrome, rather than appointed by bloodline."

That cursed Hippodrome, thought Theodora. "But how?"

Justinian smiled. "Imperial candidates would be presented to the crowd at the Hippodrome. The candidate who manages to achieve a sweeping cheer from the crowd will become the next emperor," he said and snapped his fingers. "Just like that. In a single moment, a man can grab the throne of the empire. It's democracy, anarchy, and mob rule all hammered into one terrifying process. Our friend Hypatius knows this. He knows that military officers will be out in that crowd, ready to shout their disapproval of a former war hostage who never won a single battle. If those voices carry the day, if Hypatius fails to win the crowd, then he'll be executed by the newly elected emperor. No future rivals can be left to linger. It's a fatal game, and it sounds to me like our friend is very aware of the danger. Even if Hypatius refuses to be a candidate, his bloodline to Emperor Anastasius makes him a permanent rival. His best chance to live is to become the next emperor. The question I'm trying to answer is how he'll try and play this deadly game."

Theodora's mind conjured up images of the Hippodrome, filled with those wild spirits, cheering or booing one man or another. This all seemed familiar to her, haunting even. For Theodora knew well the kind of democracy that Justinian described. Was it not democracy at work the day her pata died? Was it not democracy that day in the Hippodrome, when the people threw bread crumbs at her mother? And once the verdict came, it came quickly, mercilessly, and final, just like the snap of Justinian's fingers. "So who wins an election like that?" said Theodora.

Justinian looked down. "The man who knows how to steer the crowd."

Theodora felt a wave of heat rise to her cheeks.

A man like you.

Justinian didn't recognize her as the girl from the Hippodrome, so he couldn't have suspected Theodora's thoughts. But she saw firsthand how Justinian wielded power in the anarchy of the Hippodrome. Her mother once assured her that all battles were social battles. Democracy, after all, was a social battle for power, where the armies were the citizens, and the god they fought for was favor.

"Hypatius doesn't know how to win a crowd," she said instead. "Not that crowd."

Justinian studied Theodora as if he knew that she indeed understood *something* of the Hippodrome. He continued to rub his fingers on the table-top, and for the first time, Theodora felt as though he let slip his guard and strayed into admiring her beauty. Those deep brown eyes and black pupils bore into her again, and Theodora shifted in her seat.

Macedonia must've also noticed the look because she interrupted. "Did Hypatius mention whether he wanted to see you again?"

"Yes. There's some newly appointed governor he mentioned. They're going to have a party for him before he sets out for North Africa. He wanted me to entertain."

"Curious," said Justinian.

"Do you think the next emperor will kill Hypatius?" said Theodora.

"Yes. Do you remember the last rebellion in the city a few years back?"

The one that killed my father? "Of course," she said.

"In that last rebellion, the mob declared a man named Aerobindus as the new emperor. But Anastasius wisely reversed his policy, and the rebellion ended. That left Aerobindus suddenly stranded as a rival."

"What happened?"

"Aerobindus fled the city and has never been seen or heard from again."

Poor Hypatius, thought Theodora. Now she understood why the old man described himself as a ghost. He went from undisputed successor to a man who awaits the strangling rope of another man's rise to power. She felt sad when she imagined Hypatius dragged through the city streets, or his head pushed through a noose, or his frail body squirming from the end of a rope. He'd be a victim of the same murderous crowd that killed her father and humiliated her mother.

Why did those people get to have so much power? What makes them so infallible?

Theodora thought of her mother in a new light. Maximina went against the powerful horde that even emperors feared, and she went it alone. But there were two sides to the chaos, Theodora remembered, a Blue side and a Green side . . .

Theodora sat up, beaming with the aura of a revelation. "Hypatius said something else."

Justinian raised an eyebrow.

"Twice, he suggested that his capture by Vitalian was no accident, but a plot by his own faction," she said. "He seemed convinced that resentful Greens conspired against him and betrayed his whereabouts to Vitalian."

Justinian rocked his head back and forth as if considering the notion. "Not far-fetched."

"Yes, well, if the Greens betrayed Hypatius, then perhaps Hypatius would return the favor."

Justinian sat up and placed both hands on the table, his rings clacking against the wood. "You mean try and turn him? Make Hypatius a Blue?"

"Yes."

Theodora saw that the idea never occurred to Justinian. He seemed to consider several scenarios all at once, weighing the dangers of Theodora's suggestion. The silence broke when Macedonia spoke. "But Hypatius would never betray his uncle."

"He doesn't have to," said Theodora. "Once his uncle dies, he just has to betray the *next* candidate . . . to us. You said it yourself. The next emperor would kill him. If Hypatius believes the Greens conspired against him, then whoever the Greens back for the next emperor would be his betrayer."

Justinian could be that man in the stands for Hypatius too, thought Theodora, rising above a hostile crowd, reaching out his hand and offering the shelter of the Blue faction.

The way that Justinian looked at Theodora at that moment excited her. He'd already listened to her every word, and now he lowered his head, just a bit, and his eyes slipped into a stare that Theodora recognized in a man. If Theodora knew anything, she knew that look. And she dared to stare back at him. Their naked eyes watched each other so long that her body blushed with heat.

Finally, Justinian blinked several times and regained his focus. Theodora looked away and grabbed a length of her hair. However, she also caught the final moment of a look from Macedonia. It was an exchange between women, but Theodora recognized the warning.

Justinian sat back again and tapped a finger on the wood surface, deep in thought. He looked over at Macedonia. "What do you think?"

"It's a bold idea, but I think it could work," she said. "We'd have to establish a second go-between for you and Hypatius."

"I may be able to approach him myself," said Justinian. "If he's attending a governor's coronation, then the Palatine Guards would be posted there."

Theodora listened to Justinian and Macedonia talk. Justinian took the council of prostitutes as seriously as if he spoke with men of rank, and without the embarrassment that Hypatius succumbed to. The sight of such a serious conversation with a woman of her profession made Theodora's desire for Justinian burn even hotter. She had long clung to a girlish notion of the man as heroic, but he was living up to the idea. Theodora rubbed her teeth against her bottom lip and dared to imagine herself with Justinian alone. She wanted him. She could have any man in the city, but not this man.

Not this man.

"Can your father arrange for you to be posted at the governor's coronation?" Macedonia said to Justinian.

He nodded. "Yes."

Theodora flinched. She suddenly realized what they were talking about. If Justinian attended the governor's party, then he'd see Theodora there. He'd see her unclothed and witness her brazen theater. She never wanted Justinian to behold the Notorious Theodora. She liked that he saw her as he did now, as a woman of intellect and ideas, not as a woman who inspired the lewd calls and groping hands of drunken men.

"And this is for you," Justinian said.

Theodora returned her attention to him. "What's that?"

Justinian lowered his hand in front of her, allowing gold coins to slide through his fingertips and form two shimmering stacks. "For your masterful work."

Macedonia put her hand on Theodora's knee. "Well done, despina. You gave us a lot of good information."

"And ideas," said Justinian. "You have a beautiful mind for strategy."

"Thank you," said Theodora, feeling discomfort at the compliment.

"Do you see now the power of information?" he said. "It isn't just in knowing what your enemies are going to do, but how they think. If I have someone tell Hypatius that he was indeed betrayed to Vitalian by a fellow Green, he'll believe it. And once he believes it, he can be made to act in all sorts of ways."

"It's seduction," said Theodora, smiling. "Macedonia taught me that all seduction is about establishing authority over others."

"Our authority," said Justinian. He arose from the table, adjusted the brooch to his cape, and lowered his voice for emphasis. "Great work." He then nodded at both women and strode out of the room with an urgency Theodora admired. He paid her and left, she thought. The exchange wasn't unlike prostitution, except Justinian paid her for her mind. Theodora realized that she and Macedonia both stared after him, but Macedonia recovered first.

"Theodora," she said. "What you did with Hypatius is remarkable, more than you might realize. You gave Justinian private information about a very secretive man. But Theodora, be careful. You've impressed him. Keep your motives firmly upon serving the post and not just one man."

"I know," said Theodora. "I serve the Blues."

Macedonia sighed and gave Theodora a long look. Then she smiled, her eyes suddenly sparkling. "Are you going to even look at those beautiful towers of solidi?"

"I'm afraid to touch them," said Theodora. "I don't want them to turn to dust."

"This is four months of pay for a single evening's work. Does this feel like dust to you?"

Macedonia picked up the gold and dropped the coins onto Theodora's palm. The gold spilled over and clattered upon the table.

"What am I to do with it all?" said Theodora. "If I spend it, won't I attract attention?"

Macedonia nodded. "Yes. You must be careful with these payments. I have someone I trust holding it on my behalf. One day I'll leave Constantinople, and I'll spend it then. You should be mindful of the days ahead, when earning at the theater is no longer possible."

Theodora thought about whom she trusted. Her mother? Perhaps she could send some of the money back to help with her daughter. Perhaps she could give some of it away. Either way, the sight of so many gold coins unsettled her. Because good things never lasted.

TWENTY-NINE

Theodora danced in the center of five other performers, moving her body to a seductive street rhythm, a double-tapping on hand drums, a quivering of tiny seashells on a rod, and a soft pattering of a tambourine. They were in a private hall, so the room was dark and the music and conversation discreet.

She wore a thin, red brassiere that left the rest of her upper torso naked. Below her navel, a low-hanging belt clung to the edge of Theodora's hips, where red linen spilled down. Several metal discs, like coins, encircled her waist and jingled as she rocked her hips back and forth.

The governor's party was different from other floorshows in that the men continued their dinner talks while the women danced. Long wood tables surrounded her in a U-shape, adorned with colorful foods, candles, and many jugs of wine. Behind the tables, Theodora saw a massive hand-carved marble hearth, easily the length of five horses, with cauldrons hanging over the flames, like a string of black pearls. The whole room filled with the aroma of roasting lamb, rosemary, spiced wine, and charred fish.

Through the haze of cook-smoke, Theodora saw uniformed officers, well-dressed aristocrats, and senators wearing togas. She, though, fixed her attention on Hypatius, who stared back at her in fascination. He sat at the *lectus medius*, the head table, beside the newly appointed governor. The two men sipped from silver goblets, conversing freely and watching Theodora.

Shouts emerged from among the onlookers for Theodora to remove her clothing, followed by laughter and other vulgar demands. She, though, offered back only subtle smiles. She knew what the men wanted to see, but tonight wasn't going to be that kind of night, she decided earlier. Tonight *couldn't* be that kind of night.

She knew Justinian lurked in the periphery of that room, dressed in the white and purple uniform of a Palatine guard, probably listening in on conversations behind the stoic face of a guard on duty. More than once, Theodora's seductive stare slipped from Hypatius and to the edges of the great hall. She scanned over a few silhouettes holding spears, trying to determine which hazy shape was Justinian.

"Where's the Notorious Theodora?" shouted a voice.

"Please, lupa! Fuck something, will you?" said a man with a Latin accent. "Show us your *cunnus!*"

Theodora watched as laughter spread through the room, and a few men slapped at the tabletops. The new governor surveyed her, elbow upon the table, wrist bent, and head tilted toward Hypatius. The two men whispered, but kept their eyes on Theodora.

When the music finished, Theodora bowed to the head table and left the performing area. A chorus of lewd comments and disapproving pleas for more followed her departure. She hurried away and ran into Macedonia, who was heading out with other women for the next dance.

"Which guardsman is Justinian?" whispered Theodora.

"What?" said Macedonia, who winced in disappointment. "Theodora, focus." Then she pushed by and fluttered out to the performing area.

As a new melody began, Theodora made her way past the long wood tables of the great hall, pandering to the men in their seats, teasing them with quick comments, allowing their hands to touch her bottom or grab at her flowing fabric.

Finally, Theodora came upon Hypatius and flung her arms around the glossy-scalped aristocrat. "Rescue me from these brutes," she said.

Hypatius' arms encircled Theodora's waist as she settled upon his lap. "Governor Hacebolus," he said. "May I introduce you to the most notorious girl in Constantinople?"

"I beg that you do," answered Hacebolus, his voice deep and masculine, like the voice of a pharaoh.

"Governor," she said, flirtatiously holding out her hand.

The man kissed her knuckles lightly before rubbing her fingers with his own. "I am Hacebolus of Tyre," he said. "I'm not a governor yet, but I enjoy hearing the title in front of my name."

Hacebolus was blatantly handsome. Lean, roguish, and white-toothed, he grinned at Theodora with all the dash of the sexually depraved. He wore many gold bangles on his wrists, with bejeweled rings that glinted with emeralds and amber. Black kohl circled his eyes in the Egyptian fashion, and his thick black beard glistened with fresh oil. One smell of his luxurious perfume made Theodora pull back, unable to conceal her reflex of attraction. "Well, well," she said. "This mysterious brute can stay."

"I would hope so," said Hypatius. "It's his party."

"You told me I'd be seeing the Notorious Theodora perform tonight," said Hacebolus with a sidelong glance at Hypatius. "There wasn't much notorious about that dance."

"The evening isn't over," said Hypatius.

"Still," continued the future governor, studying Theodora. "I see the appeal. The eyes are rather drawn in by this one," he said and glanced over Theodora's body. "Beautiful women are my weakness, unfortunately."

Theodora curled her arms around Hypatius. "Tell this governor of yours to stop trying his charms on me."

"Governor," said Hypatius. "Stop trying your charms on Theodora."

Both men laughed, but Hacebolus continued. "I wish it were me fucking this one tonight instead of you, Hypatius. How's that for charm?" he said and pressed the rim of his wine goblet to Theodora's lips, tilting it. "Drink. A little wine perhaps will loosen your spirits."

Theodora took a sip. "My spirits are loose when I wake in the morning. I need no excuse."

Both men raised their eyebrows.

"You need something," said Hacebolus. "I want to see you with those clothes off. I want my imagination to run afoul with thoughts of pleasuring you."

Theodora realized that she would have a hard time getting Hypatius to talk if this governor-to-be continued dominating the conversation.

If he is arrogant, doubt him.

She laughed mockingly. "So you fancy yourself a master of pleasuring women?"

Hacebolus returned a shallow bow. "A woman's body is a garden of delicate flower buds, Theodora. And I know how to open every single one."

"Now this I need to hear," said Theodora.

"How very un-Roman of you," said Hypatius. "A man takes his pleasure from a woman. It is he who begins the act and he who ends it."

"That is where you err, Lord Hypatius," Hacebolus said."For the Levantine is different from the Roman on the matter of women. You Romans turn your women around and mount them like dogs, without imagination, without knowledge of all her possibilities. It's like using a finely crafted flute as a baton to beat your slaves with."

Other dinner guests tittered.

Hypatius nodded. "And I suppose in your household, it is the slave, then, who gives the orders?"

"Well, a slave is a slave. They aren't full men and women like you and me. But a woman. She is our ancient partner."

"Then tell us, Governor," said Theodora. "If you are a true master. What is the secret of a woman's pleasure?"

"It's not so much a secret as it is a matter of will. A man must first be willing to try. Right, Hypatius?"

"If that man's an effeminate Persian, I suppose."

Theodora sensed the tension. She knew that at any moment, Hypatius could turn on Hacebolus and use his high imperial rank to rebuke the future governor's unflattering debate. But Hypatius only blustered.

"For men, the mere sight of a beautiful woman makes us idiots," said Hacebolus. "Our intellect collapses until we're focused only on what we see. When we touch a woman's body, it's as if to confirm she's there. We see her; now we must touch her, our eyes and hands operating stupidly," he said and gesticulated.

Theodora laughed at the governor-to-be, settling into a grin. "Go on." And she felt Hypatius look away impatiently.

"Women are more complex. Nothing penetrates a woman's mind more than what she perceives by touch. But a woman too, can be reduced to an unthinking creature, as empty-headed as a man," said Hacebolus. "He need only to narrow her focus upon his touch, but slowly, skillfully. And soon, she'll have the urgent need to reach out, to touch, to feel the man dominating her and pleasuring her all at once."

Theodora's eyes slipped over the man's shapely chest and muscular arms. "A being with knowledge of a woman's pleasure, but with the body of a perfect man, you say? Well, such a creature doesn't exist," she said. "More like the strange statues I see in the city, with the body of a man, but the head of a wolf, or the wings of an eagle sprouting from behind. Such creatures are purely mythical."

Hacebolus raised his eyebrows in delight. "A disbeliever in our midst. Well then, let me take you into the labyrinth and show you what awaits you at the center."

"I like this one," Theodora said, having failed to silence Hacebolus. She couldn't resort to the blunt tool of embarrassing the man at his own coronation. For now, the governor would command the conversation.

"Yes, yes," said Hypatius, shifting in his seat. "All this talk of animal heads and human torsos is making me lose my appetite."

Theodora leaned playfully into the old man. "Are you already jealous when my attentions are elsewhere?"

Hypatius looked up at Theodora. "I'm jealous of no man."

"Can a woman not be attracted to more than one man?" she said.

"If you had to decide between two men, which quality would make you choose one over the other?" said Hypatius.

Theodora needed an answer that flattered both men but favored Hypatius. "Power," she said. "Power keeps a woman warm at night." And she ran her fingers along the purple seam of Hypatius' robe.

Hacebolus gave her a dubious look and toasted. "Power it is then. To a crown of gold, a throne of purple stone, and a bed of naked whores."

As he sipped from his goblet, Theodora stared into the future governor's eyes. He was the kind of man women like herself most resisted but moved toward quietly when eyes looked elsewhere. "So, if you're to be a governor, where will you govern?" said Theodora.

"Cyrenaica," he said in that throaty voice of his. "The Pentapolis."

As Theodora listened, she noticed Macedonia watching the conversation. Her mentor nodded at her. Apparently, she was pleased to see Theodora holding the attention of the two most influential men in the room.

Hypatius interjected. "From a military officer in Syria to the governor of Cyrenaica. Your climb is ambitious."

"I purchased the post fairly," said Hacebolus. "And I know you negotiated heavily with the emperor in my favor. For that, I am indebted to you."

"You can repay me right now and quit stealing Theodora's attention."

Both men laughed.

"Where's Cyrenaica?" said Theodora. "I've never heard of these places you speak of."

"It's at the bitter edge of the Roman Empire," said Hypatius. "In a western stretch of North Africa, a desert country far, far from here."

"It's true. Cyrenaica is a remote frontier, but it runs along beautiful coastline. It has warm skies and palm trees," said Hacebolus, leaning forward and setting his mischievous eyes on Theodora. "You should come with me. The Romans built a new palace out there in the Libyan deserts. I'm to occupy this palace and could find a cozy room for you."

Theodora grew serious. Hacebolus just offered her what all prostitutes dreamt of most: a way out of the brothels and in the private company of a wealthy man.

"A concubine?" said Hypatius. "In Cyrenaica?"

Theodora rubbed a finger along her bottom lip and held silent.

Hacebolus continued. "North Africa can be a place of exotic pleasures. You see, I make no secret about who I am. I'm a man who covets the company of beautiful women, and I mean to indulge," he said and leaned back. "If you companioned me, you could live in a naked state and fall to sleep upon crimson silks to the sound of a lapping sea. No more brothels. No more theaters. Only luxury, idleness, and pleasure."

That sounded so good to Theodora. "But I belong to this city, Governor," she said and rested her head against Hypatius. "I have family and friends here."

Hacebolus shrugged. "So? Consider my offer. I'd purchase your indenture if you agreed."

"Theodora doesn't want to be part of some North African concubinary," said Hypatius. "Have you lost your senses?"

Hacebolus shook his head and looked at Theodora with sarcastic, lazy eyes. "Forgive me. It was a rude offer." He then gulped down his wine, turned away, and fixed his gaze on the floor dancers. He looked disinterested in further conversation.

But Theodora wanted to hear more tales of the desert and the palace. Had a great opportunity just slipped away?

Hypatius gave her a friendly squeeze and whispered in her ear. "Don't mind him. He's a man who likes to possess his women, like livestock."

"You don't understand," she whispered back. "It's the best a woman in our profession can get." Not long ago she would have leaped at such an incredible offer, but now she had serious work in Constantinople. She had Justinian. Theodora searched the room again but still didn't see Justinian. She refocused on her task with Hypatius. "But I'd never go to Africa," she said and wondered if Hypatius might counter with a similar offer.

As if on cue, the music slowed to a conclusion. The men clapped as the dancers left the stage. Hacebolus looked back at Theodora, eying her with disappointment. He then stood up and slapped the tabletop to gather everyone's attention. "Good friends and Romans!" he said. Slowly, the murmur in the room fell silent. "Thank you all for attending my coronation. As you all know, next year, I set out for North Africa to take over as governor of Cyrenaica. We've been graced tonight with . . . um . . . ," and he looked down at Theodora. "Well, let's say conservative entertainment, considering the talent present."

Theodora glanced around the room as the men laughed and nodded.

Hacebolus continued. "I think we all had something different in mind this evening, more than just dancing anyway. But it seems our talent is smitten by the emperor's nephew at the moment," he said to more laughter. Hacebolus held up a hand to quiet them. "In fairness, we shouldn't blame her. A woman must favor her highest patron. But where does that leave us?" he said, provoking a mild tumult. "It does put a quandary into our evening's entertainment, and I'm not one for a dull party."

The men of the room slapped the tabletops and voiced their agreement.

"Where's he going with this?" whispered Hypatius.

Theodora shrugged. Hacebolus held the room's full attention, and she couldn't help but admire his theatrics.

"Back home in Tyre, we have a long tradition of theater, both good and obscene. Is there anyone else here from the Levant?" said Hacebolus.

One of the senators spoke. "I'm from Antioch."

"Antioch!" said Hacebolus. "Now there's a city known for its vices and entertainment. Tell me, Senator, you've been to the theaters of Antioch. Name me a play. Think of only the most depraved, most audacious, most shocking act that ever befell your eyes."

Without hesitation, the senator answered. "*Leda and the Swan.*"

Hacebolus clapped once, the sound like the crack of a whip. "*Leda and the Swan!* I knew I could rely on a man from Antioch. Thank you, Senator." He then signaled a manservant on the far side of the room, who departed as the crowd grew louder with anticipation. "Now to the women. I have summoned our swan. Who then shall be Leda? Which beauty here tonight will volunteer?"

Heads turned and searched the room. Then, commotion stirred on the far side of the room. Theodora saw a large man pulling one of the actresses toward the performing area by the arm to a chorus of cheers. She recognized the actress as Indaro, a long-legged woman with a cascade of brown hair. Indaro laughed, but resisted the man, squirming to free her arm from his grip. As the two drew near the stage, she leaned away, making a serious effort to break free. She seemed to think the whole ordeal was a jest, but the more she struggled, the more the men in the hall cheered her on. Hacebolus too, had a lingering grin as he watched.

"What are they going to make that girl do?" said Hypatius.

Theodora leaned in. "It's *Leda and the Swan*. It's an obscene version of a Greek play."

"How so?"

"Because a woman lies backward and lets a goose eat grain right off her *cunnus*," she said.

Aghast, Hypatius glanced back at the stage.

The large man pulled Indaro onto the performing area with sporadic yanks. Indaro was smiling, but Theodora recognized fear in her friend's eyes.

Hypatius lifted his lips to Theodora's ear. "These men are animals. We don't have to stay for this *obscenitas*. We can leave if you'd prefer."

"Tell them to stop," Theodora said. "She doesn't want to do the act."

Hypatius looked out at the room and sucked in his lips. "They're too well riled up."

"But you're the nephew of the emperor," said Theodora.

"Well, look at them," Hypatius said. "The governor has incited a near riot against that poor woman."

Theodora looked back at Indaro. Most of the officers and senators stood and faced the stage, cheering and clapping. The room then erupted with shock when the manservant reappeared, carrying a large circus bird, a goose, which flapped its wings and honked in agitation. Another man dropped a sack of barley onto the stage. The large man who held Indaro by the elbow reached down, dipped his hand into the sack, raised it out, and let the kernels drain through his fingertips. Again, Indaro stepped away, and again, he yanked her back.

Theodora stood up. "Stop!"

Some of the men turned to see her, but Hypatius pulled at her gown. "What are you doing?" he said.

She ignored him and shouted again. "Stop!"

Theodora strode toward the performing area, slowly gathering the attention of the crowd. She noticed that Macedonia too, watched with concern; Theodora was abandoning her work with Hypatius, after all. But she couldn't let her friend be humiliated, not at the hands of a savage crowd.

So Theodora took center stage beside Indaro. "I see that you imbeciles are finally ready for a show," she said.

The onlookers burst into applause and banged on the table even louder. Theodora smiled back at them theatrically, just as she would in between the jests of a comedic pantomime. The men seemed to believe that the whole bit with Indaro was contrived all along. The Notorious Theodora was simply making her dramatic entrance. She glanced at Indaro. "You better get out of here."

The girl covered her half-naked body, turned, and hurried off the stage.

Theodora then reached behind her back, removed her red brassiere, and flung the garment into the crowd. Piece by piece, she peeled away her clothing until she was nude on stage, despite the law against full nudity. But who in the crowd would enforce such a law?

Hands on hips, Theodora turned side to side and presented her bare body to the crowd. By the thunderous reaction in the room, these men couldn't fathom a woman who delighted in such an act as Leda. Indaro's reaction was expected. Theodora was an unnatural, erotic creature quite beyond their imaginations. And so, as always, she captivated them.

Off-stage, the goose flapped loudly as the minstrels began a light-hearted melody. She watched as the empire's most powerful men sat back in their chairs to watch the show. Hypatius too, sat back down, apparently willing to wait for her.

"Romans!" shouted Hacebolus in a grand, booming voice. "As promised, The Notorious Theodora!"

As she picked up the sack of grain, she suddenly remembered that Justinian was out there among them, somewhere, watching her become this other woman. And on a night where she tried to be inconspicuous, she was instead on the verge of her most salacious act yet.

THIRTY

Theodora sat at the empty table in the Chamber of Cupid. The shutters were closed to keep out the winter cold, but she still heard the cheering crowds at the distant Hippodrome. Their wild chorus sounded similar to the revelers from last night's final performance, only far off, at a safe distance, with chariots occupying their attention instead of geese.

And Justinian had been there, somewhere. She never saw him, but he would've seen her. He saw the Notorious Theodora at her most brazen and now he was late for their meeting. She wondered how he could ever look at her again as a woman of intelligence.

She shifted and winced at the soreness of her body, the places where the bird's bill had pinched her skin. Just as the despair crept deeper into Theodora's thoughts, the doors to the chamber opened. Justinian strode into the room, acknowledging Theodora with a nod. He sat and flung his cape over one shoulder, tossing snowflakes into the air. Macedonia wasn't with him.

"Good morning," he said. "How are you?"

Theodora blinked. She searched his eyes for any judgment on her, any hint of disgust or discomfort, but there was nothing.

"I'm well," she said. "Considering the party."

"I know," said Justinian. He then held up a small black leather coin purse and gave it a shake. The heavy coins clinked as he dropped the purse in front of Theodora. "That's for you. Twice your usual amount."

"Justinian, the reason I went on that stage—"

"There's no need to explain. I saw what happened," he said, his look stern. "But we can't talk about that right now. You and I must stay centered on our work."

"Of course." Theodora had no habit speaking about her private affairs. Indeed, she often showed the world a veneer that reflected the very opposite of what she felt. She nodded. "So, Hypatius," she said. "I spent another long evening with him."

"Is that so?"

Theodora hesitated. She couldn't quite shake the urge to justify herself to this man, the man in the stands, the man who once thought her worth saving.

Justinian smiled. "Did our friend finally consummate his arrangement? Perhaps rediscover his manhood?"

Theodora shook her head. "He didn't even try this time."

"What the hell is he getting out of all this?" he said in disbelief.

"He wants someone to listen to him," Theodora said, defending Hypatius. "He's adjusting to a lesser role in life, and I understand him. Hypatius thought the world had a special place for him. But the world passed him by."

Justinian seemed curious about the insight. "Did he tell you anything specific last night?"

"Oh yes. After the party, we had our best night yet. He mentioned you by name."

"Me?"

"In passing. But he spoke mainly about your father, Justin." She paused for emphasis. "Hypatius said that if the emperor dies without naming a successor, that it's the count of the Excubitors who directs the election. Your father."

Justinian remained stoic. "Did you sense that he suspected you as an informer?"

"No," she said. "But is it true?"

"Is what true?"

Theodora leaned forward. "That your father would control the election of the next emperor?"

Justinian studied Theodora, his eyes wide, the way a cat's eyes look from a secret corner of a room, guarded, stealthy, intelligent. "Justin's my adopted father. But yes, he's Count of the Excubitors. He guards the emperor day and night. If the emperor were to pass away, the Excubitors would place the Daphne Palace under military control. That means the Excubitors hold quite a bit of power in those hours. Since the Daphne Palace is connected directly to the Hippodrome, it's the Excubitors who'll escort each imperial candidate out to the crowds at the Hippodrome. So, my father has no power over who the mob will elect, but he's involved in which candidates the people will behold."

Theodora grinned. "But how intriguing. The path of the throne goes through your father."

"I'm helping my father gather information about potential candidates," he said. "The more he knows about who'll come forward in the election, the safer the election will be."

Theodora didn't believe that duty alone was Justinian's motive. She sensed he had a personal agenda on the matter. "So you were adopted?" she said.

"Not that this is important, but yes," he said.

"Then Justinian must be your adopted name, as in adopted son of Justin?"

He nodded.

"What was your birth name?"

Justinian's expression became formidable. "Theodora, my background isn't what I'm paying you to find out. I already know my background."

"I'm just curious," she said. "Or is your birth name a big secret?"

"Not at all."

A tension mixed with the silence that followed.

"Petrus," he said. "My real name is Petrus."

"Petrus," Theodora said again, as if testing out the sound of the word. She slipped into a girlish smile that he didn't return. The name Petrus wasn't commanding at all but had the whiff of a common man. Hearing his birth name aloud gave Theodora a soft sense of Justinian as a normal man, one capable of error or even weakness. A slight flutter emerged in her belly at an unexpected feeling of intimacy.

"Now, getting back to Hypatius," said Justinian.

Theodora ignored him. "I didn't want to do that act last night."

Justinian glanced sideways in frustration and then reset an authoritative gaze on Theodora. "Hypatius," he said.

"I was trying to help that girl. Those men were going to force her into that awful act."

Justinian sighed as if conceding a minor point. "Was she your friend?"

"Yes. And she was crumbling in the face of that horrible pressure. I hate when a crowd turns against someone like that."

"Is that why you feel sympathy for Hypatius?"

"Probably."

"Well, don't get too sympathetic. Hypatius isn't your friend and, we have work to do with him."

"I know. You're right."

Again, Justinian tilted his head to study Theodora. His demeanor softened. "If you must know, I thought what you did last night was admirable," he said. "I left the room when you took the stage for that poor girl. I couldn't see you go through with it."

Theodora glanced up at Justinian as if startled, heat filling her chest. *He did care for her*, she thought. He just broke his veneer of a dispassionate employer. "So you didn't see anything?"

He shook his head. "No. You were at that party solely at my bidding, so I felt responsible."

"I'm glad I was there," she said. "Better that I was there."

Justinian winced. "How's that better?"

"Because I can take it. I can wake up the next day and carry on. Indaro couldn't," Theodora said and continued to stare at Justinian unabashed. They were alone, and they both knew it. She wished that he'd reach out and touch her, but something in that man's mind always held firm.

He leaned forward. "Well, I'm very sorry all that happened."

"So who was your real father?"

"Theodora, we can't spend this time on personal questions directed at me," he said. "I'm paying you to inform me of the goings-on out there. Do you understand me? Our arrangement cannot afford any misunderstandings."

Theodora remained unfazed this time by his warning. "Can't I be curious about you?"

"All right, now that's enough. I pay you—"

"Yes, you pay me huge sums of gold," said Theodora, snatching up the leather coin purse and holding it up in front of Justinian. "But such a fortune only draws attention, so what can I do with it? I have a brothel-keeper, Justinian. His name is Tiberius, and if he knew about this money, he'd take most of it. If I spend your gold, if I show up at the brothel wearing fine silks or gold or rubies, he'll know. If other girls see me spending lavishly, they'll tell."

Justinian's eyes narrowed on Theodora, but confusion mixed with his show of anger.

"If I hide it, someone will find it," she said. "Someone always finds it. You should hear the stories. Some girls stash away a great fortune, only to have it stolen while they're working one night."

"Well then, what the hell are you doing with all that money?"

Theodora lifted her chin. "I have a daughter. She's being raised by my mother, so I give as much as I can to her. But again, I can only give so much, else I draw unwanted attention to them instead of me. The rest I give to the Orphanage of Zoticus."

Justinian squinted as if in disbelief. "An orphanage?"

"Yes, because at least there someone cares about the poor girls of this city. Such girls are fed and clothed there. Hopefully, they'll have a few years of peace before they grow into women and join me in the brothels."

"So why are you doing this at all?" said Justinian. "Considering the risks that come with the post?"

"Because of you," she said accusingly but wished she hadn't.

Justinian finally sat back and rubbed his forehead. He took a deep breath and exhaled loudly. "Since to this point, you've essentially done our work for free, what exactly do you want to know about me?"

"Who was your real father?"

Justinian stared at Theodora long enough for the moment to become uncomfortable. "All right," he said with an emphatic nod. "My father was from a fishing village on the Vardar River. He died of fever when I was an infant."

"He was . . . a peasant?" Theodora said, unsure she understood properly.

"Yes."

The man she gazed upon had all the polish of Roman wealth, hard angles, glinting trinkets, and a strong, masculine presence. There was no trace of past poverty on the man's face, no evidence of the countryside. Even his language flowed with alluring precision. To Theodora, Justinian was not just aristocratic, but the most aristocratic of them all. How could someone so lowborn appear to be so impressive? Was not birthright the source of advantage?

"Who's Justin then?"

Justinian hesitated, tapping a finger on the table as if musing whether to answer. "Justin is my uncle. He enlisted in the Roman army and earned a command. He was a common villager when he left, but one morning he returned wearing an officer's uniform. The idea that any person could transform themselves into something greater captured my imagination. I mean, if he could do it, so could I, right? Justin offered to adopt me and take me to Constantinople. So I left my mother behind and came here, to the capital. I was just a boy."

"And what of your mother?"

"She died."

A heavy silence settled over the room. Theodora and Justinian stared at each other for a long while. But the truth of it, she thought. Justinian was a peasant from the countryside, just like the countless other peasants who trudged in through the city gates each day. Theodora remembered watching the masses upon the street when she was a little girl, when she'd sneak out, climb a tree, and look upon the Middle Way. How interesting those dusty travelers all seemed to her. And Petrus was once in that crowd, probably staring up at the statues with the fascination of a boy, bumping into the foot traffic of an unfamiliar city. Theodora saw countless such boys in those nameless crowds.

Justinian's unexpected candidness ended Theodora's protest and shifted power back to him. "Now you tell me," he said, his voice growing colder. "What else did Hypatius say?"

Theodora sighed. "Hypatius told me that his cousin, Probus, came to him last week, more than a little alarmed."

"What alarmed him?"

"Apparently, a few people confronted Probus and asked whether he'd back a different candidate, should the Greens pass over Hypatius."

"What did he say?"

"He said he'd support whatever decision the Greens made," said Theodora. "But he only said that out of fear. His loyalty is to Hypatius and the Anastasius bloodline."

Justinian nodded. "Of course. What we really need is the *name* of the man the Greens want on that throne instead."

"Your turn," said Theodora. "What's your real interest in who becomes emperor?"

Justinian, who stared off in thought, now refocused. "I told you, to help my father manage a potentially violent transition of power. The wrong candidate could trigger a revolt."

"Surely you care beyond that," she said.

Justinian meshed his fingers together. "I care, young Theodora, because what happened to Rome could happen here."

"Why should I worry if the empire collapses?" she said.

"How can you say that? Civilization may be flawed, but it's the best effort of common people to transform themselves into something greater, to find prosperity instead of barbarism. Civilization must make a stand against the coming darkness, Theodora. That's what I want. And if the tides are to be turned, it must happen right here, from this city."

"Again, so what?"

Justinian appeared suspicious. "An odd question for a political informer."

"What do we get, Justinian?"

"Who?"

"Women like me," she said. "What do we get?"

For the first time, Justinian had no answer.

Theodora nodded. "You don't understand. It doesn't matter whether the emperor is a Blue or a Green or a Roman or a Goth; life will go on for us in the brothels. The sun will come up, we'll remove our clothes, and then we'll offer up our bodies to a city that despises us. And there's no way out. In the end, no matter what you do up there, nothing will change for us down here."

Justinian sat back, fixing his eyes on Theodora, not blinking once for a long while. He seemed to carefully ruminate the depth of Theodora's position.

"I see," he finally said. "Nothing much would change for you, would it? You know, Justin taught me that all people have worth, even the common and the poor. He said the best way to unlock a man's genius was to give him a responsibility, one where failure is possible. The truth is, I've used his lesson to gather information in the brothels. I was warned that prostitutes are a depraved class of people who couldn't be trusted with serious responsibility. And yet I've seen otherwise. I've given women tasks that might cost them their lives, and yet so many have accepted the terrible risks without hesitation, yourself included. Society ignores and condemns these women, but I don't. And so, I believe I have an advantage. I'm not embarrassed to say that I've been inspired by the courage of women, but their moments aren't often acknowledged. Last night was an example."

Theodora felt a light heat in her cheeks. *He* thought *she* was courageous? The man in the stands?

"And now I learn that my payments to these women may be a burden to them," said Justinian. "So, tell me, Theodora. What could an emperor do to help women such as yourself?"

Theodora never developed a vision of society that was favorable to women. But Justinian was asking. "Women should be able to leave the brothel if they want to," said Theodora. "They shouldn't be owned by a brothel-keeper the way a slave is owned by a master."

He nodded. "That's indenture. It's written into the chattel laws. What else?"

"Well, we should be able to keep our earnings and pay our dues willingly the way men do at the guilds." Theodora paused. "And a prostitute should be able to marry whomever she wants. Most of us meet wealthy men all the time, but the marriage laws ban prostitutes from marrying noblemen. Some women could leave this life behind if only they could marry."

"Everything you said is a boundary for women, boundaries etched in Roman law," said Justinian. "A Roman emperor can rewrite those laws."

"Ah, but would he?"

"He might," said Justinian with a dashing smile. "It would be quite an undertaking."

"Well, then it would unlock his genius, as you say."

Justinian laughed. But his smiling eyes settled into the stare of a man who saw past the beauty and admired the woman within. This time, he didn't hide his stare.

Theodora tilted her head as she watched him, exposing her neckline. And suddenly she felt the mesmerizing pull of her body toward Justinian, an upwelling of buoyancy and heat, a narrowing of her thoughts upon the need to touch another person or to be touched. Desire, after all, was a psychic urge, an exciting conspiracy that could progress without words or plans. Theodora used to indulge the sensation, but she couldn't do anything with this man. She knew better. Against her will, Theodora broke the tension. "Last night, Hacebolus offered to take me with him to North Africa. He said I could reside with him in the palace there."

"Hacebolus said that?"

"To a woman such as myself, an offer like that is a dream. We all hope a rich man will arrange to have us leave the brothels and hide us away from the world. And in a palace, no less."

"What did you tell him?" said Justinian.

"I refused. I'd rather work as I do now, for a man who sees even the smallest of people as so worthwhile."

Justinian narrowed his eyes at Theodora. Then he suddenly arose. For a moment, he stared down at Theodora accusingly, as though perceiving some trick. But the darkness slowly slipped away, and his eyes widened, revealing a disarmed gaze, one of desire. He reached out and slid his knuckles along Theodora's cheekbone, his breath slowing.

Theodora closed her eyes and exhaled audibly, having longed for such a touch. Her skin was like the still waters of a pond, and his caress sent ripples across the surface of her body. When she looked up at Justinian, the flame in his eyes strengthened.

"Sorry I'm late," interrupted a voice from the far side of the room, a woman's voice.

Theodora turned her head as if slapped. She saw Macedonia walking into the room. The look in her mentor's eyes held notes of a warning, but not quite accusation.

Justinian recoiled. "What delayed you?"

"I was on a pleasure barge since last evening," she said, coming to stand beside Justinian.

Theodora stood up, her body flush with heat. "I should probably leave anyway."

"No, stay," said Macedonia, who turned to face Justinian. "We need to deal with this, given the dangers to us all in this work."

Theodora glanced at Justinian, who folded his arms at the chest and stared at his intertwined forearms. "Nothing happened," she said.

Macedonia ignored her and continued to wait for Justinian's response.

Finally, Justinian nodded. "We need Theodora," he said, recovering his authority. "So let's allow some time to pass. In the meantime, Macedonia, I want you to serve as a liaison between Theodora and myself."

Macedonia bowed wordlessly.

Theodora tried to appear undaunted, but her mind raced at the possibility of being unable to see Justinian. She reminded herself that Macedonia was protecting the group, that private attractions had no place in their association together. But, despite the logic, Theodora still wondered whether jealousy lurked below the surface of her mentor's expressionless veneer.

Justinian looked frustrated. He stared across the room at nothing for a long while, and then suddenly turned and departed. He didn't look back at Theodora.

With great effort, Theodora faced Macedonia. "Nothing happened."

"And it must stay that way."

"So, what does this mean?"

"It means, despina, we'll take some time to recompose."

Theodora nodded, not wanting to show further guilt or disappointment. "I understand." But then, against better judgment, she asked the one question she knew she shouldn't. "But how much time?"

THIRTY-ONE

Rains pelted Constantinople through most of the day. In a brothel, rainy days were slow days. Theodora, like most of the prostitutes, sat upon a couch near the main entrance, beneath the dim crimson light of hanging lanterns and the sound of rain upon a wooden roof. This was a time of vast boredom, and the women fanned themselves with ostrich feathers, making idle conversation.

Theodora thought mostly of Justinian. She hadn't seen him since that one sweet day that ended so abruptly, when he revealed feelings for her, when he touched her bare cheek. And Theodora's work with Hypatius slowed as well. Macedonia explained the slowdown as natural for an informer, simply the ebbs and flows of clandestine activity. But not being able to see Justinian, though, if only to say "forget it happened," left the matter unresolved, less wonderful, more of a splinter in her thoughts.

Tiberius interrupted the quiet room. "Theodora," he said. "You have a caller. Let's go."

Theodora arose as if startled. "In this rain?"

"Oh yes. It's a palace client, so be quick," said Tiberius, gesturing excitedly.

Justinian?

Theodora adjusted her hair. "And I thought today would be no fun."

The other girls teased her as she made her way past Tiberius and into the rear fornices. Whoever the caller might be, he entered through the discretionary entrance at the back. There, she saw a small retinue of imperial retainers, their armor glistening with wetness, and their leather tunics dripping into puddles below. They all looked up with fascination at the scantily dressed Theodora.

She slowed and forced a smile. "Well, well. Am I to entertain one or all of you?"

None of the soldiers laughed, and Hypatius soon slipped out from between them. "I needed to see you," he said.

Hypatius wore fine attire dampened by the rain, with a heavy purple cape flung over his left shoulder and chest. The color matched the dark hues below his eyes. Theodora thought the old man looked exhausted. "It's been so long, Hypatius. I've missed you," she said and took his hands, ignoring the clammy wetness.

"I just needed to see you. And I had to get out of the palace."

Theodora led Hypatius to the privacy of a nearby fornice. He ducked in behind Theodora and glanced around at the small enclave where Theodora worked.

"Such a small space," he said.

"What I do doesn't require much space."

"I guess I always thought of you as I've seen you," he said. "A beautiful woman who makes opulence look plain."

"Does my real life disappoint you?"

"No," he said. "Not at all."

Theodora leaned over and took off the soaked purple cape. Then she gave Hypatius a cloth to dry his face and hands. Theodora had two men who needed her, she thought, two men who loved her, yet neither man could touch her, one out of weakness, the other out of strength. She sat Hypatius on the bed and rubbed his back in slow circles. "Seeing you makes me happy. I was beginning to think you lost your gleam for me."

"I came because I've been restless," said Hypatius, patting his face with the cloth. He avoided Theodora's gaze as he spoke. "I haven't been sleeping much and believe it or not, you're the one person who knows my worries best." He looked into his lap. "Or at least knows about the things of which I wish to speak."

"Of course. Anything, Hypatius. What's wrong?"

"My uncle, the emperor," he said. "He's looking old and frail, and I believe his time is coming. Soon the Lord God will take him up to the kingdom beyond life. I fear that day. In my heart and bones, I fear it."

Theodora changed her voice from soothing to firm. "You're afraid of the succession?"

"It's not just that," Hypatius said, arising and keeping his back to Theodora. "Once the emperor goes, I think I'll be joining him soon after." He turned and looked at Theodora with concern in his eyes.

She held his gaze. "You think they'll have you killed?"

"Yes," he said. "I can feel it when I walk through the palace. It's in the eyes of the nobles and officeholders. My uncle will die soon, and they're all biding their time, waiting patiently for it to happen. They know full well who they mean to replace him. And it's not me. So now I fear my brother, my cousin, and me will become the unwanted rivals to an ambitious few."

"Have you thought about ways to stop that from happening?" she said. "Thought about it? That's all I ever think about. It's all I ever dream about whenever I do find sleep. Last night, I was on my way to an imperial council. I was crossing the courtyard when I suddenly saw two Palatine guards racing from St. Stephens toward the Daphne. Their urgent speed led me to believe that the emperor had died, that the palace was being sealed off. I stood with such terror, completely unprepared. I thought, *this is it!* To my relief, the guardsmen were involved in nothing more than a drill," he said and whirled around. "Even though the emperor lived, I saw at that moment how my life would end. Someone's going to slaughter my family line like lambs."

Hypatius sat down beside Theodora again. She leaned in and rested her head on the man's shoulder. His body felt hot with distress.

"And that's not the worst part," he said. "I couldn't sleep for most of last night. I stayed up and paced in my bedchamber, hating every moment that passed. I finally found sleep sometime in the night and had the most terrifying dream. I can still feel the dream inside my body," Hypatius said, his hand clutching at his chest. "I dreamt that I was in the Triclinium. The emperor was asleep on his throne, and I stood there beside him, keeping watch. That's when I noticed a dark figure enter the throne room in the shadows. An assassin. Alarmed, I went to wake Anastasius, to warn him of the danger, and when I looked down, he was gone. The throne was empty. That's when I knew . . ." The old man's voice trailed into an icy whisper. "That's when I knew the assassin came not for my uncle . . . but for me."

"What did you do?"

Hypatius breathed irregularly, gripped by an overwhelming fear. "I just stood there. Just like I did in the courtyard earlier. I just stood in place, unable to move my legs, as if any effort to escape would be futile. All I could do was to watch as the assassin walked toward me, his blade drawn, like a silver tooth in the darkness." Hypatius faltered, succumbing to awkward sobbing.

Theodora pulled the man's wet head into her warm chest and allowed him to cry.

After a moment, he pulled back. "I awoke from the dream knowing the ugly truth. I know now that I haven't the courage nor spirit to resist what's coming. I'll stand there like a coward, close my eyes, and let it all happen. I'll let these men murder me," he said. "They'll murder my wife, my children." He covered his mouth with his wrist, frightened by such a thought. "And I'll let them do it. You don't know what this feels like."

But again, Theodora did know. More than anything else, Theodora knew the paralysis; she had spent her years trying to forget that feeling. "Who are they to take anything from you?" she said coldly. "You have to fight back."

"I can't."

"You must, for your family's sake if not your own."

"There's nowhere for us to go. Even if we fled the city, they'd find us. No one supports my claim anymore, and no one will help us. I have nothing!"

Theodora stood up and pulled the man's head so that Hypatius looked her in the eyes. "You have me," she said. "Now I know many people, powerful people. I may be a prostitute, but I'm also a woman who's invited to entertain men of all kinds. That includes powerful men who know other powerful men. I can help you, Hypatius. If you trust me, I can help you."

Hypatius collected himself. "Who do you know that would help me?"

This was the moment, she thought.

Theodora drew in a deep breath and steadied herself. "You say the Greens have chosen their candidate for the throne, but they aren't the only ones out there," she said. "I hear all sorts of talk. Men speak in front of me all the time and think I don't listen. Sometimes they speak of the emperor and succession, and when they do, I always think of you. What if I told you there is a group out there who would protect you?"

"Protect me?"

"Call me a fool, call me a stupid whore," she said. "But I believe I know these men. I even believe they'd listen to me if I suggested they help you." She paused. "As long as you offered to help them back."

The room grew silent. Hypatius looked pensive for a long while, and Theodora hid an involuntary swallow. He glanced at Theodora with a new set of eyes, as if seeing her in a different light, or possibly seeing her for the first time. Hypatius rarely met Theodora's eyes with so unbroken a stare. But the look was the most honest she yet shared with the old man. She was exposed. Now she had to wait silently at all costs.

Hypatius finally sighed, relaxed, and took Theodora's hands. "I don't think you're a stupid whore. Maybe I'm a fool, but when I hear you say that you can help me, I believe it." He laughed. "You're strong, Theodora. You're smart and capable and brave—everything I'm not."

Theodora smiled and kissed Hypatius on the cheek. "I know what it is to feel helpless."

He then squeezed both of Theodora's hands until his grip, unexpectedly, turned painful. "I know the name," he said. "I know who the Greens want for the next emperor."

"Who?"

"I'll give you the name, Theodora," he said and relaxed his grip. "But first, tell me who your friends are."

Theodora realized that Hypatius understood the situation, after all. But, if she exposed Justinian as her contact, she'd expose herself as a spy and Hypatius could do whatever he pleased with the information.

So, thought Theodora, everything they both perceived about their relationship– the intimacy, the empathy, the private confessions, and sincerity—the effects of her entire seduction ebbed back, as though a great sea drained of its water. And as those waters receded, the trust had to be there, standing like a mountain, impervious to renewed fears and doubt. Now Theodora understood in full why Macedonia had said that real seductions were rooted in honesty, not truth. Otherwise, any insincerity that lurked below the surface risked being exposed in this very moment. Theodora held his eyes. "I'm a friend of Justinian."

"Justinian of the *Scholae Palatine*?"

"Now you know," she said. "Do you want his help or not?"

Hypatius stared back with his mouth agape. Then he drew in a long, deep breath and nodded. "I like Justinian. He's a capable young man. Highly intelligent. Well respected," he said as if counting off the advantages of the alliance. "And his father is Count of the Excubitors, is he not?"

Theodora nodded.

Hypatius smiled to himself. "Clever." Then he arose. "Theodora, I want you to arrange a meeting between your friend and me. Just promise me that you're sincere in this, that you care for me as much as you show." This time, his words had no fear in them, no sorrow or pleading. He was a man at the sober end of a dire situation.

"I promise," she said. "Now let me get to work on it."

By the time Hypatius left, the rain cleared and the sun returned. Theodora, though, had to send word to Justinian. She felt a rising excitement at being needed again, at getting a chance to get involved again. She hurried across the street to the Amphitheater. Her presence was rarely welcome there, but she wasn't a stranger in the building either. Most of the thespians milled about, mingling, tossing dice or painting stage décor. Macedonia was nowhere to be found. Worse yet, none at the theater knew her whereabouts.

Twice, Theodora combed the back area of the Amphitheater until she finally believed Macedonia must be elsewhere. Like Theodora, her mentor often spent time with a wealthy class of men as a courtesan. Some visits could last days.

When nightfall came, and when Macedonia still hadn't shown, Theodora did something that could get her in trouble. She sent word to Justinian, requesting an emergency meeting . . . but to ensure his agreement, she sent the message as Macedonia.

THIRTY-TWO

Theodora splashed water on her face and cleaned her body. The young stagehand, Bacchus, arose from the fornice bed, scooped up his brown robe, and brushed off the dust. Theodora took his robe. She put on a girdle and slipped the robe over her body as Bacchus watched. The robe was long enough to cover her legs and shape. "You'll get one more for free when I return," she said and kissed the boy on the cheek.

"How long will I have to wait here?"

Theodora smiled seductively. "As long as it takes."

Then she pulled the hood over her eyes. She left Bacchus standing in the center of the room with a fool's grin on his face. She came out of the fornice and met Antonina in the hallway.

"Finally," said Antonina, grabbing Theodora's brown robe as if to inspect the garment. "You're serious about this, aren't you?"

"Remember, don't let anyone in there."

"Well, Magister Man," said Antonina in a melodramatic voice. "I do believe our time is at an end. Allow me to show you out of the brothel."

Theodora offered her arm and Antonina took it. The two women made their way through the narrow hall. A "man" tugging his hood to cover his face, accompanied by a smiling prostitute, was no strange sight. They reached the thick wooden door at the secret rear entry, and Theodora pulled her hood even lower. An old woman sat in the corner, threading a torn gown. Tiberius sat hunched over his desk in an adjoining room, holding a quill and scribbling something onto parchment. And an armed guard stood in boredom beside the entry door, but none took notice of Theodora.

"Do come and visit me again," said Antonina, kissing Theodora on the cheek. "Else I get lonely."

The door opened, and Theodora leaned out and into the hot and sunny alleyway. She immediately smelled the foul odors of the open city. She noticed the streets were soaked from recent rains and the rim of every building dripped at a different cadence. Men passed by her with a nod, and she veered out of the path of passing horse riders. How she'd forgotten the thrill of sneaking out into the city beneath a thin disguise, suppressing a youthful sense of danger, and yet confidently moving deeper into a strange world. As a girl, the faces of all those street-walking men looked so mysterious and colorful. Now she saw dozens of those faces in a single week, usually as they anxiously undressed. Theodora's natural fascination with her city nearly caused her to forget the purpose of her travel.

Theodora had to get to Justinian. She had to set a course in motion that would turn Hypatius over to the Blues and save the man's life. Her heart was split at the thought of sidestepping Macedonia to see Justinian but hoped that, given the importance of the information, they'd forgive her. In truth, Theodora didn't like working as an informer without Justinian sitting across from her at the table. He inspired her, after all. The man in the stands had once reached out for her, having helped her at her weakest, only to return and breathe life into her hopes as a woman. Never seeing the man again seemed too harsh an ending to that special and unlikely relationship. Theodora wanted to see the look in Justinian's eyes when she told him that

Hypatius wanted to meet. Such a tiding would surely validate her as an informer and serve as repayment to a longstanding debt to Justinian.

Bacchus gave Theodora detailed instructions on how to reach the Bucoleon House, the chosen meeting place that Justinian selected. Fortunately, activity upon the streets was light after the rains. Theodora made her way south alongside rows of cramped wooden buildings on her right and the towering white walls of the Hippodrome on her left. And yet the great stadium lay silent. No horse hooves thundered atop the racetrack, and no great crowd boomed at the spectacle, giving the city an almost morning-like din. Most of the foot traffic came up from the harbor. Weary horse teams towed noisy wooden carts, the axles straining beneath the weight of cargo as they trudged into the city. Already, Theodora smelled the sea. The sound of gulls and lapping waves grew louder as she followed the curving street.

Finally, Theodora passed through an intersection, turned the corner of a tall wood building, and saw the blue stripe of the Marmara Sea, a sight she hadn't seen up close before. The blue waters tossed and foamed, sparkling from sunlight, here and there darkened by the shadows of clouds, blue-black near the horizon, translucent green at the docks, and crowded with ship and sail. Out beyond the harbor, wooden vessels leaned and cruised, oars rising and falling beneath buxom red sails. She knew the ships came and went from far-off places—Rome, Alexandria, Caesarea, Tyre, and Carthage—but the harbor was a world of its own. The oddities of an empire came together at the harbor, mixing through a common purpose before dispersing, only to reform again and again in an endless rhythm, a part of the city, yet not *of* the city. And behind Theodora, Constantinople carried on with a slower rhythm of its own, with a familiar, swarthy bustle that Theodora so loved.

Her feet slapped at the cobblestone as the road sloped steeply down toward the harbor. From her vantage point at the crest of the slope, Theodora saw rooftops staggering like steps down the hill. At the bottom of the slope, she spotted a massive marble statue of a beast sitting on its hindquarters, chest puffed outward in a state of vigilance, with the muscular body of a bull but the head and curly mane of a lion. The Greeks called the creature a *bucoleon*, the "bull-lion," whose statue guarded the entrance of a massive Roman estate.

The Bucoleon House.

Two Palatine guards stood beside the entrance gates, and Theodora recognized the taller of the two as Justinian. The sight of him made her chest tighten. He shielded his eyes from the sun as he traced Theodora's approach. A moment later, he sent away the other guardsman, pulled open the entrance gates, and waited.

Theodora passed through the gates wordlessly and entered the estate without Justinian seeing her face. As the doors boomed shut behind her, she noticed that she and Justinian had relative privacy. One or two servants passed across doorways in the distance, but the Bucoleon House looked and felt empty, like a shuttered room, a place of ornament and ceremony that only came to life for certain events.

"What warrants the urgent visit, Macedonia?" said Justinian. "I have to be back at the Daphne soon."

Theodora pulled back her hood.

Justinian's eyes went wide at the sight of her face. "What are you doing here?" he said, his countenance turning hostile. "The message said Macedonia would meet me here."

"I know. I sent the message."

He stepped back and turned away as if Theodora's eyes were as dangerous as the Medusa. "This is a blatant deception. Macedonia is our go-between. Damn you, Theodora!"

Theodora stepped toward him. "Macedonia's nowhere to be found, and I have urgent news. I have good reason for what I've done."

Justinian glanced down the arching hallway in both directions before grabbing Theodora by the arm and hauling her into an antechamber.

She stood in a sitting room that had perhaps fifty animal heads mounted on the walls in rows, mostly deer as well as antelope. Justinian shut the doors with a quiet click and whirled back toward Theodora. "You *cannot* be here," he said. "Going behind Macedonia's back threatens all trust in our circle."

"Hypatius agreed to help us," blurted Theodora. "I spoke with him yesterday. He knows the Greens will kill him when the new emperor is crowned. He wants protection for him and his family."

"Will he give us a name?"

"He said he would."

Justinian pondered the news but then shook his head. "You should have told this to Macedonia. That's our chain of communication."

"Even if time is of the essence?" said Theodora.

"Yes."

"But why?" said Theodora, her voice suddenly pleading. "Why won't you speak with me anymore? I've done nothing to offend you."

"This! This offends me. You disobeying my commands and creating distrust in our circle offends me."

"I know when I'm being pushed away," she said. "I want to know why. Is it Macedonia?"

"No." Justinian folded his arms across his white chest plate. "Something came up in your past that puts your loyalty in question."

Theodora felt the sudden thud in her belly of a painful insult. "What?"

"I've been told that your family used to be strong supporters of the Green faction. You're suspiciously sympathetic toward Hypatius, who's a Green. You asked me many personal questions the last time we spoke. And now this blatant disregard for our chain of communication. You keep incriminating yourself."

"Incriminating me to what?"

"That you still work for the Greens! That you're spying on me, not Hypatius."

Heat singed Theodora's cheeks. "Who said that?"

"It doesn't matter," he said. "Is it true?"

"No," said Theodora, her voice suddenly loud. The one man who always saw her as she wished to be seen couldn't turn against her now. She couldn't bear to have him look at her with doubting eyes. Not him. "My family used to be Greens," she said. "That part's true."

Justinian took a step backward and looked heartbroken. "Damn it,

Theodora. So what made your family switch allegiances so decisively? It's not common, and it leaves your loyalties in rather murky waters."

Theodora realized that he was giving her a chance to explain, but to answer would only shatter the final barrier between her professional relationship with Justinian and the sweetened, all too private memory of him. "My father used to be a bearkeeper for the Greens," she said. "But he was killed in the Trisagion Revolt."

"Killed? By whom?"

"We don't know, and it doesn't matter. Without my father, we had no money. My mother remarried the new bearkeeper, but the Green faction turned against us. The dancing master withdrew the post, leaving us with nothing."

Justinian's gaze remained skeptical and stern. "Yes, but how did you get the Blues to admit your family?"

"Because," said Theodora, finally asserting her eyes on him. "My mother fought the Greens. She brought me and my two sisters with her to the Hippodrome. In between one of the races, we begged the Greens publicly for the bearkeeper post. But they refused. They mocked my mother, as if our lives were nothing more than a passing amusement."

Slowly, Justinian's expression changed. The tight muscles of his face relaxed, and his eyes narrowed, summoning up a hazy recollection. "Wait, a bearkeeper post?"

"A bearkeeper post," said Theodora, taking a step closer to Justinian. "But you see that wasn't the end of the story. Before we were all swept off the racetrack like dust, a single man stood up, a man from the Blue section. He rebuked the Greens for their cruelty. He offered the same post to us if only we swore allegiance to the Blues. And we did. That man, the man in the stands, saved us."

Theodora continued to press in on Justinian, knowing her every word brought that day back to life in Justinian's mind.

"I remember that day," said Justinian. "Three young girls and their mother . . . out on the track . . ."

They finally shared the same memory.

"You're the girl from the Hippodrome," he said. "The one who threw me the garland."

"So you see," she said, "I've known who you were this whole time. I've thought about you for many years, and that day when Macedonia introduced us, when I saw your face again, I realized that I'd been given a great chance to repay a heavy debt. I guess I've been spying on you in a way," she said. "But not for the Greens . . . for a girl who wanted to know more about that mysterious man in the stands."

Justinian stared at her now, his eyes soaking in the sight of her face. "I was so afraid that you worked for someone else."

"But I'm not. I'm working for you," said Theodora, stepping into dangerous proximity. "Emphatically, loyally, resolutely." She was unmasked and at his mercy. Strangely, her pleading brought an upwelling of intense sexual desire inside her, a yearning, a neediness, heart and body both.

Justinian allowed her to come up close to him. He looked Theodora in the eyes, a sweet look, a man on the verge of a tender apology. Then he darkened and grabbed Theodora by both arms. "Now you hear me. This only makes everything worse. Forget about the Hippodrome, Theodora," he said, shaking her. "I can't be alone with you like this. Do you understand me? I don't want to see you again because we absolutely can't—"

He fell silent and then kissed her. Theodora slipped into a calm and blissful state, kissing him back slowly, and reaching up to touch his face. Her body molded against Justinian like clay. The hard chest plate, the metal, the brooches, the armor all pressed against Theodora in a way that should've been painful but wasn't. He kissed her hard, angrily, and unbridled, and she matched him with sensuality.

Justinian lifted Theodora into the air as if her body were made of light silk. She wrapped her legs around his waist as he lowered her onto a table-top. Items on the table scattered and crashed to the floor. A moment later and he pulled her girdle off.

Theodora listened to the frantic fumbling of a man undressing. Her body was ready for him—urgent, heated, and soft. Justinian's eyes were aggressive, while she felt only an overwhelming serenity as she waited.

A moment later and the two were joined. Justinian was forceful, but Theodora's body erupted in pleasure. She was present for him, not as a prostitute, not as a sexual performer, but as herself. Their bodies surged while their eyes stayed fixed on one another, unblinking, as sexual as their physical exertion. Unlike any other man, Justinian was drawn in by more than her beauty and knew her beyond the brothels. The overwhelming sensation reached deeper, touching a part of Theodora's true self, her hidden self, more private and guarded than any secret.

The passion was brief, but the pleasure intense. After they slowed to a stop, her body shuddered uncontrollably, as with winter cold, though she was flush with heat. She tried to catch her breath. When Justinian leaned forward and gently pressed his dampened forehead to her chin, when their breathing was the only sound in the world, and when the wave of euphoria ebbed back, Theodora felt something very different than at similar moments in her past . . .

She felt wonderful.

THIRTY-THREE

Theodora sat up on the table and pulled her robe back over her body.

"This moment has been my greatest fear," said Justinian. "To be sitting across from you after, wondering what the hell to do next."

She meant to say words of reassurance, but only smiled brightly at him. Her mind was clouded with feelings instead of words.

Justinian returned a small but sincere smile. "Everything just became very dangerous," he said. Then he arose and reattached his belt to his tunic. "This cannot become a habit for others to trace."

"What can it become?"

Justinian continued dressing. His look changed. Theodora saw that transformation overtake many a man. After sex, men became docile, or they assumed a stoic expression, a barrier meant to ward off the disarming effects of a woman, as impregnable as the walls around the city. She didn't want that transformation to overtake Justinian, but she knew that the more she tried to prevent it, the more resistant he'd become.

"Do you think you're the first member of the *agentes in rebus* to lay with an informer?" said Theodora, exaggerating her Latin.

"Not at all."

"Come now, Justinian, mine is a world of sex and fantasy," said Theodora with a stretch and a smile. "Did you truly think you could come and go forever without consequence?"

"Consequence," Justinian said as if reconsidering the meaning of the word. "Why didn't you tell me who you were sooner?" he said.

"That memory's very private to me."

Justinian finished securing his uniform, slid his hand in Theodora's hair, and kissed her. Again, the touch was bliss. Then he leaned up against the table beside her. "I suppose that would be a difficult memory," he said. "But it explains quite a bit. You could've told me."

"Well, now you know."

"I admire your mother. I remember thinking how brave she was, going against a hostile crowd like that. How many brave acts like hers go unnoticed every day by regular people, unrecorded by any quill?"

"I still ended up in the brothels."

"That's unfair. Life would be much worse had you stayed with the Greens. I don't think a man would've begged publicly as your mother did."

"I know," said Theodora. "Because no man did."

"I always wondered what became of that mother and her three daughters. You know my views of the common man and woman," said Justinian. "I see bravery and merit in common people daily. It's like spotting gold in a riverbed."

"You have a peculiar view of people," she said.

"Great civilizations have a high place for their women. They don't humiliate them in public." Justinian fixed his eyes on nothing in particular. "I have this one memory when I was a boy, back home in Tauresium. I was hunting with my older cousins. And these were sturdy men and capable soldiers. My one cousin was famous in the village because he strangled a thief to death with just his legs. Anyway, we were all down along the banks of the Vardar, carrying a string of fish we'd caught. We came to a river bend and startled this small brown cub on the other side. It made this little crying sound that, at the time, sounded harmless to me."

Theodora knew the sound well from her childhood. Her pata coaxed all kinds of grunts and woofs from the creatures.

Justinian continued. "But the moment my cousins saw the cub, they sensed immediate danger. They fled the area in an utter panic. 'Run, Petrus,' they shouted at me."

"Did you run?"

"No. Because I didn't understand why my cousins were scared of a little cub. Well, sure enough, the cub's mother came charging out of the thickets, splashing into the river and roaring. Animals make terrible sounds when they mean to kill. I threw the fish we caught and that probably saved me. But that bear made me think. My cousins were armed and could've killed that animal. But the bear was so decisive, prepared without thought to fight to the death. A soldier does the same thing but has months or years to prepare himself for such a contest. A soldier is trained and surrounded by an army. That bear was alone. She acted absolutely. And my cousins *knew she would.* That's why they fled. Such courage was curious to me. Men calculate their chances, but a woman, a woman has that capacity to go up against terrible odds, without any training, without any support, and in a moment's notice," Justinian said and looked Theodora in the eye. "No matter the danger to herself . . . just like your mother did. If we're ever to rebuild this empire, then we need our women in the fight."

Theodora smiled at Justinian. She liked hearing him talk about women as important and brave, a viewpoint that ran counter to the rest of the world.

"I just never quite got that bear out of my head," he said. "And that day at the Hippodrome, when I saw a mother begging for the welfare of her daughters, I knew what drove her there."

"Is that why you stood up?" said Theodora, resting her head against the cool metal of Justinian's shoulder plate.

"That's exactly the reason," he said. "I admit, though, I also saw an opportunity to embarrass the Greens. Surely, I couldn't leave that chance untaken."

They both laughed.

"Well, I need to thank that bear then, wherever she is," said Theodora.

"That damn bear," said Justinian satirically before he collected himself. "I need to get back to the Palace. My father is probably wondering where the hell I am."

Theodora put her hand on Justinian's chest plate. "Don't be ashamed of what we did."

"I'm not ashamed, Theodora," he said. "But we've taken a serious misstep. We've entered a desert that has no other side. And by all I hold sacred, I meant *never* to tread this desert."

"For me," said Theodora, "it's the first oasis."

Justinian grabbed her hands, gently holding each one. "You understand that in our profession, there's no separating our private lives from our imperial lives. Once we began working together, they became the same. We'll be tempted to take risks now that could compromise vital work."

"What kind of risks, though?" she said.

"Risks like you sneaking out of the brothel to meet with me. One day, you may be followed. And should the Blues ever notice our secrecy, they'd deem our circle unreliable. They'll send you away, Theodora. They'll give you a post far away from Constantinople."

"Then, what do you wish of me?"

"For now, I want you to go back. We need to restore the chain of communication in our circle. Tell Macedonia about Hypatius and let her tell me. If the emperor is indeed unwell, we should arrange that meeting with Hypatius right away. My father needs the name of the new Green candidate," Justinian said. He opened the door and looked out into the hallway. Then he gestured for Theodora to follow.

"When will I be able to see you again?" she asked.

"You can't ask me that. Our meetings can't be designed for anything other than our work," Justinian said, but then looked down. He leaned in and whispered, "I'll come for you this evening."

By the time Theodora left the Bucoleon House, the sun was low on the western horizon. The Vespers lit street lanterns and children frolicked in the dusky light. Theodora was in disguise, but her mind was awash in distraction. She found it hard to think, and several times she became disoriented on otherwise familiar streets.

The feeling gripping her wasn't just blissfulness, but a great and complex emotion with a root that stretched all the way back to her youth—to one terrible event, from which grew a sapling, sprouting new branches over the years, barren branches, splitting off into tangles of confusing boughs, with a jagged trunk that leaned over an empty chasm. Then all at once, her moment with Justinian felt as if each empty branch suddenly erupted into a plume of deep green, rich with leaf and fruit, and the chasm below filled with rushing waters. Such an incarnation of her longing felt so satisfying to Theodora, so utterly fulfilling that she smiled like a silly fool beneath her heavy hood.

Then, trumpets.

The sound of horns wailed out into the darkening sky. For a pulse, Constantinople seemed to cease all activity. The horn blows came from the Daphne Palace, which was quite close to where Theodora stood, perhaps only the length of the Hippodrome. Was Constantinople under attack? Did Vitalian come out of hiding with a new rebel army, or did pale-skinned barbarians surprise the city and come out of the west, or Huns from the east?

The street folk wandered about bewildered, looking at each other for an explanation, but none knew the reason for the alarm. Theodora tugged her hood ever lower and picked up her pace. She wanted no part of a hysterical crowd, especially as a woman alone.

From the crest of the hill, Theodora spotted a horseman galloping at high speeds, carrying an imperial banner, and shouting. Citizens parted in his path as the rider thundered forward. "The emperor is dead!" he shouted. "Our Lord has ceased to exist as a man! The emperor is dead!"

As the imperial herald passed, Theodora held her hood in place as she spun to follow his route. Shocked chatter spread through the foot traffic up and down the street.

Emperor Anastasius was dead.

"Who's the successor?" shouted a voice behind her.

And then another voice in front of her: "Are we going to crown a new emperor before the funeral?"

Despite the summer heat of the early evening, Theodora felt a chill wave overtake her whole body. *The election!*

From behind Theodora came the sound of galloping horses. She turned to see Justinian and another Palatine guard atop white horses riding hard toward the Daphne Palace. Justinian slowed as he drew up close to Theodora, his horse rearing up and wild. He leaned down, shouting, "Get to Macedonia! We need Hypatius to give us that name. Now!" Then he steadied his excited horse, aimed it toward the palace, and broke into a rapid gallop.

Suddenly, the gongs of a church bell rang out, a solemn clanging, joined by another, more distant, one by one until the Sacred City was alive with the sound of bells.

Theodora's heart leaped as she hurried back to the theater district. The roads were choked in the heart of the city. Already, she saw Roman troops filing out of the prefectures and taking up positions on street corners. She heard voices behind her lamenting the death of Anastasius, who'd ruled for nearly thirty years, but most passing conversations centered on the *next* emperor.

By the time Theodora reached the Amphitheater, twilight had ripened. Several actors, acrobats, jugglers, and prostitutes milled about outside the theater. Audience members streamed out of the Amphitheater through the vomitorium tunnels. Theodora spotted the stage master standing on a pedestal, holding a metal cone to his mouth, and announcing the cancelation of the evening's plays. But she barely heard him over the cacophony of church bells and lively voices.

One of the dwarf actors skipped in a circle, wearing an open-faced horsehead mask, shouting, "The emperor is dead! The emperor is dead! How shall we live in a realm with no head?"

Theodora pushed through the throngs, but Macedonia snatched her in midstep. "Where have you been?" said Macedonia with concern.

"I was . . ." Theodora caught herself. ". . . with a patron."

"Come, Theodora. Much is at stake tonight." Macedonia grabbed Theodora by the elbow and guided her into the Amphitheater, through the dark tunnels, and past departing prostitutes who trotted out to join the commotion. "We'll need gold and silver for bribes if you have any."

"Macedonia," said Theodora as she pulled her mentor into an empty fornice. "I need to tell you something. You've been good to me, and I don't want a secret to come between us."

"Theodora, we haven't the time."

"I broke our rule," she said. "Just now while I was away."

Macedonia's expression did not change.

"I received important news from Hypatius yesterday," said Theodora. "When I couldn't find you, I went to Justinian directly."

"You what?"

"And we . . ." Theodora trailed off as she held Macedonia's gaze. She sighed. "We did something we shouldn't have done."

"Tell me you didn't."

"No, we did."

Macedonia stared at Theodora, her eyes blazing. "You just made an enormous mistake."

Theodora dared to stare back at her mentor, guilt and sadness blooming inside. The sound of the outside commotion filled the moment in between the words.

"You love him," said Macedonia. "Don't you?"

Theodora looked down. "Yes."

"You've loved him since the moment you first saw him."

"It's more than mere desire, Macedonia. I can't explain now, but I never meant for this to happen."

"Yes, you did," said Macedonia, her voice finally slipping with rare notes of suppressed jealousy. "I saw how you looked at him each time we met, and worse, I saw how he looked at you."

"Go ahead," said Theodora. "Slap me. Slap me and I'll not fight back. I know I deserve it."

Theodora saw the muscles at the back of Macedonia's jaw twitch, and her mentor's hand shot upward from the hip. Theodora turned her face aside, but no blow came.

Instead, Macedonia placed her hand on Theodora's shoulder. "It's not me who you betrayed, despina. You've betrayed yourself. I saw this coming. And now it's here," she said. Then Macedonia sighed, straightened, and somehow recovered. "But we haven't time for that now. The emperor's dead, Theodora. Sides are being chosen as we speak and the losing side could become enemies of the throne tomorrow. This is the storm we've been preparing for, the real thing. This other matter will be dealt with later. So, are you ready to serve the Blues?"

"What do you wish me to do?" said Theodora with a supplicating bow.

"Tell me the news that couldn't wait."

Theodora glanced up, meeting her mentor's eyes again. She almost forgot. "Hypatius. He's turned. He wants to make the deal with Justinian."

Macedonia pulled back, urgency on her face. "Get dressed. Something plain. We need to get to Hypatius before he panics. Time to aim our boats into the storm, despina."

THIRTY-FOUR

Theodora quickly washed and changed clothes. She donned a loose-fitting black robe and sandals. There wasn't much time to spare, so she made her way through the crowded streets to the Forum of Leo, where Macedonia would meet her. The square was full of vigorous conversations and stray music. Though the night was lively, the people appeared under control for now. Everything focused on the death of the emperor, and all knew that a great contest would take place tomorrow in the Hippodrome. Theodora found Macedonia in the northeast corner of the forum, standing in the arcade, holding a torch and conversing with men Theodora had never seen before.

When Macedonia saw her, she stepped forward. "Say nothing unless I command it. Do you understand?"

Theodora nodded. "Yes."

Macedonia returned her attention to the group of men around her. "The

watchword is 'autumn.' Now go to your posts and await my instructions."
She dismissed them all with a polite bow.

The group dispersed in a hurry. Macedonia stepped forward, stared hard
at Theodora, and then set out toward the city center.

Theodora followed. She felt the awful pangs of being an unwanted guest.
Her heart ached at the broken trust between herself and Macedonia. She
wanted so badly to explain herself, yet knew better than to dare speak of
Justinian unless it concerned the election.

Macedonia led Theodora down the crowded Street of the Storks. The
roadway had stone column arcades on both sides filled with people and
animals, music and firelight. The citizens clustered into different circles
and each circle occupied a different space, a street corner, an intersection, a
doorway, a taverna. In many ways, the evening resembled Theodora's memory of the revolt six years earlier, when her pata stood beside these militant
citizens. And now, Theodora was among them and this time, she followed
rather than led.

With all the sights to see, Theodora mostly watched Macedonia. The
woman strode through the crowds boldly, as one of them, a woman who
commanded the space she passed through. She no longer appeared to be a
prostitute, but an influential partisan who directed a shadowy elite. Men
moved aside, stared at her, nodding their heads as if to confirm a shared
secret. Many times, Macedonia leaned in to seemingly random people on the
street, whispered in their ear, and pressed a coin into their palm.

The whole city was alive with conspiracy.

Macedonia led Theodora past the Great Church of Holy Wisdom, which
was, itself, aglow with activity. When the Street of the Storks emptied into
the city center, Theodora beheld the swarming Augustaion, a vast public
square beneath the stars, the very center of Constantinople. This was where
the Middle Way terminated. More importantly, this was also the entrance to
the Daphne Palace. Two giant doors, known as the Bronze Gate, faced the
square and served as the entrance and final barrier to the Daphne Palace.
Three rows of infantry soldiers defended the Bronze Gate, oval shields at the
ready, swords drawn.

"Where are we going?" Theodora finally asked.

Macedonia took Theodora by the elbow and helped her up onto the back of an empty wooden cart. This gave Theodora an excellent view of the Augustaion. So many people, she thought, so many were encamped in the public spaces.

"Tomorrow morning, all these men will file into the Hippodrome," said Macedonia, pointing to the giant horse track that shared the far west corner of the square. "They'll demand a new emperor that most of the citizens agree on. This is very dangerous. Neither faction wants to carelessly elect an emperor who'll turn around and persecute them. Meanwhile, behind those closed doors over there," and Macedonia pointed at the Bronze Gate, "the ruling administration and imperial Senate are deliberating about which candidates to send out before the people. If they present unacceptable candidates, the city will riot."

This. This is what Theodora was after the day her father died, she thought. This is what she had to see and touch and understand.

"Besides husbanding the approval of the factions," Macedonia said and swung her finger toward the Hagia Sophia, which occupied the eastern half of the square, "the next emperor must also gain the endorsement of the Holy See, which means the patriarch must give his blessing to the candidate. If the candidate is unfriendly to the church, the citizens will riot. And lurking beneath it all is the presence of the army. Their commanders are out here as well. If the candidate isn't acceptable to the army, the soldiers will riot. And that means civil war. Above all, the next candidate *must* have the army on his side."

Theodora saw now that Hypatius, a failed military commander who'd been captured by the enemy, stood no chance. She understood at last why the Greens feared to back him.

"All the while, you and I will be there." At this, Macedonia pointed to the west side of the square, at the portico of a building complex across from the Hagia Sophia. "The Bathhouse of Zeuxippos."

Theodora knew the public bathhouse, but now noticed the building's strategic location. The Bathhouse of Zeuxippos pressed up against the north walls of the Daphne Palace, as if it were attached to the imperial complex, yet on the public side of the palace walls.

"We'll be in a position to pass information quickly between all our supporters," said Macedonia. "And still be in constant communication with Justinian. Like everybody else out here, we have our own mind about which candidate should become the next emperor," said Macedonia with a subtle smile. "To the best organized will go the purple."

Theodora blurted her thoughts. "Justinian?"

"Too young," said Macedonia as she leaped down from the cart. She then led Theodora through the multitudes, where Blues and Greens huddled around fires, sang songs, held vigils for the dead emperor, or tossed dice. Theodora sensed the fragile truce among the factions. But lawlessness was a single call to violence away.

Theodora and Macedonia entered the bathhouse. The interior was oppressively humid. None used the gymnasium or steaming baths for leisure as they would during the day. Instead, they crowded into whatever space they could find. On the inside, the building showed its pagan roots, having once been the Temple of Jupiter in the days of old Byzantium. Giant snow-white statues rose above the gathering, shimmering in the firelight, with adolescent boys sitting on marble limbs. Beneath the vacant gaze of the statues, thousands created a thunderous din.

"Macedonia," shouted a man, who pushed through the crowd. "We're over here."

"Good evening, Zimarchus," said Macedonia. "We've come to mourn the death of Emperor Anastasius."

"As are we all," said Zimarchus. "Eighty-eight years old. The bastard sure made us wait."

For an older man, Zimarchus was well-muscled, tall, and lively. His every manner conveyed life in the military, thought Theodora. Patches of well-trimmed white hair circled the base of his skull, leaving the scalp bald and scarred. He glanced at Theodora with suspicion. "This her? The Notorious Theodora is our go-between?"

"Yes," said Macedonia.

Zimarchus eyed Theodora in disbelief, then shook his head. "Well, let's get on with it," he said and quickly turned around. He led them through the herd of humanity and into a muggy side chamber. There, Theodora saw a group of people huddled at a stone spout in the wall that poured hot water into a tiny floor pool. They spoke in hushed voices, but all fell silent when Zimarchus entered the room.

"Macedonia has arrived with our go-between," announced Zimarchus.

Everyone greeted Macedonia but craned to peer at Theodora with fascination. There was a strange, heavy tension in the air. Theodora stared back, trying to read the many sweaty faces. A moment later, one of the onlookers stepped forward and removed his hood.

Hypatius.

"Well, now you've seen her," Zimarchus barked at Hypatius. "Are you satisfied?"

Hypatius, who looked frightened and unsure, now focused on Theodora. "I'm relieved to see you."

Theodora resisted the urge to look at Macedonia or anyone else. She perceived her involvement differently now that strange Blues surrounded her and Hypatius, like an audience. She stepped forward and took up his hands. "I'm glad you're with us," she said.

He stepped in so close that his lips grazed Theodora's ear. "I'm here to protect my family," he whispered. "Tell me that I'm not in the company of the men who'll kill me."

She pressed her lips now against his ear. "I give you my word. These people are here to help you."

Hypatius stared her in the eyes.

"We need the name," said Theodora.

Hypatius finally turned to face Zimarchus. "The Greens are going to present Theocritus, Count of the Domestics."

"Who's his backer inside the palace?" said Zimarchus.

"Amantius. The grand chamberlain of the Sacred Cubicle."

Theodora knew none of the names being discussed, but everyone in the room did because they murmured uncomfortably.

Zimarchus turned toward a group of men standing beside him. They drew in close and whispered rapidly. Then Zimarchus turned back. "We know that Grand Chamberlain Amantius has a powerful clique among the nobility, but how does he plan to win over the factions?"

"He has a great fortune," said Hypatius. "According to my cousin, he means to distribute this fortune in the Hippodrome and buy the support of faction leaders."

Zimarchus looked at Macedonia as if such major revelations required her confirmation. "What audacity," he said.

"Audacity wins support," said Macedonia.

Zimarchus snapped and wagged his finger at a Greek man who sat by the water spout. "Relay this information to Count Justin immediately."

Theodora watched in bewilderment as the Greek reached down and turned an unseen valve, stopping the water flow from the spout. He then tucked his finger into the wall's stone work and slowly pulled out a block of striped purple stone. He pressed his mouth into the opening in the wall and began speaking, though none in the room could hear him. Then he pulled back and pressed his ear against the opening, nodding, concentrating. He did this three times before returning the stone block to its place on the wall. A moment later and the spout gushed again with steaming water.

Stunned, Theodora looked at Macedonia.

"Behind that wall is the Daphne Palace," said Macedonia. "Specifically, the barracks of the Excubitors where Justin is in command. We use the old water pipes to communicate with him."

Theodora knew that Justinian's adopted father, Justin, was Count of the Excubitors, the very man who would escort the candidates before the Hippodrome crowd tomorrow morning. Theodora touched her head as if to still the dizziness. Hearing how the system worked was different from seeing the people of that system in action, making preparations, moving the pieces, and readying for a deadly revolt.

"All the chariots are rounding the final turn," said Zimarchus. "Tomorrow morning, we'll see who has the horses to win the race."

"What about Hypatius?" said Theodora. "He's done his part."

Zimarchus turned to face the imperial nephew. "We need to get you out of Constantinople. It's the best way to protect you."

"I'm Master of Soldiers in the East," said Hypatius. "My station is in Antioch. If you could get me there . . ."

Zimarchus grabbed another man by the collar and pulled him close. He whispered something. Then, he nodded at Hypatius. "This man will escort you to the small harbor. Go! Now!" Within moments, Hypatius had his hood on again and was ushered out of the room in a hurry. He looked so helpless.

"What about his family?" said Theodora.

Zimarchus splashed his face with hot water and shook his head like an animal. "What about them?"

"Justinian promised to protect them as well."

"Well, let's see how this goes tomorrow first."

"No," said Theodora, surprising even herself. "Send someone to gather his family members onto that ship as well. That was the bargain."

Zimarchus opened his mouth to argue, but Macedonia cut him off. "Do it. Hypatius is a critical ally right now. He needs to know that his trust is well-placed."

With a sigh, Zimarchus nodded and sent off a courier.

For a while, the activity settled into minor comings and goings—a messenger, a courier, someone bringing bread and water for the group. Standing in the bathhouse, at the crossroads of rapidly passing secrets, Theodora marveled at how organized the demes of the city really were. If all battles are social battles, as her mother taught, then the Blues and Greens of Constantinople controlled the battlefield. They converted the very walls, streets, and city blocks into a vast apparatus, with gears and pulleys, a great siege engine set against the palace. They called this devastating weapon *democracy*, the Greek way, the old way. And they used this ancient tradition to bludgeon any man who dared to wear a crown and declare himself their ruler. A Roman emperor was a foreign title, after all, brought into the East from a failed regime whose mother city of Rome was already dead. The eastern populace was mostly Greek, not Roman; they never asked to become a Roman capital; the people couldn't have known that the West would collapse and they alone would be tasked with the survival of the Roman Empire. Many still resisted the idea of imperial order. And it was this resistance, this process, and these people that Theodora tried so desperately to understand in the late hours.

By sunrise, the weariness of the long night fell away. Theodora watched all the men filter out of the bathhouse and into the bright morning sun. They looked tense as they set out for the Hippodrome, vigilant, ready for citizen war if events turned ill.

Not long after, Zimarchus came to Macedonia with a grave look. "Word from Justinian," he said. "They gather at the Ivory Gate now."

Macedonia sprang out of her disciplined calm and stood. "Then now's the time. Send word to the Blues in the Hippodrome! Await the watchword."

Zimarchus turned and waved his hand at a boy on the far side of the bathhouse. The boy nodded and scurried off like a mouse. "Just thought you should know," Zimarchus said to Theodora. "Hypatius and his family are on a ship that sails south to Antioch. They left this morning. And his other friends are dispersed in Blue shelters throughout the city."

"Oh, thank you," said Theodora, feeling a wave of relief.

Zimarchus bowed and departed.

Saving Hypatius was Theodora's primary concern in the whole affair. She negotiated the arrangement and turned poor Hypatius over to the Blues. It was her idea and her doing. This must be what power feels like, she thought, protecting the people who looked to her for help, having others do her bidding, and shaping events to her own will.

Theodora's smile faded as realization settled in.

She liked it.

THIRTY-FIVE

Theodora sweated as she followed Macedonia through the cave-like network of bathhouse chambers. "What's the Ivory Gate?" she asked.

"It's the gate between the Daphne Palace and the Hippodrome," answered Macedonia. "On the palace side, the most powerful men of the empire are gathered, including the entire Roman Senate. They've been quarreling over which candidate to send through the Ivory Gate. On the Hippodrome side is the emperor's Kathisma, which overlooks the horse track. Soon, the Excubitors will tear open the curtains of the Kathisma and reveal the candidate. The turn'll then pass to the people in the Hippodrome to accept or reject the Senate's choice. If most of the people approve, there'll be a great cheer from the Hippodrome benches. If too many people disapprove, then a new candidate must be chosen, and we'll be one step closer to anarchy. The men in the palace are playing a dangerous game."

Macedonia pushed open a heavy wooden door, and the two women wandered into the warm morning sun. Theodora saw a green lawn glittering with dew and scattered stone benches. They were in a courtyard at the rear of the bathhouse, and above the roofline to the north, Theodora beheld the massive corner of the Hippodrome jutting out, glowing with an amber hue of the morning sun. The Hippodrome crowd was eerily quiet, sounding almost like pleasant chatter. Birds could even be heard warbling sweetly from the treetops.

There were others in the courtyard, huddled in various circles, sending runners in and out of the bathhouse with news or instruction.

As the hour drew long, though, the great host inside the Hippodrome grew louder. At this close distance, Theodora heard individual voices shouting from behind the marble wall, followed by cheers, laughter, or boos.

"Theodora," said Macedonia, breaking the silence between them, her voice strangely soft.

"Yes?"

"You were right to go to Justinian without me," she said. "I want you to know that."

Theodora felt a surge of emotion, like guilt, like relief, like gratitude. But before she could respond, she heard a professional voice, aided by an announcer's cone, boom out from inside the Hippodrome. "Long live the Roman Senate!" the voice cried. "Where's our emperor given to us by God? Bring the new emperor before the people!"

At that command, the crowd shifted from restless to raucous. Theodora felt the noise shivering inside her body, triggering an image of her mother, standing on that horse track, pelted by bread crumbs to that same sound. She shook out the awful memory.

The Hippodrome chanted, each word like a pulse of thunder, "*Nos postulo imperator! Nos postulo imperator!*" We demand an emperor!

"The longer they take to present a candidate," Macedonia said over the din, "the better for us."

"How?"

"The greater the delay, the more the Senate will fear the people. Once they get desperate, we'll push our candidate in front of them."

"Nos postulo imperator! Nos postulo imperator!"

As fear percolated within Theodora, she saw a boy race from the bath-house doors and up to Macedonia. He cupped his mouth and whispered excitedly in her ear. Macedonia shot Theodora an alarmed glance, then turned to the boy. "Go! Send out the watchword. I want every Blue with a voice to be on their feet!"

The boy darted back toward the bathhouse.

"What's happening?" said Theodora. "Are they sending out the first candidate?"

Macedonia spun to stare momentarily at that mighty tip of the Hippodrome in the sky. Then she whirled back to Theodora. "Our supporters in the palace pulled it off. Our man is being sent through the Ivory Gate now! All our work is about to come down to a single moment. This is that moment, Theodora. The watchword instructs the Blues to hail our candidate when he appears. It'll be any moment now."

"Who?" said Theodora. "Who's our candidate?"

Macedonia opened her mouth to answer, but the chanting in the Hippodrome suddenly stopped and an eerie silence followed, as if a dark cloud passed before the sun. Both women glanced at the Hippodrome. The sudden shift in the crowd's mood was so ominous a sound to Theodora that she felt dread.

"People of the Roman Empire," shouted a voice. "The Senate gives you the Defeater of the Huns! An Orthodox man to mend our divisions! A fair-minded Blue who served our late Emperor Anastasius loyally!"

Theodora heard murmuring. A voice shouted. Then another. From the far end of the Hippodrome, she heard an upwelling of applause.

Macedonia mouthed the watchword "Autumn," and as if on cue, the Hippodrome erupted in deafening jubilation. The sound was so loud that Theodora's shoulders came up to her ears. But Macedonia remained still, her eyes sparkling with victory. "Listen to them, Theodora. Just listen to them!"

Theodora finally heard what the crowd was chanting.

"Emperor Justin! Long may you reign! Emperor Justin! Long may you reign!"

Theodora was paralyzed. Emperor ... Justin? Justinian's father was the new Roman emperor? Was that possible? Theodora looked back at Macedonia.

Her mentor nodded as if answering the unasked question. "We've done it, despina."

The great purpose at the center of the secrecy was unveiled to Theodora at last. Now, the host inside the Hippodrome called out Justin's name in one voice.

The announcer in the Hippodrome cried out, "All hail Emperor Justin, Ever August!"

This time, when the great roar thundered over Constantinople, Theodora didn't flinch. She turned to face the riotous Hippodrome. From all that chaos . . . a Roman emperor.

THIRTY-SIX

The Forum of Leo filled with men in high spirits. Theodora, along with many other actresses and prostitutes, stood in the forum, pressed against a stone pillar, smiling and swaying slowly. She thought the whole of Constantinople was on holiday. Festive music filled the public square, men drank beer and wine until they lay like dead men in the shade, and church bells continued to ring out beyond the rooftops. To Theodora, though, the jubilation was a peculiar thing. The people of the city claimed to hate a lone ruler, yet here at the continuation of imperial rule, they celebrated. Perhaps they cheered not for the emperor, but for themselves. Surely the emergence of another Roman emperor signaled new life for them in an ever-darkening world. The late Emperor Anastasius had been aging, just as the remnant of the Roman state was aging, and here, thought Theodora, here the people did not die with him; here, civilization was renewed. An emperor passes, a new emperor rises, and the city lives on, surviving yet again, and by the celebration Theodora witnessed all around her, perhaps that enduring existence had been in *doubt*.

But what of Justinian?

She saw equestrian soldiers among the crowd, clustered in the corners of the forum, but none were Justinian. None *would be* Justinian, she realized, for his father just became an emperor. So where now would he be?

Throughout the day, Theodora went back and forth from forum to fornice, fornice to forum. Men poured into the brothels, tossing coins about like seed in a tilled field. Even Tiberius was forced to help keep order with the overflow of patrons.

In the lively forum, Theodora heard her clients offer up opinions of the new emperor. A millworker informed Theodora that Emperor Justin was illiterate, a pure embarrassment to whatever dignity remained to the Roman throne. A patron from the mason's guild said Justin was merely a placeholder, a simpleton who angered no one, and the Greens would take power back as soon as he died. Still, there were supporters. A purple dyer from one of the palace workshops said at least Emperor Justin was Orthodox, a believer in the Holy Trinity, unlike the divisive Emperor Anastasius, who was a Monophysite and denied it. *Denied it and triggered a revolt once.*

And Theodora listened.

Perhaps knowing what people said about their new emperor could be useful to Justinian and the Blues. For these vital opinions, so harmless when uttered by one drunken voice in her ear, could be amassed within the Hippodrome, uttered aloud as a united roar, and set against even the Roman emperor.

Eventually, though, she removed her clothes, bent forward, and listened to the owner of that powerful voice pant like a dog. Laying with these men felt more like a tedious act now, unwanted, uninspired. When she worked, she thought of Justinian. In her imagination, it was he who took her each time that day. She closed her eyes and recalled his intense gaze, the look of his unmasked desire at the Bucoleon House, the smell of his perfume, and the sound of distant gulls. His last words to her had been "I will come for you this evening."

But the evening passed and the new day drew long. Of course, the situation had changed, but where did that leave her and Justinian? When would he come for her again?

As a dark moonless night moved toward dawn, Theodora visited Macedonia's bedchamber, took a deep breath, and knocked.

When the door opened, Theodora saw Macedonia's deep brown eyes staring back at her. "I expected you sooner," she said.

Theodora entered the bedchamber and closed the door behind her. "I just thought we should talk."

Macedonia folded her colorful gowns and set each into a pile on the bed. Theodora marveled at how clean Macedonia's chamber appeared, so meticulously arranged.

"I haven't heard anything," said Theodora. "From Justinian, I mean."

Macedonia's eyes met Theodora's for a flash. "Is that why you've come?"

"Partly. Also, to apologize."

"Despina, you don't need to apologize to me."

Theodora furrowed her brow. Macedonia seemed to be in a calm and pleasant mood, despite the uncomfortable issue with Justinian. Even a well-controlled woman such as she had to have some place in her heart reserved for base jealousy, thought Theodora. "Macedonia," she said, grabbing her mentor by the elbow. "I'm sorry."

Macedonia met Theodora's eyes. "Much has changed, Theodora, whether you realize it or not. The men we worked for are no longer just a group of Blues within the Blues. That group is gone. Now they are the imperial administration of the Roman Empire."

"But that's a good tiding," said Theodora.

"For some," Macedonia said and broke from Theodora's grip on her elbow. She gathered up a few belongings from her nightstand. "Most of Justinian's informants will now be aligned with the *Magister Officiorum*, or the Master of Offices, if you prefer Greek."

"We'll still be working for Justinian, though, right?"

"For Justinian?" At this, Macedonia stopped tidying her bedchamber, looked up at the ceiling, and exhaled. "No, Theodora. For the Blues. For the people of the empire. Your post is not about one man. We took the Daphne Palace, but now the Blues need trusted eyes and ears throughout the empire."

Theodora thought Macedonia's tone carried notes of a warning. "What does that mean?"

"It means, despina, that you've been given a new post, one outside Constantinople."

"What?" said Theodora in an icy breath.

"You're being sent to North Africa," said Macedonia. "To Cyrenaica to serve the Blues there. You've proven capable in the company of powerful men, and now the command has come down for you to companion Hacebolus. The man was smitten with you at his coronation last year. His governorship in Sozusa begins in a few months. The Blues wish you to gather information about the governor, the region, and the people and to convey that information back to Constantinople."

Theodora stepped back. "You told the Blues about Justinian and me."

"No," said Macedonia. "I concurred with the emperor's suggestion, given the knowledge I have."

"How could you?"

"Theodora, stop. You know that I serve the post in this matter. I've always served the post, never myself."

Theodora stiffened. "I refuse. I'm not leaving Constantinople."

"Then you'd be disobeying a command from Emperor Justin. It was he who bore the concern," said Macedonia, a curt note of authority in her voice, "that in your heart, you serve Justinian above the Blues."

"I serve them both," said Theodora. "Just as you do. And I'll continue to do it from right here."

Theodora expected a harsh rebuke, but Macedonia's stern expression softened. "You don't understand, despina. I tried to warn you at the very beginning that you'd be sent away if your motivations were compromised. You made the mistake of falling in love, and now you must contend with reality."

"But my whole life is in this city," said Theodora.

"There's more. You may not want to hear this, but there are other forces at work now that Justin is emperor."

Theodora looked away. "Just tell me."

"Justin is now the emperor, but Justinian's his adopted son. The plan is to name Justinian as his successor. But first, he must consolidate power."

"Justinian . . . wants to be the emperor?" she said, though the notion didn't surprise her.

"One day, God willing, yes, and unlike Hypatius, Justinian isn't betrothed."

Theodora blinked. She'd always thought of Justinian as a man who simply existed, who passed between her imagination and the real world as if he were a person of her own making, a silent guardian, a man in the stands with a special focus on her.

Macedonia continued. "Whoever Justinian chooses to wed will one day become an empress. That post may be the single greatest political station in the empire, and it's vacant. The great houses from the Diocese of Pontus to Egypt will offer up their daughters and Justinian can take his pick. He must. His marriage will strengthen his father's claim to the throne and eventually, his own. That's how critical his future marriage is now. These will be noble daughters with powerful names, Theodora. Even if you stayed here, they'd run you off."

Run me off.

That made Theodora think of the gangly dog that once lurked outside her childhood apartment. The animal had swollen teats, a tongue that twitched as she panted, and a wild look in her hungry eyes. The women of the apartment used to *run off* that dog, calling it a nuisance. For a brief moment, Theodora felt a degrading bond with that pathetic animal.

Macedonia continued. "These women have everything Justinian needs. Could you truly stand by while he courts women of the aristocracy? He'll be in the palace, and you'll be out here, doing the same things you do now. Each day, he'll forget you a little more as his new life takes hold, and each day you'll grow a little older. Even *if* the laws of the empire allowed a prostitute to marry a patrician, would it matter? He must be one of them now. It's his destiny. And it's another woman's destiny to marry Justinian and become an empress."

Macedonia's every word deadened Theodora from the inside. She knew her mentor spoke the cold truth.

Strange women would descend on Constantinople, and the man in the stands would one day hold out his hand to one of them instead. Whoever this woman will be, she'll come in silks from Asia, gems from Judea, gold from Thracian rivers, and fragrant oils from Egypt, the very luxuries of an empire crafted into the image of a perfect woman, a bride meant for the eyes of Justinian alone. Behind this woman would be a great house with powerful family members, including magistrates, soldiers, slaves, influence, power, and wealth. Theodora looked down into her lap.

Alas, Theodora was a prostitute of the theaters. She had no one and nothing behind her. The gap between herself and Justinian flung wide open, and she felt a sudden fracture in her spirit. Theodora covered her eyes and fought back the tears. Those feelings of inferiority she thought had been conquered crept in.

"I taught you how to be a woman and to hold yourself like a queen," said Macedonia. "And more importantly, I tried to teach you how to serve the post. If you truly love Justinian, then let him go for his sake and yours."

Theodora drew back from Macedonia. "Let him go. Serve. Just like always. Whether it's Tiberius or the stage master, the Blues or the Greens, I'm nothing more than a slave."

Macedonia scowled. "If you look at it with self-pity, then yes."

"But I am a slave because I've no choice."

"Tell me what you want, Theodora."

"To be the master," she said in a raised voice. "Just for once, I want to get what I want. I want someone *else* to settle for less. Why am I always the one who gets pushed aside?"

Macedonia put her hand on Theodora's shoulder. "Despina, hear me."

Theodora pulled away. "No. You hear me. I remember what you told me on that very first day. You said that I'm not Theodora, the prostitute, but a woman of my own. A woman. I used to think to be a woman meant being powerless and weak and stupid and worthless. I hated myself. Then I met you, and you showed me that a woman could be much more than the lesser of two halves. When I met Justinian, I saw that there are people out there who saw me better than I saw myself. Then came Hypatius, and I saw firsthand that any of us can be broken, even men of high titles, and sadly for some, there's no coming back. I began to like myself. I even liked being a woman. And now I love a man." She shrugged. "And it means nothing. Not being able to pursue that one course takes something away from me, something I don't want to surrender."

Macedonia looked down. "I understand. You're the most intelligent, most determined woman I know. You have a fire in you I hope breaks out one day and burns down the things that stand in your way. And maybe that day will come, despina, but it's not today. Today, you must stay your hand and *serve the post*."

Theodora felt the agony of wanting the impossible. "I hate this feeling," she said.

Macedonia reached out and pressed her palm against Theodora's cheek. The contact reminded Theodora of being a girl in the presence of her mother. "I hope Theodora the woman gets what she wants in this world," said Macedonia. "I truly do. But she must be patient."

"I'm tired of being a prostitute. I'm tired of the brothels. I don't want to be anyone else anymore."

"We must learn to wear many skins, Theodora."

"Except our own."

For a while, the two women stared at each other. Theodora realized they were equals on the matter, both of them casualties of a world that pushed them to the shadows, unacknowledged, even while they helped that world survive. Then, Theodora felt an unwelcomed wetness in her eyes, a light glaze, and this time, she made no effort to hide her grief.

Macedonia embraced Theodora. For a long moment, Theodora stood stiffly, defiant at the show of affection, but as the anguish built, she finally pressed her forehead into the fabric at Macedonia's shoulder. She felt an exhausting sadness as if she'd been crying through the night.

After a while, Macedonia pulled back. "I never wanted you to feel like this."

Theodora took in a deep breath and sighed. "Am I really to leave the city?"

"Yes."

"And what of you? What are you going to do?"

Macedonia smiled warmly. "I'm traveling too. I'm going to Antioch and won't be returning."

Theodora was stunned. "You're leaving?"

"We did what we set out to do, despina. Justin is on the throne, and Justinian is in position to carry out his great vision. But these years have passed, and I awoke this morning, and suddenly I'm thirty-one years old," Macedonia said and shook her head. "My days in the theater are few. One day, you'll see. Today, you rule men's attention like a tyrant. Tomorrow, though, there will be others. Tomorrow, these men will look to younger girls who'll view you as a relic who clings to former fame. Not even the Notorious Theodora can beat back the cruel cadence of time."

"So that's it for you?" said Theodora. "You're just leaving it all behind?"

"In this city, yes. But the Blues need informers in Antioch, and I'll oblige them as I always have," said Macedonia. "I have many friends and family in Antioch, and now it's time for me to go to them. I want to sleep in a bed away from the brothel, beside a man of my choosing and, God willing, perhaps I'll oversee a koitóna of my own one day. It's what I've wanted."

Theodora looked down again. Too much was changing and too quickly. Things always changed on her. How many times must she adapt?

"Think about the days of your life far from this day," said Macedonia. "The brothels and stage can be a tomb for the women who linger too long. Let Constantinople and Justinian go their own way. Go to North Africa with Governor Hacebolus. Live in a palace and away from the brothels. Find some peace."

Later that night, Theodora stood alone on the uppermost bench of the Amphitheater, the stage dark below her. She gazed out over the wall at the city. Above the street music, she heard the lonely voice of the monk that used to sing to her when she was a girl. Far below, two Roman troops strolled along beside the aqueduct. They still never thought to look up.

She sighed.

Constantinople would be their city. And then Theodora considered that her place had always been high up . . . in a treetop, a rooftop, a bell tower, or balcony, looking down upon them all, admiring them, discarded by them, watching, dreaming, longing for a greater part of a world that always slipped out of reach.

Theodora glanced up at the twinkling star field above Constantinople. There, she traced the path of a familiar glittering bird as it crossed the black skies. It was her bird. And it was a beautiful bird. A long time ago, she released that ghostly apparition, and it was up there still. She'd almost forgotten. The bird flew free, unencumbered by pain, untethered by duty. She watched the bird sail out and away, over the darkened Sea of Marmara, setting a course for the distant shores of Africa.

But first, Theodora had to say goodbye.

THIRTY-SEVEN

Two days later, Theodora paused outside her old apartment. She hadn't been home for two years, and the last time she was there, she was drunk. The city apartment looked so familiar and yet so different at the same time. There were more ropes stretching across the alleyways, with more clothes hanging to dry in the breezes. She saw the maple she used to climb as a girl. The tree was taller, yet somehow looked smaller than the tree of her memories. When Theodora passed by the open doors to the first-floor workshops, different women sat at the spinning wheels. Even the neighborhood children who played in the streets were unfamiliar, and for the first time, Theodora stood on that street, and no one recognized her. In her mind, this was her street, not theirs. Would the same thing happen to Theodora on the stage as Macedonia promised? Could the Notorious Theodora truly show up at the Amphitheater one day as an older woman and be recognized by no one?

When the door to her family's apartment opened, she saw Anastasia.

Her younger sister looked thin and bony, without shape, and her adolescent face bore no beauty. Anastasia never found work on the stage but stayed home to tend to the aging Maximina and Theodora's daughter. But she brightened at the sight of Theodora, dashing forward for an embrace. "Theodora!"

"Look at you, Anastasia!" said Theodora. "My little sister is sixteen years old now?"

Anastasia nodded. "Can you believe it? All us sisters are women now."

"How's Mother doing?"

Anastasia stepped back, and Theodora entered the old domicile. The smell of the place immediately recalled feelings of Theodora's girlhood. That smell came not from one source, but from many; the blankets, the wood furniture, the foods cooked here over the decades, the ash of the hearth, even the sweet scent of her mother all smelled of home, the enchanted perfume of a time and place.

Maximina sat in a chair beside the hearth. She made one effort to arise, but struggled, so Theodora walked over and settled her back in the seat. "Oh, it's so good to see you again, Mother."

But how old Maximina looked, thought Theodora. The streak of silver that used to part otherwise jet black hair now spread to more than half of Maximina's head. Her hair was longer, more unkempt, with some of the copper charms knotted in the strands. And when Theodora looked into her mother's eyes, she saw calm, rather than vigor. Her face seemed smaller, her head hunched forward, and for a flicker, Theodora couldn't believe it was this woman who once challenged the tyrannical horde that ruled the city. Home was supposed to be a permanent place where life didn't change. But even here, change was visible.

Theodora hugged her mother, and Maximina smiled broadly. "Who's this beautiful woman in my home? You look so strong and healthy, Theodora," she said. "So much better than last I saw you."

"Thank you, Mother. I feel better. Where's Samuel?"

"He's at the Hippodrome. Apparently one of the bears gave birth last night," she said. "Comito says you were dismissed from the theater."

"Oh, Comito thinks the Amphitheater is the only stage in Constantinople."

Maximina shrugged. "She never visits me either. But I'm sure a young woman in this city can become harried."

"If only you knew, Mother. I've been working on private stages lately," said Theodora. "And I do partisan work for the Blues here and there."

Her mother's face darkened. "Why would you want to work with the animals of the faction? You're too pretty and talented, Theodora. You need to go back to the Amphitheater and reconcile with the stage master while there's still time," she said. "Get proper roles again. You always give up too easily, in my opinion."

"It's not like that, Mother. The partisans I work with don't fight in the streets. It's good work with good people."

Maximina looked disappointed, so Theodora changed the subject. "Where's Palatina?"

"You walked right by her," said her mother, reclining in her chair again. "She's playing outside with the other boys and girls."

Theodora froze and glanced at the patterned wood grille covering the window, where the sounds of children's laughter came into the room. For a moment, she only stared at that window. She listened to a chorus of giggles and shrieks, each voice like a distinct musical instrument. Which of those voices was her daughter's? Palatina was no longer a squirming infant with big, hazel eyes and mindless want, but a little person who might remember Theodora's face and words, who might one day recall Theodora as the mother who chose to leave. *Would it be better not to see her at all?*

"Can you believe Palatina's almost four years old already?" said Anastasia. "She's adorable, Theodora, and so smart for her age."

"She is?" said Theodora, disarmed, the question catching in her throat.

"Come on, I'll take you to her."

Anastasia led Theodora outside. Perhaps a dozen children congregated at the lip of a wall fountain, surrounded by pigeons and snoozing stray dogs. Some played a game of kingdoms by the look of it, while others played with a wet linen sheet, shaking it and making it arch like a tunnel as one child ran through, just as Theodora and Comito had once done.

Anastasia cupped her mouth. "Palatina, I have a surprise for you! Your mother has come to visit."

Theodora saw a tiny girl trot forward, bare feet slapping on the cobblestones, her clothes soaked from head to toe. The last time she saw her daughter, Theodora had no interest. But now the girl's face bore distinctive features—sharp cheekbones, a small nose, and alert hazel eyes. She had black hair, just like Theodora, in one long braid. How comely her daughter looked, how wonderful, how youthful and vibrant. Theodora covered her mouth as unexpected guilt struck her.

Palatina studied her for a moment. Then the girl yelled, "*Mitéra*," the Greek word for "mother."

"Look at how big you've grown," said Theodora, taking the drenched girl up in her arms. "Do you remember me?"

"I think," she said. "Did you come to play with me in the fountain?"

Theodora laughed. She was going to say no, of course, but the word never came. She nodded instead. "That's *exactly* why I'm here."

Her daughter cheered and jumped down, tugging at Theodora to follow.

For a short while, Theodora played with the children at the fountain, splashing water into their giggling faces, retreating when they chased her and shrieking as they finally caught her. When they shook the linen sheet and lifted it in an arching tunnel, Theodora tried to run through but never made it out the other side. She didn't care that her hair and fine clothes hung heavy with water. Theodora knew this would be the last time she'd see her daughter. This child would grow up and lose all memory of her, but perhaps she'd remember this moment or this day, something hazy, but happy.

When they finally returned to the domicile, Theodora dried off, and Anastasia gathered a meal of bread, oil, and boiled carrots. The food tasted so plain compared to the fine cuisines Theodora enjoyed lately, served at the fine estates of wealthy Romans.

"Palatina reminds me of you, Theodora," said Maximina as they ate.

"She does?" said Theodora, recalling memories of being a girl in the same dwelling, fidgeting at the same table, and with a younger Maximina facing her. "You better latch the windows then."

"I wouldn't dare. I always let *you* sneak out," said Maximina. "Why should I stop her?"

Theodora scoffed. "You never knew when I snuck out."

But Maximina grinned and ignored the seemingly untrue comment.

"Then why didn't you stop me?"

"Why?" Maximina shrugged. "I liked that you were a curious girl."

Theodora's attention slipped back to her daughter and realized that she, herself, found Palatina intriguing. Her daughter had a loud voice and spoke her Greek fluently already. She was so lively and her face so expressive, with traces of Theodora's face appearing in the features. Theodora smiled absently. She saw how Palatina intuitively drew attention to herself, calculating her remarks and gauging reactions. Theodora perceived in her daughter a common set of eyes that looked upon the world with fascination. She dared to wonder how well she'd do now if motherhood came upon her. But as she watched her daughter, she noticed Maximina watching her. So Theodora stubbornly returned her attention to the table. "I've been delaying as long as I could, but one of the reasons for my visit is to say goodbye."

The table fell silent.

Theodora continued. "A titled man bought my indenture and so I'll reside with him in North Africa."

Palatina exaggerated a slump of her shoulders and rolled her eyes. "Where's that?"

Theodora kept her own eyes on her mother. "It's a place very far away."

Maximina dipped her bread in oil. "You said he was titled. What's his title?"

"He's to be the governor of Cyrenaica."

"A governor?" said Maximina with a big smile. She then clasped her hands together. "Oh, I knew you'd come around, Theodora. I knew Fortuna couldn't be wrong."

"What's a governor?" said Palatina.

Maximina leaned in. "A rich man, little one, just like the ones you wave at in the streets."

"Ah!" said Theodora playfully. "You wave at the rich men, do you?"

Palatina slapped a hand over her eyes in embarrassment. "I'm waving at their horses."

Maximina pressed her hands into her dark, doughy bosom. "Finally, no more of that theater life. There's no dishonor in being the quiet lady of a rich man."

"What's a quiet lady?" said Palatina. "I want to be one."

"Why did you say that in front of her?" said Theodora.

Maximina returned a stern look. "Don't shy away. Answer your daughter's question."

Theodora sensed an instruction from her mother. So, she turned to Palatina. "It's a woman who lives with a man, like a wife." But in her mind, she went on to say, *unless she's discarded on a whim.*

"Tell us about the Governor's Palace," said Anastasia.

Theodora waved off the enthusiasm. "It's newly built, but it'll be nothing like the Daphne." She knew that the distinction meant little to her mother, and for a moment Theodora enjoyed being the daughter who exceeded her mother's hopes, but when she saw the awe in Palatina's eyes, she enjoyed being a mother who impressed her child.

"But that's so wonderful, Theodora," said Anastasia.

"And what about her?" Maximina said, nodding at Palatina. "Can she go?"

Theodora stared at her daughter. "Unfortunately, no. The governor made that abundantly clear. I wouldn't want to raise her around the governor anyway," she said, her standard excuse. She wanted to change the topic. "I'll send money home to you all, just as I've always done." At that, Theodora pulled out a cloth purse tied with braided threads. She shook the purse so all heard the pleasant jingle of coins. "There's plenty of gold and silver in here."

Maximina took the purse, but Palatina reached out and said, "I wanna hold it."

Theodora watched as Palatina and Anastasia crowded her mother, hoping to behold the sight of gold coins. But again, she focused on Palatina. "I want her to have good clothes," she said. "I want her to eat well and get medicines when she's sick. I want her to have a dowry for a husband one day—a craftsman, a respectable man with the Blues . . ."

But Theodora noticed that she spoke only to herself. The others were fully distracted by the gold and silver. She considered repeating herself but realized she had no means to enforce her demands, even as the girl's mother. In the past, she always saw Palatina as an inconvenience, an afterthought. Now, Theodora saw a girl who'd one day grow into a woman, who'd be left to face an unforgiving world and may have even *needed* Theodora. Her natural authority as the girl's mother hung there for a moment. And then passed.

I'm abandoning my child.

A sudden upwelling of brutal regret struck Theodora, like an arrow in the throat, a feeling so powerful that she arose from the table and turned away.

"What is it, Theodora?" said Maximina.

Theodora came home to bid farewell, not lament past decisions. She turned back and crouched in front of Palatina, who absently jingled gold coins in her hand. "I have to go now, Palatina."

"Can we play in the water again?"

"No," said Theodora, kissing her daughter on the cheek and then on the forehead. She gave her daughter a strong hug and tried to memorize the feel of the little girl in her arms and the smell of her hair. "Just know that I kept you away from the bad places of this city," Theodora said and stood. "That counts for something, I think." She knew that Maximina didn't understand, but she couldn't linger any longer. She was glad she visited her old dwelling, but it was time to go. "Goodbye," she said, but her voice was unstable.

THIRTY-EIGHT

Theodora returned to the wagon and felt the overwhelming emotion melt into a terrible apathy. She couldn't feel anything. She had to let go.

When the wagon neared the Amphitheater, thoughts of Palatina were broken by the cadence of blacksmith hammers, the murmur of foot traffic, and the sudden applause from a play still in progress. Even the far-off cheers of the Hippodrome struck her as bittersweet. Theodora knew that all these sounds and smells, so real as they occurred at the moment, would be difficult to recall one day.

Most of her friends worked at the hour of her departure, so none, except Antonina, were there to see her off. As the carriage driver loaded her chest of clothing and perfumes, Theodora embraced Antonina one last time. When she opened her eyes, she spotted a man on horseback across the street, flanked by four Palatine guardsmen.

Justinian.

He sat upright in the saddle, helmetless, fist against his hip, his silk tunic rippling in the heavy breezes. The sight of him made Theodora's heart flutter, but Justinian didn't move. His gaze stayed fixed on her.

"Seems you have an imperial escort to see you off," said Antonina and winked. Then she grew serious. "Many fortunes, Theodora. You've always been a friend to me."

Finally, Theodora entered the cramped wooden carriage and felt the contraption lurch forward. Right away, she leaned to peer through the large aperture. She saw the black nostrils of a white stallion come into view. The horse nickered at sight of her, its ears flopping in opposite directions, its tail perched high, and its hooves clopping pleasantly upon the cobbles.

"They told me that you were leaving," Justinian said quietly, as if to himself. "Theodora, I had nothing to do with this decision."

"I know," she said through the window. "But it's the right decision. Come now, Justinian, how could I stay here?"

"I don't want you to leave. I'll arrange to have your indenture restored to your brothel. Or a different place of business. Wherever you wish."

"No, Justinian," she said, her voice penetrating the clamor of the streets. "I don't want to work in the brothels anymore."

"You don't have to go back there," he said. "What if I arranged for you to reside elsewhere, in a place I pay to upkeep?"

"As your mistress?" said Theodora, smiling at the thought. "Is that what you want of me? To dwell alone while you wed an heiress? No, I'd stare out the window and wither away."

Justinian faced her from atop his horse, staring more intently at her now. "I need you here."

Just yesterday, those words might have entered into Theodora and spread through her like soothing warm water. But an idea had taken her, an idea that hardened almost at once. "My sister always said that I never knew when to get off a stage," she said. "Well, now I know better. My bit part in this play has ended, and this time, I'll not linger."

Justinian steered his stallion around the foot traffic before pulling back alongside the carriage. "It's not as you say. My father is emperor, yes, but that doesn't change how I feel about you, Theodora. You'll never be an unwanted guest to me," he said. "Never."

"You say that now," she said. "But eventually a day would come where your new life will clash with the old. Today, you answer to no one, Justinian. Tomorrow, there will be a wife."

"A political union. She'd be my wife in name only."

"But a wife . . . ," she said, unembarrassed, the word echoing a sweet-sounding bond between herself and Justinian, one that almost seemed possible when spoken aloud. "Is that not the greatest alliance of men and women? Is that not how they face the world together?"

Justinian only stared at her accusingly. "You demand what isn't possible and then profess a lesser role to be unfit," he said, his voice rising. "Yet you ride out this very moment to be the concubine of this Hacebolus. Why him? Why not me?"

"Because I can be such a woman for him," she said. "A lesser role for a lesser man. I could never be that woman for you."

Justinian led his white stallion even closer to the wagon. He leaned so close that his head came right up to the opening, their faces close enough to arouse desire in Theodora. She felt it in her belly, her chest and mouth.

"Don't leave," he said as if issuing a command. "We'll find a path through."

Theodora shook her head. "I wish to leave while I can remember you as you are now, as a man who wanted me to stay. That'll be enough for me. And for you? I hope you get your chance to remake the world. I hope you get everything you dream for, Justinian. You deserve it."

Justinian wore the look of a man who expected to get his way and only now realized he'd fall short. He seemed to consider a thousand retorts, but instead, he leaned down from his horse and kissed Theodora through the aperture. The two stayed joined at the mouth, and her mind emptied of all words while a sweet sensation coursed through her body. But the uneven motion of the carriage and his horse pulled their lips apart. Theodora caught her breath and recovered. "There's just no place for me in your world, Justinian," she said. "Not anymore."

At this, Justinian yanked violently back on his reins, turning his horse sideways in the street and coming to a stop. He stared at Theodora with forceful brown eyes, his clothing rippling in the salty gusts as the carriage pulled away. His mounted guards gathered up at his side. She watched as the whole of Constantinople rose up behind him, the rooftops hazy, the city walls so mighty. The sounds and activities of the city filled in around him, a man who might one day become an emperor. Theodora stared at Justinian through the window until he was a small figure on the streets silhouetted against many.

When the carriage turned toward the bustling docks of the Golden Horn, Theodora lost all sight of Justinian. She felt a pop in her chest, the final crushing of her heart. She released a heavy, uneven breath, fell back onto the bench, and succumbed to tears. A ship awaited her. She'd sail far from home, into a foreign land and a new life.

The course before her was no longer one forced upon her. As always, Theodora made that path one she imposed herself. Her choice. And for the first time, she felt truly alone.

PART 3

EXILE

THIRTY-NINE

Two years later
520 A.D.
Sozusa, North Africa, Byzantine Empire

Theodora awoke at midday to the sound of swans. She blinked
until the blurry world came into focus. For a moment, she
thought herself back in Constantinople, in her bed at the
brothel, somewhere near the cheers of an unseen Hippodrome
crowd. But the dream dissolved.

And the heat of the desert greeted her.

Theodora yawned and stretched, taking in the mixed aromas of sea salt
and sand lilies, breathing slowly with the lingering spell of sleep. The bright
sun flooded the chamber, revealing two other women laying with her in a
large bed, Helena and Sophia the mute. The women were naked and slept
peacefully. For a while, Theodora merely listened to the sounds of the world
through the open windows. She heard the soft gush of ocean waves, the cries

of seagulls, and voices from the city streets. From the pools outside, she heard the gentle honks of the governor's prized swans.

Eventually, Theodora sat up, threw on a silk robe, and strolled to a row of open windows. The view before her was far different than any view from Constantinople. From the second floor of the palace, she looked out and saw a sweeping blue-black stripe of sea that stretched across the horizon. White wood smoke billowed into the sky from the lighthouse, and a slight bustle stirred on the streets below. The whole of Sozusa looked like one tiny section of Constantinople laid out along a desert coastline. No great sea walls faced defiantly out to the horizon and no Hippodrome loomed above the rooftops.

This was the sparse frontier of the Eastern Roman Empire. She counted only three basilicas, a bathhouse, a small theater off to the east, and a modest harbor lined with perhaps a dozen ships. Directly below Theodora was the main imperial highway. The roadway ran alongside the Governor's Palace and stretched into the hinterlands both east and west.

Sozusa was one of the Five Cities that made up the Pentapolis of Cyrenaica, and now it was Theodora's home. She felt the burn of the Libyan sun upon her skin and the hot salt air in her lungs. Whereas Constantinople was a young city, a fortress behind impregnable walls, surrounded by naval dromons and home to the Roman emperor, Sozusa felt ancient and un-guarded by contrast. The white-robed folk who roamed the streets seemed unhurried, barely connected to the events of the capital. Caravans moved lazily across the coastline, following the shade of fig palms that swished in the breezes. And every time Theodora watched a merchant ship sail out the harbor gates and head east, she wondered whether that same ship would ap-pear in the Golden Horn. Would that ship be in the background as Justinian rode his horse down the Middle Way?

"Don't leave," he'd said.

Theodora dropped her head and shook out the thoughts. Such recol-lections never helped and, besides, Sozusa was her home now. And in Sozusa, she hadn't the burdens of the theater or brothels. Life was as she expected . . . dull and without applause. She couldn't tell herself that she was happy, but she no longer felt the anxiety that used to stalk her each day in

Constantinople. In her heart, Theodora knew that such a life was the best a woman could hope for, and she had that life. Yet beneath the oppressive boredom of a concubine, Theodora felt, but couldn't stop, the ever-creeping preference for idleness. Laziness was a numbing luxury. If she wished, she could slip back into the cool silk of colored blankets, lay her head upon plush, log-like pillows, reposition, and fall again to sleep.

But Theodora did have one unspoken purpose left. She still passed information on to the Blue faction. Her information traveled from lips to ears all the way back to Constantinople, and, at least in her imagination, to Justinian. As always, though, there was little to tell, usually the names of foreigners the governor met with, rumors about the Vandal kingdom, and gossip she overheard during the governor's many parties. She wondered, though, who in the Sacred City cared about the goings on at the bitter edge of the empire?

"Theodora," said a woman's soft voice. "The governor called for you."

Theodora glanced over to see Samira, a tall Ethiopian woman, whose skin bore a beautiful sheen of dark brown, as smooth as polished wood. Her face was perfectly shaped and symmetrical, with prominent cheekbones, plump painted lips, and a tight hood of patterned blue fabric. Theodora liked Samira's look, particularly the gold bangles along her forearm and the layers of colored fabric around her neck and collarbones. Apparently, she'd been the illegitimate daughter of an Ethiopian prince before Hacebolus brought her to the palace. "What does he want?" said Theodora. None of the concubines had any authority in the palace, so it was unusual to be summoned during the day, especially when the governor was with his advisors.

"He wants to talk. I'm not sure what about," Samira said with a shrug. Her words carried a heavy African accent that Theodora found pleasant, even noble.

"Any word from my contact?"

Samira looked around to be sure no one overheard. "He just arrived. He's waiting downstairs."

"Can you tell him I'll be with him shortly?" said Theodora. "Right after I find out what the governor wants. Thank you, Samira."

Samira nodded and vanished. She too, was an informer for the Blues and had a knack for knowing the events of the palace before anyone else.

Theodora quickly readied herself. She donned a red and yellow silk robe that left a large "V" shape of bare skin from her collar to her navel. She tied scarlet sailcloth around her waist and felt the silk, as cool as water, cling to her figure. Around her neck, she wrapped a triangle of golden lacework, dotted with polished onyx, and then she attached topaz earrings to dangle below her lobes. After she painted her face, she then made her way through the Governor's Palace. She reached the mosaic-tiled floors of a breezy atrium, where an open archway led out to a courtyard.

"Ah, Theodora, come, come, come," said Governor Hacebolus from beyond the archway. "You move slower than a wounded camel, I swear it."

Theodora meandered out to the courtyard where Hacebolus sat. The local traders called the courtyard a "caravansary," a stopover for caravans to rest and trade wares. A shaded colonnade traced the perimeter of the sand-dusted square, centered with a gushing fountain. And in the scorching heat of the Libyan desert, no sound was sweeter to Theodora than the trickle of fresh water.

The advisors and creditors surrounding him all glanced at Theodora when she approached. Typically, concubines stayed away from prying eyes, since the Christians did not approve of the practice as the old Pagans did. The governor, though, sat at a small table, eating a midday meal. He'd gained weight since the days she'd met him back in Constantinople. No longer did he project a dark male virility. After two years of demanding imperial oversight, his dark face had thickened, his black beard showed flecks of gray, and his muscular frame included a protruding belly.

"I have guests coming in from Ravenna," said Hacebolus without looking at Theodora. "Friends of King Theodoric. They've requested quarter here on their way through to Alexandria."

"Barbarians?" said Theodora. "Here?"

"Yes, wealthy barbarians. Members of the Ostrogothic nobility. From what I hear, decades of prosperity have tamed them a little. In a few days, they'll quarter here, and I intend to treat them as guests. It could help relations with the Gothic court."

Theodora already felt desert sweat forming on her forehead. She didn't care about the governor's guests. "Why are you telling me this?"

"They're expecting to be entertained in the Roman style. They'll want the kind of lowborn entertainment you were known for. So, I want you to put something together for these men when they arrive."

Theodora flinched. "Have one of the other girls do it."

The governor stopped and glanced up as if offended. "Mind yourself when you address me, Theodora. We're not at leisure here," he said. Then he signaled his advisors, a mix of Romans and Libyans. "You men should've seen what she did at my coronation. They still talk about it in the capital."

Theodora glanced at the advisors. They held stern faces, but looked over Theodora's body, making no effort to hide their imaginings. She pulled the edges of her robe tighter. She knew she risked angering the governor, but pressed him anyway. "You said I wouldn't have to do that kind of work anymore."

"I said you wouldn't have to work in the brothels. Besides, it's just one night."

But one night was all it took, she thought. One night of performing and she'd be back to entertaining every guest who visited the governor.

"When would I have time for any of that?"

"Time?" Hacebolus laughed loudly with food in his mouth, his black beard oily in the sunlight. "Woman, all you have is time."

The advisors joined in the laugh, and Hacebolus returned to his meal—strips of cooked antelope, a side of glazed figs, and an exotic peeled orange from Morocco. He then tossed bread bits over to his swans at the pool; they snatched the bread greedily. "That's it, Krikou. Easy, boy," he said. "Anyway, I want the Notorious Theodora for a night. Shock them a bit, make them laugh like fools!" He shrugged. "Sophia the mute can help you. She worked in the theaters of Tyre before I brought her here."

"But I haven't done that kind of thing for almost two years," she said. "The show would be dreadful."

Governor Hacebolus stopped eating and dropped his fists on the table. "That's enough. I'm not making a request." With a flick of his fork, he returned to his meal. "It'll all come back to you. Like I said, get with Sophia. And remember, these are barbarians. To them, fine art is a painted handprint on a horse's ass," he said, and the men around him tittered smugly.

Some part of Theodora wanted to give the performance. The thrill of removing her clothes in front of a lusty audience again, the clamor of men calling out as if for mercy, and pleasure from unfamiliar men afterward—all of it still stirred her. Somewhere. But the numbness crept back, stilling her, and she sighed. The urge to do anything at all didn't last anymore.

Before Theodora could respond, a manservant approached. "Some Berbers are here with wares for trade, Governor."

"Ah yes. I nearly forgot," he said.

Theodora heard the squeal of the iron entrance gates as two Roman soldiers strode backward, pulling each door open. She watched camels, mules, and robed men amble through the opening, lightly dusted in sand.

"Go on, Theodora. You have your tasks," said Governor Hacebolus without looking at her. Then he stood, wiped his mouth, and greeted the caravan.

As Theodora turned to leave, activity near the rear of the caravan caught her attention. She shielded her eyes to get a better look. She watched as a stream of women exited the back of a wood wagon, each wearing tattered clothing around their waist and chest. One by one, they emerged and lined up before the governor.

Was he considering yet another concubine?

One of the women had skin as brown as the Berber, while another looked pale with yellow hair, and yet another had the awful wrinkle of burned flesh aside her face and only a stump for an arm. The last to emerge wasn't a woman at all, but a girl with unkempt black hair and sun-darkened skin.

"What's this?" Theodora asked aloud.

The advisors glanced at her, but none answered. They all reset their attention on the caravan women with fascination.

Theodora sighed in exasperation and strode away from the gawking advisors. She ran into Samira near the entrance archways but brushed past her friend. "The governor's considering another concubine."

Samira spun and followed Theodora. "But there's already no room in our quarters."

"I doubt he cares," said Theodora. "He seems only to want more." She quieted as they passed two Roman guards. Then Theodora turned to Samira and whispered, "Is the priest ready for me?"

"Yes. He's in the chapel waiting," said Samira. "But I have to go. The governor wants me in his bedchambers after his meal."

"We'll talk more after."

Samira nodded and set off. Theodora pulled open the chapel doors and peered inside. She saw a dark Christian sanctuary with shimmering gold mosaics and half-melted candles. On the far side, a lone priest was polishing the reliquary, which was a large sarcophagus-sized container. He was another contact for the Blue faction, which used the network of churches to pass information throughout the empire. At the creak of the door's hinges, the priest turned to see Theodora. The priest had sharp angles in his cheeks, small eyes, and a conical beard of black and gray.

He walked to the altar and knelt. Theodora knelt beside him and they both clasped their hands together in prayer.

"What news?" he whispered.

"Very little," said Theodora. "I overheard the governor complaining about the cost of this year's wheat festival. So Constantinople can expect a large grain shipment this season," she said. "And something else just came up."

The priest didn't move. "Yes?"

"I heard this only moments ago outside, but the governor intends to quarter men of the Ostrogothic court. They're coming in from Ravenna, and he plans to host them for an evening. He seems to think it'll help form ties with Italy."

"A waste of time. Italy's lost to the empire," he said. "Anything else?"

"For now, no. What news in Constantinople?"

"Well, Emperor Justin turned the religious situation around. After years of infighting under Anastasius, Justin's making some headway with uniting the churches."

"And Justinian?"

"Justinian reopened a dialogue with Pope Hormisdas in Rome, but that has angered Pope Timothy in Alexandria," said the priest, frustrated. "Justinian believes the papal feud is purely a matter of wording. He's trying to write a single doctrine that all three popes can agree on."

"Well, if anyone can find the right words, he will," she said.

The priest turned to face Theodora. "He also sent another message this time. This message comes from Justinian himself and is meant specifically for you."

"For me?" Theodora felt a flush of heat in her cheeks. "What did he say?"

"Justinian wished to tell you that he thinks of you still. He says that the Sacred City has become a dull place without you in it. He says that your departure has left him seeing the world in a faded hue. He described it as colored linens made pale in the sun."

Theodora met the eyes of the priest and for a moment, she felt as though she looked into Justinian's eyes through the man. "Is that all he said?"

"No. He said he hopes that you've found happiness in the desert."

An aching filled Theodora's chest. The words of intimacy filtered right into the undefended center of her heart, the very place where daydreams still filled her soul with longing, where sweetness stayed sweet, no matter what happened in the world outside.

"Do you wish to send a message to him?" said the priest.

Theodora shifted and removed a pin at the top of her hair, letting her long, black locks fall free. Then she tucked her finger under the beard at the priest's chin, leaned in, and kissed him. Theodora closed her eyes and imagined Justinian in the darkness beyond her lids. Her lips stayed pressed on the priest for a good long time, the bare contact being the sole focus of her conscious mind. Even as she pulled back, she savored the slow peeling away of his lips from her own, her mind sensing only Justinian in the kiss. When Theodora slowly opened her eyes again, the stern face of the priest was replaced by a stunned and boyish expression. She whispered seductively. "Will you tell him what I've said?"

The priest swallowed involuntarily and then nodded rapidly. "Of course. Well . . . I'll try to find the right words. I'm not sure how to . . ."

Theodora grinned at the dazed man before arising. She took the single gold coin he'd been clutching in his fingers, her informer's payment. She then left the altar, but paused beneath the archway of the narthex and turned around. "Tell me. Has he found anyone yet?"

"Justinian?" said the priest with a sympathetic smile. "My colleagues in the capital tell me there are many ladies at the imperial court. But there's no word he's pursued union with any of them."

Theodora bounced on her feet as she turned to leave the chapel. "Good," she said with satisfaction.

FORTY

By the time Theodora returned to the concubinary, the pleasant feelings had worn off. Now, she smelled perfume in the sweltering air—notes of jasmine, cinnamon bark, and African ginger—a fragrance that was strongest whenever the women began stirring for the day. She looked for Samira but didn't see her. She spotted Sophia the mute reclining on a couch draped in leopard pelts, coolly fanning herself beside a sago palm in a vase. She was bare-breasted and wore a green cotton headwrap with billowy, loose linens around each leg.

Theodora approached Sophia. The couch was large enough for both women, so she sat beside her friend. "I've news for you," she said.

Sophia raised an eyebrow and smiled. As always, the young woman radiated with warmth, thought Theodora, silent and feline. Her inability to speak made Sophia a natural mime, ideal for the theater. Her eyes sparkled with mischief and her every subtle body movement signaled a vast inner sensuality.

"The governor wants us to put on a silly show," said Theodora. "A theater show for guests."

Sophia brightened.

Theodora shook her head. "I told him we didn't want to *perform*. But he's insisting."

Sophia placed her hand gently on Theodora's knee as if to affirm something pleasant. Her eyes danced with excitement.

"You like the idea?" said Theodora.

Sophia nodded.

Theodora reclined sideways, fist to temple. "But if we do this one show, the governor will bother us all the time."

Sophia shrugged, shook her head, and held up one finger.

"One show only?"

Sophia nodded.

Theodora scowled playfully. "Well, if we're to do just one show, which should we do?" she said. "The governor wants something bawdy, of course."

But as Theodora combed her thoughts for the right play, Sophia's attention shifted toward the door. Theodora turned to see Samira holding open the scarlet curtains at the entrance of the concubinary. She ushered in an unwashed girl, no older than thirteen, the same girl Theodora had seen with the caravan outside. "Who's that with you?" she said.

"This is our newest sister," said Samira. "The governor relieved her from the caravan, and she's to stay with us."

There was a beat of full silence before all the women spoke at once. In every corner of the room, words chirped and chattered and created an unfriendly din. Theodora and Sophia exchanged a concerned glance.

"Stop it. All of you," said Theodora, and the volume in the room receded. "It's not the girl's fault she's here."

On the other side of the room, a concubine named Helena, who played a game of backgammon with another woman, spoke up. She was a curvy woman who talked with the fiery temper of a street girl. "The Christian priests are already against us being here," she said. "This girl gives them the perfect excuse to turn against all of us."

The room chattered in agreement.

Theodora shook her head. "Where's she to go?"

Helena counted off on her fingers. "Back to the caravan, one of the brothels, or the orphanage. But she can't stay here."

"Yes, she can," said Theodora, rising to her feet.

The concubinary was, in effect, an egalitarian circle of women. The ease of their lives removed the need for a competitive hierarchy; so the sudden note of authority in Theodora's voice hushed the women and put them on guard. She felt their kohl-lined eyes narrow on her as she crossed the room to stand beside Samira and the girl. She looked down at the girl and then back at Helena. "Come now, who here actually believes the governor will do anything we tell him to do?"

No one answered.

Theodora continued. "We can't send this girl to some brothel. I can't believe I heard you suggest it, Helena. She's better off here with us."

"But, Theodora, every girl's better off here with us," said Helena. "We can't take them all in. Where is she going to sleep?"

"We'll find a place."

"And I suppose you'll be the one to look after her?"

"We'll all look after her," said Theodora, feeling the anxiety of taking an unpopular position.

"Well, I certainly won't," Helena said. "And I'm not afraid to tell you or the governor what I think. If he wants to pack this room with more women, then I say we fight him on it!"

Theodora kept her voice even. "But she's not a woman, Helena. She's a girl."

"Even worse. Let him pay for little girls at the theater or brothel like everybody else."

The voices of the concubinary agreed but then fell hush all at once. Theodora watched as every eye shifted to a space just behind her. When she turned around, she saw Governor Hacebolus standing there, with his body-guard and chamberlain. His eyes glittered with the satisfaction of having caught the women by surprise.

Theodora noticed the other concubines stayed silent, blank-faced, fanning themselves with peacock feathers, trying to appear casual.

"No, please," he said and stepped into the room. "Do continue. I seem to have walked into a serious council. Such elite minds. Such logic and resolve. Please, Helena," he said with sarcastic concern. "Enthrall me with a concubine's wisdom. You were saying?"

"But Governor," said Helena, her voice no longer defiant, but pleading. "There's no more room. We're overcrowded as it is."

"Truly?" he said. "Overcrowded? Well, you're the largest one of the bunch. You've enough bread dough above your hips to feed the poor on Sunday. If I'm sending anyone to the brothels, it'll be you, Helena. Now, were you advising me or were you just braying like a donkey?"

Theodora watched Helena flop back into her chair, her face pouting.

"Anyone else care to advise me?" said Hacebolus, looking around the room. "No? Just a bunch of bleating and braying from my painted women?" Then he straightened and smiled. "I thought so. Now I've spared you fine women from your public lives. I let you roll around in here like lazy hogs in the mud. So, do I care if you're displeased? Helena? Answer me."

"No, Governor," she said.

He held up a finger. "No, I don't. Remember what happened to Constantina when she decided to advise rather than please me? I threw her into the streets and locked the door. You all heard her pounding on the doors, and you all remember when she finally gave up and skulked away. So unless you wish to wander beggarly upon the streets, dressed as you are now, remember your duties here. Theodora?"

"Yes, Governor?" said Theodora, stepping forward.

"You seem like the only one with any sense in here. You're to make sure this girl is properly trained for her duties. Make a good girl out of her."

Theodora felt a thud in her chest. "Yes, Governor. We've had our say and know what to do."

"We're doing this girl a favor," he said, looking back at Helena. "Better here than out there. Show some compassion."

Theodora hated hearing a man who purchased slaves speak of it as compassion. She felt the gnawing anger that used to lurk below the surface back in Constantinople. It was Magister Origen's bargain all over again—accept the favor of a powerful man, and he'd press his claims upon the body with or without consent. Theodora knew the path of resistance led nowhere and she hadn't felt that hard sting for many years.

When the women appeared to lose interest, the governor faced Theodora, and his voice became conversational. "I'm counting on you."

She hesitated. "I understand, Governor."

Hacebolus studied his newly purchased girl. "Now I paid extra for this one," he said. "She's an unspoiled girl," he said and rubbed off a dirt smudge from the girl's cheek. She pulled away. "I've never sampled the fruit at first ripe. So, instruct this girl on her duties here and have her ready tonight."

"All right," said Theodora with irritation in her voice. "Can I take her down to the baths now?"

His gaze lingered on the girl a bit longer. "Yes," he said. "Give her a wash and a good hot meal. Let's welcome her properly. You hear me, girl? No longer will you feel hunger or thirst. Not here. So listen to Theodora. She'll teach you what you need to know so you can enjoy all the hospitality I have to give. You have a good life ahead of you now."

Governor Hacebolus glanced at Theodora and nodded, apparently convinced that he'd assured the girl of his kindness. Then he, his bodyguard, and his chamberlain left the concubinary.

When he was gone, Samira placed a hand on Theodora's back. "Do you want me to help you?"

Theodora sighed through her nose. "I don't like this." She looked down at the girl and saw weary eyes staring back at her. "Come on. Let's go wash up."

As Theodora ushered the girl out of the concubinary, she heard the other concubines whispering.

"I'm sorry if I'm a bother," the girl said.

But Theodora was in no mood for conversation. "You'll be fine."

"Am I to be a handmaiden here in the palace?"

"Of a sort," said Theodora as she entered the baths at the rear of the palace.

Two older female attendants were busy changing out the incense ash. Theodora handed the girl off to the attendants, then sat down in the corner of the room, crossed her legs, and leaned forward. The room smelled like a well with hints of burnt wood, while the tangling luminance of water danced upon the stonework and ceilings.

Theodora watched the attendants remove the girl's sand-worn caravan garb and guide her into the hot waters. Every now and then, the girl glanced back at Theodora as if trying to get a better read.

The governor caused a serious problem with this girl, thought Theodora. Of course, he knew nothing of the reality of quartering a girl her age; he'd merely shrug at any mention of difficulties and expect Theodora to solve every burden without a word. Theodora meant to keep the girl away from the caravan, but she hadn't been prepared to care for the girl. She was never a good mother as it was.

Theodora sat back on the bench and thought of her days at the koitóna. She recalled Madame Glyceria, a woman whose face had faded over the years. She remembered how the old woman so easily sent her off with the magistrate, never once alerting her to the devastating reality. Perhaps Madame Glyceria thought it better that Theodora find out on her own.

Now, Madame Glyceria's task fell to Theodora. She understood the old woman's quandary. Training a girl to be a prostitute seemed cruel and inhuman, an immoral undertaking. And yet without such training, a girl would be unprepared for what was to come, just as Theodora was unprepared. She couldn't change the role this girl would fill in the world. So what then could she do?

Was there a *good* way to train a child for prostitution?

Theodora suddenly squeezed her eyes shut and dropped her head. She knew the answer, but that didn't change the task at hand.

FORTY-ONE

After the bath, Theodora took the girl to the wardrobe, where she dressed her in a white gown. A small gown was difficult to find. As she ushered the girl through the palace, many slaves and servants took notice of their passing, since concubines rarely walked about in the open.

Finally, a welcomed sight arrived when Samira came down a staircase and joined Theodora. They entered the kitchen, where the two women gathered items for the girl to eat—a warm bread loaf, a cup of oiled olives, goat cheese with sea salt, ripe tomatoes, and a bowl of almonds. To drink, Theodora poured the girl fresh water, and herself, wine. She seated the girl at a table where slaves typically ate, and then she stood, leaning against the back worktop, a ledge adorned with clay bowls and iron pots.

The girl ate like an animal. Her cheeks bulged as she chewed and she squeezed her eyes shut when she forced down food with each swallow. When she drank, water spilled over her chin and streamed down her throat. She spoke not a word.

"I don't know if I can do this, Samira," said Theodora, far enough away so the girl couldn't overhear. "How's it my duty to instruct this girl?"

Samira sidled up beside Theodora. "Do you want me to do it? I fear the governor has overburdened you. First the play, now this."

"It's not that," said Theodora. "It's this training."

"Well, she has to learn sometime. Better it come from you."

Theodora eyed the Roman girl. "I used to wonder why people looked away when bad things happen to girls. I used to hate them for looking away, for leaving me alone when something terrible came up close, for not caring."

Samira spoke. "Come now, lying with a man isn't of itself so bad a thing. It's all about how you present it. You know how fun it can be with the right state of mind."

"I'm sorry, Samira, but there's nothing fun about sex when you're forced to do it."

"Theodora, I've never seen you so melancholy. What is it? You haven't even taken a sip of your wine," Samira said.

"I've never been on this side of it," said Theodora. "This has always been a private matter for me."

"I can see this weighs heavily on you. Why don't you let me instruct the girl tonight? Go back upstairs and—"

"No," Theodora said. "I remember the madame who trained me. She kept silent until it was too late. People don't like talking about these things, so nothing ever changes." Theodora sighed. "I also remember the first time I sought a man out for myself. I learned what every girl learns, that I could lay with a man and the world didn't end afterward. I was still me the next day and everything goes back to normal. That's when I decided that I'd never again be helpless. Not me. So I came up with my own path through. I'd master a world that frightened and fascinated other women. I became bolder than they were. I taught myself to ignore all caution and do anything with a man, never to refuse, never to hesitate. And, surprisingly, I liked it. Perhaps I betrayed some part of myself, but I didn't care. The more I hurt myself, the more I wanted to hurt myself." And Theodora shook her head. "So strange is the world inside us. But you see, that was *my* choice. That's how I did it," she said and lowered her voice. "It's quite a different thing to pass this on, like a mother to a daughter. Maybe that's how you know when something is evil, when you have misgivings about teaching that thing to a child."

Samira pressed her dark forehead against Theodora's shoulder as if she too felt a private ache from her past.

Theodora said nothing for a while, but the heaviness filled her body now, an ugly feeling. "In here where it's safe, we privileged women giggle and play and indulge every demand upon us. Then we pass it on, out there to all the girls we don't see . . . they pay the heavy price."

The Roman girl slowed her eating and took long drinks of water. When she saw Theodora staring at her, she smiled.

Theodora smiled back, but it was forced. "I was so focused on saving this girl from the caravan, I didn't even think about what came next. Now she's in my care."

"Then she's in good hands," said Samira.

"You know, I used to daydream that someone would come and fight men like the governor," Theodora said. "The men who take what isn't theirs."

"Me too," said Samira.

"But no one ever did . . ."

Samira seemed to sense the dangerous line of thought. She gave Theodora a friendly shake. "Because you'd have to fight everyone everywhere. It would be a fight you couldn't finish, and so you'd fight alone. And a woman should never be so alone."

Theodora looked at Samira and smiled. "You're right." Then she tilted her head and sighed, trying to break the bitter spell. "So tell me, should I be honest with her? Should I tell her exactly what the governor expects and shatter every illusion all at once? Should I seduce the girl, be the older sister who corrupts the younger? Or should I do what the Madame did to me? Say nothing. Look away."

"Just be you," said Samira. "Tell her what she needs to know to the best of your abilities. That's all you can do. At some point, every woman must make this her own burden."

"Because this is where it all begins, Samira," said Theodora. "With a child and an adult. And the terrible truth of it is that too many times, a grown woman is standing there who either tells a girl that this is the way of the world or looks away."

The soothing smile on Samira's face waned. "What are you saying?"

Theodora cleared her throat and drained the glass of wine in a single gulp. "I don't know what I'm saying. I guess I have to get this over with."

Theodora left her friend standing, perplexed. She touched the Roman girl on the shoulder and led her out of the kitchen.

FORTY-TWO

Through the windows, Theodora saw the skies were pink with yellow clouds and that Vespers lit the city streets. The people of the palace also busied themselves at lighting the thousands of candles in every room.

"What's your name?" asked Theodora while they walked.

"Valeria Sidonius," she said. "Daughter of Marinus Sidonius."

A girl of the nobility.

"Well, my name's Theodora, and I'm going to get you ready for your duties here, which for you, start tonight."

"I'm glad you're teaching me my duties," she said. "I knew right away you were the good one here."

Theodora ignored the compliment as she took Valeria up a flight of stairs. She knew the girl might soon change her opinion. "You speak Latin well, Valeria. Where are you from?"

"Rome. My father was a tribune there before we left."

"Really? Why'd you leave?"

"Because my father was removed from his post by King Theodoric."

"The barbarian king," said Theodora.

"We're not supposed to call him that. Back home, the king's people are called Goths, and they control everything. They're very mean to the people, especially if you're Roman."

They reached the top of the stairs and Theodora led Valeria into the vacant salóni. Several mirrors reflected the two when they entered. The room smelled strongly of perfume. Glass vials with colored liquids adorned the shelves, while enamel bowls of water and cloth scattered the benches. Nothing was more precious to a concubine than clean skin, vivid colors, and exotic fragrances.

"Sit, please," said Theodora.

Valeria sat on a seat with a plush scarlet cushion. She bounced on the chair and smiled. "Everything in here is so wonderful. The governor must be a great Roman to hold so high a post."

"He bought his post, like everyone else," said Theodora, lighting the wick to a large lantern.

"My father didn't. He was appointed by the Senate. He was good friends with many senators."

Theodora crouched beside the girl. "Do you miss your home?"

"Very much," she said, her smile fading. Then she brightened. "I miss sneaking down to the courtyard at night, stealing sugared chestnuts, and looking up at the stars. I used to be able to see the Coliseum from our rooftop."

Theodora winked at Valeria. "But pretty girls aren't supposed to be climbing onto rooftops, are they?"

Valeria shrugged and grinned.

"Good for you," Theodora said and nodded in approval. "I used to climb onto the roofs back home too. My mother scolded me, but my father always winked at me, like it was our secret."

Valeria laughed. "Our fathers sound like the same man."

They were nothing alike, thought Theodora, recalling the odor of bears that once clung to her pata's clothes. The two of them came from opposite corners of the empire, from opposite upbringings, yet they both ended up in the same place. "How'd you end up in the caravan?" she said instead.

"Because my father thought Rome had become unsafe for Romans. He decided we should leave Rome and live in an eastern city. We didn't leave alone either. Five other families came with us."

"Where was your mother in all this?"

Valeria looked away briefly. "My mother died when I was little."

So, no Maximina for this girl, thought Theodora. "Where was your father trying to take you?"

"To Caesarea. We got on a ship, but when we stopped at our first port, men boarded the ship and took my father away."

Theodora eyed Valeria. The girl spoke of such terrible events as if detached, without sadness or fear. "Weren't you scared?"

"Yes. These were very bad men. They hit one Roman sailor with a sword, knocking him down. Blood spilled onto the decks from his stomach, and they kicked him until he stopped moving."

"You seem quite calm despite all this."

"Because my father said he'd come back for me and never to lose hope. My father always means what he says."

The girl's blind faith in her father only reminded Theodora that she still spoke with a child. She sighed and grabbed the bowl of kohl. "Have you ever been painted?"

"Yes. Whenever my father attended public festivals or coronations, I'd get painted."

That was a different kind of paint, thought Theodora, the doll-like paint of a nobleman's daughter. She leaned in and stroked lines of kohl along the bottom of Valeria's eye. "Were there any handsome boys back home?"

Valeria looked up so Theodora could better apply the kohl. But a broad smile crept across her face. "Yes."

"What's his name?"

"You can't tell anybody if I tell you."

"I promise, I won't."

"Roderic," said Valeria and lowered her voice. "He's a Goth."

Theodora pulled back with a conspiratorial smirk. "A Goth, you say?"

Valeria giggled. "I know. But he has big blue eyes and golden hair. He's tall and strong."

"Sounds handsome," said Theodora, completing her black ring around the girl's eyes. Then she grabbed scarlet powder and dabbed Valeria's cheeks. "Did you say goodbye to him?"

"In secret, because my father hates Goths. The day I left, Roderic came to our villa in the early morning. I snuck out to see him," said Valeria and covered her mouth. "We kissed."

Theodora wrinkled her nose playfully and smiled at the girl but realized this was her entry point. "Did you like the kiss?"

"Oh yes," she said.

"That's good," said Theodora, arising. She wet her hands and stroked lengths of Valeria's long black hair until the strands were straight and wet. The two looked at each other's reflection in the mirror. "Well, tonight, I want you to think of handsome young Roderic for me."

"Of course."

"Valeria, do you know what's expected of you tonight?"

She didn't answer.

"Valeria?"

"No."

"Well, when Roderic kissed you, did he want you to do anything else?"

"No. He brushed my cheek and said he'd never forget me."

Damn you, Roderic. Why couldn't you have been more of a bastard? "Valeria, did he try and touch you anywhere?" said Theodora.

The girl only shrugged and avoided Theodora's eyes in the mirror.

"Valeria, it's all right. You can tell me. You won't be in any trouble."

After a long wait, Valeria said, "A little, but nothing vulgar."

"Up top or down below?"

Another pause. "Up top, but I pushed his hand away."

"Well, this evening will be a little bit like that," said Theodora, now brushing the girl's hair.

"A little bit like what?"

"The governor," said Theodora, cursing her sudden difficulty with words. "You'll be with the governor tonight, and he'll put his hands on you the way Roderic did, only tonight, you'll let him do it."

Valeria turned around to look at Theodora, incredulous. "I will not. I'm a young lady, and the governor's an old man."

"Exactly, a man. And men like women of all kinds and this man happens to like you."

"Well, I don't like him."

"I know that," said Theodora. "But you'll have to be with him tonight nonetheless. That's why he bought you from the caravan. That is why you're here. It's why we women are all here, including myself."

"You let the governor . . . touch you, and you don't even like him?" said Valeria.

"I let him touch me and more," said Theodora, irritated. She turned Valeria around to face the mirror again. "In exchange, the governor gives me things that I want, like living in this palace. I don't have to deal with the harsher world anymore, just as you no longer have to deal with that caravan. I also get luxuries that—"

Valeria interrupted. "Are you sending me to the governor's bed tonight?"

Theodora stopped brushing. "Yes."

Valeria waited for a moment and then stood up, slapping away the brush. "I'm not a dirty prostitute. Like *you*. I thought you were helping me. But you're just helping the governor."

Theodora pointed to the chair. "I am helping you. Now sit."

"No," said Valeria.

"A girl needs to *know* what she's up against." Theodora grabbed the girl and set her firmly back in the seat. Discomfort washed over her at the physicality, but she tried not to think about it. "This is going to happen tonight, Valeria, whether you like it or not, whether I like it or not. I'm trying to advise you."

"I don't need any more of your advice. Your advice is to be filthy with a grown man, and I'm not going to."

Theodora brushed Valeria's hair again. This was her chance to do what Madame Glyceria never did for her, to warn, to improve something ugly, to *care*. Theodora couldn't give up. "I'm telling you exactly what's about to happen so you're prepared. Wouldn't you feel betrayed if I didn't tell you anything at all?"

Valeria stared at herself in the mirror, and Theodora could feel the girl's feelings. She remembered hating the sight of herself in that mirror, the stupid red of the lips and the stupid black of the eyes. None of it mattered when the magistrate turned her onto her stomach, when he did what he wanted while she cried.

"You're fortunate to be in here," said Theodora. "Most girls like you and me are out in the city tonight and crammed into small rooms. They'll be awake until morning, sharing a bed with four or five different men over the course of the night."

Valeria winced at the thought.

Theodora continued. "Oh yes. That's the hard truth. You and I have it easy."

"When I tell my father what you're saying—"

Theodora stepped in between the mirror and Valeria. "Listen to me. You may have been part of a noble family once, but that's finished. You and your father have been sold into slavery. Pirates capture Roman refugees headed east all the time, and this time they caught you. Do you understand? Your father's not coming back for you."

"Yes, he will, he—"

"He's gone, Valeria. I lost my father once too. You're alone now just like the rest of us," she said, then softened. "This is it now, and it can get worse if you're not careful. If you fight the governor, he can sell you to one of the brothels, and believe me, you don't want that. So yes, I'm teaching you how to handle something you don't want so you can get something out of it that you do want."

Valeria folded her arms and glared at the ground.

Theodora watched the girl's expressions. She needed to see that Valeria appreciated hearing the truth. But Theodora only saw a lump ripple in the girl's throat. Then, the black kohl at the eyes bled a bit. "Don't cry. You'll ruin your paint."

Theodora paused. Something sounded familiar. Then she realized that Magister Origen once said the same thing to her. Those exact words. The phrase, uttered in the magistrate's voice, lay imbedded in her mind, preserved there as a fragment of a nightmare. Yet she just heard the phrase spoken aloud in her own voice.

"What's wrong?" said Valeria.

Theodora didn't look back. Didn't Origen try to break her resistance with words first too? She sniffed and cleared her throat. She turned back and brushed Valeria's hair again. Then she stopped. "The world doesn't end afterward," she said as if rehearsing the lines of thought that once soothed her as a broken girl.

Then she heard a knock at the door. "The governor is in his bedchamber early for the evening," said Samira. "How much longer until the girl's ready?"

Theodora and Valeria stared at each other in the mirror.

"Hello?" said Samira.

"I heard you," Theodora said curtly. "We'll be there shortly."

Valeria spun around and grabbed Theodora's gown with both hands. "Please. Don't make me go to the governor's bed. My father would be so ashamed of me. It's not supposed to be like this."

Theodora crouched in front of the girl. "It's not supposed to be like anything. Better to deal with things as they are."

"Theodora, I don't want to do it."

"Neither do I, but we go anyway."

Valeria pressed into Theodora, squeezing the gown with two fists. "Can't you stop this?"

Theodora didn't answer because the answer was barren, plain, and undeniable: Valeria didn't *have* a choice. At the end of the path, if the girl could not be convinced to lay with the governor, then she would be forced. A thought slipped into Theodora's mind, one she'd been intentionally resisting. She imagined her daughter sitting in the chair, moments from being sent to a man's bed. As an image of Hacebolus smiling at Palatina came into her mind, Theodora shook her head and cleared her thoughts.

Valeria wasn't her daughter. Theodora wiped the kohl that bled from the girl's bottom eyelid and spoke in a soft voice. "Valeria, it's time to go."

The girl looked down slowly, mouth agape, as if finally perceiving the truth of her situation.

Theodora lowered her voice and in the gentlest tone, she spoke. "The governor's going to ask you to remove your clothes in front of him. You can turn your back when you do this. Try talking to him. The more familiar he is to you, the better. Now he may prompt you to speak. To everything he says, just reply, "I don't feel like talking." You can repeat that phrase as many times as you want. "I don't feel like talking." If, during, he starts hurting you, instruct him to go slower. If ever you feel like crying, just close your eyes. It'll end eventually, and I'll be there for you afterward. Valeria? Do you understand?"

Valeria seemed far off. Then she turned her head away. "I don't feel like talking."

Theodora winced as if insulted. "Say that to the governor, not me."

But Valeria stayed fixed.

Theodora pulled back to full height. "If that's the way you want it."

FORTY-THREE

T heodora opened the door to the salóni and gave Valeria a gentle push forward. The other women saw the two emerge. They fanned themselves from behind peacock feathers or sipped wine from silver goblets, idle and bored. After a cursory glance, woman by woman, they each looked away. To other concubines, Valeria was just another girl facing reality. Only Samira stood with a show of concern.

"Will you be all right?" Samira asked Theodora.

Theodora glared back but said nothing. Then she led Valeria out of the women's chamber, into the adjoining rooms, and toward the governor's bedchamber. She walked slowly to delay the ordeal, but with each step, Theodora felt more like a warden escorting a prisoner. Valeria was sedate, perhaps already distancing her private inner self from the real world. Theodora knew the silence and knew the emptiness. It was the mask forming for the first time. And the walk through the palace seemed to go on forever, itself a kind of torture, without any words passing between them. Theodora's discomfort grew amidst the sound of their footfalls. Like echoes in a well, distant tremors of old and blackened feelings came back to her—memories of shrinking in the face of coercion, of being cornered, of participating in her own debasement, as surely as if it were an obligation.

Theodora wasn't improving Madame Glyceria's handling of the matter. She just made it worse. Because Theodora emerged now as a true accomplice, putting *herself* in the role of coercer instead of the governor. Memories of Magister Origen flashed through her mind in waves now, vivid once again. And the magistrate's voice returned to her.

Ambitious girls must learn how to favor the men who help them.

Theodora shook her head, clenching her teeth until she felt her jaw muscles bulge in the corners. So then, there would have to be two Theodoras one last time, she decided, the Theodora who taught Valeria the ways of the world, who did not lie about the role this girl would serve, who met the harsh reality head-on, and then there would be the other Theodora, the one who . . .

. . . the one who looked away.

Theodora stopped walking in midstep. For a moment, she and Valeria stood motionless just outside the governor's bedchamber, where two Roman guards stood, flanking the doorway.

Valeria turned around and stared curiously at Theodora. "What is it?"

"You're not going in that room," said Theodora.

The despondent expression on Valeria's face lifted, and for a moment, the girl's youthful glow came back.

But the governor's bedchamber doors opened, casting yellow light onto the stone floors between the guards. His shadow appeared in the light, and then he stepped out, draining a cup of wine. He wore a silk robe, open down the center, showing a gold medallion hanging against a chest of gray and white bristles. He saw Theodora and Valeria standing there, watching him.

"Ah, my little sweetmeat has been baked and now served," he said but narrowed his kohl-lined eyes with suspicion. "What are you two doing, just standing there?"

"I've had a change of heart, Governor," said Theodora. "Just now. Tonight's too soon for this girl to share her first bed."

The governor scoffed. "She looks perfectly fine to me. She can rest in my bed after."

Theodora stepped in front of Valeria. "No, Governor," she said. "She won't. I offer myself as a replacement."

The governor's face darkened, but Theodora quickly parted her shawl and set the fabric on the outer side of her breasts. She drew in a deep breath, bulging the round flesh of her upper chest, her nipples pressing out from beneath the gown.

Hacebolus stared at her breasts, raised an eyebrow, and sighed. "Well now, I won't be able to shake that sight from my mind."

Theodora turned back to Valeria. "Go back to the salóni," she said.

"No, no, no," said Hacebolus in his theatrical and throaty voice. "You've piqued my interest. I'll have you both in my bed tonight."

Theodora flinched. "You run afoul with such thoughts, Governor."

Irritated, Hacebolus looked at one of the Roman guards. "Cato, when I tell you to do something, do you feel obliged to weigh in on the merits of my judgment?"

"No, Governor," said the soldier without looking.

Hacebolus handed the empty wine cup to the guard. "Do you offer me alternatives, Cato?"

The guard smiled. "I do not, Governor."

"And yet I have this spoiled whore who can't follow simple directions," Hacebolus said. He grabbed Theodora by the arm and yanked her into the bedchamber. "Get in here."

Theodora didn't resist, but when she noticed the guard push Valeria into the room and shut the door, she shrieked. "No! Leave her alone!"

"Damn you, Theodora," said the governor, letting go of her arm with a shove. "Enough. I spend my day trying to keep Cyrenaica from falling apart, and here, in these hours, this is where I get what's mine." He straightened. "I want you and that girl in my bed right now."

Theodora rubbed her arm where the governor grabbed her. "She's not sharing your bed, Governor, and I won't stand aside if you insist."

"You won't stand aside?" the governor said but stiffened as if he suddenly realized Theodora meant to resist in full. He lowered his voice. "Now I've been lenient with you, Theodora, especially you. But if you cross me one more time," he said and then shouted, "I'll throw you into the streets and lock the doors! Just as I did to Constantina. You can beg and whore your way back home."

Valeria slid behind Theodora at the frightening sound of the governor's voice.

If he is threatening, then face him.

That's what Macedonia had said.

Face him.

At last, Theodora understood the cold truth in Macedonia's instruction. This was about power. This was about Theodora's authority on matters she cared about, and if she ever intended to wield power, then she was to refuse, absolutely, the authority of those who opposed her. She steadied herself with a long, deep breath.

"Good," said Hacebolus after the silence. He began removing his robe. "Now undress and get into my bed."

"No," said Theodora and the word held the moment.

The governor paused in his undressing and slowly turned back to eye Theodora.

She continued, this time to Valeria. "Go back to the women's chambers."

Valeria took a few steps toward the door, but the governor's voice boomed out, like a crack of thunder. "Do not leave this room!"

The governor broke forward, but Theodora stepped into his path. "I said leave her alone."

Governor Hacebolus grabbed Theodora's wrist and yanked her out of his way. "I don't take orders," he said and then pointed at Valeria. "You. Sit down!"

Valeria stumbled back into a nearby chair, tears in her eyes and horror on her face.

"Now it's my turn," said Hacebolus, his grip tightening on Theodora's wrist.

Theodora looked at Valeria and in a calm voice said, "Close your eyes."

The girl squeezed her teary eyes shut.

And with a violent yank, Governor Hacebolus swung Theodora around and pushed her toward the bed, his knees prodding the back of her legs angrily. When she bumped into the bedframe, he pressed against her from behind, his chin pushing through her hair, his breath on her ear. "You disrespect me?" The governor's hand came around, grabbed the collar of Theodora's gown, and tore away the fabric, exposing her breasts. Then he grabbed a handful of her hair and pulled her head back. "I'll show you how it *feels* to be disrespected, you conceited whore."

Theodora turned her head and met the governor's eyes through tousled strands of her hair. "Show me," she said.

The governor flashed his teeth and flung Theodora onto the bed. He was upon her in an instant. She felt her gown constrict around her belly and hips before ripping from her body, leaving her suddenly naked.

"You say this girl isn't ready for her first bed," he said. "Then, you'll give her a demonstration." Hacebolus flipped Theodora violently onto her belly and placed his large palm against the side of her face, pressing her head into the pillow. "Don't you move," he said.

As brutal as the next few moments would be, thought Theodora, Valeria would be untouched. She saw that the girl still squeezed her eyes shut, but her face showed open terror at the noises in the room. But Valeria would know now there was a beast in the palace, thought Theodora. She would learn the real lesson.

Theodora clenched her teeth and winced as the governor forced himself into her. Hacebolus grabbed her at the bend of each hip, repeatedly pulling her body against his until the penetration became fluid.

But this was about power, Theodora reminded herself. This time, Theodora felt neither powerless nor humiliated. She wasn't hurt. She wasn't unprepared. And she'd been through worse.

The power of violence is not the violence itself, but whether you obey afterward.

And Theodora would not obey.

The governor became more forceful. He yanked her by the hair, leaned in, and growled an obscenity, his spittle spraying her face. Then he released her head with a shove. But there, in the midst of that wicked intercourse, Theodora knew the act itself meant nothing. Because for the first time, she knew she was going to fight back and with all her strength and power. And so, a new path opened up for Theodora, the one path that always sat plainly in front of her, the only path she ever feared to tread.

Her own.

FORTY-FOUR

 hen Theodora and Valeria returned to the concubinary later that evening, the women were already asleep. Samira, though, arose from the shadows and came to Theodora.

"We heard your fight with the governor," she whispered. "Are you both all right?"

Samira always knew the goings-on in the palace. Theodora brushed Valeria's hair with her fingers. "We're fine," she said. "The governor left her alone tonight."

"But you . . . ," said Valeria, the gleam of tears still upon her cheeks.

Theodora crouched in front of Valeria, her body still aching from the forceful encounter with Hacebolus. "I'm perfectly fine," she said in a show of confidence. "You see? The governor didn't hurt me at all."

"Why did you tell me to look away?"

"Because what happened was between me and the governor."

Valeria fell into Theodora for an embrace. "I never want to go to the governor's bed."

"You never will," said Theodora, stroking the back of Valeria's head. "For now, get some sleep. Close your eyes and dream of things that make you smile, green things, beautiful things."

Valeria nodded, and Theodora tucked the girl into the fine blankets. After some time, Valeria breathed heavily. She finally looked peaceful to Theodora. A moment later, she and Samira crept over to the dark salóni to speak privately.

"I've come to an important decision," Theodora said. "I'm leaving the palace and taking this girl with me."

Samira pulled back and placed her hand over her mouth.

Theodora continued. "I have many connections to powerful people in the Blue faction, and I intend to use them all. My friends are more powerful than Governor Hacebolus, so I needn't fear him."

"Where will you go?"

"Home. Back to Constantinople."

"Theodora, what has gotten into you?" said Samira. "You're not yourself at all. Your great humor has left you, and now this fight with the governor. Perhaps you should sleep, and we'll talk tomorrow."

"I've been ruminating," said Theodora. "And something's changed. I know what I want now and what I won't accept."

"But Theodora, is it worth it? We have everything we need, and whether we like it or not, that girl's better off here than out there. If not the governor, then someone else will take this girl," said Samira. "And who knows what kind of person that will be."

"That person is me."

"But it's a Hydra, Theodora," said Samira. "Cut off one head, and you'll find two more in its place."

"I know, and I've stared into many faces on that Hydra. I'm not scared of it anymore. This fight isn't about destroying the Hydra. It's about committing to our own choices, regardless of the consequences. I'm trying to get Valeria to a better place. And I'm convinced it's not hopeless."

Samira shook her head in disbelief. "What are you going to do?"

"Well, I'm not going to tell any of the other women, lest they inform on me to the governor," said Theodora. "I'm telling you because I trust you."

Samira nodded. "No matter what you decide, I'll keep my silence."

"I need to know if you'll help me further," said Theodora, shifting from warm to assertive. "And whether you wish to come with me."

Samira stared back, the whites of her eyes blazing. "Come with you? To Constantinople?"

"Yes."

"How would we get there?"

Theodora smiled. "By ship. I'd have my contact here in Sozusa arrange for our travel aboard a Roman vessel. We'd sail east and could reach the Sacred City in a month."

Silence followed. The sounds of the outside sea and the heavy breathing of sleeping concubines filled the wordless pause.

Samira seemed to consider the plan, and right when Theodora thought she'd agree, the flicker of excitement faded. "I don't think I can go that far. I'll help you however I can. But sailing away on a ship to Constantinople . . . that's too much. For me, the palace is a good place."

"I understand. I'll be sure not to involve you too deeply."

Samira squeezed Theodora's hand. "What do you want me to do?"

"Arrange a meeting with my contact in the chapel tomorrow," said Theodora. "The Blues are going to work for me whether they realize it or not."

"If you truly believe that you can get Valeria out of the palace and down to the harbor, if you truly believe it, then I'll help you do it."

"Thank you, Samira," she said. "I'll know more about everything tomorrow. For now, let's get some sleep. I've had enough of this day."

Samira nodded, and soon the concubinary grew silent and all was still. But Theodora couldn't fall asleep. She lay upon the silken blankets, feeling luxuries that no longer appealed to her, staring up at the darkness, thinking.

After a while, Theodora arose and walked to one of the large windows, rested her hands upon the sill, and peered down at Sozusa. So quiet, she thought. Dots of torchlight lined a maze of black streets. Beyond the city, the moon showed white and luminous, hanging low above the horizon and casting light upon the ceaseless ripples of ocean waves. North Africa was beautiful country, she thought, a desert coast both majestic and perilous. But it wasn't her country. Theodora fixed her eyes upon the silhouettes of ships that rocked in the harbor. One of those ships would sail east and take her back to Constantinople.

To Palatina.

A sweeping ache filled her heart as she imagined looking upon her daughter's face again. Girls were so vulnerable in the world, and yet Theodora left her own daughter behind. And she felt the crushing anguish of knowing she fell short where her mother did not.

I abandoned my little girl.

As with the last time, Theodora gasped and tears came quickly. Her focus had been so inwardly aimed, she never thought much about her daughter. But Theodora thought of Palatina now. She stared into the dark haze at the horizon to the east. Life went on out there, she thought. Somewhere behind that blackness awaited the world and the people she truly loved. Valeria may not have been Theodora's daughter, but she was someone's daughter. The fate of any girl, or any woman, could suddenly slip into the dark corners of the world, just as it did for Valeria and herself. Just as it could for Palatina one day.

No more.

But how to escape?

Her thoughts became convoluted from countless scenarios and outcomes that converged and diverged in her imagination. As she considered one plan after another, the skies above turned from black with white stars to dark indigo, then to the eerie azure light of early morning. The next day drew up, and she didn't have a final idea for escape. The harbors stirred now with men and carters, mules and gulls. Theodora imagined herself leading Valeria toward the harbor, dressed in hooded robes. She knew how to wear a hood and how to hide the face beneath. But how to get past the guards in the palace? She could seduce one man, surely, and occupy his attention, but she'd need to seduce an entire palace.

Her eyes grew heavy from exhaustion. Just as she was about to succumb to sleep, a line of yellow light erupted at the horizon, separating sea from sky. Dawn beset the coasts of Sozusa with the rich colors of the earth—amber and blue, brown and green. To Theodora, the rising sun looked like the eye of God slowly opening, gazing over all Creation, and spotting her at the window.

The thought of being looked upon by a great and divine eye triggered a revelation in Theodora, one that mixed with her old and most painful memories. Of all those eyes that sought her out through the years, that stared at her, that watched and desired her, there were other eyes too. Theodora recalled the eyes of a youthful Comito upon the Middle Way, looking for direction during the rebellion; she recalled the frightened eyes of her mother that day in the Hippodrome, when it was Theodora who acted, who raced decisively toward the Blue section; she recalled the eyes of Hypatius when he looked up at her in shame, an abandoned man who feared death; she recalled the frightened eyes of Indaro upon the stage, while a crowd cheered on the woman's humiliation; she recalled the eyes of Justinian through the carriage, as he pleaded with her to remain in the capital, seeing her as a woman too valuable to leave; and she saw the eyes of Valeria, the girl's face painted as she begged not to go. And then there were the eyes of Palatina the day Theodora left Constantinople, who looked on her as a mother, but a mother who'd be leaving. All those eyes stared back at her now in her memory. How many had turned to Theodora in their moment of despair?

Theodora never considered that these people looked on her as an actual leader.

But she was a leader who always walked away in the end, thought Theodora, fearing herself too weak to be trusted. Because hadn't Magister Origen exposed Theodora as weak? She was just a woman who could be cast aside if she wasn't careful. Women couldn't lead, and if they did, not for long.

All those unfulfilled feelings hung there invisible. Theodora wasn't going to walk away this time. This time, she would lead or die trying. She'd go all the way. That was the covenant Macedonia spoke of. And so Theodora gasped as she felt the sweet pinprick of hope. For such a thing as hope promised her nothing, yet offered up everything, a scintillating vision of something better, something worthwhile, something impossible that she still believed in. If only she had more time. As fatigue finally overtook her, Theodora moved to the silk blankets and pillows upon an empty bed. There, she instantly succumbed to sleep.

FORTY-FIVE

S he awoke to a large hand shaking her at the shoulder. "Stop," she
said. Theodora turned to see Governor Hacebolus staring down at
her, a bodyguard behind him.

Hacebolus handed Theodora a cup of water. He looked fresh-
ened and smelled of sandalwood oil. "How are you this morning?"

Theodora took the water and drank. "I'm well."

"I hope you're not dwelling on last evening," he said in a quieted voice.

The governor never downplayed insubordination from his women, so
Theodora eyed him suspiciously. "Should I dwell?"

He grinned until every white tooth appeared. "It was rather enlivening,
though, wouldn't you agree? Such passion, such anger, and hate, yet so intense the pleasure."

"Yes, and all in front of the girl, you fool," said Theodora with a scowl.

"Oh, she'll have nightmares for a while, I'm sure of it. But one day, she'll remember last evening with a woman's mind. She'll understand it then. I should try and anger you more often."

Theodora glanced around the concubinary. The other women listened in to the conversation but scattered their attentions as Theodora noticed them. Samira wasn't in the room.

"I have news," said Hacebolus.

Theodora took another sip of water. "Oh?"

"This morning I received word. The Ostrogothic delegation from Ravenna will arrive today, a full day earlier than expected."

Theodora said nothing. A visitation from foreigners would ruin everything. The palace would stir with heightened vigilance.

The governor shook her pleasantly at the shoulder. "Well? Have you and Sophia come up with the evening's entertainment?"

That's why he's so forgiving. He needs me for that stupid show.

Suddenly, an idea fell into Theodora's mind, one so dark, so horrifying that she knew at last how she'd strike back at the governor and escape his world. As a nightmare. In front of everyone. With finality. "Oh yes," she said.

"Well, what is it?"

She looked Hacebolus in the eyes. "*Leda and the Swan.*"

"*Leda and the Swan?*"

Theodora knew he remembered that night back in Constantinople, when she last performed the salacious act during his coronation.

"I love it," he said, his voice triumphant. "I thought you'd fallen off, Theodora, like a chariot horse with a lame leg. And yet I see I haven't lost you yet."

"It's my last performance," she said. "So, I'll bow out boldly."

Governor Hacebolus pressed his palms against both of Theodora's cheeks. "What dark pit did you crawl out of?" he said. He then kissed her on the forehead and bellowed, "The Notorious Theodora, indeed! The world may never see another like you." He arose and pointed at Theodora. "If you and Sophia pull this off, I'll forget about your obnoxious fit last night."

Theodora shrugged.

He suddenly clapped. "And we'll use Krikou, a true swan for *this* performance. It'll be unforgettable."

For once, Theodora agreed with Hacebolus.

FORTY-SIX

"Leave us," said Theodora, her voice echoing in the bath chamber.

The two bath attendants, older women dressed in white gowns, bowed their heads. They dried their hands and retired to the servant's quarters beyond the doorway.

Theodora and Valeria sat submerged in a pool-sized bath, which occupied most of the floor space in the chamber and filled the air with humidity. Stone columns surrounded the pool, alit by foggy sunbeams that angled down from above. As in a cistern, the ubiquitous sound of dripping water echoed off the damp stonework.

"They won't be able to hear us," said Samira, who locked the doors. She then removed her robe to reveal a dark chestnut body, with silken skin and muscled legs. She lowered herself into the steaming pool and nodded at Theodora, who nodded back.

"Well, Valeria, I'm going to help you—if you want my help," said

Theodora in a low voice. "I have a plan for us to leave the palace. We'll set out for Constantinople, where I'll help you find your father."

Valeria looked taken aback.

"But hear me," said Theodora. "This'll be dangerous. If we go against the governor, there's a good chance we fall short. We'll be putting ourselves at great risk. I want you to think about that." And Theodora lifted her head and spoke as if addressing a grown woman. "There's a choice here, Valeria. You can live against your will with a master who takes care of you. Or you can face the dangers on a path you choose yourself. Both paths are harsh," she said. "So, I'm going to ask you to become a woman for me and choose for yourself. Do you wish to stay here or come with me?"

The whispers of the bath chamber fell silent, and for a moment only the sparkle of water light tangled upon the girl's face.

"I'm going with you," said Valeria. "I want to find my father, and I never want to see the governor again."

"Then I'm going too," said Samira.

Theodora glanced at Samira and searched the woman's deep, brown eyes. "What?"

"Last night, I realized that I'd regret it if I stayed behind. If you two came to harm, I'd regret not being able to help. If you succeeded, then I'd regret not coming with you. Besides, you'll need my help if you're to travel with this girl."

Theodora smiled warmly as she took up Samira's hand. "Very good. Then we go all the way."

Samira and Valeria nodded.

"How are we going to get out of here?" said Valeria.

Theodora leaned back. "The governor is preparing the palace for visitors, which means most of the servants will be readying the palace. To be unseen is to be forgotten today. Tonight, though, during the governor's party, I'm going to create a diversion. While all eyes are on me, you and Samira will slip out the eastern doors. Once outside, you'll meet with partisans from the Blue faction who'll escort you both to the harbor. There, you'll board a ship."

Valeria tilted her head. "How will you get out?"

"I'll join you on the ship, but *after* the play's finale."

"Theodora," said Valeria. "I'm scared."

"I know." Theodora felt the girl's fear. She grabbed Valeria's hand beneath the water. "Uncertainty is always frightening. But we'll go anyway."

The sounds of conspiracy faded back to the echo of water drops. Then, Theodora arose from the steaming waters, dried her body, and left the girl in Samira's care.

Theodora felt the same dread as when she was a girl that one night in the koitóna, when she crept down the warbling staircase with a knife tucked in her gown. The task was so daunting, and Magister Origen so intimidating. The goal had been to escape then too. But she was just a frightened girl then, defeated in the battle, and discarded in disgrace. Not today. Today, Theodora was a woman in full.

She donned a silver robe embroidered with white and black swan patterns from collar to ankle. When she left the salóni that morning, Theodora concealed her anxiety, fear, and exhilaration behind the pleasant mask of a quiet lady. With sidelong glances, she observed the comings and goings of the servants. She surveyed the Roman guards who conversed near each doorway. She leaned briefly out window openings to study the cobbled streets below, tracing their course all the way down to the harbor. Such a distance, she thought, much further on foot than it seemed from her view at the concubinary. Theodora knew that she was like a ship still moored in the harbor. But the anchor had come up. She was adrift among the other ships around her. Soon she'd break toward the eastern horizon in view of all. For now, though, she moved amongst them, a background onlooker to the palace's preparations.

Theodora followed the arcade around the central courtyard and made her way to the palace chapel. Midday drew on and the heat, even in the shade, suffocated her. By the time she opened the chapel door, she heard singing. Robed men stood in the nave of the chapel, facing the wood templon and singing a solemn Christian hymn. Numerous candles filled the enclosed room with fragrant and ghostly smoke. When the priest noticed

Theodora, he quickly broke away from the congregation and approached her. "What's the meaning of this summons?" he said in a whisper.

"Something has come up, Father," she said as they slipped behind a large pillar of gray limestone. "I need passage on a ship bound for Constantinople and three partisans of the faction, men who know the streets of Sozusa. And I need this arranged by tonight."

"For what?"

"To escort myself, Samira, and a young girl out of this palace."

"Under whose authority?"

"Mine," said Theodora without raising her voice.

"But you have no authority."

"Of course I do. There's a girl upstairs who I don't want to see sullied by the governor. My time here is done, and I'm leaving this palace."

The priest looked stunned. "This is a completely unreasonable request. The Blues can't assist you in that. They'd never cross the governor over a handful of . . . of women."

"Stop and think about who I answer to in Constantinople," Theodora said. "Do you remember the last message I gave you?"

The priest's face relaxed as he seemed to recall Theodora's kiss from the other day. She waited as he connected the kiss to Justinian, the heir apparent of the Roman Empire. "I remember," he said.

"Helping me will bring you favor, not scorn," said Theodora, speaking softly as if to a friend. She wanted the priest's obedience without threatening him. "I'll see that you are rewarded for your services to me. But I need partisans and a ship. Can you make this happen or not?"

The hymn of the choir rose and fell on the word *Hallelujah*. The next verse began, and the priest finally sighed. "Plenty of ships sail for Constantinople, so arranging passage on one will be easy. But where exactly do you want these partisans you ask for?"

"I need two outside the palace back there," said Theodora and pointed. "The eastern door behind the chapel. It opens to a side road that runs the length of the palace. I'll be sure that no guard is at that door tonight. Samira and Valeria will meet you here and then depart through those doors."

"And you?" he said.

"I'll leave the palace through the north gate. Have another man positioned across the street. I want this done in secrecy, so you're not to alert the leadership of the Blue faction," said Theodora. She wore the same blank mask that used to veil a deep humiliation, but now, she hid nothing and looked the priest directly in the eyes.

"I'm taking a grave risk on your word, Theodora. But I'll do as you ask."

Theodora gave her first command, and the priest obeyed. So, she thought, authority came with a feeling, surety, a readiness, intuition. Her commands put people who trusted her at risk, and yet she insisted. "Thank you, Father," she said.

"I'll pass this on to a select few, and I'll say this comes from Justinian directly. I'll find you a captain and a few partisans. Here, take this," he said and removed a thin silver chain from around his neck. "This is an amulet of St. Christopher. He's a protector of pilgrims and travelers."

Theodora slipped the necklace over her head. She leaned in, kissed the priest on his cheek, and stepped back.

"God be with you in this," he said.

As Theodora departed, she gave a reflexive bow to the crucifix at the fore of the chapel. She nodded at the priest and then left.

But her work wasn't done.

She needed to rehearse *Leda and the Swan* and the performance had to be good. Theodora found Sophia in the concubinary and smiled at the silent woman. "Well, are you ready for a little rehearsal?"

Sophia grinned as if she'd been awaiting the request all day.

Theodora and Sophia descended the stairs and went outside to the caravansary. A few other administrators in colored robes congregated nearby, standing and talking, paying the women intermittent attention. The sweltering heat and blinding sunlight forced Theodora and Sophia to the shaded end of the courtyard.

"So, the governor wants this to be a shocking comedy," said Theodora. "He probably just wants the final act, but I want the play to be set up properly, to build anticipation," she said. *And to allow enough time for Samira and*

Valeria to make their escape. "Since I'll be Leda, you'll be Tyndareus, the king of the Spartans."

Sophia dropped her head and set malevolent eyes upon Theodora. She swept through a series of poses that projected masculine dominance, flexing her legs and arms, altering her facial expressions and doing so effortlessly.

"That's it," said Theodora, laughing. "I wish I could perform like you, Sophia. I just never had the talent," she said, realizing she made her first confession of weakness. She felt not a sting, but joy in recognizing the great skill of her friend.

Sophia, though, stayed in character and dismissed Theodora's last comment.

Theodora flung her hair to one side and continued. "So now, the king will come into his bedchamber after a long day. He sees Queen Leda." Theodora twirled away a few paces. "She's locked away in the king's palace, bored beyond her senses. She dreams only of adventure and love," she said, but paused. She and Leda weren't so different after all. "Anyway, now the way the story goes, the king comes to take his queen, intent on making love to her but gets summoned away instead. At that point, you'll exit the stage. I'll remain and tease the men in the audience about being left unsatisfied. You change costumes and return to the stage as Zeus. He'll spot poor Leda, a woman in heat, and he succumbs to desire himself. Since you're a typical Greek god, you devise a ridiculous way to satisfy your sexual urges."

Sophia spun away, twirling and exaggerating her body's contortions. Already, the onlookers in the courtyard became distracted by the two women, a good sign, for distraction was the aim of the play.

Theodora continued. "Here, Zeus takes the form of a swan. You'll leave the stage a second time, and that's when you'll send out the swan."

Theodora turned and set her eyes upon Krikou, the governor's favorite swan. The bird floated in a pool alongside another swan, their necks like shepherd's crooks, their orange bills aimed downward. The bird looked so much bigger than a goose. Theodora dreaded the size of the animal when she imagined the bird up close.

Sophia put her hand on Theodora's shoulder. As the women exchanged a glance, a single blare from a horn rang out. Six Roman guards trotted across the caravansary toward the main entranceway.

"Attention," shouted the Palace chamberlain, striding through the courtyard and clapping his hands. "I need this area cleared out. Everyone, return to your quarters until called for. Go on now."

Theodora watched the people of the caravansary slowly disperse and vanish into the surrounding arcades. She looked at Sophia. "Shall we don our costumes?"

FORTY-SEVEN

The chapel was dark and empty. Theodora knelt alone at the altar of the crucifix, her hands clasped together, the soft light of candles upon her. She wore the costume of Leda, a gold band at the forehead, braided black hair in the old Spartan fashion, and heavy kohl around each eye, with tails like bird wings at each corner. Over her body, Theodora donned a flowing white peplos with an open seam along the right side. The partition revealed a nearly unbroken stripe of bare skin from the neckline, down along the shoulder and ribs, allowing the naked hip to protrude, and exposing one full leg. Only a crimson belt held the opening together above the hip. Beneath the belt, though, Theodora hid a knife. She sewed the handle into the fabric so the weapon couldn't slip out.

"God," she whispered. "I'm not one for prayers. I don't know if You can hear me or if You're even there. But if You are there, then help me tonight. I know I've lived a shameful life in Your eyes, but help me spare Valeria from the same life," she said, staring into her clasped hands. "And I'll spend my days sparing others from this fate to the best of my abilities, and to whatever end." So strange was a prayer, she thought. Words entered the space around her and met only an oppressive silence, a kingly silence where no voice would ever answer. She felt only a presence, real or imagined, a sense that her request was heard by a great and concealed power. When she looked up, she saw the serene face of Christ upon the crucifix, His head slumped away from her, His eyes closed.

Again, the silence.

"Amen," she said.

Then, Theodora suddenly felt the presence of Macedonia fill her heart. For those early and grueling lessons always felt like they were about much more than mere spy work. Had her mentor long foreseen the coming contest? When Theodora arose, she saw Macedonia standing beside the door, dressed in one of her beautiful gowns. So vivid. So surely present. Her mentor stood perfectly still, hands clutched below her navel, chin high, eyes set hard on Theodora.

"It's time, despina."

Theodora's throat tightened. "I know."

Macedonia nodded and stepped aside. Theodora sighed, leaned in, and pulled open the chapel door, where she immediately heard music and boorish laughter from the outdoor caravansary. Luminance from the fire basins fell short of where she stood. When Theodora glanced back at Macedonia, the apparition was gone, replaced by crushing anxiety.

A few moments later and Theodora heard footsteps. Samira appeared soon after, her dark skin blending with the colors of the night. "It's done. I've passed word to every last guard not to miss your show tonight," she said in a quiet voice. "All will be watching."

"And Valeria?"

"I dressed her in a black cloak and hid her from the other women. She's ready."

"Good," said Theodora. "You'll both have to be as swift and silent as the wind tonight."

Samira craned her neck and looked up into the night sky. "At least the moon has waned."

"The night may grow even darker," said Theodora. "Once you're free of the palace, don't stop for any reason. Go with the partisans and head straight for the harbors."

"How long should we wait for you?"

"Until the ship disembarks," said Theodora. "If I haven't made it out by then, then I'm not getting out. Do not wait for me."

Samira looked worried. "What should we do if we reach Constantinople without you?"

"Seek out the Blue faction there. Ask to meet with Justinian, and he'll give you everything you need."

"But how will he know who we are?"

"Tell him . . ." Theodora searched for words that would identify Samira as her trusted companion. "Tell him you were sent by Theodora, the girl from the Hippodrome. He'll know what that means."

"How are you getting out?"

"Right through the front gate."

The quiet conversation was interrupted by the voice of Governor Hacebolus, which boomed from the caravansary. "Come, come! Where are my performers?"

Theodora sighed, but slowly, collecting herself. "Here we go. I'll see you on the ship."

Samira touched Theodora ever so gently on the shoulder, stared for a moment, and then nodded. Theodora knew there lurked the uncomfortable possibility of never seeing each other again. Samira pulled away and slipped back into the darkness.

Theodora turned to face the caravansary. She saw white-skinned Ostrogoths and local Romans sitting outdoors around four long tables, grabbing and eating roast lamprey, raw oysters, boiled eggs, bread loaves, and ruby-like pomegranate seeds. The barbarians laughed so loudly that their guttural voices carried into the skies. Everyone looked as though they were good and drunk, some clapping and stomping to the music. Torches surrounded the courtyard, casting a soft orange light upon the governor's Gothic guests. And, of course, swans waddled about the group, heads twitching as they searched for morsels of food.

When Theodora emerged from the arcade, Hacebolus spotted her and gestured for her to hurry along. So she made her way to the performing area. Sophia was already there, wearing the costume of King Tyndareus—a wooden crown painted gold, long red cape, and exaggerated brooch.

"Ready?" said Theodora.

Sophia struck a commander's pose, fist over chest, and gave a brooding nod. Theodora laughed, relieved by a lapse in her biting anxiety.

But Hacebolus clapped his hands together loudly and all the lively voices fell quiet. "And so the evening moves to entertainment," he said, gesturing toward Theodora. "Let's begin with an introduction to this evening's leading and most infamous performer."

Theodora watched as each head turned from Hacebolus to search the performing area. She stepped into the shimmering fire light, and she bent her knee so that her oiled thigh and hip slipped through the seam in her peplos. Immediately, the Ostrogoths groaned, howled, and slapped the table in approval of her provocative appearance. In the darkness beyond the torchlight, Theodora watched as Roman guards wandered away from their posts, congregating at the edges of the courtyard, eager for a glimpse. She then raised her arms above her head and lowered her fingertips to touch the top of her scalp.

"Lo! Esteemed guests and beloved countrymen," thundered Hacebolus. "I've brought this deadly flower to the desert from the very heart of the Roman Empire. A woman of such depravity in Constantinople that the Romans call her the Notorious Theodora. A whore! A whore with a cleave between her legs that has swallowed more men than all the beasts of Africa. She's been known to bring ten noblemen to exhaustion during a single party, only to move on to their slaves and servants, which sometimes number thirty or more. I've heard her rebuke nature for giving her only three openings, a cruel limit to the gluttonous commerce of her body..."

Theodora closed her eyes. She listened to every defaming word followed by bellows of disbelief from the dinner guests. She drew in deep breaths and thought of Valeria and Samira. They'd watch from the chapel and await the right moment to flee the palace.

". . . and so cast your eyes upon her!" said Hacebolus, cueing the minstrels to position their instruments. "I give you . . . the Notorious Theodora!"

Brass horns blared the fanfare of Old Sparta, accompanied by a rumble of drums. Theodora bowed low, and when she arose, she was Leda, Queen of Sparta.

She arched her back and slipped into a sway, her arms outstretched and head tossed sideways. She spun in place so that the peplos parted further, allowing more flesh to be seen.

A moment later, Sophia scurried onto the stage as King Tyndareus and circled Theodora, her head lowered and eyes set hard upon the queen.

Theodora twirled with unusually crisp balance, her dance steps nearly perfect. Sophia took Theodora into her arms, and the audience laughed at the height disparity, with Theodora, the queen, towering over Sophia, the great king. The two women spun in place until the laughter died down. Sophia went to kiss Theodora, but paused, glanced up at the men, and goaded them for encouragement.

The Ostrogoths responded loudly with a string of vulgar suggestions and drunken cheers.

As Sophia listened, Theodora reached up and pressed her mouth against Sophia's, kissing her forcibly. Instead of a demure queen, Theodora dominated Sophia, taking the lead in the pantomime. Why hadn't she ever performed like this before with such fluidity and grace, such precise steps and exciting improvisations? Why only here at the end did she suddenly get it right?

Sophia followed Theodora's lead, but the comedic poses strayed into more artistic body movements. The absurd became the dramatic. Sophia then slid her hand into the seam of Theodora's peplos and pretended to arouse the queen with exaggerated gestures, her hand rising and falling. Theodora threw back her head and broke the strict code of silence during a pantomime. She cried out in pleasure, the bell-like chime of a female voice, a single note that cracked the air with sexuality. The raucous laughter fell suddenly silent. The men now watched Theodora with the focus of gathered predators.

But Sophia abruptly spun away from Queen Leda, having been summoned from afar, and the king slipped off-stage. While Sophia changed costumes, she smiled broadly at Theodora, clearly giddy at the unexpected synchronicity of their performance.

Theodora continued on the stage alone. She arched, she bent, she snapped into alluring postures. She strode along the edge of the stage, teasing the men by peeling away the partition in her garments, the desert air cooling her oiled body. She dared the Ostrogoths to try and quench her carnal thirst. But with each blond-bearded lord who arose from the table, she waved off in dismissal or shoved him back if he approached the stage. Every rejection met with a chorus of riotous laughter. Only one of the Goths had a gentleness to his countenance. He sat beside Governor Hacebolus and watched the performance with an intense gaze, perhaps even admiring Theodora artistically.

Theodora risked a glance into the darkness of the arcade and caught a glimpse of fabric passing through a spot of moonlight. Samira and Valeria were leaving.

There was no turning back now. Every beat of the hand drums counted off the footsteps of her friends from the palace.

Theodora looked at Hacebolus, who showed no sign of suspicion. He sat back in his seat, one leg outstretched, knuckles at the mouth, teeth showing from a grin.

With a flurry of notes from the horn, Sophia returned to the stage, dressed now as the pagan overlord, Zeus. She wore a gold-leaf head laurel and transparent toga that revealed the silhouette of her body, the gown catching at her nipples. While the men cheered at the shapely sight of the Greek deity, Theodora brushed her hair to the elegant lutes and sweeping lyres. Sophia gestured for the men to look at Theodora—*should a god take this mortal woman?*

The men roared in approval, pounding so loud upon the table that wine cups fell sideways. Theodora encouraged the heavy clamor, knowing the furious noise masked any sounds of escape. The guards still huddled in the periphery, and so Samira and Valeria must have slipped past them, now out of the palace, now into the night . . . away . . . away . . .

Finally, Sophia conceded to the crowd. Zeus would take the queen. She tossed up a handful of orange and yellow ribbons and spun out of the performing area. The music grew loud and then hushed.

From out of the pitch blackness, Theodora saw the white shape of a swan emerge, coming toward her, wings outstretched. As always, the crowd roared in disbelief at sight of an actual bird upon the stage. Any lingering doubts as to the shocking final act quickly gave way to anticipation.

Upon seeing the swan in her bedchamber, the queen of Sparta fell to her knees, seduced by the crude animal masculinity. She rubbed sensually at her thighs, the peplos smearing against her oiled skin.

The audience fell hush.

And so, Theodora arched back and dipped her hand into the grain sack. The kernels were as cool as fresh linens. Krikou snapped his head up and looked on with beady, animal eyes.

She laid back on a bed of pillows, spreading her knees apart so that the peplos flowed in between her thighs. Then Theodora positioned her fistful of grain above the soft hump of skin at the crest of her sex. The music intensified. She felt a fresh wave of anxiety as the swan waddled toward her, bent, and wiggled its head beneath her peplos. Right away, Theodora felt the hard bill of the bird pecking at her hand, pinching and snatching up wheat grains.

Beyond her, the men howled at such a sight—a beautiful woman, laid back, legs apart, and the head of a swan bobbing about beneath the fabric. Theodora drew the warm desert air into her lungs and flushed it through her lips, singing out with a luxuriant sigh. Then another moan. At her hand, where the swan's head burrowed against her fist, she felt heat coming off her tender loins, an erotic heat. The pleasure became real, fueled by the knowledge of the chaos that she'd soon invite into her world. So, she gasped and moaned again, her voice carrying up into the stars above, the audience growing quieter as her pleasure quickened. She need only to lift her peplos and reveal the perversion.

Now, the final act.

Instead, Theodora wrapped her free fingers around the hilt of the hidden knife. With eyes open to the stars, with her blissful moans falling into the hushed gasps of a female at the height of her pleasure, like lovely chimes of glass, Theodora grabbed the neck of the swan.

The bird jerked.

She set the blade of the knife against the exposed neck of the swan, and the creature lurched to free itself. She cut forward and backward, feeling the feathers fray, the bird beating its wings in panicked flaps. The crowd was cheering when the blade came free.

A wave of blood splattered the inside of her peplos all at once, followed by gasps from the audience. The body of the swan bounced and tussled about, with all the vigor of life.

The clapping and music trailed off as Theodora slowly arose, clutching the flapping, swinging body of the swan by the neck, holding it out beside her. Blood yet pumped from the open neck, spraying her face with hot liquid. Theodora stood there, stoic, queenly, staring at Hacebolus with eyes that issued a judgment against him, against all those like him.

Governor Hacebolus sprang to his feet in shock and from the side of the performing area, Sophia the mute . . . screamed.

Theodora flung the decapitated carcass at the governor, and the bird landed at his feet with a flat smack, its wings still twitching.

Hacebolus, though, set a furious gaze upon Theodora. "That was my swan!"

Theodora only stared back at the governor, free of his authority.

He drew in a few hateful breaths. "I see. So, you *want* me to throw you out," he said and approached her. "So be it."

Theodora watched as the governor closed in on her. He walked leisurely, but his jaw and chin twitched side to side with anger. When Hacebolus came to a stop, Theodora, who was still on stage for all to see, lifted her chin proudly. He struck her across the face. Her head lurched to the side, but she stood fixed in place and reset her gaze upon the governor.

"Governor!" shouted a commanding voice from the far side of the courtyard. All attention turned to the voice.

Across the caravansary, Theodora spotted a guardsman standing with Helena. The guard shouted again. "We believe Samira and that new girl have run off! The east doors are wide open."

Theodora cursed Helena under her breath as two Roman guards seized her at each arm, their breath against her ears. Freedom, home, a ship had been just a few moments away. She felt one guard peel away the knife in her fingers as Hacebolus looked upon her anew, finally perceiving the full deception. An eerie calm overtook him as he thumbed the rings at his knuckles. "You Goths will get a show tonight," he said, then nodded at the guards.

Both guards released Theodora and backed away.

Her scalp chilled as she sensed imminent violence in the air. She knew then what the governor meant to do. So, the unconquered woman always wears her burial shroud, recalled Theodora.

Wear it proudly.

She drew in a deep breath, straightened her posture, and stared Hacebolus in the eyes.

He struck her.

The blow sent Theodora twirling backward, almost dance-like, and collapsing upon the ground. She spat blood onto the stonework.

Stand tall and dare him to do it again.

Theodora quickly rose to her feet and turned to face the governor again.

"So that's how you want it to be," said Hacebolus, nodding. He reared back and struck Theodora full in the face as if striking a man.

She stumbled backward, clutching at her face, but caught her balance. Her head throbbed with pain, but she shook it out. Theodora resumed an upright stance, leaning toward the governor, challenging him.

The governor bared his teeth and struck Theodora much harder. Her head pitched backward, her feet went lifeless, and she didn't know she'd fallen until her body crashed against the stone lip of the fountain and then the stone terrace. Blackness settled in but faded. Dizzy now, she stumbled again to her feet. But the governor grabbed her peplos at the collar and struck her with an open palm repeatedly. The blows smacked nakedly against her face, and now the brute impacts stunned Theodora, rattled her skull, and filled her mouth with the taste of blood. She'd never been hit like this before. When the blackness of her vision faded, she saw Hacebolus. She mustered a breath and spat into his face.

He flung her to the ground and kicked her repeatedly in the belly. Theodora sucked in a strained, loud gasp, but the precious breath suffocated her.

"Is this what you wanted?" yelled Hacebolus, bending near Theodora's face. "To be beaten like a dog?"

Theodora crawled forward, barely able to breathe or see. The world around her looked shadowy and muddled. Blood seeped from her mouth, like thick, red honey. Exhausted, she climbed slowly to her feet, always on her feet, no matter the pain. Soberly and breathing wearily, Theodora stood up once more, wavered, but faced Hacebolus.

This time, the governor glowered at Theodora for a long while. "No one will ever look on you again and see beauty," he said. "I'm going to take that from you." He then turned and snatched a baton from one of his guards.

Theodora kept her eyes on the governor, even as the baton went up.

With a final blow, Theodora entered a blank space somewhere in between waking life and beautiful death. She did not collapse but instead flew backward and upward as if caught in a great gust, ascending into the sky above the caravansary like a bird. Perhaps her mind had seized upon the fragments of a dream.

Ever skyward, ever brighter.

Triumphant.

She knew then that the Notorious Theodora had been destroyed forever.

And yet there was the other Theodora who was not beaten, nor harmed, nor touched at all, the flawed and beautiful girl who'd been there all along. There had indeed been two Theodoras; the one who died upon a stage somewhere in Africa, and the one who did not.

FORTY-EIGHT

Theodora felt cool water trickling onto her face. She thought to sit up, but pain beset her entire body. Each breath brought searing, sharp, excruciating pain in her ribs, just below the breast, while her face and head throbbed everywhere. Indeed, her entire conscious mind was aware only of pain, insufferable pain that brought out a long and inhuman groan.

"Mother?" said Theodora in a raspy whisper. "Mother, I can't open my eyes."

"You've been badly hurt," said a man's voice. He spoke in Latin, but his words carried a thick, barbarian drawl.

Theodora tried to peer through swollen eye slits, but brilliant light intensified the pain in her head. She tried to swallow, but her throat was so dry. "Water," she whispered.

Trickles of water pattered onto her desert-dry tongue, spilling to the back of her sore throat. She was parched and suckled the water until she coughed, groaned, and fell still.

"Slowly," said the voice. "Try not to move."

"Where am I?"

"Beyond the gates of Sozusa," he said. "You're safe, though. Rest."

Theodora realized only then that she was outdoors. Sunlight warmed her body. "Who are you?" she said.

"I'm Vermundo Odomalia, son of Eiriks Odomalia of Ravenna, and loyal godson to King Theodoric. I've spent the last two days wondering whether to bury you beside this road."

"You're a Goth?"

"I'm a fellow Christian," said Vermundo, his voice tender. "And Christ the Pantocrator has cleared away the darkness of death for you. He has given you life."

Theodora suddenly remembered that she'd been performing a play of some sort. She recalled Sophia, dressed as a man, as a king even, twirling, smiling, and all to the sound of laughter and applause.

Theodora forced her eyes open and saw a beach scattered with perhaps a dozen green pavilions. White-skinned men milled about the tents, saddling horses or conversing. Theodora lay on a cot padded with blankets. Above her billowed a small patterned canopy, which was suspended between two tree trunks and was thin enough to show sunlight and silhouettes of tree branches. Theodora risked a glance to the side. She noticed rows of thick, twisting tree trunks, and rich canopies of green leaves and purple olives, like grapes. *An olive orchard?* And there, nestled beside her, lay Valeria, her body rising and falling with the slow breaths of deep sleep. Despite all the pain and confusion, the serenity of the grove created a dream-like calm.

From further away, a familiar woman's voice spoke. "Is she awake?" A moment later, Samira appeared at the edge of the cot and took up Theodora's hand. "You don't know how wonderful it is to see you right now. They told us . . . well, we feared the worst."

"Your beautiful friend's been worried about you," said Vermundo. "She and the girl haven't left your side."

Theodora peered through one eye. "Samira, why aren't we in the Palace?"

"You don't remember, do you, Theodora? You helped me and Valeria leave the palace. For good. And now we're camped outside the town of Naustathanos. Don't you recall your fight with the governor?"

Then . . . a swan . . . a knife . . .

Theodora remembered. She'd been performing *Leda and the Swan*. She was to distract all the men while Samira and the girl slipped out of the palace under cover of darkness. But she couldn't summon up a single memory of how the play ended. She remembered the plan, though. "You're supposed to be on a ship with Valeria, heading to Constantinople," she said. "I told you not to wait for me."

"Yes, you did," said Samira. "But we came back for you anyway, Theodora."

"The three of you are under my protection," said Vermundo.

"These are the Ostrogoths who visited the Governor's Palace," said Samira. "The ones in the audience during your performance."

Theodora finally looked at the strange man tending to her. Vermundo was a comely man, small for a Goth, with oiled locks of short blond hair and a clean-shaven face. He still wore the trousers and jerkin from the night of the play, but he was more prince than barbarian. And his sky-blue eyes were not violent, but sensitive whenever he looked on Theodora. He pressed a wooden bowl of water to Theodora's mouth. When she felt the liquid wet her lips, she leaned forward and gulped like an animal at a trough, then she caught her breath. "What happened?" she said.

"Well, as guests, we're to honor the hospitality of our host," said Vermundo. "But beating a woman nearly to death was too much. I demanded he stop and he refused. His men and my men shouted at each other, and he finally apologized. But we broke our quarter that evening anyway and took you with us."

"That's when I spotted you," said Samira. "We were across the street with your Blue partisans. When we saw the Ostrogoths leave the palace with you in this cot, we came for you. We meant to board the ship, but the Blues warned us that the governor might search departing ships. So, I changed the plan."

Theodora smiled at Samira, though doing so was painful. "Then you did well." Theodora looked back at Vermundo. "Thank you," she said. "Why hasn't the governor sent anyone after us? It's not like him just to let go of his possessions."

"My men and I travel east to Alexandria under the banner and protection of King Theodoric," said Vermundo. "The governor wouldn't attack foreign envoys over a few women. He'd be a fool to even think it."

"To Alexandria? In Egypt?"

Vermundo padded the water cloth along Theodora's forehead. "My men and I have been sent to the Holy See of Alexandria on the wishes of our king. We're to meet with His High Holiness, the Patriarch, Pope Timothy the Third. Once we get there, I'm sure you can arrange safe passage to Constantinople."

"How many days will it take us to get there?" said Theodora.

"Twenty days overland," said Vermundo. "And tomorrow we'll reach Erythron, where we can get more medicine and dressings for your injuries. We have twenty-one men in our procession, and now we've added two women and a girl. Provisioning will be critical."

Theodora adjusted her body and winced. "No matter which way I lay, this pain in my side won't go away. Every breath feels like a knife in my ribs."

Vermundo nodded, examining the bloody dressing around Theodora's torso. "I've tended soldiers before. The governor broke your ribs, and now that your fever is gone, you'll heal in full. But for now, you need rest."

Theodora felt Samira's fingertips stroking her forehead. The soothing caress sent her slipping back to sleep.

FORTY-NINE

When Theodora awoke again, she jostled in the back of a wood wagon. Daylight ached her eyes and pain streaked through her body from the erratic motion. She watched an unlit lantern swing freely from the ceiling, and the sounds of rattling wood and axles prevailed. Outside, she heard the Ostrogoths singing a cheery song in their strange, hard language. The pain in her ribs, though, became so great that she couldn't help but moan.

"Theodora!" said Valeria, leaning over. "You're awake."

Theodora smiled when she saw the girl's dark hair and youthful Roman face. Then she lifted an aching arm and pressed her palm against Valeria's cheek. Joy flooded her senses, for Theodora had made a stand, she had followed through, and now they were on this other path. A moment later and Samira appeared beside Valeria, their bodies rocking and swaying with the motion of the wagon. Theodora saw that their faces were smudged, and their hair was dry and wild from the sun, but they appeared otherwise healthy.

"Samira told me your fever broke yesterday morning, and I wept in joy," said Valeria. "Vermundo told us all how you showed no fear of the governor, even as he attacked you."

Memories of fists against her face came back and the pain in Theodora's body intensified. "Yet I seem to have led us into the wilderness."

"But we're away from the governor," said Valeria. "To whatever end. That's what we all agreed on."

Theodora squeezed Valeria's hand. "How have the Goths been treating you?"

"Good," said Samira. "Vermundo recites poems in the evening and speaks more like a Roman than a Goth. I think he's rather handsome."

Valeria interjected. "He tells us stories about how sneaky the Gothic court is, and when he describes the countryside of Italy, I can almost see my home again in my mind. I asked if he knew my father, but he said he didn't."

Theodora thought back to that night at the palace. She vaguely recalled Vermundo's face in the audience. He'd sat beside the governor, coolly slapping the table during drunken uproars, smiling instead of shouting, watching with interest instead of lust. "I'm so tired, Valeria," she finally said. "So tired."

Theodora drifted in and out of consciousness for the next several days. Sometimes, she awoke to the glow of daylight with Samira and Valeria smiling down at her, and other times, she awoke to darkness and the sound of a crackling campfire, sometimes to laughter, sometimes to the swish of an ocean. Each time she awoke, she felt more pain in her body and became aware of individual injuries. Soon, the raw pain settled into an overwhelming body ache. The stiffness of her fixed position became a torture of its own, worse than anything she'd experienced in her past. And if she tried to adjust to alleviate the agony, searing pain erupted somewhere else.

For the first time since she could remember, Theodora couldn't clean herself. She didn't like anything foul on her body that couldn't be controlled with water, color, or perfume. But upon the highway, tending to beauty proved impossible and a heavy musk hung about her skin, mixing with every breath. She relied on Samira and Valeria to scrub softly at her skin each morning with a wet cloth. They often pressed against injured areas but did their best to wipe off the fine sand that invaded every space of Theodora's body. During this painful part of the day, Valeria often spoke about her father. Theodora found it odd that despite all she'd done for Valeria, the girl's thoughts stayed fixed upon her father, as though she couldn't conceive of her existence without him. She knew, though, that Valeria was simply a daughter with a missing parent.

There were nights when she listened to Valeria cry. Theodora would whisper words of assurance and promise an end to the misery in time. How strange that a woman's show of confidence could soothe a child, she thought. Was that a mother's duty? To walk into the dark headwinds of a brutal world, only to turn around from time to time and show sweetness, poise, and serenity to the fearful souls who followed, no matter how blind the way forward? Was she to stand in the path of beasts and face down all that threatened the fragility of life?

Only once Valeria fell asleep each night did Theodora marvel at the peace upon the child's face. That any child fell asleep in so harsh a world and felt safe was itself a sweet miracle. They were both untethered from the world; free, but far from home. But this was the uncharted territory she meant to traverse.

And perhaps soon, Theodora might see the daughter she left behind. Random details of Palatina came and went from her thoughts—the tiny hands, the baby-like skin of her knuckles, the miniature fingernails, the lovely sound of Greek in her daughter's voice. She remembered Palatina's thin, wispy hair as an infant, and then the thick black hair that hung in a braid the last time she'd seen her. If Theodora left the brothels behind when she returned to Constantinople, she could pass entire days with Palatina, perhaps teach the girl lessons or letters.

She needed something pleasant to think of because the North African sun soon became her greatest enemy. Theodora drank bowl after bowl of sun-warmed water, heavy with the taste of metal and earth, but each mouthful and forced swallow was a precious luxury. And there was never enough.

Hunger also stalked Theodora. The Goths were generous with their provisions, but food still had to be rationed on a journey. Theodora couldn't chew hard foods like meat or nuts because of the insufferable pain in her jaws and teeth, so she ate only sweetbread, honeyed figs, and the soft meat of cured fish. Taste meant nothing. Chewing and swallowing meant everything. When she could finally chew through a bite of steaming hot mutton, she savored the flavor, relished the heat in her mouth, and learned to value the richness of meat.

The pain in her ribs from breathing became tolerable after about eight days. Every now and then, she sat up in the wagon to gaze out the window. She, Samira, and Valeria watched the coastline as the wagon lumbered onward.

Theodora saw soldiers, farmers, and shepherds with bleating sheep. When she spoke to other travelers, she encountered Christian pilgrims who traveled eastward for Jerusalem or westward for Rome. So many people from such far-flung places moved about on the highways, thought Theodora, and all of them were part of the vanishing Roman Empire. She realized during her recovery just how big and diverse this thing called an "empire" really was. But what held all these people together? Just what were the common bonds? Why did some rape and murder, while others sang and shared bread?

Theodora remembered that her mother too, once journeyed overland. She used to envy her mother's stories, but now she thought differently. Adventures were awful things that took place in far-off countries, with haunting loneliness and crushing despair, where exotic sights became no longer wondrous, but commonplace, where vast boredom numbed the human spirit, where food was scarce and tasteless, where sickness stalked, where the body withered, and only uneasiness persisted. Surely an adventure became glamourous only when it ended, once the comforts of life returned and the strains of a bizarre reality faded into the past. But until that day, there was only the miserable voyage forward—the crossing of a continent—step by step, hour by hour, day by day, without relief.

In the late evening, Theodora often heard the sounds of lovemaking. Quiet pulses of Samira's voice slipped into the air, different from a brothel sound, for in the wilderness, the sound was sweet. When Samira fell silent, Theodora recognized Vermundo's voice as the two spoke quietly to each other, and it made her smile.

On the fifteenth day of the journey, Theodora finally arose from her makeshift cot. Her body was unwashed, her injuries still bore pain, she stood with a hunch, but at least she could stand. Theodora let Valeria steady her posture, and the girl caught her whenever she faltered. Then she, along with Samira and Valeria, walked barefooted out to the beach and into the sea. Cold water gushed over her ankles, and soon she waded out into the ocean with her friends, letting the cold water rise to her waist, hopping as the waves surged by her, and giggling like sisters. The muscular force of the ocean water freed her skin of all sand and grime. Theodora finally felt clean, if only for a moment.

By the eighteenth day, Theodora felt strong enough to walk alongside the wagon, holding Valeria's hand. She stared up at the sun as if willing the death of a hated enemy. Her skin had darkened. Her bare feet were blistered. But Theodora trudged along with a vagabond's silence, marching between exhausted horses, creaking wheels, and silent barbarians. And the voluptuous beauty from the theaters of Constantinople seemed a hazy memory.

On the twenty-first day, Vermundo pointed to the eastern horizon. "There," he said. "The Lighthouse of Alexandria welcomes us at last. We'll be in the city by nightfall."

Beyond the dunes, Theodora saw a thick plume of white smoke rising into the sky. The sight made distant Constantinople feel suddenly reachable, even if only by her own two feet.

FIFTY

Affter three weeks of pain, despair, and exhaustion, Theodora
approached the city of Alexandria. She was awestruck. The
city looked as large as Constantinople, but with palm trees
instead of cypress, and white sand instead of green hills. The
defensive walls were thinner, shorter, less impressive, but they encircled the
sprawling city, snaking south into the hills and vanishing before reemerging
along the seafront. Unlike Constantinople, Alexandria was flat, built upon a
wide strip of beach, bordered by the sea to her left and an oceanic waterway
to her right.

Theodora gathered Samira and Valeria so they could walk outside the
wagon and see the beautiful sight. They all seemed eager for open air and a
view of the city.

The Goths led the convoy toward a massive arching gate flanked by
Roman soldiers. Foot traffic clustered at the gateway, with people of all colors coming and going in clamorous droves. The smell of animals, foul brine,

and cook smoke filled the air. Theodora watched Roman troops search through wagons and cargo, shoving back unruly migrants, and questioning the travelers at the gate. In some cases, migrants were hauled away. Some of the travelers encamped among the beach dunes, less eager to enter.

The din grew louder as Theodora drew closer to the gate. The entry checkpoint was garrisoned by roughly fifteen Roman soldiers. The remaining troops rested on their shields nearby and watched the foot traffic through unfriendly eyes.

After hours of waiting, a sweaty Romanized Egyptian waved Vermundo forward. "State your homeland, Goth."

"Ravenna, the great capital and home of King Theodoric."

"What's your interest in Alexandria, Goth? Looting, rape, or murder?"

The Roman soldiers behind the officer all laughed.

"We're here by diplomatic request," said Vermundo, handing the Roman officer a scroll case. "We've been sent to seek the counsel of His High Holiness, Pope Timothy the Third. We come in peace to your magnificent city as admirers of Roman culture."

The Roman officer read through the scroll. "A bunch of dogs dressed in finery," he said. "You think wearing highborn clothes disguises you? One misstep inside our city and we'll beat you all out." He then shoved the scroll case back to Vermundo. "You're in the East now, Goth."

After Vermundo kicked the sides of his horse, the Gothic cavalcade trudged into the great gateway, waved on by Roman soldiers with hostile faces. Theodora entered Alexandria as a migrant, from beneath a foreign flag, and before the suspicious eyes of her own countrymen. For the first time, she tasted the bitter sting of being an unwelcomed guest of the empire.

When she stepped out from the gate's shadow and into the sunlit city, she beheld a beautiful and bustling metropolis. The main boulevard looked like an enormous horse track, with two straightaways divided by a long, palm-lined median. Thousands filled the sand-swept boulevard on both sides. Roads didn't spill down into each other from burgeoning hills, but intersected at regular distances, as if each city block was perfectly square. Alexandria gave the appearance of intelligent planning, a city like an orchard, patterned in rows and orderly buildings, whereas Constantinople, at least as Theodora recalled, was more like a great forest of civilization that grew wild upon the hills.

Theodora took in a deep breath of foul city odors, listening to the din and marveling at the chaotic pulse she so enjoyed. She was a woman of the city, after all, of bricks and mortar, of chariots and crowds, of grand monuments and thunderous applause. So, after weeks trudging upon the sweltering highway, Theodora felt the embrace of a sprawling imperial city.

But cities had a dark underside as well. As she followed alongside the Gothic procession, she noticed women standing in the arcades on the side of the street. The women beckoned the foot traffic, and when men looked in their direction, they let slip their gown to reveal a bare breast, or parted a robe to flash a slender, naked body. There were so many prostitutes, thought Theodora. And men broke from the crowded street, took a prostitute by the hand, and vanished into the shadowed arcade. The view served as a reminder to Theodora that she hadn't yet spared Valeria, Samira, or herself from such a fate.

"Don't look at them," said Theodora, turning Valeria away.

Valeria resisted. "I want to see."

Theodora relaxed her grip on the girl, letting Valeria peer at the prostitutes. Theodora knew that most women, even girls, bore some natural fascination with the ancient profession. For a prostitute was the inverse of the chaste mother, a shadowy opposite of each woman, the dark feminine, a being of sexual power and social powerlessness alike.

"They look happy," said Valeria. "They all smile."

"They smile to attract men," answered Theodora. "An unhappy woman won't bring men to her, and she won't get paid. It's that plain. The more a woman looks like she wants a man, the more men will seek her out. And sometimes that practiced smile becomes real."

"Then what's so bad about it?"

Theodora watched another prostitute smile and throw her arms around an approaching man. "I used to ask the same question. If that life truly brings joy to a woman, then she should pursue it. But once you cross into that world, you must be owned and governed. The truth is, you lose control of your life. Some of us feel enlivened by that loss of control," said Theodora, recalling her own feelings as a younger woman. "But most of us . . . most of us get beaten down by it. Most of us just get lost. Most women wish to leave that life, just as we left at the Governor's Palace. They just don't know how."

Valeria grabbed Theodora's hand.

Theodora found comfort in being able to teach the girl a true lesson, one without the cloud of servitude over their heads. This was a lesson between two free women.

"What will become of me? Or you?" said Valeria.

"I don't know," answered Theodora, feeling the nag of uncertainty. She stood up to the Hydra, but its many eyes could still spot her passing, and the great serpent could yet reclaim her. "I plan to send word to find your father. If he's alive, then the Blue faction will find him."

"What if he's not alive?"

Theodora squeezed Valeria's hand. "No need to ask that question just yet."

As Theodora and the Goths traveled deeper into the city center, the streets became more and more crowded by the dispossessed. Refugees in sand-stained robes, livestock, chickens in crates, crying babies, horses, and freight carts all occupied the roadways. The streets looked like the caravan camps Theodora had encountered on the imperial highways. But how strange to see them in an urban interior such as Alexandria.

"Who are all these people?" asked Valeria.

"I've no idea," Theodora said. She craned to trace the long line of refugees to its source. Further down the road, where the crowd seemed to converge, she saw a white building with a large Christian cross rising above the roof line.

"That is the Holy See of Alexandria," said Vermundo, interrupting Theodora's curious stare.

She turned to see Vermundo atop his horse, trotting toward her. "Are we here then?"

"We're to quarter at the residence of His Holiness," he said. "You,

Samira, and the girl will have a proper bed, a bath, and a hot meal. We made it, Theodora."

Theodora smiled and hugged Samira and Valeria. For a moment, they all embraced and a sense of relief seemed to pass among them. An arduous journey found a reprieve.

Vermundo dismounted, took up the reins to his steed, and walked alongside Theodora. "We'll be here for one week before we return home to Italia," he said. "You seem to be mending well."

"All thanks to you," said Theodora. "My ribs are still tender, but I'm indebted to you and your men."

Vermundo shrugged. "You owe us nothing. After what I saw at the Governor's Palace, you've already paid a steep price."

"Why did you intervene?" said Theodora. "You could've looked the other way, and none would've judged you poorly."

"Truthfully? Because you remind me of another woman, one I admire back home."

Theodora smiled as a co-conspirator. "Is that so?"

"Yes," said Vermundo, but didn't return the smile. "Like you, this woman is very beautiful. And, like you, she's smart and capable in the company of men. When I saw you stand up to the Roman governor, I couldn't help but think she'd do the same."

"What's her name?"

"The princess, Amalasuntha. She's the youngest daughter of our king."

Theodora thought the name sounded unflattering, as did most Gothic names.

Vermundo continued. "She could probably rule the whole of our king-dom if called upon."

"Do Goths have many women rulers?"

"No," said Vermundo. "But she's not like other women. The princess studied Greek philosophers and Roman historians. She speaks Latin, Greek, and Gothic perfectly. She envisions a Gothic kingdom as educated and skilled as ever once the Romans were."

"She sounds like a woman of great vision."

But the odor of unwashed human bodies, urine, and feces suddenly filled Theodora's mouth and nostrils. She pressed a handful of her dry hair over her nose and mouth, just to block the stench. One of the other migrants on the street bumped into Valeria, and Theodora instinctively pulled the girl closer. "Who are all these people?" said Theodora.

"These?" And Vermundo looked around with revulsion. "These are your empire's Christian refugees, deemed heretics by Emperor Justin. Many have been displaced by his Orthodox policies. Roman emperors stay locked away in Constantinople and see nothing of the outside world. A few of these sorry souls might make their way to Emperor Justin to plead their case, but he'll only look on them as poor beggars from a remote province. He won't see them as people."

Theodora didn't like hearing Vermundo speak of Justinian's father with such harsh words. If people saw the Roman emperor as an agent of evil, then perhaps so too might they see Justinian one day. "What did Emperor Justin do to cause this?"

"He wants a single Christian doctrine to unite all three popes. He's so desperate to get Rome back into the Eastern fold that he'll do anything," Vermundo said and waved his hand at the refugees. "Look around you. To win the favor of Pope Hormisdas, your emperor is persecuting the Monophysites. And so, they come to Pope Timothy for shelter. Christians persecuting Christians."

Theodora was still a Blue informer. She may have been far from the capital, but she knew intrigue when she saw it. She knew that it was Justinian himself, more so than Justin, who sought the alliance with Pope Hormisdas in Rome. When Justinian told Theodora that he'd reunite the East and West churches and end Vitalian's rebellion, she thought his idea smart and common sense. But here, in the distant reaches of North Africa, that common sense looked so different.

She saw an opportunity in the situation. And a way to help.

"Monophysites against the Orthodox," she said and shook her head. "This dispute sparked a rebellion when I was a girl, and my father was killed in the fighting."

"I'm sorry to hear that," said Vermundo. "Kingdoms used to fight over territory. But this is a different age. Now we fight over the definition of God."

The delegation drew up to Saint Mark's Cathedral. The building's roof curved like a giant arch, with a front wall facing the street, all painted in beautiful white. A large cross protruded from the crest of the roof, rising and casting a crucifix shadow upon the refugees.

"So small for a Holy See," said Theodora.

"I like it," said Samira. "It's dignified."

Vermundo pointed at the church. "Saint Mark is buried inside that building."

"I'm more concerned about the living at the moment. Will you let me come with you to meet the pope?"

Breaking an unspoken courtesy, Vermundo put his arm around Theodora. He smiled warmly. "I'd be a fool to bring you this far only to deny so simple a request. Let's meet the Pope of Alexandria."

Theodora turned again and took in the sight of Saint Mark's Cathedral. Once again, she had to cross into the domain of the Christians.

FIFTY-ONE

When Theodora entered the Cathedral of Saint Mark, the bustle of an overcrowded city fell almost silent behind her. The high, arching ceilings reminded her of being a girl, when the children of the neighborhood shook a linen sheet, arching the fabric like a tunnel while Theodora ran through. But this tunnel towered overhead, cavernous, with stone pillars, like giants instead of neighborhood girls, lining up alongside the tunnel. Beams of sunlight angled down from the clerestory, the tiny flower-shaped openings high on the walls. And the smoky aroma of frankincense mixed with the stench of unwashed bodies. Like the Hagia Sophia in Constantinople, the walls of Saint Mark's glittered with mosaics. The artwork depicted strange men looking upward, their eyes sullen, their heads framed in golden circles. Refugees filled the pews. Some knelt with hands clasped and heads bowed. Some whispered words in silence, some wept, while others spoke aloud in their native tongues, begging the favor of an invisible, but overpowering presence.

Now that she stood inside, Theodora immediately felt the contrast between her dusty highway attire and the clean, ornamented space of the temple. But she felt safe. The downtrodden were clearly welcomed here.

After a brief wait and a chance to freshen their appearance, the pope summoned the Goths. Vermundo led the way, following two red-robed priests. Each priest wore a white onion-shaped headdress with a white cloth that fell back behind their ears and neck.

They all entered an antechamber where two chamberlains leaned in and pulled open a set of doors. As the room beyond came into view, Theodora heard a loud clang, like metal on stone, followed by a man's commanding voice. "You're in the presence of his High Holiness, the thirty-second Alexandrine Patriarch, Pope Timothy, the third of his name."

Vermundo and his men entered a humble audience chamber and dropped to one knee, bowing their heads. Theodora, Samira, and Valeria mimicked the gesture.

"I am Vermundo Odomalia, son of Eiriks Odomalia of Ravenna, loyal godson to King Theodoric, who is himself the ruler of Italia, the regent of the Visigoths, and the people-king of the Roman Empire in the West."

Vermundo's words echoed until the chamber fell silent.

"Please rise, Vermundo, son of Eiriks," said the pope.

Theodora heard the shuffling of clothing, and she again followed the cue and arose from her kneeling position. She set her eyes upon Pope Timothy. He sat in a chair of white fabric with gold leaf edges. He looked to be a man in his late fifties, with sun-brown skin and an unruly white beard. His eyes shone with compassion, but the hard creases on his face hinted at stern authority and the worry of troubled times. He wore no crown, but a simple white hood that clung to his scalp and cheeks.

"We've been sent by our king to discuss the state of Christendom. And to find common ground against the persecution of your flock," said Vermundo.

"How unexpected. But we welcome the concern," said Pope Timothy. "It seems our emperor has sided with the Orthodox Church and rendered all others invalid. His view of unifying Christendom is nothing more than the silencing of dissenting voices."

At the mention of Emperor Justin, Theodora flinched. Now she paid attention to every word.

"We believe Pope Hormisdas is exploiting a simpleton emperor," said Vermundo. "Pope Hormisdas pretends to work with this illiterate Caesar, but seeks sole authority over all Christians. The emperor doesn't know any better and so, here we are."

"But what is your interest in all this, Goth?"

"Pope Hormisdas rejects the doctrine of Arias as well," said Vermundo. "He sees my people as barbarian heretics, so we know well the sting of persecution. That is why we seek a common stand against the policies of the Eastern Empire."

"Well, we both agree that Emperor Justin must be dealt with," said Pope Timothy. "But as with any resistance, the question is how?"

Theodora was stunned. She realized that she stood in the center of a critical negotiation, one that took place between two men who opposed Emperor Justin. Worse, she knew the campaign for a unified religion came not from Justin, but from her beloved Justinian.

Pope Timothy looked over the men in Vermundo's delegation, ending with a long look at Theodora. She wondered whether he regarded her presence as suspicious. Her instincts told her not to look away from the pope as he stared on, but she bowed her head in reflex.

"And what of these women?" said Pope Timothy. "Who are they? Companions of the highway?"

Vermundo glanced at Theodora. "No, your High Holiness. I brought these women all the way from Sozusa. They were maltreated by the Roman governor there. This one is Theodora—"

Theodora stepped forward. "I'm a friend of Emperor Justin," she blurted. The name of the reviled emperor echoed in the chamber and caused a murmur. Vermundo wrinkled his eyebrows at Theodora and stared at her in contempt.

Pope Timothy's expression darkened. He lifted his bearded chin and narrowed his eyes on Theodora. "You choose poor friends," he said. "Emperor Justin has turned against our Holy See and caused many Monophysites to flee their homes."

"I'm also a friend to any people who suffer, Your Grace," she said. "Eight years ago, my father died over the policies of a Monophysite emperor, so I detest the fighting. I never understood the infighting as a girl, and to be blunt, I didn't care. But I've seen with my own eyes how widespread this divide yet runs."

"Young woman, do you believe in the One Nature or the Three?"

The room fell silent as all the men, both Goth and clergy, turned to look at her. Dread struck Theodora. For this was the great question of the age... was Christ born half man and half god with *one* unique nature of his own, as the Monophysites believed? Or was Christ a simultaneous father and son, united through a holy spirit in trinity, as the Orthodox believed? She cleared her throat. "I don't know, Your Holiness. But in your house, I'll honor the ways of the host."

"How is it you came to be in the service of these Goths?"

Theodora looked at Vermundo, who still looked perplexed. "This man was of great assistance to me, my friend, and this girl."

"And in what capacity did you *serve* the governor of Cyrenaica?"

"As a concubine," said Theodora. "As a quiet lady."

There was another murmur as the holy men in the room grew uncomfortable.

Theodora raised her voice. "I'm not ashamed of this, Your Holiness. But I've had a change of heart on certain matters. My friend and I have turned away from such services at great cost to ourselves. We did so to remove this girl from the concubinage of Governor Hacebolus. We've traveled far to escape that bondage, and now we seek sanctuary in your Holy House."

"And you shall have it," said Pope Timothy. "Just as I must grant shelter to the thousands outside my doors right now." Then the pope softened and smiled warmly. "But my laments are unfair to you. I see that you've sacrificed much to get here. Why did you announce your friendship to the Roman emperor? Do you seek an intercession?"

"I ask that you send word out for this girl's father, Your Holiness," said Theodora, and she pulled Valeria in front of her. "Her name is Valeria. Her father was a former tribune in the government of King Theodoric before attempting to immigrate to the East. While in transit, their vessel was attacked, and her father was taken from her. We believe her father may still be alive."

Silence.

"I offer to plead your case to Emperor Justin," said Theodora. "As a first-hand observer to the suffering of your people."

"And what do you want for yourself?"

"Only to return home to Constantinople."

Pope Timothy sat back in his gilded seat and tapped his fingers against the armrest. He ruminated and then glanced over at Vermundo. "Magister Vermundo, you and your men shall have all the hospitality you desire. I'll treat further with you tonight, and you'll have my full attention. In the meantime," said the pope as he arose from his seat, "I wish to speak more with these women."

Vermundo looked at Theodora with frustration showing on his face. She nodded at him, hoping to convey solidarity with the Goth, despite her interruption.

Then a white-robed chamberlain pounded a gold scepter and a definitive clang echoed out. Vermundo scowled at Theodora, but bowed to the pope and departed with the other Goths. Theodora, Samira, and Valeria only huddled closer together.

Pope Timothy approached Theodora and took up her hand. Immediately, she felt the old man's weight and steadied him. "Thank you, Your Grace," she said.

"I know your intentions are pure," he said. His voice no longer bore the notes of authority but sounded soft and sincere. "I know this because it would have been smarter for you to keep quiet and overhear the discussion that would've taken place. The emperor would have paid well for such information. But you were forthright, and I see that you have other matters on your mind," he said with a gentle nod at Valeria.

"I do, Your Holiness," said Theodora.

The pope reached down and tucked his finger under Valeria's chin. "And how are you, young one? Has Theodora been a blessing to you?"

"She has," said Valeria. "I don't even know what to say."

"Say 'thank you,'" he said.

When Valeria looked up, Theodora saw the girl's eyes were glassy. "Thank you," said Valeria.

The emotion was contagious. She, Samira, and Valeria were so focused on getting through each day on the highway that none thought of how they'd feel when the journey found a reprieve. Theodora squeezed the girl's hand.

Pope Timothy signaled two other robed assistants, who quickly opened a door in the path of the pope. Theodora felt hot air sweep over her. Beyond the doorway, she saw a green lawn, a view of the sea, and groves of palm trees painted white at the base of the trunk. They all walked out into a courtyard and sat on a curving stone bench, with Samira helping the pope settle into his final, restful position.

Pope Timothy pulled back his hood to reveal a balding head and unkempt white hair. "That's better. When you get to my age, walking about in heat like this isn't so easy."

"It's not easy at any age," said Samira as she sat beside Theodora.

After an exhausted sigh, the pope looked at Theodora. "Now, young woman, tell me exactly how you would plead our cause to Emperor Justin. And tell me what you expect in return."

Theodora knew how to speak to men of power. She fixed her eyes on the pope and meant to be direct and exact in her words. But the compassionate expression on the old man's face caught her off-guard. An unexpected upwelling of sorrow overtook her, perhaps from the relief of a strenuous journey, perhaps from the serenity of the courtyard, perhaps from the focused attention of an old man who wished to listen. As she felt the muscles in her face tightening with emotion, Theodora looked down at Valeria, hoping to stave off the anarchy of an all-consuming grief. But when she saw that the girl also faltered, Theodora broke.

She dropped her head and tears came flooding out. "I want to go home," said Theodora, her voice catching on the word *home*, stretching into a long, child-like wail. "I abandoned my little girl. I left everyone behind—"

Pope Timothy pulled Theodora's head into his collar. She felt his hands on the back of her head and then felt both Samira and Valeria lean against her back and embrace her. She heard Valeria crying as well. And for endless moments, Theodora wept in the silent embrace of Pope Timothy. Her sobbing bore no dignity. It was loud and unrestrained. She pressed her open mouth into the pope's robe to stifle the sound of her weeping. Theodora's body shook with irrepressible spasms. And when she tried to catch her breath, the air stuttered in. Her cheeks and jaws ached. Her throat constricted. The anguish of eight years poured into the dark space of shadow and wet fabric at the pope's chest.

Theodora reached out and pulled Samira and Valeria as close as she could. They all had lost their families along the way. They all risked everything to make the terrible journey. They all had stayed strong while suffering. Such strength in the face of hardship finally caught up to all three women.

After some time passed, Theodora pulled back in spent exhaustion. She sniffed and rubbed away the tears that clung to the bottom of her eyelids. Pope Timothy, who said nothing during the bout of weeping, now smiled gently. He took up Theodora's hands.

"Some of us must wander before we come home," said the pope. "And a person's true character can shine through a thousand misdeeds. As a believer in the one nature of Christ, I also believe in the one nature of people. The person we truly are beneath is the very person we eventually become in the world, no matter how long we may act to the contrary. I've seen holy men reveal a wicked character upon temptation. And now, in this courtyard, I've seen agents of carnality reveal themselves as truly brave."

Theodora looked up at him, sparked by his words. For years she wrestled with the two Theodoras, and here the pope breathed life into her private reflections. "You don't believe that people can have two natures?"

"No," he said. "We have one nature given by God, and we follow that nature. Some try to hide this nature by inventing a second one. But this second nature is a deception, a façade that merely conceals the true self."

Theodora considered the remark. "But what if . . . a deception . . . is the only way to live with oneself?"

"That's not living with oneself. That's dying with oneself."

"But a child, Your Holiness. When evil comes up close, a child may not understand it. The second nature, even if it's just a façade, may be the only thing that can," and Theodora searched for the right words, "ward off the evil."

Pope Timothy grew stoic. "You've seen the beast then?"

Theodora nodded solemnly.

Pope Timothy placed a gentle hand on Theodora's shoulder. "Would you consider a confession?"

A Christian custom never occurred to her, but now she imagined herself telling someone everything. What if, just once, she hid nothing? "Your Holiness, there are many things I've seen and done that I'm struggling to let go of. And I know I must let go."

"Most confessions allow us to face our sins. But often, the most powerful confessions come when we say aloud the sins of others we carry with us, like heavy stones, sins that went unspoken in this world. Those sins can poison us for a lifetime, child."

Then she felt it, like a shadow befalling her every sense, an ambush of her worst emotions.

No, no, don't look at me.

Theodora quickly pressed her hand over both eyes and turned her head. The *shame* was still there. Had she forgotten?

Don't look at me!

She clenched her teeth and felt her body growing hot. There, at the heart of the one Theodora was a fragile fourteen-year-old girl. Without the powerful and notorious Theodora to beat back the world, her younger self lay suddenly exposed. And now, she was stepping forward and asking once again: *Was any of it my fault?* Because she never got an answer. Her question had been buried beneath an unbearable, unlivable shame, and then forgotten altogether. Despite everything, she never knew for sure.

Was it my fault?

Theodora rubbed her hand against her eyes as hard as she could, the shame a chokehold. Perhaps now was the time to face that day as a grown woman. "Yes, I want to confess."

FIFTY-TWO

nd so, on the following day, Theodora met Pope Timothy in his private chambers. The room held a dignified silence, with many strange objects that cluttered the area, yet in stillness. She sat in a chair beside a low wood table. To her left arose a wall of shelves, crisscrossing into wide diamond shapes with rolled scrolls filling the bottom half of each diamond. She looked around. The chamber seemed to be a place of learned study, solitude, and private meditation. She noticed that the pope hung dozens of blue glass ornaments around the frame of his doorway. Each amulet bore a single eye, staring out lidlessly, with some eyes centered in the palm of an upturned hand. Even here, thought Theodora, eyes befell her. Even here she had a watchful audience. "What are those?" she asked.

"Those are wards against evil," he said. "The source of all evil begins with a covetous eye."

Theodora recalled the gaze of Magister Origen at her father's funeral.

His covetous eyes had beheld Theodora's youthful beauty, while his dark imagination spun webs, impelling him to act. Later, such eyes multiplied, filled rooms, stared, and always, always impelled men to act.

"Would you like some wine and bread?" he asked.

"Just water. I still have the thirst of the desert in me. How was your talk with Vermundo?"

Pope Timothy filled a wooden cup with water and then sat beside Theodora. "He and I had a fruitful discussion about your 'friend' Justin this morning."

"I apologized to Vermundo last night," said Theodora. "I had no idea what he came here for until he addressed you."

"He understands why you spoke out when you did," said the pope. "I think Vermundo's a man of culture and goodwill who wants prosperity for his people."

Theodora smiled, but just as quickly felt anxiety bloom in her body's center. She knew why she was in that room and she knew what she planned to talk about.

The pope must have noticed her sudden uneasiness. "Try not to worry," he said. "In here, nothing you say will be judged. Later, we may speak of worldly affairs, but nothing you say to me in this room will be shared or used to that end. In here, I am a man of God, and I listen with an open heart."

Theodora looked into her lap. "There's a world inside us, Your High Holiness. I think when something bad goes on unspoken and unpunished, the world inside us burns. Since no eye can see the burning, you realize you can hide it. And hiding it becomes your sole focus."

"And now you need hide nothing," he said.

Theodora stared into the pope's eyes for a long stretch, fearing to trust anyone with her heavy burden, her dark life of secrets.

Pope Timothy nodded with eyes closed.

And so Theodora spoke of those things that had no prior voice. She told Pope Timothy of her great happiness as a child, admitting her childish pride and arrogance. She told him about the death of her father during the

Trisagion Revolt, the hopelessness of the family, and the help of Magister Origen. Then, Theodora spoke aloud the words that reconstructed the event that happened so long ago. She recounted her rape at the hands of Magister Origen. It was the first time she ever used the word "rape" to describe the blackness in her memory. The rape existed in her mind in separate parts, as a constricting feeling, as horror and shock, as smells and words and random objects nearby, as voices and noises, all heaped in her memory like a million shards of colored glass. She wept before the pope as she might when alone. And the deep agony turned apathetic when she told of those faces who knew the evil but looked away. And then her apathy darkened when she spoke of those who denied her the truth, who defamed her, and left her estranged.

Theodora also described how the evil spread inside her, just as a single drop of poison turns the whole vessel to poison. Time and time again, Theodora descended into the awful prison of tears, where speech is impossible and grief suffocates the human spirit. For grief was the closest thing in the world to death.

As the sun set beyond the window, Theodora told of her mother's humiliation in the Hippodrome and how a stranger from the enemy faction, the man in the stands, appeared and saved her family.

As the evening drew on, Theodora told the pope of her rebirth as a sexual performer. Innocence was to be expunged because innocence was blindness; innocence was ignorance, separating her from those numerous others who knew evil and therefore, had a great and mysterious power over her. Resistance to dark masculine forces *without* this knowledge was to thrash blindly at a creature she didn't understand. Better to be a woman who knew the nature of a man like Magister Origen than to be a weak girl who no one wished to see, who no one wanted to hear, whose grievance bothered all and left her despised.

She explained how she had become pregnant when she was sixteen and how each night, while drunk, she'd gulp a foul-tasting cup of roots to quell the baby within, and how the baby came anyway. She confessed she had no interest in Palatina because she could not earn in the theaters with a needy baby at her breast. But so too, did she refuse to raise her girl in the brothel, as most women did.

Pope Timothy listened to Theodora's every word, never interrupting or losing focus or looking tired. As the night matured and moved toward morning, Theodora detailed her life in the theater. To be beautiful and willing was to be invited to a secret table, to partake in carnal pleasures, and to experience the thrill of self-indulgence while the waking world toiled. Surely, they were the fools.

Theodora's crying eventually slowed and her words came under control. She told Pope Timothy how she had met Justinian and began clandestine work for the Blues. The responsibility appealed to her. She spoke of Hypatius and his tortured mind and how she contrived a plan to protect the old soul. She confessed to her special relationship with Justinian and admitted for the first time that she loved him. Then she bespoke the pain she felt in leaving them all behind.

She confessed that, on the eve of her departure from Constantinople, she found it difficult to leave her daughter, that she admired Palatina and wondered for the first time, if only briefly, about the role of motherhood.

Finally, Theodora spoke of the governor and Valeria and the long trek across North Africa. When she finished, no tears wet her face. She looked on Pope Timothy as if awaiting some kind of judgment. But the pope's countenance bore no trace of judgment. He merely returned a fatherly smile. "You have endured the hardships of a lifetime already, Theodora. How old are you?"

"Twenty-two."

"What arrogance you've seen in men, with their attitudes," he said, "you have matched with an arrogance of the body."

"Yes."

"We live in a Roman world, and it's a harsh world, an effort by man to conquer the material realm. But God offers an alternative to Caesar."

"Both are tyrants," she said. "God permits too much evil in the world for me to regard Him much."

"And Caesar does not? Those who reject God are always left turning to

Caesar, for what else has the power to grant favor in this world if not his government? They despise Caesar with all their heart, bending their minds around his corruption as Caesar oppresses them. But they are quick to hail him when he oppresses those they despise."

"What choice do we have? It seems to me an all-powerful being wouldn't allow so many bad things to happen to His people. I've prayed to your God before, and even He looked away."

"I think God has answered your prayers."

"I prayed to go home, not to be beaten nearly to death and forced to march across a desert. If God truly meant to answer my prayers, why be so cruel?"

"You misunderstand. You mentioned two prayers. The first was when you were a girl, after Magister Origen enacted his evil upon you. You told me you prayed for strength and power. The second prayer was to deliver you and Valeria from the governor. You describe your flight from the palace as the cruelty of God, but I see it as nearly the opposite. I think God is answering your first prayer."

"How?"

The pope pulled back with a grave and startled expression. "You sought God for power."

"But I have no power."

"Oh, but Theodora, you do. Just as when the Israelites left Egypt, there's only one path ahead," he said. "And this path is not safe. Misfortune will come sweeping in and overturn your life. Real inner strength comes not from birthright or godly magic, but from terrible atrocity, from devastating loss, and brutal hardship. It's dark and traumatic, a path fraught with the possibility of your own destruction at the hands of evil."

Theodora swallowed involuntarily.

"On such a path have you now tread, young woman. You wanted strength, well, this is what it looks like. No longer are you intrigued by the dark underworld. No longer are you conflicted about the people you love. You defeated the evil designs of a wicked man and withstood his effort to destroy you. You risked your own life in protection of others, and here you come from out of the desert. Out of exile. Your hardship has given you a boon of strength and wisdom. What you do with this boon is up to you now."

Theodora stared back at him. "Are you saying that men like Magister Origen and Governor Hacebolus are part of some godly plan? They're the tools bringing goodness into the world? You're telling me that evil is useful because it creates strength and goodness in people?"

Pope Timothy finally leaned forward and raised a finger. "No. Not that at all. That's a logic that works backward and gives a kind of justification for evil. No. Because for each one like you who limps forward, having survived with wisdom and strength, there are countless others who did *not* survive. Their lives have been spent, crushed beneath a worldly evil, never to return to us, never to heal, never to gain strength. Their voices are silent at this moment as you and I here now speak. In that process, evil only destroys. And it will continue to do so until a weak and unlikely soul makes a stand, survives, and learns how to fight back. And you can fight back now, Theodora. You can continue to risk yourself." Pope Timothy smiled warmly. "It's why God favors the downtrodden. Many beg God to intervene and wipe away their problems, to make their life free of suffering, free of degradation, and struggle. But they unwittingly seek to be relieved from the burdens of life itself. No wisdom can be gained by us if God is the doer of the most difficult deeds."

There was a long silence as Theodora mulled over the pope's words.

"Would you consider being baptized?" said Pope Timothy. "A washing away of the poison, to be born anew, here in Alexandria, before I send you home?"

Thoughts of clean, cool water went through Theodora's mind. A baptism. She never thought of such a thing, perhaps because her mother so strongly opposed it. Such a ritual was too . . . Christian . . . and she wasn't Christian; she wasn't a part of this religious happening that spread to every corner of the Roman Empire and inspired such vitriol in people. But she saw now that these strange forces also brought light and wisdom, a sanctuary from the darkness, a code of conduct for men. And to be forgiven? To be reborn?

These new ideas stuck in her mind like splinters of wood in the flesh. "But don't I need to convert to be baptized?"

"Yes."

"Your Holiness," Theodora finally said. "I'm not comfortable with religions or rituals. Let me think about your proposal. For now, I wish only to remain in Alexandria until we hear news of Valeria's father, good or ill. Until that day comes, I offer to help you with the refugees. You needn't pay me so long as I have a bed to sleep in."

"I accept," said Timothy.

Theodora arose. "Thank you for listening to me, Your Holiness," she said, feeling confidence and authority returning to her. "But for me, there's still work to do."

FIFTY-THREE

Aweek after arriving in Alexandria, Theodora stood in front of St. Mark's and embraced Samira. Her Ethiopian friend was the first to depart. She was to travel first to Carthage, and then sail home to Italy with Vermundo and his men. Apparently, their bond on the highway was more than a fleeting companionship. The Goths sat atop their horses, packed and ready to travel.

"Thank you," said Samira. "What you've shown me will stay with me forever."

"This doesn't have to be goodbye," said Theodora, smiling. "Vermundo is a member of the Gothic court. From time to time, I'll send word from Constantinople."

"I'd like that."

There wasn't anything else to say. After a final embrace and a long stare into each other's eyes, Samira backed away. She turned and hurried excitedly over to the Gothic convoy. Theodora watched as Vermundo dismounted, took Samira into his arms, and kissed her. They both looked happy. He led Samira into the back of the wood wagon that had been Theodora's home for three painful weeks. Once he closed the wagon, Vermundo paused and looked back at Theodora, squinting in the sunlight. After a moment, he bowed in a show of respect.

Theodora bowed in return.

And then she watched as horses, wagons, and mule trains stirred from their resting positions and lumbered westward, back the way they'd come. The Ostrogothic convoy moved out and soon merged with the congested streets before vanishing into thousands of anonymous people.

Theodora hoped that soon she too, would depart. But not until she finished what she began. Valeria was safe from Governor Hacebolus, but Theodora felt responsible for the girl's welfare. She told herself that this was the price of empowerment. She was free to choose her course, but now she must stay the course.

True to his word, Pope Timothy dispatched inquiries as to the whereabouts of Marinus Sidonius, the former tribune and father of a Valeria Sidonius. As Theodora watched the pope's couriers set out, she knew that such a search would take months or more. Valeria's father could be in exile, begging in an alleyway, or worse, dead and unable to respond. Even then, Theodora figured word might reach someone who knew Marinus and end the uncertainty.

So, Theodora remained in Alexandria as the months went by. The time was not without its rewards, and unexpectedly, the contentment came from hard work. She and Valeria labored alongside the Monophysite Christians of the Holy See. Each morning, she awoke with Valeria while the skies were still dark. They drew water from the wells together, carrying the heavy buckets to the church. Afterward, they walked through the dusty horde of refugees encamped outside the Holy See. Theodora saw the weary faces of Monophysites from all over the empire and some from beyond imperial borders. They came from every corner to seek the protection of Pope Timothy. As Theodora and Valeria passed among the refugees, they handed out warm bread loaves from the ovens of St. Mark's. Valeria held the sack, while Theodora reached out and pushed bread into the skeletal fingers of the destitute. How close she and her family once came to such a fate, she thought. If cruelty tore the world apart, then surely compassion mended it back together.

At midday, when the sun overhead was hottest, Theodora and Valeria brought water to the asylum-seekers. Theodora dunked a ladle in the bucket and held the utensil at each weary mouth. She watched as cracked and sand-speckled lips sucked eagerly at the fresh and glinting water. Despite her sweat and thirst, Theodora never drank a sip of water in front of the downtrodden.

At the Vesper's Hour, when a purple twilight befell the Egyptian skies, the Alexandrine monks marched in procession through the streets. They sang hymns and swung ornate brass thuribles, mixing incense with the heavy odors of livestock and humanity. That was when Theodora and Valeria finally rested. They retired to the courtyard at the rear of St. Mark's to wash their dirty hands and faces in the fountain.

As the days bled into months, and as the months grew on, Theodora sent word to Justinian. She pressed a quill to parchment and began an official correspondence, her first. Theodora's mother ensured that her and her sisters learned to read and write, and for years, the skill seemed almost unnecessary, a novelty of the upper classes to collude against the public. But here, in the lonely months, she saw the power of literacy. She was amazed at how mixed ink and scribbled words became an actual voice, no longer a muddle of feelings and ideas, but an articulation of her private thoughts laid bare. Theodora informed Justinian that she intended to return to Constantinople in the coming months, and how she meant to see him again. And when, after five weeks, he responded, Theodora curled up beneath a candle and silently read his flowing script, written by his own hand. Once read, the sound of Justinian's voice flooded her mind with stunning intimacy, which only deepened her longing.

While Theodora corresponded with Justinian through writing, she also continued her discussions with Pope Timothy, face to face. They mostly talked about her work with the refugees, and from time to time he asked if she still sought a baptism. And, as always, she refused.

In early spring the following year, Theodora and Valeria sat atop sandy dunes, sharing bread at sunset. To the north, a whipping flame crowned the monumental lighthouse, while the tower beneath seemed to quiver in the shifting shadows. Theodora watched the Pharos of Alexandria funnel white smoke into darkening skies, its fire a beacon to the scattered ships on the horizon.

"What if no word ever comes?" said Valeria, breaking the silence, as she stared at the lighthouse. "You can't stay here forever."

Theodora drew in a long, slow breath. "Pope Timothy asks me the same thing from time to time. I'll tell you what I tell him. I stay until this task is complete."

"But you know what I'm asking," said Valeria. "For my father, I'll hold out hope forever. But you? When will you decide to give up the wait?"

"I'll never give up anything ever again. I led us down this path, Valeria," she said, almost drearily. "I do my chores, I enjoy my time with you, and I remind myself that soon I'll be home again. That keeps me going."

Valeria paused. "But surely this time would be better spent with your own daughter, not me."

Theodora finally looked at Valeria and smiled. "You're a strong girl," she said, "to talk of difficult things. Well, when I return home, I plan on being a mother this time. But what kind of a mother would I be if I let the most important tasks go unfinished? My daughter needs a mother who finishes what she starts and doesn't give up when things are bleak."

"But you're already that kind of person," said Valeria. "I've thought about you a lot lately and don't feel good, knowing I'm keeping you from your daughter."

"You're not keeping me away from her," said Theodora sternly. "I'm choosing to be here with you until we hear back from your father. I'm happy to do this."

Valeria fell quiet again. Then the girl leaned in and rested her head on Theodora's shoulder. After a few moments passed, she continued. "Theodora?"

"Yes, Valeria?"

"If I don't hear from my father by the end of the month, I'll return with you to Constantinople. I'll wait for my father there."

Theodora rested her head on Valeria's. For a while, the two just stared out at the magnificent lighthouse as the skies darkened like a shade over the earth. She heard Valeria sigh, and it made Theodora smile. This is what the girls of the world needed, someone who cared, who went all the way.

Fourteen days later, Theodora and Valeria carried buckets of water into the basilica for morning prayers. They stood near the apse when Valeria suddenly dropped her bucket and gasped. Theodora jolted in alarm, but the girl fled from her side, racing down the center aisle and toward the entry doors.

A man stood in the doorway.

Theodora watched Valeria run toward the tall older man. He spotted her, crouched, and caught the girl, embracing her and lifting her into the air until her legs dangled. They stood silhouetted in the open doorway, the sunlight blurring their outline. Marinus Sidonius had come for his daughter at last.

Theodora covered her mouth. She smiled as she watched inaudible words pass between Valeria and her father. He stared at the girl with eyes that only good fathers have for their daughters, utterly biased, nodding, smiling, and embracing her again. Then Valeria turned and pointed in Theodora's direction, and the man craned to see. When their eyes met, Theodora straightened her posture, suddenly aware that this Marinus was a real man, no longer just a spoken name.

Marinus arose to full height. His visage was that of a marble Roman statue, but one weathered and chipped from centuries of neglect. He had a gray-stubbled jawline, an aquiline nose, and large brown eyes. He still bore the upright posture of a former station-holder despite his drab clothing. Marinus approached Theodora, pausing when he came within an arm's length. Then, when words failed him, Marinus drew in and embraced Theodora. Finally, he said, "I owe you my life."

Theodora squeezed him back. "You owe me nothing. The truth is, your daughter saved me too."

When Marinus pulled back, he held Theodora at both shoulders. He gave her a light shake that conveyed gratitude. Then he turned around and succumbed to joy at reuniting with his daughter.

Theodora slipped away to give the two more privacy. Her heart thumped as she wrestled with the new reality. After fifteen long months in Alexandria, her stay was abruptly unnecessary. Now, Constantinople loomed large in her mind.

Later that evening, Pope Timothy invited Theodora, Marinus, and Valeria to sup with him. All had endured much and the time came for laughter and thoughts of simple things. At first, the conversation stayed light and pleasant. But eventually, Marinus told of his release from bondage, and how he became a migrant laborer, working his way from Leptis Magna to Carthage in search of his daughter. There, he found legal work inside the Vandal Kingdom. When he heard the news about Valeria from messengers of Pope Timothy, he set out immediately for Alexandria.

"What will you do now that you've found Valeria?" Theodora asked after dinner.

Marinus laughed, but the laugh melted beneath a show of emotion. "I don't know," he said. "You don't understand. I have my girl back. My mind hasn't moved beyond that one thought."

But Theodora understood. For she too, had a daughter in a far-off place.

A few days later, it was Valeria's turn to leave Alexandria behind. Her father decided to return to Carthage, where he had a life and decent earnings.

Theodora stood on a pier in the Harbor of Alexandria. Massive wooden ship hulls, like puffed-out chests, towered above, rocking visibly upon the water.

So strange the farewell, thought Theodora. There were tears and sorrow that felt more exhausting than sad. Perhaps they both yearned to be free of a city that wasn't their home. Or perhaps they simply desired to resume a familiar life after so much uncertainty. They bore an unbreakable, unforgettable bond, yet their lives had converged from two different paths, and now those paths were to split again. They would've been strangers in this world after all. Theodora saw that the girl beamed with anticipation.

It was the future that held promise, not the past. And now Theodora was a lingering agent of that recent and extraordinary past. So, there on the pier, the sisterhood between Theodora and Valeria, one that came into the world so suddenly and endured so strongly, drew to a close.

"I'll never forget you," Valeria said as she gave Theodora a strong and lasting embrace.

Theodora cried openly. "Nor I."

A few moments later, Theodora watched a great hulking vessel drift backward, with dozens of oars rising and falling into the water. Valeria and Marinus stood at the prow, waving at Theodora. As the ship's red sails unfurled and went taut with wind, and as the vessel turned out to sea, Theodora felt an unbelievable weight slip from her heart.

That was it.

She had completed her task.

She could return home as the woman she set out to be.

Theodora left the harbor and made her way back to St. Mark's. The slow amble that had slipped into her pace over recent months soon sped to a brisk walk. Then she trotted through the foot traffic. And when the revelation of total freedom befell Theodora in full, she burst into a full run toward the church. She lowered her head and smiled as she ran. She reached the Holy See and dashed through hallways, causing priests to leap aside at her passing.

Theodora ran directly to Pope Timothy. He was in his study, hunched over, and peering at a scroll up close. When he looked up and saw Theodora, he smiled warmly. "Did you say your goodbyes?" he asked.

"It's time, Your Holiness," Theodora said, trying to catch her breath. "It's time for me to go home to my daughter."

FIFTY-FOUR

T
he next morning, Theodora stood outdoors, alone with Pope Timothy. In the distance, Theodora heard crowing roosters, church bells, and wailing prayer songs. The baptistery looked like a bath-sized pool set into the courtyard, an elongated rectangle with a widened circle in the center. The water rippled as if a natural spring churned below. At her feet, three stone steps descended into the water.

Theodora had spent long hours with the pope over the months, studying the doctrine of the Monophysites. She still didn't understand all the nuances of the One Nature belief, but she did know that there couldn't be two Theodoras. Her own two natures were irreconcilable. One Theodora. One Nature.

Pope Timothy submerged into the baptistery, his robes floating to the surface, the water reaching to his mid-abdomen. He then looked up at Theodora and nodded.

She slipped off her robe. Warm desert air graced her bare skin. She was a catechumen, a convert facing baptism, and as such, she was to face God unclothed. This was the first time she undressed before a man where her sexuality meant nothing, where she was just a person unclothed. Unexpectedly, Theodora wanted to cover her breasts.

"Jewelry must also be removed," he said.

She realized she still wore the Amulet of St. Christopher that the priest in the Governor's Palace had given her. She removed the necklace and dropped it onto her crumpled robe. Then, wordlessly, Theodora descended the steps and lowered her body into the baptismal pool. The water was cold and churned near her ankles.

"Blessed is the one whose transgressions are forgiven," said Pope Timothy. "Blessed is the one whose sins the Lord does not count against them."

Theodora felt Timothy's hand touch her back, so she leaned backward, her hair spilling into the water, while the pope held her up.

Timothy continued the psalm. "When I kept silent, my bones wasted away through my laments. For day and night, Your hand was heavy upon me; my strength was drained as in the heat of summer."

Theodora now gazed directly up into a beautiful cobalt sky. The water came up to her cheeks now. As her ears submerged, the Pope's words fell mute.

Silence.

She felt water pouring onto her forehead, once, twice. Her eyes widened, her body relaxed, and tranquility befell her in full. Her life before was washing away for good. She smiled, even as tears filled her eyes. She felt again that hopefulness that had once sparked her as a child.

And there, high up in the skies, Theodora saw a majestic, glittering bird flying freely in the heavens. It was her bird. And it was a beautiful bird. Now, the bird circled above in slow, lazy arcs. She watched as it banked into a slow descent as if answering its master's call. As she imagined the beautiful avian approaching, the wings dissolved in mid-sky, and its form vanished into nothingness; at last, a haunting mirage that was no more.

When Theodora arose from the water, she held her robe against her wet and naked body. She closed her eyes and lifted her head to that once devastating sun. Her face warmed, and the desert breeze cooled her cheeks and forehead. She stood there for a long while, listening to the swishing palm tree fronds and the gushing sea. She felt a deep and satisfying serenity.

When Theodora finally opened her eyes, she saw the pope standing there. "It's time for me to leave Alexandria, Your Holiness."

FIFTY-FIVE

During her stay in Alexandria, Theodora often thought of the journey back to Constantinople. Naturally, she thought of all the people she would see again, and how'd they'd react when they saw her. But when the pope told Theodora that she'd return home by ship, Theodora knew she'd disembark in only one city. Antioch.

More than two years earlier, Theodora left Constantinople for Sosuza, while her mentor, Macedonia, set out for Antioch, and that seemed to be the end of it. But Theodora wrote Macedonia, sending word of her passage home, and her intent to visit her old mentor. Their relationship felt like all the others—spectacular, intense, and then silent. She didn't intend to drift away from these beautiful people, like flotsam upon an ocean of time, consigning their faces to memory. And Macedonia had been one of the best.

Reaching Antioch was not an easy task. Unlike Constantinople and Alexandria, Antioch was not in view of the sea. Her ship sailed north up the coastline of Syria, where it ported in Seleucia Pieria. There, along with a group of Monophysite priests, Theodora changed vessels. They boarded a smaller merchant ship, which was laden with Egyptian grain, and entered the estuary of the Orontes River. She stood at the rail of the ship as it navigated an inland waterway, gliding through valleys of green hills and even mountains, bald with beige stone. Village upon village passed before her eyes. When fishermen or caravans hailed her vessel with lazy waves, Theodora waved back. Now that she was a Christian, she somehow felt closer to the world and all these people. She was one of them now, a person who was a part of the most powerful, most passionate ideas. She'd taken a side. And soon, when she'd eventually speak on the matter, she'd be speaking to the most powerful people of the empire.

Eventually.

When Theodora finally saw Antioch, a city in the hills, she thought the metropolis looked like home. The one difference was a breathtaking mountain range to the east. Great walls snaked through the hillocks and along the waterfront, while heaps of buildings clustered at the river's edge, sprawling outward and stretching to the forested horizon. Theodora realized that this was the furthest inland she'd ever been. Her ship entered a canal with high walls on both sides, passing beneath an arch of a stone bridge. Sure enough, Theodora spotted a hippodrome, which sat in the western half of the city.

When her vessel finally moored in the harbor, Theodora heard the chatter of countless voices and the peculiar accents of the Antiochenes. She grew so accustomed to the ship that when she finally set foot on the wood piers, it was the solid, unmovable earth that felt unnatural. And the ubiquitous smell of mossy fish, wet wood, urine, and salt brine became as familiar to Theodora as ginger, lavender, and sweet rosewater had once been.

She wore no cosmetics. Theodora dressed plainly—a crisp brown robe, washed hair that hung flat and neat, and clean skin unadorned with jewelry.

One of the priests accompanied Theodora until they crossed into what was clearly the theater district. When she spotted an animal trainer, looking bored as he led a fire-orange tiger out of an amphitheater, she realized she knew this part of the city. She didn't need a guide or hood. So, Theodora dismissed the priest and walked unaccompanied upon the street, smiling as the male foot traffic took notice.

Theodora met Macedonia at a small wood koitǫna on the north end of town. When she entered the building, and when she drew in a deep breath, the taste and scent of the air flooded her with memories of her life at age fourteen, during those bitter months after her father's death. But then Theodora spotted Macedonia leading a dance lesson, guiding a dozen or so adolescent girls through a series of balance exercises. She wore a dark yellow but sleeveless dress, an Oriental fashion. Theodora smiled and the anxiety slipped away. This was a welcoming place for girls. This was a koitǫna as it should have been.

When Macedonia saw Theodora standing in the foyer, she smiled. Then she grabbed a metal baton, tapped a bell, and ended the lesson. As the girls dispersed, Macedonia came up to Theodora, smiling as if to say she knew this day would come.

"Wonderful to see you, Theodora," she said. "Even in plain clothes, you stand out like no other. How are you?"

"I'm well. Excited to be heading home again."

"Of course."

Theodora spoke of her ship travels as the two women meandered up a staircase, one that did not warble, and into Macedonia's residence. Her former mentor had a large dwelling atop the koitǫna, decorated beautifully with colorful woven rugs that covered the walls and floors alike.

"Is your husband here?"

"Daniel's working down at the Amphitheater. He's the stage master for the Blue faction here," she said. "I think you'd like him, Theodora."

"I'm sure I would. I always wondered what kind of man the great Macedonia would take," said Theodora.

"Come," said Macedonia. She led Theodora through a doorway and onto a massive wooden balcony, shaded by a canopy and draped in curtains. Her maidservant brought a bowl of fresh green figs, along with a jug of coan wine, which was a red wine lightly blended with sea salt.

There, they told each other all that had happened over the intervening years. This time, Theodora mostly listened as her mentor spoke. She learned that Macedonia still informed for the Blues and still managed several girls in the city. At her age, though, she no longer danced in a chorus line, but trained others.

Even with the years spent since the election of Justin, Theodora still struggled to raise the topic she so wished to discuss. But when the conversation met a pleasant lull, she finally did so.

"I've been corresponding with Justinian," said Theodora.

Macedonia didn't react. She only took a small sip of wine. "*Consul* Justinian these days. And, yes, I know."

"Of course, you know." Theodora nodded to herself and looked down. "I suppose that's always been the way of it." She drew in a deep breath and met her mentor's eyes. "Well, I'm sure you know that he resides now in the Bucoleon House, near the Daphne."

Macedonia nodded. "A beautiful little palace."

"It is," said Theodora, recalling her passionate moment with Justinian there. "Well, did you know that he's offered for me to reside there with him upon my return?"

Macedonia's statue-like stoicism never wavered, yet in her eyes, Theodora spotted a subtle darkening, perhaps confusion.

She didn't know.

"What do you mean, 'reside there with him'?" said Macedonia.

"Exactly that. To live in the Bucoleon House. With him."

Macedonia's eyes narrowed, but not in bitterness. She seemed to contemplate the news fully. "But you're an unwed woman, a former . . . actress from the lower classes," she said. "And he's in the high aristocracy, the son of the emperor. With all the eyes and ears in the palace, he could never hide you from all the women suitors."

"I don't think he means to hide this arrangement."

Again, Macedonia wrinkled her brow. "It's an impossible arrangement, though. The law forbids him from marrying you. And I know he'd never indenture you as a concubine."

"I wouldn't accept such an arrangement anyway," said Theodora.

"What then? A permanent mistress? The scandal alone would be devastating for the emperor and Justinian alike. And you . . . the nobles would be horrified," she said. "What has the emperor said on the matter?"

Theodora shrugged. "He hasn't told the emperor yet."

Macedonia recovered from her rare bout of confusion. She reclined, looked down at the streets, took a sip of wine. Then she faced Theodora and smiled genuinely. "Well, you must be very happy."

Theodora, though, didn't smile back. "I know I should be." She set her wine cup on the tray and arose, restless. "But things are different now. Or maybe things are the same, and I just see them differently."

"Tell me what you mean."

"I just left the opulence, the generosity, and protection of a powerful man. I had all those things I thought I needed or wanted. But when I think about it now, I see that those things trapped me, made me dependent on Hacebolus, made me more like a slave. And as time passed, he treated me more like a slave. Only at the end did I realize that indeed, that's all I was. You see? I'm not so sure now that I should rush into that same net."

"You've changed, Theodora," said Macedonia. "And I'm happy to see it. You're free for the moment now. You're strong. But you'll learn that freedom and strength are enigmas, aren't they? Elusive. They'll weigh on you. The prospect of sliding backward, of returning to dependency and weakness will always be present."

"Yes," said Theodora with a sober nod. Finally, she smiled and laughed quietly. "I see you still have lessons for me, after all."

"No. This isn't tradecraft, and you're no longer my pupil, Theodora. Here, we're two women. And we're talking about your life."

"Well, what's your advice?"

"First, tell me what you're afraid of in this."

"That maybe I haven't learned anything. That no matter what, I'm still destined to live under the mastery of a man who can discard me at any time. If Justinian ever treated me the way the governor did, I'd be no better off." Theodora met Macedonia's eyes. "I'm afraid that in the end, while we women can be strong, we simply have no real power in the world. That's what I'm afraid of."

Macedonia nodded. "So Justinian would still be your benefactor, and you'd be dependent on his loyalty and whims? And although you love this man, the basic bargain is the same as it was with Hacebolus? Accept the hospitality and status a man can provide, but cross him and you're finished."

"Yes. And that's what pesters me. After all this, I'd still be entrusting my life and the life of my daughter with one person. Justinian has the power to cast us both aside, while I lack the same power over him."

"Is that what you want with Justinian? Equal power with him?"

"Yes."

Macedonia leaned forward. "Well, you don't have it. Even if the laws gave you this power, you would depend on others to enforce it. What I recommend is far greater than anyone's notion of equal power, so far as I can see."

"What's that?"

"An equal partnership."

Theodora didn't respond.

"Think about it. You once chose to leave your daughter behind. Are you going back to her now because a law says you must?"

"No."

"Or are you doing this because you fear retribution if you don't?"

"None of those things. I go back to Palatina because I want to."

"So it goes with men," said Macedonia. "If you genuinely love this man, then equal power is not what you seek. He must choose you every morning, day after day, just as you must also choose him. No amount of coercion, manipulation, or threat will change this basic truth. Focus on your partnership with Justinian and learn whether you can live with each other. Real partnership requires no law from Caesar. It requires no soldier to enforce and no threat of harm. A partnership is between you and him. And it revolves around both your decisions, freely, to keep one another and to work together."

Theodora sighed. "But what if he one day turns against me?"

"Your daughter may yet do the same. But you choose that risk with certain people because you build trust with them."

"But it's different with a man. If I am one day cast out—"

"Theodora," said Macedonia, setting down her wine cup with a clack, polite but curt. "You'll never be cast out again. Because you wouldn't allow it. In the future, you'll leave of your own choosing before it ever comes to that."

"But how would I raise my daughter?" Theodora said, her voice unexpectedly loud. "I risk impoverishing her as well as myself."

Macedonia smiled. "We come to it at last, despina. Your fear isn't being cast out. Your real fear stems from your lack of independence. You're afraid you can't make it without a man."

"Well, I saw it firsthand with my mother, after my father died."

"Indeed. It happens to women all the time."

"So how do we get around this?"

"Never depend on a man before you've learned how to depend on yourself," said Macedonia.

Theodora swallowed involuntarily.

"You'll be a woman who chooses the men and the people she depends on, and never the kind who has these choices imposed upon her. Not anymore. If you end up trusting Justinian, or any other man for that matter, with the welfare of yourself and your daughter, you may choose to sever the arrangement at any time. Using this authority leads to permanent outcomes and invites confrontation, and so we fear to use it." Macedonia held up a finger. "But not you. I know many a woman who depends on a man but is unwilling to upkeep herself without him. She clings to hope, even while her partnership degrades. That woman will struggle. She chooses his authority over her own and then laments her situation. In that lies her slavery."

As always, Macedonia spoke with such soft authority, delicate, like a light breeze, but with a volley of arrows that riddle the target. "So, it's not about power this time?" said Theodora.

"To retaliate? That power is for our enemies, despina. Do you want Justinian's loyalty only because he fears you?"

Theodora thought about it. "No."

"Do you think that Justinian sees your worth as that of a concubine or servant?"

"No."

"Then work on that kind of partnership," said Macedonia. "Equal to each other here and now, without rank or class or status. But you must be brave enough to assert yourself to Justinian. He'll need that from you. Otherwise, the alternative is to have no partnership at all. In that life, fear of having unequal power will come to rule over you, embittering you, causing you to withdraw. And I do not teach women to withdraw." Macedonia paused. "We may not have equal power, but we will risk ourselves in pursuit of equal partners. It's the greatest power there is."

A long moment went by. Many noises from the streets below filled the silence between the women. Theodora thought about Justinian. She thought about Palatina. She thought about her own desires and needs. Finally, Theodora stiffened and lifted her chin. "When I return to Constantinople, I won't go to Justinian right away. If he waited for me this long, he can wait a little longer."

Macedonia tilted her head, her eyes sparkling with curiosity. "What then?"

"I'll be with my daughter and learn to raise her on my own. I'll learn a skill that is not of the brothels or theaters. I'll find a life I'm prepared to return to if or when I must. Once I learn to do that, then I'll go to Justinian. I'll choose this partnership with him, as you call it, and we'll see what the two of us can become."

"And for your earnings?"

"Below the dwelling where my mother lives, there is a workshop. I've seen women working the looms and spinning wheels down there," Theodora said and looked into her lap. She nodded. "They earn money from their labor, just as men do elsewhere in the city. I'll learn the trade, and I'll learn to be a mother in my way."

Macedonia reached over and took up Theodora's hands and rubbed them. "If you go to him in such a way, despina, I believe he'll never want to leave your side."

"That's not all," said Theodora. "If I'm to reside with a man who manages the affairs of the empire, then I mean to contribute."

Macedonia's smile waned, and her eyes again searched for meaning. "What are you talking about?"

"I believe Justinian is a brilliant man," said Theodora. "But he hasn't seen the empire beyond the walls of Constantinople. He knows nothing of North Africa. He hasn't seen what I've seen in Alexandria. And he's never listened to what words are spoken by those far from the capital, nor has he mingled with the discontented. I have. If he wants me, then he'll get someone who can truly help him, someone who has experience that exceeds his own on certain matters."

A church bell rang out somewhere nearby and Macedonia stared at Theodora for the duration. When the bell stopped, she blinked and looked away. "Well then, despina. I've no more advice to give you. What you're about to do, no one has seen yet. Not like this."

EPILOGUE

SEVEN MONTHS LATER
522 A.D.
CONSTANTINOPLE, BYZANTINE EMPIRE

Theodora's skin prickled. The Christian hymn resounded over the hundreds who filled the Hagia Sophia Basilica. A choir of about two dozen men sang out as one powerful voice, their verses filling the smoky ceilings of the church, joined by the mighty voices of the congregation.

Women couldn't join the main congregation, so Theodora stood in the crowded aisle on the side of the nave, listening. She was dressed in her finest, with hair held up in pins, and a crocus flower set above her ear. Beside her stood Palatina, now a lanky eight-year-old girl. Her daughter gazed in disbelief at the opulence of the church. Every time Theodora caught her daughter smiling admiringly up at her, she winked.

On Theodora's other side stood the rest of her family—Maximina,

Comito, Anastasia, and Samuel. They all wore colorful garb but were markedly less impressive than the ornamented nobility that crowded the central nave.

Theodora bent beside Palatina and pointed to the front row of the congregation. There sat the Roman emperor, Justin, adorned in shiny silks, layer upon layer of purple, gold, and white, as was his wife, Empress Euphemia. Bejeweled crowns of gold sat atop their heads. And beside the emperor was Justinian, like a Roman prince, a man who could one day rule the empire. He watched the ceremony, but turned sideways and peered in Theodora's direction, searching the crowds for her. He knew she was there.

Three days earlier, Theodora finally sent word to him. She told Justinian of her life at the spinning wheel, of her joys in raising her daughter, and how she found happiness again in Constantinople. He responded by inviting her to the morning services, and she accepted.

Sometimes she thought Justinian smiled at her from afar; other times she couldn't tell if he saw her at all.

But she saw him.

And how grand he looked beside the Roman emperor, their two profiles showing similar features. He too, wore scintillating attire, as decorated as Theodora ever saw him. Justinian's brown locks lay flattened beneath a single gold headband. She couldn't take her eyes off of him. He looked picturesque and reverent as the choir thundered the triumphant verses of the hymn. She once thought that she'd never see Justinian again, and now he stood in view, dressed as if he embodied the Roman Empire himself. She once shared so many private hours with him in small, quiet places. So now she found it strange to look upon him with so great a crowd in so public, so opulent a place. Would he act the same toward her in the presence of so many powerful people? Or would his tenderness and respect wane in the presence of the emperor and his court?

Theodora held her breath as she tracked the approach of Justinian, along with the rest of the imperial family members, who filed in behind the departing priests. She pulled Palatina in front of her and waited. Soon those who ruled the empire all passed by her. And finally, Justinian met Theodora's eyes with certainty. She smiled exuberantly at him while he returned the dignified nod of powerful men, but his eyes smiled back.

As the procession moved by her and out the front doors, Theodora's family, along with the nearby crowd, exited as well. She held Palatina's small hand as they walked through the front doors of the church and out into the open sunlight. Here, the final hymn was replaced by the pleasing sound of warbling birds, the snorts of idle horses, and lively conversations.

"Are we really going to meet the emperor?"

"We're going to meet the emperor's whole family."

Palatina's eyes widened as she slowly spun to gaze upon the emperor's entourage, who stood behind a row of purple-clad guards and beside the Bronze Gate.

"Come on," said Theodora. Slowly, she led her family through the crowd and ever closer to the man she so desired to see. As Theodora approached, the Palatine Guards glared at her with unfriendly eyes. They stood in a row, resolutely separating the public from Emperor Justin.

"Let her through," said a man's voice in pristine Latin.

As the guards nodded and pulled back their spears, Theodora saw Justinian standing there. He held out his hand, and she took it. She let him pull her in close, and the sudden proximity flooded her with buoyancy and anxiety alike.

"At long last," he said. "I get to speak with Theodora here and now. I've gone through so many quills writing you that the birds here have threatened a revolt."

Theodora laughed. Although she was a member of the lower classes, she saw that Justinian spoke easily to her, a clear break with convention, his countenance that of a man comfortable around anyone, even in full view of the nobility. "My family and I are humbled by your invitation," said Theodora. "Consul, this is my daughter, Palatina."

She watched as Justinian bent forward until he was at eye level with Palatina. "What a beautiful little girl you are," he said. "And you have your mother's eyes. Are you pleased that your mother's back home?"

Palatina shrank away from the attention, twisting behind Theodora, but peering back at Justinian.

"She's very happy I'm back," said Theodora. "But not as happy as I am. I see her every day now."

"Well then, she's the lucky one," he said. When Justinian finally tore his intense eyes off of Theodora, he spotted Maximina. "And this is the great matriarch. Honored to meet you finally in person."

Theodora helped her mother forward. Though frail, Maximina smiled girlishly at the heir apparent. "So handsome," she said. Then she boldly placed both hands on either side of Justinian's face and kissed him square on each cheek.

He laughed and looked back at Theodora, then her sisters, then again at Maximina. "I see this is somewhat of a reunion."

Theodora suddenly understood the truth of Justinian's comment. They'd all been together that day in the Hippodrome, so long ago. He was the man in the stands, a Blue partisan, while her family teetered on total ruin. How far they all had come.

Justinian nodded. "I'd like you to meet my father, Emperor Justin, who agreed to hear your plea for Pope Timothy."

Theodora finally glanced at the man behind Justinian. The emperor was shorter but wore a stern face, a commander's face. He nodded quickly and shallowly. "Honored, young woman," he said, his words revealing traces of a lowborn draw. "Your past work for the faction has been explained to me. Naturally, I'm grateful."

Theodora bowed, wondering just how much the emperor knew of her involvement during the election.

Justinian gestured again. "And this beautiful woman is Empress Euphemia."

Theodora bowed even lower to the empress, who wasn't beautiful at all. But the empress returned only a cold stare, merely nodding an acknowledgment.

As if sensing the disapproval of the empress, Justinian steered Theodora away from the imperial couple. "And this," he said, holding his hand out, "one of my closest associates, whom I believe you know."

Before Justinian completed the salutation, Theodora spotted Hypatius approaching the group. The old man looked younger, more alert, a glow of self-confidence upon his face. He walked briskly up to her with the warmest of smiles. For the first time, she felt as though she got a glimpse of the Hypatius that came before she knew him, the Hypatius who could've been an emperor. He took both of Theodora's hands and kissed them. "Wonderful to see you again, Theodora," he said. "You look absolutely breathtaking."

She smiled and felt a sincere joy at seeing the former imperial nephew. "Hypatius. I thought of you often while I was away."

"And I, *you*," he said. "When Justinian told me of your return, I was glad to hear the news."

The greetings continued to circulate. Theodora also noticed Comito looking at her in amazement. Not since they were girls had Theodora seen her older sister stay so reserved and quiet. She remained in the background, less sure of herself in the company of the East Roman court, despite Comito's own modicum of celebrity.

As the conversations drew on, Theodora found herself staring at Justinian for longer and longer durations. He noticed her watching him, but maintained a sociable coolness, commanding, unhurried. Soon, though, he turned to Theodora. "Will you walk with me around the palace gardens?"

Anxiety surged inside Theodora's chest. It was time to speak privately.

Maximina waved off Justinian's words and turned to Theodora. "Go, walk with him. I'll take Palatina home."

"I've come too far for that. Palatina goes where I go," said Theodora, turning to her daughter. "Palatina? Would you like to see Daphne Palace?"

"From behind the gates?" she said.

Justinian answered. "From behind the gates."

"I want to see," she said as if she feared the opportunity would slip away. She darted forward to Justinian; her earlier reservations seemingly gone.

He leaned down and hoisted Palatina into his arms, something Theodora could no longer do with her eight-year-old daughter. But Justinian was a strong man, with broad shoulders and sturdy posture. Theodora never saw her daughter in this light, with a man who might care about her well-being. She saw that her daughter looked at ease with Justinian, one arm around his shoulder, absently peering out at all the extraordinary people.

Justinian gave the Palatine guards a nod, and they pulled open the mighty Bronze Gates. The Daphne Palace grounds appeared before Theodora's eyes, a wonderland of green gardens, manicured trees, Roman columns, all bathed in sunlight and shadows. When she looked over at her family, they looked back at her in disbelief.

Theodora opened her mouth to speak, but her mother again shooed her away.

Justinian and two guards led Theodora and Palatina through the Bronze Gates. They strolled down ornate arcades, upon walkways overlaid with beautiful and elaborate mosaics. Theodora felt as though she tread upon artwork. Would she truly grow accustomed to such magnificent sights?

Justinian set Palatina down and let her wander as she pleased. Most of the Daphne was outside with one courtyard after another. Large buildings loomed above the ornate colonnades, and two upright Palatine guards flanked each portico. And there, above the clay tiled roof, she saw the entire rim of the Great Hippodrome up close.

"Can I pick these flowers?" Palatina called out.

"No," said Theodora.

"Of course, you can," said Justinian. "As many as you can hold."

Theodora held her breath as her daughter plucked what looked like priceless flowers.

"I was happy to read your latest letter," said Justinian. "But surprised to learn that you've been in Constantinople for seven months already."

"I know," said Theodora. "Part of me feels as though I've only just returned."

"But seven months," he said, his tone serious as if their conversation were now a formal negotiation. "I'd assumed that my offer to you would've taken precedence upon your return. Seven months suggests otherwise."

"You offered for me to reside with you in the Bucoleon House, Justinian.

Such an offer has been in my thoughts ever since and has weighed on me heavily. I take your offer as seriously as a woman can. That's precisely why I didn't rush to judgment. But, you must understand, your offer didn't take precedence over *all* else."

They both watched Palatina bend down and take in the fragrance of dozens of colorful flowers.

"I see."

"After all, I had to learn a different line of work," said Theodora, smiling at him, hoping he'd acknowledge her intimate jest. He didn't.

"But, Theodora, my offer gives you all that you need. You need master no trade, nor toil as a man toils for wages. I thought that was understood."

"I understood."

"Then why?"

"I want you to know what you're getting into as well," she said. "I have things in my life that I intend to pursue with my whole heart. I intend to raise my daughter and to teach her things about the world. I intend to work hard, helping other women break away from the brothels if they so choose. And I wish to help the Christians I met, who suffer in North Africa today."

He stopped walking. "So, what are you saying?"

"I have my own mind about what I want in life now," she said and shrugged. "And I set forth a path for myself that I intend to follow regardless of where I live or with who."

Justinian looked at Theodora with a furrowed brow, his brown eyes dancing with both intensity and confusion.

Theodora knew she risked herself by speaking plainly with Justinian. Even the surety she had in her position didn't spare her from the clutches of anxiety. She still felt heat on her face and neck. Her body still flushed hotly beneath her clothing. "Does that bother you?" she asked.

"No," he said, but fell silent, as if collecting many thoughts. For a moment, Theodora feared he would send her away, finally recovering an aristocratic sensibility, the spell of desire vanishing all at once. He clutched his hands behind his back and turned to face the courtyard. For a while, he seemed only to watch Palatina. "It's good that you have your own mind on matters, Theodora. The truth is, you've been a big part of how I see the world. Before I met you, I spent my entire life fighting against the idea of aristocracy. I've passionately rejected the idea that excellence in people comes from birthright, and my experiences thus far have rewarded my beliefs on such matters. For me, excellence was a manly pursuit, a matter of will and daring, bringing a man's intelligence to bear upon his vision. I believed that it did not matter where a man begins in life. He could become great, perhaps rise in society by the merit of his actions. My father did it; I did it. I thought I had a new outlook on the world. That was until I began my clandestine work in the brothels. First, I met Macedonia, then yourself, then others." Justinian turned and looked at Theodora. "Many questions came to me during that time, causing me to revise my outlook. Could the common woman also follow a path of excellence? Did the common woman even want that path? Could women too, rise to face a great undertaking, regardless of their station? What did women know of courage? Well, I learned that they know quite a bit." Justinian looked down. "I think what frightens me the most, Theodora, is that here you are. You're exactly the kind of woman I've wondered about," he said. "I knew it early on when I met you. And here, this is the first time that such a woman has confronted me directly about matters of the world as well as the heart, asking me to go a little further. I realize as you speak that this is what such a woman sounds like, this is what she cares about, and these are her terms. Now they are your terms to me," he said and looked her firmly in the eyes. "And I accept them wholeheartedly."

A quiet euphoria made Theodora's throat constrict. Was all this happening? She took Justinian's hands. "Then I'm yours."

He pulled both of Theodora's hands up at his chest, bringing her closer to him, and the hard gaze of a man in negotiation slipped away. He finally looked at her the way she'd wanted him to look at her. And then he kissed her. Theodora nearly forgot how long she'd waited for that kiss, but her heavy emotions dispersed like flower petals in the wind. She too, felt the sweet sensation of knowing there wasn't another living man who could contend with Justinian for her heart. Now she understood what Justinian meant a moment earlier, when he spoke of fear. Getting exactly what she wanted was wonderful and terrifying alike, merely a new beginning for Theodora.

"Did you just kiss my mother?" said Palatina.

Justinian pulled back, and Theodora saw Palatina standing in a garden, squinting as bumblebees buzzed around her.

"I did," said Justinian as if answering a dignitary.

"Mother?" said Palatina, concerned. "Did you agree to that?"

"Yes, I agreed to it."

Palatina considered the answer and then shrugged. "All right," she said, returning her attention to the garden. "But you should give my mother flowers first. Here, I'll get them for you."

Theodora glanced at Justinian, who raised his eyebrows, clearly impressed that Palatina questioned him.

"I see you've taught your daughter well," said Justinian, but then became serious again. "Theodora, you realize our arrangement will be completely unprecedented. We can't marry. You're not my courtesan, nor mistress. You're not a member of the aristocracy. The nobility will never let either of us forget your social class or former profession. Residing together in the Bucoleon House will be a flagrant scandal. And if I include you in imperial affairs, they'll resist in full. There could be quite a storm ahead."

"Well, I accept," she said.

When Palatina returned with a bouquet of flowers, Justinian kissed Theodora again. She heard a horn blare from the Hippodrome, followed by a booming cheer just beyond the tree line. The crowd was maddened and joyous. And there, after all these years, Theodora finally felt what they felt . . . a passionate, powerful, uncontrollable joy.

EXCERPT FROM THE NEXT BOOK

Theodora stared into the Triclinium. She drew in a deep breath and pressed a fist into her lower lip. Tomorrow she'd sit upon the throne for the first time, alongside Justinian. She couldn't suppress the crushing anxiety in her chest. The feeling reminded her of girlhood, of looking upon something so much larger than herself and trying to make sense of it. She took in the scent of fresh polish on the purple marble floors and watched the torchlight shimmer upon the thick marble columns. Finally, she beheld a golden gossamer curtain that hung like a ghostly partition in front of two thrones. In the morning, the partition would part and unfurl like bird's wings to reveal herself and Justinian, dressed in the full regalia of empress and emperor. She and Justinian would come face to face with hundreds of courtiers, delegates, clergy, and military officers.

A throne room.

In this place, words are born from the mouths of Roman rulers to persecute, to set free, to decree, to make justice, to muster armies for peace or war, then to travel through the hallways, beyond the walls to penetrate the minds of scheming people, impelling dangerous opinions, spreading out further, expressed as rumors and news, as information and intelligence, into the streets, as uncontrolled as the gales of a great storm, passing into the ranks of soldiers and the company of caravans, into the brothels and taverns, into the forums and markets, and upon the decks of seafaring dromons, changing languages out on the sea lanes or winding highways, over hillocks and lakes, into the countryside, entering the farmhouses and outposts, by daylight and moonlight, reaching distant cities, into the ears of other rulers and out again upon their breath, in praise or denunciation, repeated in the echoes of distant halls before falling silent, where those living words finally settle upon the drying ink of the men who write histories, etched there to stand against time and dust on brittle pages, to be read one day by those unborn generations who will know not this time and place, nor the people who dared to speak the course of empires.

Theodora shuddered at the brute power of spoken words in this place. And tomorrow, she would speak. Yet she knew that when she spoke, there will arise a hesitation in the chamber, an unspoken doubt about the new empress. She'd see the entire East Roman Court take in her face and appearance with unguarded fascination. They'd imagine her as she must have been not long ago, as a poor girl in a brothel, as a woman who'd been beneath them and stained by scandal. The esteemed court will freely wonder at the body their empress once displayed so brazenly to the lowest of lowborn men. Then their eyes will narrow, and they'll grow suspicious about the erotic creature who sits upon the Roman throne while they do not. And at that moment, when their disbelief is left unanswered, when their loathing is at its highest—they'll hear the sound of the imperial scepter bang upon the floor.

And they will bow.

For details on the release of this and other works from the author, visit DouglasABurton.com.

WHO ARE YOUR FAVORITE HEROINES?

I am actively seeking your thoughts about heroines.

The Heroine Project is an ongoing study into the distinctive expression of heroic women in fiction. How heroines are portrayed in film and literature do more than merely entertain us; they model perspectives, attitudes, and strategies that generate dynamism within our culture. The heroine archetype likely has its own secrets to teach us.

I feel that this topic hasn't been fully explored yet.

Do you agree? If you'd like to get involved, then I'm listening. I'd love for you to participate in the discussion. Your feedback will provide critical perspectives for my next book, *The Heroine's Labyrinth*, which aims to advance a more complete look at the human phenomenon of heroism in general, and in heroic women in particular.

JOIN THE RANKS

Join me at www.DouglasABurton.com.

http://bit.ly/DynamSurvey

WHICH HEROIC PERSONALITY TYPE ARE YOU?

When it comes to heroic action, each one of us is equipped with gifts and weaknesses, preferences and tendencies, habits and attitudes that make us who we are. Results are based on the Myers-Briggs personality type indicator.

TAKE THE QUIZ

http://bit.ly/HeroicQuiz